Earl o

CW01095677

Jacqueline Reiter

© Jacqueline Reiter 2017

Jacqueline Reiter has asserted her rights under the Copyright, Design and Patents Act, 1988, to be identified as the author of this work.

First published by Endeavour Press Ltd in 2017.

Table of Contents

Chapter One

April 1778

John checked his pocket-watch as he crossed Cavendish Square and quickened his pace. It was nearly noon already and he had promised Papa he would not be late.

He reached the rented townhouse on Harley Street and tugged at the bell until the porter let him in. John hammered up the stairs to his room, tossed his scarlet coat onto the back of a chair and threw off his officer's sword. The clatter of the polished brass hilt on the floor brought Wood to the door. 'Lord Pitt?'

'What's the time?' John groaned, hopping on one foot as he tugged his boots on.

Wood had been John's valet since John was a child. He spoke promptly, as though he had known John would ask and had checked a clock beforehand. 'A quarter to 12, my lord.' John swore under his breath as he battled his buttons. 'Shall I assist you?'

John shook his head. He was going to miss the appointed hour and felt a swell of anxiety at the thought of what his father would say. Not that Lord Chatham was likely to notice when he had William by him. John wondered whether he would find Papa better than he had been, and dread shifted in the depths of his stomach.

It was nearly half past 12 by the time John wove his way through the queue of sedan chairs, chaises and coaches clogging the expanse of Old Palace Yard. The coffee houses clinging to the crumbling frontage of Westminster Hall swarmed with customers, most awaiting the debate on the Duke of Richmond's motion regarding the state of the nation.

'John!'

The cry cut across the babble of voices. John turned to see his brother elbowing through the crowds. William was easy to spot, for even at 19 he towered half a head above the next tallest person. His long face glistened with anxiety. John could see at a glance that all was not well, and his chest clenched.

'You did not come, so I went to find you,' William said by way of greeting. He grasped John firmly by the upper arm and dragged him through the archway into Westminster Hall. 'The debate will begin soon.'

The brothers jostled through the Court of Requests and pushed through airless corridors, the ancient floorboards creaking underfoot. Both had often accompanied their father to the House of Lords, and the labyrinthine corridors of Parliament were familiar to them. Only the crowds kept them from making swifter progress. The debate on Richmond's motion was a big draw, but the prospect of a speech from Lord Chatham had attracted the crowds in earnest. Everyone wanted to hear William Pitt, Earl of Chatham, victor of the old wars and scourge of France, decry American independence.

'Papa said noon,' William said as they went. 'Are you incapable of keeping an engagement?'

John took in William's tight expression and knew there was no point reminding him of General Boyd's last-minute summons to his aides-de-camp, or that the convoy was due to carry him to Gibraltar in less than a month. He wondered whether William truly expected him to place military duty below his obligations to his father. He also wondered why he felt guilty for not doing so. 'I'm here now.'

'Do you seriously expect me to congratulate you for turning up at all?'

'I don't expect congratulations for anything,' John snapped, 'but since you mention it, a little more respect towards the future Earl of Chatham would not go amiss.'

'If you want my respect, keep your appointments. You're not head of the family yet.'

John's irritation flared, but he suppressed it with practised effort. This was familiar sparring ground between them, and had been ever since they had been small, when John's status had been the only advantage he had to wield over his favoured and startlingly precocious sibling. Today he could tell William's heart was not in it. His brother's jaw was tense, his thoughts clearly elsewhere. John softened immediately. He did not like this duty any more than William did. 'Is Papa no better?'

A pause. 'Worse, I think.'

'Did you not try to dissuade him from staying?'

'Of course I tried,' William said, and John immediately knew the severity of the situation. If William had been unable to persuade Papa to return home, then nobody else stood a chance.

The stillness of the Painted Chamber struck John immediately in contrast to the hubbub outside. Sunlight poured through the long, recessed windows and projected diamond patterns onto the walls, once covered in colourful frescoes but now hung with tapestries depicting scenes from England's past. John's father sat near the empty fireplace, a glass of wine in his hand. His gouty feet, swathed in linen, were propped on cushions. Behind stood John and William's brother James, carrying Papa's crutches and wearing an anxious look. Nearby was Charles, Lord Mahon, husband of John's sister Hetty, his sparse black hair unfashionably bare of powder. Mahon flashed John an eloquent look.

The reason for Mahon's warning stood a few paces away: John's uncle Richard Grenville, Earl Temple, his heavy-lidded grey eyes aflame with anger. 'For the sake of my sister and your children, Chatham, go home to Hayes. Why are you even here?'

Chatham's hook-nosed profile pierced the shadow of his curled wig. 'Did you think I would stay away, today of all days?' He raised the glass to his lips. He had to use both hands to steady it. Once the bells of every church in England had rung to celebrate the victories he had masterminded as Secretary of State: Guadeloupe, Quebec, Minden. Broken and ill, his once-brilliant mind shattered, Chatham was a shadow of his former self. His stumbling repetitions pierced John to the heart. 'I had to come. I had to.'

'You would have done better to remain at home,' Temple said, quietly. 'I know Hester would not have let you go without a struggle.'

'She does not understand. I lavished my health in the effort to secure America for England, only to watch Lord North stumble into this useless, wasteful, stupid war. But stupid or not, we must fight to the finish. It is a matter of life or death.'

John suppressed a shiver and placed a hand on his father's shoulder. Beneath his fingers, Chatham jumped, as though a shot had been loosed by his ear. 'Papa, William and I have arrived.'

'Pitt.' Papa's smile transformed him into the doting father of John's childhood who had romped through the fields searching for butterflies and delighted in his sons' Latin compositions. But as always there was a doubt there, a nugget of criticism. Papa pinched John's plain brown sleeve. 'Why are you not wearing your regimentals?'

Another pang of guilt. 'I did not want to be recognised.'

Chatham sniffed; he had always enjoyed the pomp of fame, never travelling without his coach-and-six with eight liveried footmen in tow. 'A shame. I wish to show the world that, if my day is past, my sons will save England's future. Pitt in the army; James in the navy; and William will continue my fight in the House of Commons.'

'I agree your sons are all of them fine young men,' Temple said. 'I agree with you even more strongly that your day is past. You made Europe tremble and the world take notice, but that was 20 years ago. Now, you will only make them laugh.'

'How dare you, sir!'

'I dare because I care for your family.' Temple pulled John sharply towards him. John could feel his uncle's gnarled fingers trembling round his arm. 'If you cared for them, too, you would give this up. Pitt is but 21. What do you think he would rather preserve – America, or his father?'

'Uncle,' John protested, horrified, but Temple ignored him.

'Pitt is as much a patriot as I am!' Chatham shouted, but he could not maintain the strength of his fury. He groaned and pressed the heel of his hand to his forehead as though his head ached. 'He knows I must defend what I believe to be right.'

John's gaze crossed William's. His brother's eyes were wide in his pale face. Nobody here had any doubt Chatham was unfit for debate; only Chatham himself seemed not to see it. William had failed to persuade him to return home, but John was the eldest son: surely Papa would listen to him? John licked his lips and said, 'Papa, Uncle Temple is right. I – I think you should go home and rest.'

'You too?' Chatham said, the fatherliness he had shown only moments before dropping away, replaced by naked disappointment. John stammered to a halt, but his father moved on. 'I have come for a purpose and no man alive will prevent me fulfilling it. Not His Grace of Richmond, whose motion I am here to oppose. Not Lord North, His Majesty's so-called Minister. And certainly not you, sir,' to Temple, 'openly supporting the lunatics who are losing my colonies; nor you, sir,' to John, the betrayal in his tone tearing the boy's heart, 'who know how important this is for me.'

Tears of humiliation rose to John's eyes and he fought them, trying to remember his father was ill. Beside him Temple said, ashen-faced, 'My dear friend, what you have said proves you are not yourself. Go home, I beg you.'

'And have you lose my colonies while I am gone?' Chatham roared, and again John noted he said "my colonies" as though they were his personal property. Chatham planted his hands on the armrests of his chair and pushed himself to his feet. James scurried forwards with the crutches. John moved to help but Chatham waved him away and beckoned William and Mahon instead. William threw his brother a helpless look but obeyed Papa's summons. John could do nothing but stand back, cheeks flaming, as William took his place.

With nothing to do, John and James went to watch the debate by the empty Throne of the House of Lords. The steps beneath the red silk canopy thronged with spectators pushing and jostling for space, but a respectful path to the front opened for the eldest son of Lord Chatham. The high vaulted ceiling and the walls hung with tapestries depicting the defeat of the Armada resounded with hundreds of excited voices. Journalists stood by, paper at the ready, pens tucked behind their ears and inkpots in their pockets.

The instant Chatham entered, the entire House rose in a spontaneous gesture of respect. They remained standing until Chatham lowered himself into his seat and William and Mahon joined the others by the Throne. John's heart raced and he was beginning to regret not eating anything since breakfast. He met the gaze of his younger brother. William looked frightened, but the moment their eyes met his lips jerked into a half-smile, as though in apology. John returned it, but knew many of those present would have noticed the second son doing the duties of the eldest. Did they wonder why?

He did not have time to dwell on it, for the debate began immediately. The Duke of Richmond rose first, his bald head gleaming in the candlelight from the irregularly-placed wall sconces. His eyes rested uneasily on Chatham as he spoke. The British force in America had been smashed at Saratoga. Now that France had entered the fray on America's side, with Spain and Holland likely to follow suit, cutting ties with

America and focusing on the European dimension was the only way to retire with dignity.

Lord Weymouth answered for North's government. The Lords had heard Richmond out in silence, but now they fidgeted impatiently; Weymouth, aware his audience was not with him, wrapped up fast. John's heart clenched as his father struggled onto his flannelled legs. Papa's voice, as thin and insubstantial as a whisper, barely reached his ears.

'My lords. I thank God that I have been enabled to come here this day, to perform this duty. I am old, and infirm, and have one foot … more than one foot in the grave.'

The tightness in John's chest intensified as his father went on speaking. It was worse than he had feared. Chatham's mind wandered and he stumbled from sentence to sentence. The lords sat through it all without interruption, without, it seemed, even drawing breath.

'I will not consent to the dismemberment of this ancient and most noble monarchy. Let us make one effort for America's sake. If we must fall, let us fall like men.'

John willed every muttered word out of his father's mouth, straining with every nerve as though he could lend his father his own strength. By the time Chatham sank back into his seat, John felt as exhausted as though he himself had spoken. One glance at his brothers' grey faces told him they, too, had experienced a similar ordeal. But it was not yet over.

The Duke of Richmond looked as though he would rather do anything but debate with a man plainly unfit to defend himself, but courtesy obliged him to respond. He did so as gently as possible. 'The name of Chatham will ever be dear to Englishmen; but the name of Chatham cannot perform impossibilities. It cannot gain victory without an army, without a navy, and without money.'

Richmond sat down. Chatham made to stand, but had considerable difficulty getting up. Even from across the room John could see something was wrong. Papa made a noise and staggered. He swayed, and would have fallen had the Duke of Cumberland and Lord Fitzwilliam not caught him.

Sudden coldness stung John's eyes and stole the breath from his mouth. Every detail of the scene pierced his mind with the precision of a knife: the colourful tapestries, the faint light from the high windows, the prostrate form of Lord Chatham staring sightlessly up at the vaulted ceiling. Then, as though time had finally caught up with the tableau, the house exploded into chaos. John felt himself shoved against the Throne by spectators crowding forwards for a better look. Even the journalists stopped scribbling and peered.

Chatham lay motionless in the arms of Cumberland and Fitzwilliam, Lord Temple gripping his hand. Lord Stanhope rushed in with a bottle of salts. Lord Townshend raced past shouting for water. He was closely followed by Lord Camden: 'Strangers out! Get out!'

The crush eased. John leant against the padded arm of the throne as the world spun around him. He felt someone grip his arm and turned to face William.

'My God, Will,' John gasped, 'Papa—'

William dropped John's arm and shoved his way towards their father. John left Mahon and James behind the Throne and followed. The peers stood aside respectfully as they passed.

Chatham's face was white. The muscles in his neck stood out like cords and he stared in confusion at the men moving about him. John hung back, too horrified to move, but William sank down by Papa's side so abruptly his knees made a cracking sound against the wooden boards. He pressed Papa's hand but Chatham's eyes stared blindly, without recognition.

Lord Temple said, 'We should take him away from here and fetch a doctor.' He glanced up and John realised Temple waited for his orders. A new horror took root. In all the confusion he had not realised the full import of his father's collapse. So long as Papa was incapacitated he, the eldest son, must make any necessary decisions. The shock of seeing Papa fall returned, like a physical blow.

'Yes, yes ... a doctor,' he muttered.

Lord Shelburne ran out of the room to find one. At John's nod four peers carried Chatham into the Prince's Robing Room. John followed, feeling helpless but unwilling to leave his stricken father.

Chatham lurched back to consciousness just as the doctor arrived. John moved forwards the moment his father's eyelids started flickering but William was there first, rushing past John to take his father's hand. Chatham's face was lopsided as though the seizure had loosened the muscles in his left side, but he gave a soft, crooked grin at the sight of his second son and tried to speak.

'Hush, Papa,' William said, his eyes filled with tears, and John came to stand by him. Before he could say a word, however, the doctor turned to William and said, as though he were addressing the eldest son, 'Dr Richard Brocklesby at your service, sir. I saw you carry Lord Chatham to his seat earlier. His Lordship has come round well, but I am anxious to have him moved to a quieter location. If you give the order, I will accompany him to his coach.'

John realised his mouth was open as though to speak. He shut it. William turned to him in embarrassment. Brocklesby's florid face flushed more as he realised his blunder. 'My apologies, sir. I assumed …'

'It doesn't signify,' John stammered. He glanced back at his father. Chatham lay against a cushion with his eyes closed. His loose fingers had twined themselves round William's as though his son's touch were the only thing rooting him to life. John felt the knots inside tighten further as the accumulation of responsibility pressed down on him like an unbearable weight, exacerbated by an unexpected and disorientating stab of loneliness.

A sickening rush of saliva filled his mouth. He turned away and pushed past James, who was just approaching. William shouted his name but John was deaf to all but his inner turmoil. He shoved through a crowd of reporters waiting in the lobby for news, cut a swathe through the people thronging the passageway and bowled out of a side-door into the riverside gardens. He drew deep breaths to steady himself, but the coal-filled air was laced with the unsavoury stench from the Thames and did nothing to refresh him. John raced down the five steps to the gravelled path, skidded to a halt behind the shrubbery and vomited into the undergrowth.

Ever since Papa had accepted the Earldom John had known he would one day succeed to the title. As a child, he had gloried in it: the riches, the lands, the gilded coach with the earl's coronet, the ermine robes with three black bands across the right breast. *A little respect towards the future Earl of Chatham would not go amiss*, he had said to William that very afternoon. And William had replied, *You're not head of the family yet*.

Papa had always seemed so strong, so powerful, so … immortal. A million miles from the limp body slumped across the bench of the House of Lords. John's stomach heaved again at the memory. The moment Temple had turned to him in the Robing Room for instructions everything John had ever known – his role, his identity, even his name – had crumbled into uncertainty.

Chapter Two

May 1778

The servants of Hayes Place waited for John at the head of the stairs. Two days after their master's death, his father's retainers – no, his own now – wore sombre mourning instead of their usual blue and silver livery. Their faces were shadowed in the dim light filtering through the crepe-hung windows. Not one of them met John's eye, but bent into bows or sank into curtseys at the new Earl of Chatham's approach.

Papa's valet came forwards to greet him. The old man's grip shook as he bowed over John's hand. He had been in the family for 30 years, and the sight of the old man who had served Papa so long and so well sent a pulse of emotion through John. 'What will you do now, Bradshaw?'

'There will always be work for me as Lord Chatham's man,' Bradshaw replied, deliberately omitting to mention the fact that, at 65, he was unlikely to find other employment. John hesitated, but as the new Earl his father's household were his responsibility. If he could not help Papa's most faithful retainers, what could he do?

'I am certain my father has left you ample provision in his will. If he has not, I will arrange a pension for you.'

He entered the library for the reading of Papa's will. The old drop-leaf table stood unfolded in the centre of the room. Only a few years ago he and his siblings had used it as a school desk; now it was covered with large leather folios and folders stuffed with legal and financial records. Uncle Temple sat next to John's mother, holding his sister's hand and speaking softly to her. Lady Chatham wore her widow's weeds. The sight of it brought the reality of his father's death back like a knife-thrust. For the second time in a handful of minutes, John found himself blinking back tears.

James, whose leave had been extended only out of compassion for his dying father, had already returned to his ship, but John's brother William and sister Harriot were present. Like Temple and Lady Chatham they, too, held hands. John fought a pang of isolation at the sight. He had not yet had time to examine his own feelings at losing his father, afraid of what might happen if he did. He was the head of the family now; his mother and his siblings all depended on him. He had no time to grieve. Papa would have expected no less.

All rose when John entered, but his eyes were inexorably drawn to the two sombre figures at the other end of the table: William Johnson, his father's man of business, a tall, grizzled man in his early sixties; and a heavy-jowled stranger with pouched eyes.

Johnson's lined face wore an expression befitting the solemnity of the occasion. 'My lord, my profound condolences on the death of your father. I heard the fleet is soon to sail to Gibraltar, and your regiment is to go with it. I take it Your Lordship will not now go?' Decades seemed to have passed since John had raced back from Horse Guards to attend Papa in the Lords. John felt as disorientated as though the question had been addressed to the wrong person. Johnson gestured towards the stranger, who stepped forwards. 'May I introduce Mr John Skirrow?'

'I am pleased to make your acquaintance, Lord Pitt,' Skirrow said.

'I beg your pardon, Mr Skirrow,' Johnson interrupted him with a watery brown eye on John, 'but you are no longer addressing Lord Pitt. You are addressing the Earl of Chatham.'

Skirrow's heavy-set face flushed with embarrassment. At the use of his new title John felt loss slice through him yet again, as though his father had died a second time. Only the need to remain strong for his mother and siblings prevented him staggering beneath the blow.

'My lord,' Skirrow began once John had taken a seat, 'your father was my partner's client for many years. When Mr Nuthall died, your father's will passed into my care. I have it here.' He laid a brown leather folder tied with red silk ribbon on the table. John expected Skirrow to open it at once, but the solicitor laid his hand on it and hesitated. 'My lord, as you were a minor when this will was drawn up you will forgive me if I address the Countess of Chatham. Madam, was your late husband in sound mind when he made this testament?'

Temple clicked his tongue in disapproval. The rustling of Lady Chatham's crepe gown was the only outward indication of her emotion. 'Yes, sir, he was.'

As unpleasant as it must have been to ask such a question, Skirrow looked as though his ordeal had only just begun. 'I fear there may well be difficulties ahead, particularly for you, Lord Chatham. Mr Johnson and I have been in conference for much of last night and this morning, and I regret to say … But perhaps I had better let the will speak for itself.'

Skirrow untied the ribbon and fished a pair of spectacles out of his pocket. He cleared his throat and peered at the thick, gilt-edged foolscap in his hands. 'His Lordship made this will in April of 1774. My Lord Temple, here present, he appointed executor. The estates at Hayes Place, Kent, and Burton Pynsent, Somerset, and all revenues derived thereof, pass to the Countess and second Earl of Chatham jointly. All remaining provision concerns the three youngest children. The Honourable William Pitt is left a sum of £15,000. Lady Harriot Pitt receives £10,000. The Honourable James Pitt inherits £5,000.'

John had known it would take all his strength to sit through Papa's final wishes unmoved. As Johnson read he felt shock dawning, but not for the reason he had anticipated. *Fifteen thousand*! *Ten thousand*! He had no idea how much money his father had had at his death, for Papa had never spoken of such things, but £30,000 …! It was a fortune.

He licked his lips and forced himself to ask the inevitable question. 'How easily will these …' he swallowed back the word "enormous", '… these sums be raised?'

His words fell into deep silence. Skirrow looked at Johnson, who turned to Lady Chatham. 'Madam, was it not a condition of your husband's last loan that his eldest son be informed at his majority of the extent of the debt he stood to inherit?'

John stared at his mother. She ducked her head away from his gaze and fixed her eyes on her gloved hands. 'I did mean to tell him, sir, but I did not find a suitable moment. My husband's health has been poor for many years, and my first duty was to him. I am sorry.'

Johnson shook his head. 'Well, it cannot be helped. I am afraid, Lord Chatham, that you and I must talk privately on the full extent of your father's debts.'

'The legacies?' John pressed, as though prodding at a wound. Johnson's lips lengthened.

'The legacies stipulated in your father's will were to be paid from his estates at Hayes and Burton Pynsent. Burton is heavily mortgaged, and the revenues from the estate will merely pay off the interest. As for Hayes …' Johnson paused, picking his words. 'Your father sold the house and repurchased it at great expense. He was forced to take out a number of loans to do so, and has taken out more since to underwrite improvements to the property.'

'What manner of loans?'

'The last sum amounted to just over £10,000.' The enormity of the sum felled John in his seat. Johnson must have seen the look on his face, for he said, 'Do not despair, my lord. Parliament intends to pay off the bulk of your father's debt, if a vote in the House of Commons next week goes through. There is also talk of settling £4,000 a year on the Earldom of Chatham, which will enable you to maintain the dignity of the title.'

The implication of that was not lost on John. 'Without the pension I could not do so?' Johnson said nothing. The leaden sensation in John's stomach intensified. 'What if I sold Hayes?'

'If you were to sell for more than £20,000, you might cover the immediate interest payments on the loans.'

'Then it is impossible to fulfil my father's dying wishes,' John concluded. His own voice sounded calm but distant, as though the words were spoken by someone else.

'Not impossible, my lord. With careful management, you may expect to pay off the legacies over a period of years – say 30, perhaps 20 if you are frugal.'

By now John was inured to bad news and it no longer had the power to shock him. He still could not look at William and Harriot, to whom he was now so heavily indebted; nor could he look at Temple, in case he turned out to be a creditor. That left him with nobody but his mother, but she was too embarrassed to meet his eyes.

Johnson and Skirrow took their leave, bowing solemnly. William approached John, but all John could think of was of how much he was now indebted to his brother. That £15,000 would have allowed William to pursue the political career Papa had planned for him. *William will continue my fight in the House of Commons.* A bitter taste came into John's mouth. He turned away to find his mother hovering anxiously.

'I meant to tell you,' she said, 'but your father never could bear to talk of money, and you know his state of mind of late ...'

'I know,' John muttered. Lady Chatham put a hand on his arm. Her fingers in her black gloves grasped him, too tight.

'I pray you never know the misery of seeing one you love destroyed from within.'

'I understand, Mama.' And he did – but did she? An hour ago he had been planning pensions for Papa's faithful servants. How naïve he had been. Did she know Papa had frittered away his children's inheritance for the sake of a few more acres, a new wing for Burton, another carriage for six more thoroughbreds to draw? Did she realise Harriot might never have a dowry suited to her rank, that William and James would struggle to live as gentlemen? That he, John, bore a title as hollow, as empty, as ridiculous as if his earl's robes were of straw and his coronet of paper?

Of course she did. He could see it in the lines on her face. She opened her mouth to continue but John could not bear any more excuses. He disengaged himself from her and walked as steadily from the room as his shaking legs would allow.

Once out of sight he broke into a run, down the stairs and through the connecting passage to the nursery wing where he and his siblings had grown up. He burst into the chamber that had been his as a boy, pulled back the curtains and raised the sash. The estate, with its lakes, cedars and beech trees; the oriental carpet beneath his feet; the great mahogany bed with its green brocade hangings – all had been purchased with money his father never had. John had been born at Hayes, and had always loved it. Now he felt himself hating it.

He parted the hangings, sat on the bed and pushed his trembling hands between his legs. He was twenty-one years old: his father was dead and the world he knew lay in fragments. He wanted to live up to Papa's expectations, but he could not do it. He had never been able to do it. He took a deep breath of the room's stale air and tried to catch a hint on it of his childhood. He wished with all his heart that he was still ten, and that he could enjoy the innocence of plain John Pitt again.

****

When John returned to the library half an hour later he found William and Harriot at their mother's side. Harriot held Mama's hand and William touched her arm. At the sight John felt the void in his own heart fill with loneliness and despair. His mother and siblings had each other to rely on; but he, placed unexpectedly in a position of obligation to them, had no-one.

William looked up and saw John watching. 'Is Uncle Temple gone?'

'Yes. He said he would write with the outcome of the debates on Papa's debts.'

'That is unnecessary,' William said. 'I will attend the debates in the gallery myself.'

William's words betrayed his assumption that John's remaining at Hayes was a foregone conclusion. John's sense of entrapment swelled until he could hardly breathe. He said, 'I imagine you will not wish to leave Mama and Harriot alone at Hayes.'

'I won't be leaving them alone. Surely you will remain here with them?'

'I hardly need remind you the convoy to Gibraltar departs in a few days.'

Harriot dropped her mother's hand. William stepped back as though John had struck him. 'You cannot intend still to go?'

Lady Chatham, too, was startled. 'John, you are head of the family. I grant you much of the work to be undertaken can best be done through Mr Johnson and Mr Skirrow, but the estates must be examined, the servants paid, the funeral arranged—'

John felt his breath constrict more and more with every word. He cut in desperately. 'Parliament has voted for a public funeral. The arrangements for that are already out of my hands.'

'But who will be Chief Mourner?'

The memory of his brother pushing him aside in the Prince's Robing Room to take Papa's hand cut into John's mind unbidden. 'William can do it,' he said, more bitterly than he had intended, and his brother flinched.

Harriot's hooded blue eyes, so similar to John's own, turned to her older brother in contempt. 'William is 19. You cannot expect him to take your place.'

'I don't,' John protested, trying to remain calm. 'I know I have responsibilities to you, but I am under orders—'

'General Boyd would have released you from them!' William finally found his voice. John had not seen so much emotion on his self-possessed brother's face since their father had fallen ill. 'Many disasters might befall you in Gibraltar, should Spain join the war. You may never come back. Your first duty now is to your family … to us.' John said nothing, silenced by William's uncharacteristic outburst. 'Papa took the

Earldom of Chatham as a gift from a grateful King and a loving populace. For God's sake, be worthy of it. It is the one thing Papa asks of you.'

Stung, John said unevenly, 'Papa is dead. He asks nothing of me.' William's face drained of colour and John cursed his clumsiness. 'I only want to make my name.'

'You are Earl of Chatham! You have the greatest name in England!'

'No,' John shouted, giving in at last to his anger and fear. '*You* have received England's most famous name. All I have inherited are debts.'

His words echoed in silence. Harriot braced her hands on Lady Chatham's shoulders, her face tense. William's grey eyes were wide. Suddenly his gaze hardened. 'How could you be so selfish? But then it has always been that way, has it not? Always late, always unreliable. You never think of how others might feel. I will not allow you to load your troubles onto my shoulders. You cannot abandon us all because you are jealous of me.'

'I already told you,' John insisted, white-faced. 'All I want to do is make Papa proud.'

'As you correctly observed,' William hissed, 'Papa is dead.'

'That is enough!' Lady Chatham leapt between her sons as though to stop them physically attacking each other. 'How can you quarrel with your father lying dead upstairs?'

The reminder that their father's body still lay in the great bedroom where he had drawn his last breath shocked both brothers into silence. John realised he was trembling. William turned to Lady Chatham, his chest heaving. 'Tell him he cannot go, Mama. Tell him.'

Lady Chatham looked wordlessly at her eldest son. John fancied there was a shade of guilt underlying her grief, guilt that her omissions, as much as Lord Chatham's extravagance, had placed John in such an impossible position. To his relief, he saw she had no intention of stopping him. She gave William an apologetic glance and said, 'John, are you certain?'

'I am, Mama.' He added, more for his benefit than anyone else's, 'I must go.'

He saw that she comprehended him, as William did not. She kissed him once on each cheek. Her breath trembled as though she fought tears. 'God be with you, my son.'

Harriot led her mother out. Left alone, John turned back to William. He had no wish to part with his brother on bad terms. 'Will, I am sorry, but I have to go. I need to know what this all means for me – for us. You must understand—'

'I do understand, too well,' William interrupted. 'And I hope you understand that I will not forgive you for this.'

The door thudded closed behind him. John, crushed by the bitterness in William's tone, could not find the words to call him back.

Chapter Three

June 1779

'We could make a surprise of it.' The Duke of Rutland leaned back against the velvet upholstery and tugged off his gloves. 'We will have to leave the coach elsewhere; my panelling might give us away. But just think of when your mother will come into the drawing room to find you waiting!'

'I don't want to startle my mother into a fit. Besides, she already knows I am coming.'

'You, Chatham, are dull. Although I am impressed you remembered to give her notice of your return to London. Either Gibraltar has matured you, or you are an impostor.'

John could not help laughing, although the prospect of facing his family again after the way he had left them did not amuse him at all. But that was Rutland for you. Barely a fortnight had passed since he had succeeded to the dukedom on the death of his grandfather, but in or out of mourning, he was utterly incapable of remaining serious.

Charles was a steadfast friend who could be trusted with anything; not for nothing had John made his way immediately to Rutland's house on Arlington Street after disembarking at Dover. Rutland was also close to William, and knew more of the two brothers' history than any other person. He was the son of the famed Marquis of Granby, whose largesse to the men he had commanded in battle had enabled many of them to start new lives as tavern-owners. Everywhere Rutland went, he was likely to see a public house named 'The Marquis of Granby' in his father's honour. Rutland knew what it was like to be a hero's son; John often wondered whether it was this that bound them together more than anything else.

Even now Rutland's heavy-lidded brown eyes rested on him shrewdly, and John suspected his friend knew more about what was passing through his mind than he was letting on. 'You have been away for nearly a year. Do you not think your family will be pleased to see you?'

'Of course Mama will be happy,' John protested. Rutland blew out his plump cheeks.

'That goes without saying. But what of William? I think you are not so sure of him.' John said nothing. Rutland's lips twitched. 'So it stands thus. You have been on active service in Gibraltar; William has hardly stirred from his Cambridge college. You fear you will have nothing to say to each other.'

'On the contrary,' John said quietly. 'I fear we will have too much.'

'Then worry not. William has begun studies to become a barrister, but he has not relinquished his ambitions to sit in Parliament. He is thoroughly qualified to talk the hind legs off a donkey whilst not listening to a word you say.' Rutland leaned forwards, suddenly serious. 'In all honesty, do not fret. William has been talking about your return to England since February. Had you heard him you would have no doubt of the warmth of his regard.'

Rutland's carriage drew up in Harley Street. Just over a year ago John had hurried from here to meet William the day Papa collapsed. The memory of that day seized John like a superstition. He gazed up at the house's tall, blank sash windows with dread. 'Will you not come in?'

Rutland gave an exaggerated sigh. 'Do you think it's me your family wishes to see? Get out, Chatham, before I tell my coachman to use his whip on you.'

John got out and the carriage clattered off across the muddy thoroughfare. John turned to the large, polished front door. He took a deep breath and pulled the bell.

A moment later the door was pulled open by his brother-in-law Mahon, an excited look on his long, scholarly face. He stepped across the threshold and clasped John into a tight embrace. 'Lord Chatham! We have been expecting you since yesterday! Welcome home!'

John stiffened instinctively, mindful of the audience of curious passers-by who had already been attracted by Rutland's handsome coach and four, but his brother-in-law had never heeded convention. Mahon called up the stairs and John's embarrassment transformed into a thick, choking emotion that took him entirely by surprise; for there was Mama running down the staircase shedding tears of relief, his sisters close behind her.

John found himself the centre of a whirlwind of arms, faces and questions, barely aware of anything except the ball of unacknowledged homesickness lodged in his throat. He had looked forward to this moment so much, but now he could think of nothing but how much he had missed the scent of lavender in Mama's hair, or Hetty's musical laugh, or Harriot's habit of wrinkling her nose when pleased. Then he raised his eyes and saw William at the stair-head.

William stood in silence with one hand braced against the bannister. John disengaged himself from Hetty's arms. 'Well, William, are you not pleased to see me?'

For a heartbeat William did not react. Then he broke out of his stillness, hammered down the stairs and threw himself at John. 'John! Good God, John, of course I am pleased to see you!'

'Thank goodness for that,' John joked. Even to his own ears his voice held more sincerity than the jest ought to permit, but nobody seemed to notice. He clung to his mother, brother and sisters as though to let them go would be to sail away once more and lose them forever.

****

A few days later the new Earl of Chatham appeared in the House of Lords for the first time. Like his return to Harley Street, John's appearance in the chamber where his father had suffered his spectacular collapse brought back so many memories he had to fight the swell of emotion threatening to overcome him as he stepped over the threshold.

'I, John, Earl of Chatham, do truly and sincerely acknowledge, profess, testify and declare ...' John took a deep breath and peered at the dog-eared card held out for him by the Clerk. He was going hoarse, for he had already read out the Oaths of Supremacy and Allegiance before the Lord Steward. '... in my conscience, before God and the world, that our Sovereign Lord King George is lawful and rightful King of this realm ...'

It took him a good few minutes to get to 'I do make this recognition, acknowledgment, abjuration, renunciation, and promise, heartily, willingly, and truly, upon the true faith of a Christian', by which time he felt he had learned more ways of expressing the verb 'to swear' than he had ever known existed.

He could feel curious eyes on him as he bent to inscribe his name in the register. He had seen the journalists staring at him and scribbling notes when he entered the room. John knew they were thinking more about his father than about him, but it only made him more aware of the duty he owed to the name of Chatham. It was part of the reason he had chosen to appear today in his regimentals. The dense scarlet wool of his coat lay as heavily on his shoulders as the title he bore.

The formalities over, John clambered up to take his seat beside Rutland. His friend was still mourning his grandfather the third Duke, although characteristically the black velvet straining across his paunch was cut to the height of fashion. 'So you've joined us old hands at last.'

'You've been a member of the House of Lords ten minutes longer than me. I'd hardly call you an "old hand".'

'Ten minutes is an age in politics, believe me. Will you look at that?' Rutland pointed at the two pedigree rolls on the clerk's table, neatly tied in red silk ribbon and deposited by Garter King of Arms in accordance with the procedure of admitting new members to the House. 'My pedigree's bigger than yours.'

'They probably use more calligraphic flourishes for Dukes. Be serious, Rutland, as befits the august chamber of which we are now both members.'

'Be serious? Who do you take me for?' Rutland said, with a mischievous twinkle. 'Very well, if I must. But unless debates have changed since I was in the habit of watching behind the Throne, you will soon regret forbidding my jokes.'

While the Lord Chancellor laid out the preliminary business for the day a number of the opposition front bench turned to extend a welcome to John and Rutland. Lord Shelburne gave them both a long, appraising stare from beneath his large, mobile brows. The Marquis of Rockingham, head of the Whig opposition, took John's hand and shook it. He was a small, thin man who looked older than his 49 years. 'I am pleased beyond measure to see the sons of the Marquis of Granby and the Earl of Chatham join us today.'

John's uncle Lord Temple leaned across. There were genuine tears of pleasure in his eyes as he pumped John's hand. 'My dear boy. I am glad to see you have returned safe and well from Gibraltar. I was afraid you would not be able to leave before Spain declared war.'

'I was lucky,' John said, touched. Temple smiled.

'It is good you are returned. We have much need of an Earl of Chatham here, now we are at war with half of Europe.' John began to feel a little uncomfortable, hoping Temple did not expect him to take his father's place. 'England needs you.'

'I will do my best,' John stammered, but to his relief Temple did not seem to notice his discomfort. The old man laid his hand on John's shoulder in a paternal manner, his fingers lingering on the gold braid of John's epaulettes.

'Hester tells me you will not be returning to Gibraltar when your leave ends, but to the West Indies?'

'Indeed, uncle. His Grace of Rutland has raised a new regiment, and I have obtained a captaincy in it. We leave for the Leeward Islands in the new year.'

'You were lucky not to be sent to America,' Lord Shelburne cut in. 'Most newly-raised bodies are being sent there. I hope Lord Chatham's son will never find himself obliged to wage war on our colonial kin.'

'I had the foresight to request that my regiment not be sent to the Colonies,' Rutland said. 'Lord Chatham is as dear to me as a brother. I cannot prevent him being sent abroad, but I would not wish him to draw his sword against his political inclinations.' John did not know what to say, surprised and moved at Rutland's words. Rutland himself looked abashed and said, after everyone had returned to their seats, 'Listen to me. I must sound like your mother.'

'Believe me, Rutland, you are nothing like my mother.'

'Well, that's a relief.'

The debate was about to begin; the Lord Chancellor, Lord Thurlow, had taken his seat on the Woolsack, adjusting his robes and glaring at the assembled lords from beneath his bushy black eyebrows. John looked across at Rutland. 'Shall we take in a debate, Your Grace?'

Rutland returned his expression with a lopsided grin. 'Why of course, my Lord Chatham. By all means, since we are now both Peers of the Realm.'

The Realm so many people here hoped the Earl of Chatham would save. John smiled nervously. Rockingham's welcome had unsettled him, for it demonstrated how much both he and Charles stood in their fathers' shadow already. John had told Temple the truth: he would do his best. Only time would tell whether his best would be enough.

He settled down on the bench beside his friend and tried to concentrate on the debate.

January 1781

Parson Alford stood with his fingers curled around the edge of the pulpit. There were no pews, only family stalls arranged against the whitewashed walls; the poorer parishioners stood in the middle of the church with bent heads and clasped hands. Every now and then a few of them glanced up at the Pitt stall, their eyes lingering on the lozenge-shaped hatchment above it, and the dark mourning worn by its occupants. Then their eyes dropped again.

'Our minds must turn to the trials of the season,' Parson Alford said, his words echoing off the coarse barrel-vaulting above. 'We must turn our thoughts to those less fortunate, who have little to keep them warm when the snow lies thick on the ground. We must remember those in our parish whose sons have fallen in the war and will not now come home; those who have lost parents, to old age or disease; those who have lost children.' Alford's deep-set eyes, too, were drawn to the Pitt stall for a moment. 'These are wounds that will not easily be healed.'

John risked a glance at his mother. Lady Chatham sat with her hands clasped before her, elbows resting on the worn oak stall. Her face was hidden behind the black lace of her veil. John could not tell whether she had heard Alford, but she was certainly taking his invitation to pray to heart. The words she muttered carried to him on a whisper of air: ' … for the Lord will not cast off for ever … but though he cause grief, yet he will have compassion according to the multitude of his mercies … for he doth not afflict willingly nor grieve the children of men …'

William and Harriot flanked her, straight-backed in their close mourning. They gazed out at Alford with set, pale faces, their solemn expressions so similar they might have been twins. John suspected that, like him, they were too accustomed to tragedy to find prayer of any comfort. Even Mama, for all her references to God's compassion, sounded more desperate than devout; and well she might, for of a family of seven they were now the only four that remained.

****

'Don't go back, John,' Lady Chatham blurted out halfway through a listless Sunday dinner. She pressed the back of her hand to her mouth as though to brace herself and repeated, 'Don't go back to the Leeward Islands. Please. For my sake.'

John had been expecting this ever since he, William and Harriot had arrived at Burton Pynsent with news of James's death. It was only six months since Hetty had died of a consumption following the birth of her third daughter. John knew his mother was only wondering when the next blow would fall, and on whom. 'I must go back. My regiment is there, and I am under orders.'

'I do not think I can bear it.' To John's alarm his proud, unshakeable mother was on the verge of tears. 'I lost James to fever. I cannot lose you as well. Do not go back. I beg of you.'

'I know it is hard for you,' John said, gently, 'but I must return.'

He did not say that he would gladly have stayed, given the opportunity, for the West Indies was a difficult billet. He dreaded the long journey back he would have to make when his leave ran out at the end of February. The voyage would take six weeks and pass through dangerous waters, beset by the weather and stalked by Spanish and French ships. Once there, he would be threatened by the constant, horrifying spectre of the disease that had killed his brother.

John had seen too many cases of yellow fever to have any illusions about how much James must have suffered in his last hours; he had already determined never to tell his mother about it. The Leeward Islands were beautiful with their white sands fringed with lush green foliage, but it was a dark, hard beauty, for a large proportion of those who saw it died there.

'Please, John,' Lady Chatham insisted, as though she had read John's thoughts. A pair of tears coursed down her cheeks and she shook her head as though to deny their presence. John looked across at William and Harriot, bent over their plates with every sign of not wanting to be involved, and felt a pulse of irrational anger. He understood his mother's reasoning, and he had not forgotten his argument with William after Papa's death over the disastrous decision to leave for Gibraltar. He was determined not to make the same mistake again, but he still felt the unfairness of being the one who always had to make sacrifices for the good of the family.

He swallowed his frustration with difficulty. 'Very well. I promise I will seek the first opportunity I can for an exchange.' He did not know how easy it would be to find an officer desperate enough for promotion to take the place of a man serving in the West Indies. He could not help adding, although he knew it would do no good to point it out, 'It will be expensive.'

'Your life is more valuable than money,' Lady Chatham said. She looked relieved and John knew he had made the right decision for his family, if not for himself. He turned back to his plate and wondered, bitterly, if he could ever reconcile them both.

****

'This is not the way I had planned my election to Parliament,' William said. He flicked a mote of dust off the ivory tip of his cue, then leaned over the table to line up his next shot. 'I imagined myself bringing the good news to Burton. I imagined Mama's joy. I thought James would be with us.' His voice started to tremble. He hit the ball awkwardly; it bounced off the cushion of the billiard table without striking any of John's.

'Forfeit,' John said, sadly. William flashed him an uncertain smile and laid his cue down.

'Let's take a pause. My hand is none too steady tonight.'

John poured two glasses of port and carried them to where William stood by the window. Darkness had fallen, the shadows drawing their way across the expanse of Sedgemoor beyond the trees bounding the house's estate. John wondered whether William was remembering when the Pitt children had played on this very terrace, pretending to be Indians, or American frontiersmen, or Frederick of Prussia's army; remembering when there had been five of them. He set down his empty glass. 'William, you are too hard on yourself. I know James's death was not the news you had meant to bring; but your election was just what we needed to take our minds off the tragedy.'

'I just thought Mama would be so pleased for me,' William said. His voice sounded muffled. 'I know the borough of Appleby isn't a grand prospect, but it is a good sound seat, and Rutland tells me Sir James Lowther does not intend to control me.'

'Lowther is a character,' John observed. 'He is notorious for placing pressure on the men who sit for his boroughs. Now that you are one of those men, can the two of you rub along together?'

'Long enough for me to establish myself,' William said with a faint grin. 'Besides, it was Rutland found me the seat. I am obliged to him, not

29

to Lowther, and you know well how closely Rutland and I are likely to agree.'

William cradled his empty glass and stared out of the window. His white face contrasted strongly with the black of his clothes. The family had hardly packed the mourning wear away from Hetty's death before the news of James's demise had brought it out again. As though he knew what John was thinking William said, 'I wish James could have known of my election.'

John knew it was impossible; at least six weeks were required to carry news to and from the West Indies, and although James had died in mid-November he guessed he had been ill and delirious for some time prior to that. To make William feel better, however, he said, 'Perhaps he did.'

He had a feeling William knew he had not spoken the truth, but to his relief his brother changed the subject. 'Another game?'

'What stakes?'

'John, I'm a barrister. Unless you expect me to pawn my lawyer's gown, we'd better not play for money.'

They set to, but William's mind was still not on the game and he helpfully potted several of his own balls to save John the effort. John waited for him to explain what was on his mind. A year ago he would have doubted whether William would talk, but after three months of leave in William's company he was certain that he would. He was willing to be patient, for he knew now how precious a thing brotherly ties could be.

At length William said, 'That was good of you, promising Mama you would leave your regiment.'

John did not answer for a moment, gauging his next shot. 'I did not promise her I would leave. I promised her I would consider procuring an exchange. I meant what I said: it will be expensive; not many men want to serve in the West Indies.'

'It will be worth it. Mama cannot afford to lose you. Neither can I.' William bent back to the billiards table. Another of his own balls spun off into a pocket.

'My word, William, you are off your game tonight,' John remarked. 'I'd stand more chance of losing playing against the candelabrum.'

William did not look at him, rolling his cue back and forth between his fingers. 'When your ship was nearly shipwrecked on its way home from the Indies we thought we could not be so unlucky as to lose you and Hetty in the same year. Now we know we were even more fortunate than that. You, Hetty and James. John, Mama would not have survived it.'

'And you, as my heir, would never set foot in the House of Commons.'

William looked at him fully for the first time and John saw the depth of his emotion: pain for Hetty and James, fear for John. 'Do you think I care about that even for a moment?'

'I am whole and well, and I promise you I will seek an exchange, whatever the cost.' John took aim for his next shot. 'Whatever my ambitions, I never stood any chance of military glory in this war anyway, not without serving in America – and what chance would I have of distinguishing myself in such a wretched struggle?' He changed his aim to a different ball. 'My place is here, in England, with you, Harriot and Mama.'

William said nothing for a space, as though gathering the strength to ask a question. 'You said, "whatever my ambitions". What exactly is your ambition? You did not say.'

'Must I have one?' William frowned and John grinned. 'Oh, I don't know … I am easy to please. Perhaps to have a fast horse and a good pack of hounds, and to sleep till past noon every day if I wish it.'

'John, you've spent too much time in Rutland's company. Be serious.'

'I am serious.' John laughed at William's moue of disapproval. 'Very well, very well. If I must have an ambition, let it be to get married and provide an heir to the earldom. That should be easy, if I can find a pretty enough girl, that is.' William opened his mouth and John held up his hands. 'In all seriousness, are they not worthy aims? Unless you'd prefer me to say I wish to bring about peace with the American Colonies?'

'They're worthy,' William said, and the smile he gave was sincere enough. 'You can leave the peace-making to us statesmen.'

'And right gladly. I'm not sure that one would have been so simple.'

They settled back down to the game. William seemed in lighter spirits, talking about what he intended to do once he had taken his seat in Parliament. His game improved markedly too. John's, on the other hand, declined in quality. The last exchange had thrown him more than he cared to admit. *What exactly is your ambition*? The question had caught him off-guard, and he was only now realising why: because he genuinely did not know the answer.

John watched William bend over the billiards table and felt a prick of resentment. At twenty-one William was following the path that had been marked out for him from the cradle. He had always known he would one day sit in Parliament, just as John had always known he would enter the army. But for John things were different. His obligation to his father's politics kept him from action in America. His duty to the family had brought him home early from Gibraltar, and would shortly curtail his career in the West Indies. He was the eldest son, the Earl of Chatham, and that would always colour the course of his life, for he was the head of the family and William was not.

The Earldom of Chatham is a mark of esteem for you to wear your whole life. For God's sake, John, be worthy of it.

To be worthy, to do his duty: that was the summit of his ambition. What was required to fulfil it? Would he ever know if he had been successful? He was not certain, but it mattered very much to him; and perhaps that was enough.

February 1781

'My lords, Mr Pitt is on his legs.'

The whisper travelled along the benches of the Lords as rapidly as flame. It was not clear who had started it – probably some messenger had run through the corridors and up the twisted staircases to carry the news that Lord Chatham's son was making his maiden speech. Ever since William had taken his seat at the end of January such a summons had been eagerly anticipated, but nobody had expected it to come so soon.

John himself was surprised. When he had last asked William when he intended to make his maiden speech, William had laughed at him. John tugged Rutland's sleeve. 'Did I hear aright? My brother?'

'Is speaking, yes. On the Bill to regulate the Civil List.'

Several lords rose and took their leave, curious to see whether young Mr Pitt was as good an orator as his father had been. John and Rutland followed them. John felt an unaccountable nervousness, as though he himself were expected to stand and talk.

They were not the only ones who had heard of Pitt's intentions. The coffee houses were emptying of customers, and the crowds got denser the closer they got to the House of Commons. Somehow, John and

Rutland managed to elbow their way through the mass to find a space in the House itself.

'The name of William Pitt still works its magic,' Rutland observed, before he was shushed by another member of the audience.

The galleries above the green cloth-covered benches heaved with people. John felt the pressure weighing down on his brother from all these curious faces. He imagined what it must be like to be subject to the same scrutiny, and felt faint. He was sure it would have been the same had he given notice of a speech. He too, after all, was Chatham's son.

Wedged between the wall and another man, hardly able to raise a hand to touch his face, John tried to pick out his brother on the benches stacked against three sides of the tiny chamber like choir stalls. He could hear a voice, deep and pleasant in tone, speaking in a measured, calm, fluent manner. Surely that could not be William? And then he saw him, three benches back on the opposition side. William spoke calmly and firmly, in command of every word, every gesture, moving from point to point with breath-taking confidence.

'The noble lord,' William said, bowing his powdered head in the direction of Lord Nugent, scowling through a pair of spectacles on the government bench, 'has declared that if the Bill would apply all monies derived from reductions of Crown expenditure to the public service, then he would become one of its warmest advocates. He believes, however, that the savings will be appropriated towards a fund providing for the Royal Family. This clause he claims to have found in the Bill before us now.'

Rutland gave a deep breath and whispered wonderingly, 'My God. He's making an answer. He's actually *engaging in debate* for his maiden speech.'

William paused. Many men of twenty-one speaking in the Commons for the first time might fall dumb out of fear or embarrassment, but John could tell William was aware of the effect he was having and enjoying it. When Nugent said nothing, William gave a flicker of a smile and dug a copy of the Civil List Bill out of his pocket. 'I beg leave to take issue with the noble lord. There is a clause which expressly states that monies arising from the reductions proposed will be directly applied to the public service. The only merit I can claim in competition with the noble lord is that my eyes are somewhat younger than his, but he should not trouble himself, for I will read the clause to him.'

The House burst into laughter. Nugent went red and folded his spectacles into his waistcoat pocket. William meanwhile read out the clause to which he alluded as though he sat by the fire in the library of Hayes or Burton Pynsent. Apart from Nugent, John did not think he could see a single person William had not won over. Even Lord North himself, on the Treasury Bench with his arms crossed over his ample belly, listened with benevolent interest.

After a further quarter hour of clear, polished oratory William sat down. Almost immediately the House and galleries began to buzz with excited conversation. Several oppositionists leaned over to clap William on the shoulder. Across the House Lord North nodded vigorously and several of his colleagues looked impressed. The only person who appeared unmoved was William himself, and even his cheeks were flushed. The name "Chatham" hung in the air, as though William and his great father were one.

Rutland leaned over. 'Was that not excellent? I know he's no fool, but did you ever suppose Pitt would be so good?' He belatedly caught sight of John's expression. 'What's amiss? You think he did badly?'

'No, no,' John said. 'He was marvellous.'

Rutland beamed. 'I agree. Nearly as good as the late Lord Chatham, in fact!'

The present Lord Chatham smiled weakly. John was glad beyond measure William's rite of passage was over, and glad it had been so successful. But William's success was salt on a wound he had barely known he had. For if William was his father's son, so was John, who would soon be forced to leave the profession his father had selected for him – at the same moment William was making his name in his.

Only now was John beginning to realise just how far his little brother had already outstripped him.

****

That night Rutland treated the entire subscription room of White's to several bottles of the cellar's most distinguished vintage of burgundy wine, raising a toast to "his new pet orator". 'I always wanted to tell my grandchildren I brought William Pitt back to Parliament,' he announced.

'Mr Burke told me himself our young friend was not a chip off the old block, but the old block himself. Chatham redux!'

'Chatham redux!' the others echoed, their eyes turned to William. John, leaning against one of the window seats, swilled the wine around in his glass and downed it in silence, but nobody paid him any heed.

The next evening John and William went to dine with Thomas Townshend, Lord Sydney. Sydney was an old associate of their father who had served him well over the years. His country house, Frognal, was close to Hayes, and the Pitt and Townshend children had grown up together. John had met with Sydney several times in Parliament over the last few months, but he had not seen Lady Sydney or the children since before his father's death.

He was under no illusions as to why he and his brother had been invited now, but old ties could not be ignored. The two of them arrived at Albemarle Street shortly after five. Sydney was a solidly built, fleshy man with twinkling dark eyes and a ready smile. He and his wife Elizabeth greeted the two Pitt men as though they were part of the family, which was not surprising as they had known them since they were barely out of the cradle.

The youngest Townshend children stayed only to make a brief bow before going back to the nursery, but Georgiana, Mary and John, the three eldest, accompanied their parents to dinner. John Townshend was soon to go to Cambridge, and spoke with William about the university. Georgiana prattled to John about a new spaniel she had acquired; John smiled and nodded but found her relentless stream of inane conversation rather tiresome. In contrast, her younger sister Mary said very little, and kept glancing at him across the table.

Sydney kept an excellent table: game from his Frognal estate coupled with tender lamb and a magnificent pie. The party had hardly sat down before Sydney turned to his guests. 'I am delighted to see both of you tonight, particularly as we see so little of Lord Chatham since he has been serving abroad.' He nodded at John, who acknowledged the compliment, then turned eagerly to William. 'As for you, my young orator, I cannot tell you how pleased I was with your speech. You were every inch the man your boyhood promised you would be.'

John guessed he would be no longer required in this conversation. He drained his glass and began ladling some sauce onto his meat. Across the table William laid down his knife, a blush creeping across his cheeks. 'I am glad my speech found favour with you.'

'I know of no-one with whom it did not find favour,' Sydney said. 'Parliament has been waiting since your father died for a successor worthy of his memory. Here you are at last, and his own son, no less.'

John fumbled the ladle and a splash of sauce landed on the table. He mopped at it with his handkerchief. Miss Mary handed him hers without a word.

'It has long been my ambition to follow in my father's footsteps,' William said.

Sydney beamed. 'I know. I told Lady Sydney only this morning how I remembered your father taking you to the stables at Hayes, setting you on a coach block and making you address the horses in their stalls as though they were Members of Parliament. What did you think, Chatham?' John froze, his fork halfway to his mouth. 'I saw you there behind the Bar. Was it not the most perfect maiden speech you have ever heard?'

John considered the question. 'If I am to be perfectly frank, it is so far the only maiden speech I have ever heard.'

'But was it not sublime?' Sydney pressed him.

'I thought it very good, yes.'

'Very good? It could not be bettered! How many young men would throw themselves into the midst of a heated debate in getting on their legs for the first time? It was splendid, Pitt, splendid!' Sydney stood up. He refilled his glass, raised it and looked William directly in the eye. 'Had your father been here he could not have been prouder. As it is, I tell no untruth by saying he is back at Westminster at last. To your health, sir, and your father's memory. May Lord Chatham live on through his son!'

John raised his glass with the rest but wished Sydney had chosen different words. He did not begrudge Sydney's comparing William to their father, but Sydney did not seem to remember that another of Chatham's sons had already been at Westminster for over a year.

Sydney had clearly not read John's mood accurately. He refilled John's glass and said, 'Would you name the next health, Chatham?'

John blinked into his glass. His mind raced. He knew Sydney was only doing his duty in naming him as the highest-ranking person at table, but he knew very well everybody would expect him to drink to his brother. Tonight was William's night; to judge from William's performance, every night henceforth would be his night. John supposed he was just going to have to get used to it. He was fair enough, and loved his brother enough, to give William his due.

John rose, forced a smile and said, 'To the orator.' A slight pause; he felt something else was needed to persuade William of his sincerity. 'Our father would be proud.'

William beamed, and John immediately felt better for having made the effort. The others at the table echoed the toast. Everyone looked at William save for Miss Mary, who watched John over the rim of her glass of wine and water.

****

Sydney's footmen cleared away the remaining dishes. The silver plates, centrepieces, bowls and tureens were removed and the tablecloth taken away. The polished walnut surface of the table glistened in the candlelight. Decanters were arrayed on the sideboard and fruit, nuts and sweetmeats arranged in dishes on the table.

After the loyal toast the ladies retired to the drawing room. John could see Sydney already preparing himself to quiz William and felt a sudden need for fresh air, certain that he could not last out the evening unless he managed to clear his head. 'Might I take a quick turn in your garden?'

'Of course,' Sydney said. 'Are you not well?'

'A headache, that is all. I will return shortly.'

Leaning on the stone balustrade looking down into Sydney's narrow townhouse garden John felt a little better. The air was crisp but dry, and with his coat pulled about his shoulders he did not feel the cold. The light from the house behind cast his shadow past the ornamental water-feature into the depths of the garden. John stared through the clouds of steam pooling from his mouth and nerved himself to re-join Sydney's uninhibited adulation of his brother. He had known it would be like this, and had thought he would not mind. He was disturbed to find that he did mind after all, and rather angry at himself for it.

The creak of the tall French door warned him he was not alone. Sydney must have sent a footman down to see if he needed any assistance. He turned to dismiss the man and found himself unexpectedly face to face with Miss Mary Townshend. She still wore the pink satin gown she had worn at dinner, but she had pulled on a fur-lined pelisse on top of it. She said nothing, but blinked to adjust her eyes to the darkness.

John did not feel like making conversation, particularly when the topic was likely to be his brother. 'Should you not be in the drawing room with your mother?'

'I saw you here and thought you might need some company.' She jerked her head up at one of the windows on the first floor. 'If it's my reputation you fear for, my mother is just above us and can see you as well as I could.'

She stepped out onto the balcony and came towards him. She stumbled on one of the steps down to the balustrade and he thrust out his arm to steady her. 'I can be so clumsy,' she said with a shy smile, but her fingers dug into his upper arm for support. A memory came to him from his youth of Lady Sydney writing for herbs from Hayes' kitchen garden to make compresses for little Mary's hip and knee. He could not recall if she had had a childhood accident or not, but now that he thought about it he could see she walked with a noticeable limp.

She leaned next to him on the balustrade and drew in a few long breaths. A few chestnut strands of her hair had come loose from her braided chignon and danced in the breeze. He had vague recollections of her as a slim, pale child with dark hair and solemn blue eyes, practising dance sequences or playing blind man's buff. A glance at the curve of her hips and swell of her breasts, just visible under the pelisse, was enough to show John she was no longer a child. How old was she now? Seventeen? Eighteen? She glanced up and he became aware he was staring. He blushed and looked down.

'I much admired what you did for your brother tonight,' Mary said at last.

That was unexpected. John tried to remember doing anything other than bite his tongue all evening. 'What did I do exactly?

'You know as well as I.' Mary focused her attention on a stray lock of dark hair which she coiled round her finger. 'I cannot imagine being in your precise situation, but I think I have an idea of what you might feel. Georgiana is older and prettier than me. She is not lame like me. She thinks of nothing but dresses and balls but that will not stop her making a much better marriage than I will ever make. I have watched her dance for an hour without pause, while the rest of the company did nothing but praise her lightness and beauty.'

'I do not think Georgiana is prettier than you,' John blurted out, and felt himself go red instantly. Mary looked startled, but not displeased.

'My father is a good, kind, clever man, but often speaks without thinking. Sometimes tonight he spoke as though you were not there. Had I been you I do not think I would have held my tongue; but you did, for Mr Pitt's sake.'

'Hardly matter for admiration,' John noted dryly, and Mary gave him a curious look.

'I think you were very generous. You were the highest-ranking guest and my father spent almost the whole evening ignoring you. I'd say you had every right to feel slighted, and yet you ceded your right to prominence to your brother without protest.'

She turned away as though she felt she had said too much. John could see nothing but the fringe of her dark hair, a few loose wisps trembling in the cold breeze. He knew he would probably regret what he was about to say, but he was so amazed to find his innermost thoughts articulated aloud by her that he could not help it. 'Of course I am happy for my brother. Parliament has long been his aim and I am delighted he did so well; but I cannot but wish …' He tailed off, unable to finish.

'I could see it was not easy for you,' Mary prompted.

John drew a deep breath to steady himself. 'No. It was not easy.'

'When you make your first speech, they will—' Mary said, but John laughed mirthlessly.

'They will not.' Mary was stunned into silence by the self-deprecation in John's tone. He tilted his head back up to look at the stars. 'Sometimes I wonder what would have happened had William been the eldest son, and I the younger. Would Papa have lavished as much attention on my education as he did on William's? Would I be the toast of London's political salons now?'

'Do you want to be?'

John shuddered at the thought. 'No. And that is the oddest thing, because I still resent William's success, even though I would not want it myself.' He gave a small, bitter laugh. 'I always suspected he was the better man of the two of us. What I just said probably confirms it.'

'I do not agree,' Mary said.

'But it is the truth.' The agony he had been keeping inside all evening was spilling out now, almost beyond his ability to stem it. 'I always knew it would be difficult to follow my father, but at least when I came to Parliament everyone knew who I was. Now they all look through me as though I'm not there. William has stepped ahead of me and I've fallen into his shadow. Everyone is talking as though his arrival in Parliament is nothing but a return home. And I? I belong nowhere. I have no presence, no role, nothing but a name, and even that is more William's than mine now.'

'And yet despite all this you still toasted William's success with a glad heart.'

'Of course I did,' John said. 'He is my brother.'

Mary turned to him in palpable amazement. 'You truly do not see it, do you?' she said at last. 'You truly do not understand why I find your sacrifice so admirable.'

'What sacrifice?' John frowned, genuinely confused. Mary drew a long, shuddering breath.

'You said you had no role. You are wrong. Your role is to know when to step back and allow others to shine in your stead. A thankless role, perhaps, but one that takes the most strength, and deserves the most applause.'

'Strong?' John snorted in derision. 'Even if I were, nobody else would believe it. Nobody sees me, not with my brother around.'

'I see you,' Mary said.

John stared at her again, more sharply this time. She looked alarmed at her own words, but moved one of her hands slightly apart from the other and nudged his gently. It was no more than a brief tremble of a touch, but coupled with what she had said he could not have been more amazed if she had thrown her arms around his neck and kissed him on the mouth.

A tapping on the window above broke the spell. Mary withdrew her hand as though scorched. They both looked up to see Lady Sydney waving at them to summon them inside.

'I think my father and your brother have come to the drawing room,' Mary said. She gave John another smile that, this time, John returned. 'We should join them.'

John nodded and helped Mary back inside. He knew he was going back to Sydney's unbounded raptures over William, but he no longer minded.

For the first time in a long while he felt he had an ally, someone who understood him.

Chapter Four

July 1782

The queue of carriages for entry to the landward entrance of Vauxhall pleasure-gardens stretched down Kennington Road, the shadows of their bored occupants – gauze-wrapped women in expansive hats, men in powdered wigs and evening finery – still perceptible in the dusk light. Mary cast an eye over them from the ferry and felt glad she and her family had come by river.

Her father helped her step down from the boat. For a moment all Mary could think about was placing her feet in the right place without her hip giving way, for Georgiana had helped her select the most beautiful cream-coloured satin and the thought of trailing it in the muddy shallows made her shudder. Once safely on solid ground she raised a hand to her hair to check it was still pinned up securely. She did not usually take such pains with her appearance, but today she wished she were prettier.

As though Georgiana had read her mind Mary heard her whisper: 'Do not worry, you look perfect. *He* won't be able to keep his eyes off you.'

'Who is *he*, exactly?' Mary muttered back, looping her hand through her older sister's arm. Georgiana elbowed her gently.

'Only a certain officer our father has invited this evening, in the hopes that some of the company at table might catch his eye.'

'George!'

'No *he* in particular, then.' Georgiana winked. 'I have said nothing.'

They showed their season tickets and passed through the entrance gate at the manager's pavilion. Vauxhall's legendary thousand lamps guided their path as the natural light fled. Violins, flutes and cellos trilled from the orchestra pits concealed in the undergrowth, filling the air with invisible music. Guests enjoyed a discreet cup of tea in the alcoves around the Rotunda, in full view of the large ornamental fountain. Liveried waiters bustled from table to table, taking orders, bringing wine and food.

The rest of their party awaited them in an alcove painted with scenes depicting Odysseus and Circe. Lady Harriot Pitt sat between her brothers, listening with parted lips and great attention to the conversation of William's friend Edward Eliot. She was so engrossed that she did not notice the Sydneys until they were only a few feet away. 'Lord and Lady Sydney!'

'Many congratulations, my dear sir.' Mary's father clasped William by the hand with genuine admiration. William's eager face was flushed with his usual odd combination of pride and self-consciousness.

'Thank you, sir. I accept them, although I suspect being a member of Lord Shelburne's government will be far from a sinecure.'

'Chancellor of the Exchequer!' Lord Sydney said, in some wonder. 'At twenty-three! My dear sir, I had hoped you and I would one day be colleagues in office ever since you first opened your mouth in the House of Commons. I never knew it would happen so soon.'

'Come and join us,' William said, gesturing towards the rest of the alcove. 'Harriot will be glad to see you. I think Mr Eliot's been boring her.'

Mary had not received that impression at all, but she was no longer looking at Harriot, or Mr Eliot, or Mr Pitt. She had seen plenty of the Earl of Chatham over the last few months: he had acquired a commission in the 3rd Foot Guards, a London-based regiment, and he and his brother had taken a house in Berkeley Square close to Albemarle Street. Even so Mary always felt a thrill at the sight of him, as though every meeting was their first.

Lord Chatham's frizzed hair showed dark even through the abundant powder, much of which had fallen onto the tall collar of his elegant woollen coat. His heavy-lidded blue eyes returned Mary's scrutiny with approval. Their gazes met and he gave a slow smile that sent a warm shudder warmth through her. She blushed, but kept her eyes fixed upon him. Nothing in the world would have persuaded her to look away.

'How is the beauty of Albemarle Street?' John murmured into her ear.

Mary had never considered herself a flirt, but she felt one eyebrow rising as though of its own volition. 'Georgiana is well. You may ask her if you like.'

John laughed, and his sideways glance at her stirred a strange mixture of admiration and yearning in her stomach. 'I shall make a note to ask her later.'

As though she had heard her name, Georgiana spoke from across the table. 'Have you made any great speeches, Mr Pitt?'

'Hardly any, I am afraid,' William confessed, 'great or poor.'

'Come now, do not be modest, Pitt,' Mary's father said. 'Your speech on parliamentary reform was much acclaimed.'

'Perhaps, but we lost the vote.'

'Only by twenty votes. That's the closest reform has come to passing in nearly a generation. Even your father never succeeded so well.'

William looked pleased. Eliot broke away from his flirtations with Harriot and gave his friend a prod in the arm. 'He wasted it all on that one speech. I can vouch he has spoken nothing but nonsense since.'

'You think you could do better?' Harriot teased. Eliot gave her a fond look.

'I wouldn't presume. Your brother is the best pedlar of nonsense in the country.'

'Now he is a minister he will have plenty of opportunity to speak more frequently,' Lord Sydney said, benevolently. 'I'd say we shall hear young Mr Pitt very often, since he is virtually the only high-ranking minister in the House of Commons.'

'It will not be easy,' William observed, although in Mary's opinion he did not look displeased at the prospect of the challenge.

'I daresay it will not,' Lord Sydney nodded. 'This may be your last night of leisure as a private citizen, sir. Enjoy it, for you may not find yourself at liberty again until we have secured peace with America.'

Mary privately agreed. She knew the situation well, from overhearing her father's conversations with other politicians and scouring the morning newspapers in his study. Persuaded Britain could ill afford to lose America's trade and friendship after a major war, and reluctant to grant full independence without a single concession, Lord Shelburne wished to make trade and defensive pacts a fundamental part of the peace process with the rebellious colonies. Lord Rockingham's followers, however, preferred cutting all ties and focusing on the continental war with Spain and France. Rockingham's death a few weeks previously might have left them leaderless, but they were still acting as a bloc, and had uniformly refused to take office under Shelburne. Rockingham's most talented protégé, Charles Fox, had made it clear he would openly oppose the new ministry in the Commons.

Yet despite the severity of the situation, Mary's father still looked optimistic. He reached across and patted William on the shoulder in an avuncular fashion. 'You will rise to the challenge. You are your father's son.'

'My lord, you flatter. Lord Shelburne has only called me to office because his government is weak, and he needs my Pitt name to strengthen it.'

There was a chorus of protest. Lord Chatham's low, deep voice made itself heard above the others, drowning them out. 'No, William, that is not true. Why, had Lord Shelburne simply wanted a great name to buttress him in office, he might have asked either of us – but he chose you.'

William blushed. 'Had Shelburne offered you a government post, John, I would have no hesitation in supporting you now, as you are supporting me.'

'But he did not,' John said. To Mary's ears, his nonchalance when he spoke those words did not entirely ring true, but the sincerity behind what he said next moved her. 'I've told you before, William. Politics is not my ambition. I do not begrudge you this opportunity, not in the least. Lord Sydney is right. You are Papa's son, and worthily so.'

John raised his glass and William grinned back in response. Mary watched Lord Chatham with a sense of admiration she was accustomed to feeling in the presence of the two brothers. John was right: Shelburne's offer of office might have belonged to either of them. But if John was disappointed, or jealous, he was hiding it very well. Mary had seen so much evidence of John's self-effacement since her father's dinner to celebrate William's election to Parliament, but it never stopped being any less amazing to her – particularly as nobody else seemed to realise the scale of the sacrifice he was making, least of all John himself.

John met her gaze over the rim of his glass and smiled. Mary felt the blood rush to her cheeks and glanced away in confusion. She spent the next few minutes staring at her lap, winding the ribbon from her hat around her forefinger, but when she risked glancing up John was still looking at her. His gaze warmed her pleasantly, despite the evening chill.

They were interrupted by the first strains of a minuet drifting across from the Rotunda. Georgiana, whose attention had quickly strayed from the earnest politics of the conversation, clapped. 'Time for dancing! I can try out my new slippers!'

William invited her to partner with him, and Eliot approached Harriot with a similar request. Mary watched them leave. She knew what was going to happen next even before John Chatham stood beside her.

His eyes were dark in the flickering light of the oil lamp. For all his outward poise, he was as awkward in her company as any schoolboy. The thought at once pleased and terrified her. 'Will you do me the honour of a dance, Miss Mary?'

She remembered from when they were small how much he loved dancing. They had occasionally been partners then, learning their steps under the watchful eye of the dancing-master Monsignor Gallini. Mary could remember admiring the graceful way he moved through a figure long before she had grown aware of the ties weaving them together. She longed to accept his offer, but after three quarters of an hour of sitting still her hip ached powerfully. She did not think she could walk as far as the Rotunda, let alone dance a half-hour set. 'I would very much like to, my lord, but I dare not.'

She saw in his disappointment how much he had been looking forward to the dance. For a heady moment she wondered whether she should change her mind and take the risk, but then his mouth twitched into a smile and he dropped back into his seat. 'Then I shall stay and keep you company.'

'Do not let me keep you from the dance,' Mary protested. John moved his chair closer.

'I had much rather stay here with you,' he said. He took her hand and she felt a flood of excited emotion at his touch. It was the first time he had taken the liberty and she was too surprised, and too pleased, to take it back.

They sat for a few minutes without talking. Mary dearly wanted to tell him how much his forbearance while everyone paid court to William impressed her, but she could not find the words, and in any case she suspected John would take it amiss. His pride was a fragile, but very real, part of him; she could almost see it beneath his skin, pulsing through his veins like electricity.

'Does your hip pain you very much?' John said, at length. 'Have you considered visiting Bath, or Tunbridge Wells? Or one of the seaside towns? My father would take us to Lyme when we were children. Sea bathing did wonders for his gout.'

'Perhaps a visit to a spa might help but Dr Warren's advice mostly seems to be to bleed me half to death, then plunge me into cold water and feed me camomile tea till I am sick.'

'Does it help?'

'Help? Heavens, no. But I have developed an undying hatred for camomile tea.'

'Then I shall make sure to serve you only coffee,' John said, and grinned. Mary grinned back.

'I find your attitude refreshing. My aunt Courtown whispers about my lameness and talks in euphemisms as though I might drop down dead from it at any moment. You treat it as the fact it is, and I like that, truly I do.'

'I am glad,' John said.

He did not let go of her hand. The evening was cold and Mary was shivering, but the warmth of his touch through her gloves stilled her shaking. She could smell the lemon from his hair powder and see the hint of darkness on his chin where he had shaved that morning. She could hear her parents talking on the other side of the table, but they seemed suddenly far away, as though they lived in a different world and she and John were alone, bound by a nameless bond neither yet completely understood.

September 1782

John followed Rutland through the long grass, his gun resting on his shoulder. About them the rolling land stretched for miles, broken on the horizon by copses of beech and elm. Here in the sporting field John's world did not stretch far beyond the whistling wind, the calling birds and the warm gun in his hands. A fortnight's shooting at Belvoir Castle in the company of his friend Rutland never failed to chase the cobwebs from his mind.

A brace of partridges flew into the air in a burst of feathers. John and Rutland discharged their shots and two birds fell.

'Might we expect your brother here any time soon?' Rutland enquired while the two grooms collected the kill. He poured powder down the barrel of his gun from the inlaid powder-horn at his waist and rattled the ramrod up and down with a practised hand. 'It would be a shame if he did not come. I have not seen him for some weeks.'

John sighted along the polished barrel of his gun. It was a beautiful piece, Italian-made, its mottled walnut stock smooth and firm against his shoulder. 'You will perhaps be surprised to hear it, but neither have I.'

'Truly? That does surprise me.'

'He has his own house in Downing Street now.' Since his brother had moved out John's enormous Berkeley Square house, its pilastered staircase and vast open drawing rooms seemed somehow bigger, and emptier, without William's boisterous humour to fill them. 'Possibly it is just as well, for Cabinet members and House of Commons orators keep unsociable hours. The days when he and I slouched over the breakfast table after a night at the opera are over.'

'Not, I understand, that Lord Shelburne gives Pitt a great deal to do,' Rutland said.

'Indeed. My brother often complains that Lord Shelburne is unwilling to entrust him with larger duties than counting pennies, and presiding over a department whose members have been in politics since before he was born … although he says none of them has been so impolite as to remind him of that.'

Rutland took a flask from a groom and took a long swig from the contents. 'So what's keeping Pitt in town? The peace?'

'That, and endless rounds of Treasury meetings, Exchequer boards and parliamentary committees.' John raised an eyebrow and added, pithily, 'Superintending the finances of a defeated, bankrupt nation is no sinecure.'

'That I can well believe! How go the peace negotiations? Has Pitt any information from Paris?'

John snorted. 'You know how Lord Shelburne plays a devilish close game. William will probably get first news of peace with America from the *Courier* or the *Morning Chronicle*.'

'Do you think the peace treaty will be signed by Christmas?'

'Perhaps. The last of the troops have been evacuated from America, so little remains to be discussed save for the terms.'

'Lord North will not let it go unchallenged,' Rutland said. John shook his head and raised his gun. The shot loosed with a smooth kick and a sound like ripping silk.

'Neither will Charles Fox. He hates Shelburne almost as much as he hates Lord North. Thank God Fox still blames North for the American war. If they ever combine, Shelburne is sunk.'

'Is that likely to happen?'

'God only knows. We live in interesting times.'

The two friends walked on through the tall grass. Rutland's dogs bounded ahead, delighted with the exercise. Rutland paused to load again. As he poured the charge down the barrel he changed the subject to one less gloomy. 'What of your family? How is your mother?'

'She is well, all things considered.'

'Your sister?'

'Also well, and with my mother.'

'No news of Mr Eliot?' Rutland said, taking aim.

'I am sure I do not know what you mean.'

'Yes, you do.'

John laughed. 'Very well. He has not yet asked for Harriot's hand, but I expect he will propose soon.'

Rutland lowered his gun without loosing the shot. He placed it on half-cock and handed it to one of the grooms, then sat down on a nearby tree stump, settled his hands across his paunch, and looked slyly at John. 'Speaking of proposals, what is this I hear about your being smitten with Miss Mary Townshend?' John's stomach muscles tightened at Mary's name. He ran his thumb over the tooled leather strap of his gun and felt the blood rush to his face. Rutland regarded him triumphantly. 'Do not insult me by pretending you do not know what I mean by *that*.'

'I know what you mean,' John said. He was aware of a foolish smile spreading across his face but he could not help it. Rutland arched his eyebrows.

'Well? I wish to know more about this Aphrodite.'

'There is not a great deal to say.' John thought about Mary nearly all the time, but for some reason talking about her was suddenly the most difficult thing in the world. 'We see a great deal of each other.'

'Well, then, the papers will have married you off ten times over,' Rutland observed. He added, as though he was not greatly interested in the answer, 'Do you love her?'

The weight of the gun was heavy in John's hands, still warm from the shot he had fired. He rubbed at a smear of gunpowder near the mouth of the barrel, but he had no need to search within himself for the answer. 'She has taken my heart.' He added, more warmly, 'I know it must appear odd to you, but without her I am incomplete, as though she carries a part of me.'

Rutland's eyebrows shot up. 'I never knew you were so sentimental, Chatham.'

'I must apologise. That was foolish stuff.'

'But instructive,' Rutland said. 'Although I advise you to leave the eloquence to your brother. He's much better at it than you are.' He stretched, then took his gun back from the groom. 'Well then, Chatham, I had better take advantage of you in your bachelor state, for I doubt very much you will wish to spend time with rakehells like me when you are respectably married off; but you are my closest friend, and I look upon you as family. Please believe how sincerely glad I am for you.'

'I know,' John said, touched by the warmth and sincerity of Rutland's words. Rutland took John's hand with his free one.

'I mean it, Chatham. You have had a hard run of it since your father's death. I know better than most how hard it is to exist in the shadow of famous relatives. I very much hope this represents a turn in your fortunes for the better.'

Chapter Five

February 1783

'Tomorrow, gentlemen, His Majesty's Government will lay the preliminaries of peace before both Houses of Parliament.'

Lord Sydney's jowled face was uncharacteristically solemn as he made his announcement. John glanced quickly round Sydney's Albemarle Street drawing room, which was full of government supporters. Lord Shelburne sat by the door. William stood nearby, a tight expression on his long face.

'I will now read out the Address,' Sydney continued. He cleared his throat and read: 'We move that a humble Address be presented to His Majesty, to express our satisfaction that His Majesty has laid the foundation for a treaty of peace with the United States of America, which we trust will ensure perfect reconciliation and friendship between both countries.'

The phrase "United States" appeared to draw away all the air in the room. Even the fire seemed to burn lower. Sydney licked his lips and went on.

'We assure His Majesty that we shall diligently turn our attention to a revision of our commercial laws and endeavour to frame them upon such liberal principles as may best extend our trade and navigation.'

The only sound that could be heard for a few moments was the crackle of paper as Sydney folded the Address back into his pocket with trembling hands. Every member of the government looked as though Sydney had just read them their death sentence. Even William chewed on a thumbnail and looked preoccupied. He made brief eye-contact with John and shook his head.

'I see little to disagree with,' one of the backbenchers said after a space. 'The sentiments are loyal enough.'

'You think the Address will pass unopposed?' Lord Shelburne rose from his chair. His deep, melodious voice sounded like silk, smooth but cold. 'I wish I agreed with you.'

'We will have a hard struggle tomorrow,' Sydney agreed grimly. 'Those who resigned after the death of Lord Rockingham will make their voices heard, and Lord North cannot be expected to approve any treaty that condemns his war policy. The terms we have managed to secure are as favourable as we can expect, but we are a defeated nation. America has taken all our territory – from the Great Lakes to the Mississippi River; they have taken our fishing rights in Newfoundland. The opposition will fasten on all this, and will no doubt say we have been too generous in returning territories to France and Spain.'

'There is worse,' another voice spoke up: Henry Dundas, Treasurer of the Navy and Lord Advocate of Scotland. Dundas' deep-set brown eyes were grim under his sandy brows. 'Today I received word from Lord North. He and Charles Fox have come to an accommodation.'

The room burst into incredulous, horrified noise. John gaped with the rest of them. Charles Fox, scion of the Rockingham interest, ally himself with Lord North, the author of the American war? John threw a look at his brother and knew immediately that William was as shocked as he was. William stared at Dundas as though begging him to announce he had spoken in jest.

'Yes indeed,' Shelburne put in. His complexion was grey from lack of sleep, his eyes deeply pouched. 'It is almost beyond belief, is it not? Fox and North together – this very same Fox who once called North "the most infamous of men". But the prospect of toppling our government and scrambling into office has put an end to all that. Against both parties in conjunction the ministry cannot hope to stand … and Mr Fox knows it.'

The meeting broke up. Shelburne's supporters bowed and left. The next day's debate promised to be long and acrimonious, and John guessed most of those present wanted an early night in preparation for a sleepless one on the morrow.

'Fox and North,' Eliot groaned, his voice brim-full with despair, as they waited for their carriages outside Sydney's house. 'Can you credit it?'

'You heard Mr Dundas,' John said.

'He's gambling for office,' William observed. 'Only time will tell if he has judged the stakes well enough.'

William's face was grey: as the highest-ranking government orator in the Commons, the weight of the government's defence would fall on his slender 23-year-old shoulders. John gave his brother a worried look. In his opinion William did not look well, and he was all too aware of how frail his brother had been as a child. Could he withstand the strain of supporting Shelburne's government? The previous summer's celebrations on William's coming to office seemed so far away now, blown away by the cold February wind.

'Will you be able to stop Fox?' John asked. The moment of tense silence that followed his question worried him; normally William was breezily optimistic, but his confidence seemed to have buckled beneath Dundas's startling revelation.

'I do not know.'

'I am certain you can,' John said, but secretly he doubted it.

And he was right to do so. The Address on the peace was read on the 17th and 21st of February amidst a riot of publicity, for the downfall of a ministry always attracted the biggest crowds. They were not disappointed. The House of Commons sat at four in the afternoon and did not rise till seven next morning. Charles Fox and Lord North's unholy alliance put the government in a minority of 17, and even the most inspired, most desperate eloquence from William could not counter it.

Shelburne retained the seals of office, but he had lost the peace and the confidence of Parliament. His ministry was as good as over.

****

'What is going on, Will?' John asked the minute he and Harriot stepped across the threshold of his brother's official Downing Street house. 'Has the government fallen? Why have we been told nothing?'

'I am afraid you will hardly believe me when I tell you I do not know,' William said with an air of frustration. 'I do have one piece of news: Shelburne resigned yesterday.'

John had been expecting that and so was not taken aback by the news, but Shelburne's resignation left William in a difficult position. John looked anxiously at his brother, half-afraid to hear the answer to his question. 'Do you retain the Exchequer?'

'Until further notice, yes. I have not been told to relinquish it, at least not yet.' William's expression hardened. 'But I will not serve under Fox and North.'

John led Harriot up the cantilever staircase. He had been staggered at his first sight of Downing Street's enormous pillared rooms with their painted fireplaces, moulded ceilings and glittering chandeliers, but familiarity with the building had stripped away much of its grandeur. It consisted of a four-storey townhouse and a three-storey stately home inexpertly tacked together. Staircases went nowhere, doors opened into brick walls, and the older part of the house dripped with damp. Many of the floorboards bowed so that the furniture, beautiful and gilded as it was, had to be propped up on wedges. Half the house had been shut up for maintenance since William had moved in, and John wondered whether his brother would not be glad to get out before the place collapsed about his ears.

One other guest waited for them: Edward Eliot. John had expected the evening's dinner to be a family affair, but when he saw Eliot kiss the back of Harriot's hands he remembered only Eliot's lack of a declaration stopped the young man falling under the description of kin.

The sounds of Downing Street preparing for dinner filled the silence. The recently restored kitchens below stairs were no doubt a noisy mess of cooks and scullions dressing meat and arranging dishes ready to bring to the dining room. From the vast study overlooking the gardens came the sound of footmen packing up William's trunks, boxes and papers ready for the inevitable move.

William poured them all a drink of brandy and raised his glass to John. 'Well, brother, I would drink to the prospect of my becoming your lodger once more.'

'So long as I have a house you will always be welcome there,' John said.

'Do you not find it odd that Lord Shelburne has remained so quiet?' Eliot asked. Harriot laughed bitterly.

'Would it not have been more amazing had His Lordship communicated with anybody?'

'Certainly Shelburne's closeness is typical of the man,' William said. 'When we met in Cabinet he told us that he had resigned, and that we should know more by and by. But lest I disappoint you in your expectations, he gave us no hint of who was to succeed him.'

'Who do you think *will* succeed him?' John said.

'The Duke of Portland, under the thumb of Fox and North?' Eliot suggested, and William smiled humourlessly.

'Who else? There is no alternative.' He hesitated then continued, like a child prodding at a sore limb. 'The coalition between Fox and North means any new government will face the same forces that outvoted Lord Shelburne. The only chance of success would be to split the Coalition … and what do Fox or North have to gain by parting from each other so close to their goal?'

John rose to refill his glass. He paused by the decanters to look out of the darkened window at the garden below and Horse Guards beyond, the dark outline of the golden clock just visible through the blackness. The sound of the doorbell echoed through the floorboards. A few moments later a footman came in bearing one of the red leather boxes through which the King corresponded with his ministers of state. William eyed it in irritation. 'What in God's name does His Majesty want with me now?'

'Does he require an answer?' John put down his glass. William pulled a face and unlocked the box with a key he kept on the watch fob at his waist.

'I suppose I had better find out.'

The box was empty save for a small piece of paper folded into an envelope and sealed. John peered over his brother's shoulder as William broke the seal. He saw two lines, hurriedly written in the King's angular handwriting and signed 'GR'.

'His Majesty requires me to attend him at St James's,' William said at length, throwing the paper back in the box and snapping the lid closed.

'Tomorrow?'

'Now.'

The clock on the mantelpiece struck six. The smell of roasted partridge drifted up from the kitchens. John saw his own thoughts etched on his brother's face. With a flippancy he could hardly have felt William said, 'It seems His Majesty may want to invest a new Chancellor of the Exchequer after all!'

'Shall we wait for you?' Harriot asked.

'I shan't be away more than an hour.' He smoothed down his waistcoat and buttoned up his coat. 'Start dinner without me.'

Dinner was a subdued affair. The prospect of the end of the government hung over it like a cloud, and John hardly tasted the food that came up from the kitchens. He, Harriot and Eliot spoke of a variety of inconsequential things, but not politics. Up until William had left for St James's they had spoken of nothing else; the confirmation that William would soon have to give up his office and his house had turned the subject sour.

The evening stretched on and William did not reappear. The clock struck nine, ten, eleven. John fingered his glass and wondered why the King was keeping William so late. The street fringed a conglomeration of stews and brothels, and the King's Head and Axe and Gate taverns at the entrance to the cul-de-sac attracted a host of unsavoury types. One glance at Harriot and Eliot's tight faces told him they were having the same thoughts.

When the clock struck midnight John walked over to the window and peered outside. A thin sleet had started to fall and the oil lamp hanging from the wrought-iron arch cast a dim light over the cul-de-sac.

'I should be going,' Eliot said, at last, but made no attempt to get up.

'What do you suppose has happened?' Harriot asked.

John was about to reply when a movement caught his attention. A tall, familiar figure walked briskly to the front door, his way illuminated by the torch of a link-boy. Relief swept through John and only then did he realise how much he had feared for his brother's safety. 'Here he comes at last.'

A few minutes later William came upstairs, still brushing the damp sleet from his hair. The others leapt to their feet the moment he walked in.

'Thank goodness,' Harriot said, coming forwards and taking his hands. 'I was beginning to wonder if you had been set upon by cutpurses.'

'Mighty poor form of His Majesty to keep you from your dinner for so long,' Eliot said. 'We kept you some partridge, but it will be cold by now.'

'I take it we are addressing the late Chancellor of the Exchequer?' John proffered his brother a glass of wine. When William did not immediately take it, or even respond, John peered at him more closely. William returned his scrutiny with wide, dark eyes in a pale face. That was the moment when John, with a lurch, realised the issue was much more serious than simply resigning the seals.

'Good God,' Eliot stammered, having evidently reached the same conclusion. 'Pitt, what has His Majesty said to you?'

William collapsed into a chair as though his legs could no longer support him. Harriot and Eliot exchanged an anxious glance. John pressed the glass of wine on William again and this time he took it. He drained the wine in several convulsive gulps.

'What happened?' John asked.

'I am not certain I am at liberty to say.' William looked from one face to another. 'No, I might as well tell you. You will find out soon enough. His Majesty offered me the Treasury.'

John fell back, stunned. He frowned, and saw the same frown come on the faces of the others as they each tried to work out which part of the sentence they might have misheard.

Finally, Eliot said, 'What, Secretary to the Treasury? Under Fox and North?'

'No.' William shook his head. '*The* Treasury.' He stared into his empty wine glass. 'Shelburne's old place.'

'He asked you to head a government?' John asked. William nodded. A throb of excitement pierced John's disbelief as the full import of what William had been offered struck him.

The others, however, could not get over their bafflement. 'Offer you the Treasury?' Eliot burst out. 'Has His Majesty gone mad? I do not mean to impugn your ability, Pitt, and God knows I have always fully expected to see you head a government one day. But not now! My God, Pitt, you're twenty-three!'

'Did you accept?' John asked eagerly. His brother's eyebrows twitched at John's tone, but William's voice remained level.

'I asked for some time to consider the offer.'

'Some time?' John repeated, incredulous. William was acting in a manner John found inexplicable. Yes, the offer was unexpected; yes, William was uncommonly young. But he was already a Cabinet minister, and John knew his brother well enough to know he was more capable than most men twice his age. 'What does Shelburne say? Have you seen him?'

'Yes,' William said reluctantly. 'He was with me at the audience. It seems he suggested me in the first place.'

'Then why should you not accept? With His Majesty's confidence and Shelburne's support, how can you go wrong?' William said nothing. 'God, Will, you cannot possibly turn the King down!'

William's voice was taut. 'Part of me wants to accept, I cannot deny it.'

'But?' John could hear the word hanging in the air even though William had not yet spoken it.

'But there is something about the whole business I do not like.'

'Christ, Will! How many men of three and twenty are offered the Treasury on a plate? Do you not realise what an opportunity this is? Is this not precisely what Papa trained you for?'

He had supposed this was what William wanted to hear, and was completely unprepared for the violence of William's reaction. 'Do not dare bring Papa into this! This has nothing to do with Papa!'

'Oh yes,' John snapped, cut to the quick by William's tone, 'because the King obviously made you Chief Minister in recognition of your transcendent administrative abilities.' The words had hardly left his lips before he regretted them: William had no need to be told the premiership had not been offered to him on the merits of his talents alone. 'Will, trust me. In the army, it is far preferable to hold a position of strength under disadvantageous circumstances than hesitate and lose the moment. Show those who wish to use you as a puppet that the son of Chatham is not so easily to be played.'

'If you want me to trust you, for God's sake do not make use of military metaphors. Your limited experience of garrison duty hardly fits you for it.' John was too horrified to formulate a suitable response. William's ears belatedly caught up with his tongue. An expression of dismay crossed his face. 'Dear God, John, I'm sorry. I did not mean—'

'No,' John interrupted, thinly. 'I daresay you did not.'

'John—'

'I see precisely what you think of my opinion.'

William bristled. 'I did not even ask for it!'

'Because clearly my position as head of the family counts for nothing?'

Harriot, who had so far sat helpless next to Eliot while her brothers fought, snapped out of her trance. '*Enough*! Enough, enough! You're like children.' John's chest heaved. William wiped his brow with a shaking hand. Harriot waited until she was sure the argument had subsided then continued. 'William, what you have told us tonight is incredible, to say the least, but do not blame John for what is not his fault.' William bowed his head. John looked down on him triumphantly, then flinched when Harriot brandished her finger at him. 'As for you, John, this is not your battle. Do not fly at William for choosing not to take your advice.'

John should have known Harriot would take William's side. 'Well and good,' he snapped, 'but I reserve the right to tell William he is a fool when he acts like one.'

'*I* am the fool!' William's face rose from his hands, suffused with colour. Harriot raised her eyes to the moulded plaster ceiling.

'Unbelievable! Simply unbelievable! Can you two not be civil to each other for one moment?'

'Be civil yourself,' John said. 'I have had enough of this.' He turned his back on William, left the room and slammed the door behind him.

****

The journey back to Berkeley Square was a silent one. Harriot was in a sulk; John had no intention of opening a conversation with her. He finally got to bed at about half past four, but was too agitated to sleep. Staring up into the darkness the realisation gradually crystallised in his mind that leaving without talking with his brother had very much been the wrong thing to do.

By the time he gave up the fruitless battle for slumber it was about half past six. The sky was still dark and he had to break a film of ice on the water in his washbasin. He decided a pre-breakfast ride in Green Park might clear his thoughts.

The Park was empty at such an early hour. The leafless trees sparkled with icicles in the faint morning light. Without quite knowing why, John left the green expanse and rode down the Mall. On the right loomed the crenellated Tudor brick entrance to St James's Palace, flanked by scarlet-coated grenadiers. This was where William had received his startling offer the previous night. The Royal Standard had been run down the flagpole; the King must have gone back to Windsor, secure in the supposition that his offer would be accepted. John took in the empty flagpole and knew what he had to do. He morosely turned his horse back towards Downing Street.

William was busy, so John had to wait. He entered the drawing room so quickly he did not at first notice he was not alone. Only when he moved towards the bell-pull did he see his mother sitting by the fire.

'Mama! What are you doing here?'

'Waiting for you, my son.' The pale grey of Lady Chatham's fur-lined tippet and muff, the impenetrable look in her blue eyes and the straightness of her back, all put John in mind of a fairy-tale ice queen. 'I knew you would come back eventually.'

'I thought you were at Hayes.'

'Indeed I was,' Lady Chatham said with a gentle inclination of her head. 'I was roused by a message from William early this morning. He told me of the extraordinary offer he has received, and expressed a strong desire to see me—'

'And so you came,' John finished for her, unable to suppress a treacherous doubt that she would have done so had he issued the same plea. 'If William summoned you, should you not go to him?'

'I have already been with him. Now I want to speak with you.'

'Why?' Even to John's ears the syllable sounded defensive. His mother looked at him.

'Because you, too, are my son; and, as I trust you will recollect, William's brother, and bound to support his decision in this matter.'

Guilt vied with indignation in John's breast. 'I am also the head of the family.'

'Head of the family you may be, but you are half Grenville, and a Grenville always holds family paramount to all other considerations – even pride.' Lady Chatham waved her hand. 'I know of your argument with William. The details of what happened are immaterial. What I want is for you to forget your dignity and give your brother the support he needs.'

John experienced a stab of wounded disappointment. It seemed to him that he had done nothing else all his life but sacrifice his best interests for the family good. 'Would you say the same to William, were I in his position?'

His mother's expression sharpened with anxiety and suspicion. 'Do you think you *ought* to be in his position?'

'Of course not!' John felt his cheeks go hot and cold by turns at the prospect of facing the kind of decision William did now. 'You know full well I have no intention of standing in my brother's way. Of course I want to do my duty to him, but I also owe a duty to myself.'

John's response was prompt enough to dispel the clouds from Lady Chatham's brow. 'In that case you may find fulfilment in giving your brother the support he requires. There are some hard decisions to make, and when he makes them he will need you by his side. I know you will never let harm come to him – even should you not agree with him.'

She rose and took John's hand. He bent down to receive her kiss on his cheek, as he had done so often as a child. 'William may be the one the world is watching, but your actions, John, your choices, are just as important. He will always need you, even if he cannot bring himself to tell you so.'

****

William had a succession of visitors all day, so John did not get a chance to say his piece till evening. He found his brother alone in the study, straining to read some papers by the light of a branch of candles. Outside the frost-laced window the weather was cold. The chill was reflected in William's face as he looked up at John. 'I thought you had gone back to Berkeley Square.'

John flinched at William's tone but he could see the strain in the grooves round William's mouth. 'I had. I came back.'

'You came back,' William repeated.

'Yes, I did. Although had I known I would spend this long waiting, I'd have made an appointment to speak with you next Thursday.'

The joke fell rather flat. William stared at John for a moment then crossed to the large mahogany desk and locked his papers away. He carried a candlestick round the sconces and lit the candles. Part of the vast room was bathed in a warm, rich glow.

'I came to your house this morning to speak with you,' William said at last. 'You were not in.'

So William had come to see him after all. 'You did not know I was here?'

'My secretary probably told me, but I may have been deafened by the noise from the carpenters,' William admitted, and indicated the direction of the works in the south-west corner of the house with a grimace. There was a short silence.

'I suppose you will be glad to leave then,' John murmured.

Relief chased across William's face. 'I might still stay, John. Believe me, this is one decision I will not make in haste.' William fell into one of the high-backed chairs by the fire. John took a seat opposite and waited for more, hands resting on his knees. A flush of colour came over William's cheeks. 'I am sorry for last night. I was taken by surprise by His Majesty's offer. I took my confusion out on you and I apologise for it.' His blush deepened. 'I am particularly sorry for what I said about your military experience.'

'You had received a shock.' John forced the words out with difficulty. 'You spoke without thinking. I can understand that. But when you seemed to hold my advice so cheap … I admit, Will, it hurt.'

'I know.'

'It matters little. I too owe you an apology. I was so pleased for you I could not comprehend why you yourself were not.'

The excuses were over. John felt as though a weight had been lifted from his soul, but a sense of oppression remained. The furrows returned to William's face only moments after John had stopped speaking. John glanced at his brother and sat forwards. 'What did Mama tell you?'

'She thinks I should consider the offer well.'

'I think she is right, until you are sure you know what you have been offered.' John gazed at his linked fingers then looked up. 'But I still think you should accept.'

William's eyes met his and John felt he could see right into his brother's soul. 'It is not so simple, John. You may think it is a clear-cut decision – yes or no – but you will not be the one to fight both Fox and North in the House of Commons.'

'That is true,' John said, 'but you owe a duty to your former colleagues. I know you received a message from Lord Sydney today: I recognised the livery. I would wager he did not write to dissuade you.'

'You are right. Lord Sydney wrote to offer me his support. And yet …' William passed his hands through his hair. He spoke bitterly. '… I have spent this whole day in conference with the King's messengers. Richard Rigby. John Robinson. Henry Dundas.'

'Followers of Lord North all of them.'

'*Former* followers of North, as they were at pains to impress upon me. Robinson brought me estimates of the way he thought Parliament might vote if I were minister. I was looking at them when you came in.'

'What did they say?' John asked, although from the haunted look on William's face he thought he knew the answer.

William nibbled his lip for a moment in doubt. He did not reply, but said instead, 'Tell me. Why do you think I should take the premiership?'

John was half-staggered by the question; he could not remember William ever asking him for his opinion before. 'Because such opportunities hardly ever come twice. If you refuse the King now, he may never forgive you.'

'Do you not think His Majesty's turning to a man of my limited experience will doom my ministry from the start?'

'No, I do not,' John said without hesitation. 'You are young, Will, but you have talent. You are a great orator.' The expression on William's face made John blush. 'Not only that, but you have the support of many of your former colleagues – and of Lord Shelburne.'

'That does not worry you?' William said wryly.

'Why should it? Besides, if you join with Fox you need not have Shelburne at all. With the King standing behind you, how long do you think Fox's marriage of convenience with Lord North will last? Act now, before they find something in common to stand on.' William nodded, but his frown deepened. John's words had not convinced his brother to accept; on the contrary they seemed to have had the opposite effect. John felt a pulse of disappointment, but at least he now knew William would explain his reasoning. He took William's hand and squeezed it. 'And yet you will refuse.'

'Yes.'

'I have been candid with you. Now I want you to return the favour. Why, Will? Why decline the King's offer?'

William spoke softly. 'Because were I to accept, it would not be my ministry, but Shelburne's.'

'I never imagined you would head any other combination of men than the ones who have served with you over the last few months,' John said.

'You misunderstand. As soon as His Majesty made me the offer last night I began to wonder why Lord Shelburne suggested me in the first place.'

'Because you are Papa's son,' John urged. 'You are William Pitt.'

'I thought so too for a while, but I am convinced it is not so.' William looked bitter. 'Shelburne has lost the confidence of Parliament, and God knows he has only been a hair's breadth from losing that of his Cabinet. What if he has found, in me, a way to retain power while appearing to relinquish it? All by playing the benevolent patron and sponsoring my rise to prominence?'

John thought he was at last beginning to grasp the point William was trying to make. He swallowed hard and fought to sound nonchalant. 'Shelburne knows you will not ally with North; he suspects Fox will not have you, and he may be right. In which case …'

'I will have no-one to turn to but Lord Shelburne himself.' William turned hollow eyes to John. 'You see now why I must decline. So long as Fox, North or Shelburne call the tune, I refuse to dance.'

John nodded. 'I think you are right,' he said, and William smiled in relief.

The two brothers sat in companionable silence. John glanced around at the green wallpaper, the gold-edged plasterwork, the imposing marble fireplace which, on closer inspection, turned out to have a pronounced lean towards the centre of the room. Downing Street was a grand house in appearance but, like the King's offer, it looked better on the outside than on the inside. John cast another eye around the gilded room in which his brother, in his shabby blue coat and worn leather breeches, looked so out of place. 'Will you miss this house?'

'Of course I will.' William laid a proprietorial hand on the edge of the writing desk. There was a spark of contumacy in his expression, a challenge launched at the rest of the world that John had seen more than once in the eyes of their father, before the bitter disappointment of political reality had worn him down. 'But I will return.'

Chapter Six

July 1783

'My Lord Chatham, if you will repeat after me ...'

Mary's heart beat hard in her chest as Dr Courtenay, the parish rector, took the ring off the Bible and slipped it onto her finger. Opposite her John wore a cream silk suit trimmed with silver to match her gown, his hair immaculately curled and powdered, and his eyes held hers with an intensity that made her throat constrict. He echoed Courtenay's words, precisely and with great concentration.

'With this ring I thee wed. With my body I thee worship, and with all my worldly goods I thee endow. In the name of the Father, and of the Son, and of the Holy Ghost, Amen.'

'Those whom God hath joined together let no man put asunder,' Courtenay said. John put his hand over Mary's; the sensation of his warm flesh pressing the cold band of the ring into her finger sent a shiver of excitement through her. 'I pronounce that they be man and wife together.'

The wedding guests applauded as John leaned down to bestow a chaste, self-conscious kiss on his wife's lips. Mary saw his eyes dart towards her parents, who sat beaming a few feet away. Arrayed beside them in the Sydneys' drawing room were Mary's six siblings, from Georgiana to three-year-old Horatio, sucking his thumb on his eldest sister's lap. Behind were William and Harriot, both grinning broadly.

Mary wrapped her arms around her husband's neck and murmured into his ear. 'Does Mary, Countess of Chatham not return your kisses so sweetly as Miss Mary Townshend?'

His face cleared instantly. 'Perhaps we should put it to the test.'

He cupped her chin and kissed her again. In an instant her world narrowed to the sensation of his lips against hers and her father's elegant drawing room, with all its inhabitants, was lost to her.

Mary kept her hand in John's as the guests came over to congratulate them. Her father and mother led the way, smiling broadly. Lady Sydney kissed John on each cheek and Lord Sydney pumped his hand up and down, unable to say anything other than 'Well done, Chatham, well done indeed,' as though John had just won Mary in single combat. Last came William and Harriot. Harriot slipped her hand through her new sister-in-law's arm and William clasped John's hand with genuine pleasure. 'My congratulations.'

'Marriage suits you,' Harriot observed. Her eyes were like John's: they had the same almond shape, the same shade of greyish-blue flecked with brown, but Harriot's were full of mischief. 'Why, you nearly look *handsome*.'

'Only nearly?'

'As far as I am concerned you look splendid,' William said. 'Lady Chatham too.' Mary glanced over her shoulder, half-expecting to see John's mother there, then realised William was talking about her and felt the blood rush to her cheeks. 'Congratulations, my lady. Welcome to our family.'

'Too late to change your mind I'm afraid,' Harriot put in.

'I don't think I want to,' Mary said, with a coy glance up at her husband. John smiled back and dropped a brief kiss on her lips.

'I am glad to hear it!'

Harriot and William laughed, but Mary detected strain in his voice. When he was not paying attention, she looked at him more carefully, peeling away the silver-lined coat, the pomaded, curled hair, the aura of quiet gentility and pride he wore like a cloak, and thought: *He is as nervous as I am*. She wondered if she was the only one to notice, for even William and Harriot continued to mock him as though they did not see his jaw tighten further with each joke.

Mary felt as though she could see him better than anyone else in the room, as though her love were a filter stripping away everything but the raw thoughts and emotions that made him John. She took his arm and he turned to her with a smile she was beginning to recognise belonged only to her. The connection between them felt more than physical, as though if Mary withdrew her arm she would still be holding him, even if they were hundreds of miles apart.

****

Upstairs, Lady Sydney unpinned Mary's voluminous gown with its shimmering silver thread. Harriot and Georgiana tackled the hoop and the stays, then retreated with a parting grin. Lady Sydney picked up a lacquered hairbrush and began brushing Mary's hair out of its back-combed, powdered mass.

Mary peered at herself in the mirror. She wore nothing but a fine cambric chemise; the prospect of coming before John like this was at once intoxicating and terrifying. She made eye contact with her mother in the mirror. Lady Sydney spoke reassuringly. 'Not long now. Lord Chatham will be waiting for you.'

A thrill of excitement raced up Mary's spine. 'What must I do, Mama?'

'Whatever he asks. He is your husband.'

My husband. One question had needled at Mary's mind ever since she had started thinking seriously about the wedding night. *How do I know this is John's first time as well as mine?* She had led a sheltered upbringing, but one on the fringes of the court, and she knew from hearing the servants gossip how few men came untouched to their wedding bed. As much as she wanted to ask, however, she could not, certainly not to her mother. She kept her mouth closed and prayed silently and desperately she would not disappoint him.

The bridal bedroom had been carefully prepared. The bed and walls were hung with fresh damask roses, all releasing their heady perfume into the warm evening air. John was there already, wearing a shirt that hung down to his knees. Mary noticed his long, muscled legs and the triangle of skin visible at the base of his throat. Something shifted, not unpleasantly, at the base of her spine. The sensation intensified when he caught sight of her and smiled.

'Good evening, Lady Chatham,' he said, and she felt herself blush.

'Good evening, Lord Chatham.'

John put his candle on the side table and they climbed into bed. They faced each other without touching, eyes wide in the semi-darkness, then John reached out gingerly and put his arms around her. They lay like that for a while, accustoming themselves to the sensation of their bodies in such close proximity. Under John's nightshirt his muscles were tense. Mary realised with a shock that he was as shy of her as she was of him.

He kissed the top of her head. 'Nervous?'

'No.' Mary's voice came out muffled. After a hesitation, she corrected herself, 'A little.'

'You don't have to be.'

She bit her lip, then blurted out, 'Harriot says you have left a string of broken hearts all over the world.'

'Well, I wouldn't believe everything Harriot says.' John kissed her again, then gently untied the ribbon holding her cap in place. His touch sent flickers of flame across her skin. He undid her braid and laid out her long, dark hair on the pillow. There were glints of gold in the depths of his eyes; he did not take them off her for a moment as he pulled at the string of her chemise and slipped it off her shoulders.

He guided her fingers to the buttons of his nightshirt and helped her ease it off him. Her eyes widened at the sight of his dark chest hair and his lips twitched at her obvious astonishment. He smiled reassuringly, brought his mouth down onto hers and rolled her gently onto her back. She let him do it, waiting for him to tell her what to do, tensed for the moment she knew could not be far away.

He seemed to have lost all trace of his former nervousness; his kisses were firmer, his touch lighter, swifter, more sure. Her body tingled as he cupped her chin then traced a line down her neck, between her breasts, across her stomach and below her hips. Her own fear began to melt away into a riot of sensation. She shuddered and dug her fingers into his skin. He kissed her ears and throat and she followed his lead, amazed at how pleasurable it was, how intoxicating it was to feel him so close, to smell the sweat and the desire on him.

The longing at her core focused to a sharp ache, so intense she was almost relieved when he kissed her long and lingeringly, pushed her hair back from her face and said, 'Ready?'

She caught her breath, then buried her face into his shoulder and nodded. The fire between her hips overrode her fear, but she still could not help closing her eyes involuntarily when he shifted on top of her. She felt his lips curve as he kissed the corner of her eyelid and eased himself in. She gasped in discomfort, but then she felt herself opening inside like a flower, every inch of her body alive with wonder and love.

They lay entwined for a while after they had finished. The candle had burned down to nothing, and Mary gazed up into darkness. This, then, was the end of the journey she had begun on Albemarle Street's terrace when John had shown her his heart. He was like a child who had yet to find himself. She felt a wave of love for him, and the intensity of it robbed her of breath.

As though he sensed her sudden swell of emotion John's arms around her tightened. 'You see? You had no need to be afraid of me.'

'I wasn't afraid of *you*,' Mary said, and John laughed.

'What were you afraid of, then?'

Mary did not respond for a moment. With one innocuous phrase, John had brought back all her doubts. The unspoken question she had swallowed back from her mother remained in her mind. She was certain now she knew the answer: John's caresses, his ability to bring her pleasure with the lightest touch, all of it spoke of experience. The realisation had much the same effect on her as plunging into a cold bath.

John rolled onto his side. 'Mary, what is wrong? Did I hurt you?'

'No!' She hoped the promptness of her response would convince him. 'You were very gentle.'

'Too gentle, perhaps? You think I found no enjoyment in it? It was the best experience of my life.' *Experience.* Mary's mouth went dry. There, she had it from John himself. She was just another *experience.* John leaned over to kiss her and she twitched her face away automatically. 'Mary, please, tell me what is amiss.'

'Nothing,' Mary said, but she knew she was being unfair. She did not want theirs to be the kind of marriage where secrets were kept: she wanted their union to be true and open, forged on the hard iron of trust. She rolled over to kiss him fiercely, possessively. 'There is only this. I love you so very much. I cannot express how proud I am to be your wife, but all this is new to me, whereas you have done it all before ...'

She tailed off into silence, but John had understood everything Mary could not bring herself to say. 'I told you not to believe a word Harriot says. Mary, I will not trifle with you. Tonight is not the first time I have lain with a woman.' She blinked at the frankness of his admission, but then he kissed her and her last doubts melted away. 'I promise you it is the first time I have given a woman my love ... and that she has, and always will have it all.'

'I know,' Mary said. She felt the warmth of his hand against her cheek and cupped it with her own.

'We have been married less than a day and already you know me better than any other person. I may have a great title, but you remind me of who I truly am. You alone can do that.'

'I just don't like the thought of sharing you,' Mary murmured, her words muffled against his shoulder.

'I am your husband. There are some transgressions a wife should not be asked to forgive. If you ever feel I am neglecting you, that I have forgotten your happiness, you may remind me of this conversation. You have my word.'

'I don't need your word. I only need you.'

'That you have, I promise you.'

She smiled and let him take her in his arms.

****

'Stop fidgeting, Mary!' Georgiana snapped. 'Stay still or you'll never be finished! Surely you realise this is the most important day of your life?'

'More important than my wedding day?' Mary said, then gasped as her maid tugged at the laces running up the back of her stays.

'Think of it, Mary. The last time you went to court you were not even a peer's daughter. Now you will outrank half the women in the room!'

'I do not want to think of it, thank you.' Mary steeled herself for the next effort from her maid. The prospect of appearing at court half-terrified her, but John had been planning their official presentation as a couple for weeks and she knew her husband needed to make a show.

The maid tied the basket hoop round her waist and Georgiana helped Mary into the heavy silver brocade petticoat. 'Almost finished,' her sister soothed as Mary staggered under the weight of the fabric. 'Nearly there.'

Mary gazed anxiously at her reflection as the maid pinned the gown to the embroidered stomacher. Her chestnut hair had been frizzed and pulled as high as it could go, powdered and strung with pearls. Three ostrich feathers bobbed towards the ceiling, matched by a pair of lappets stretching halfway down her back. An enormous amethyst necklace – a wedding present from her husband – hung above her breasts, which thanks to her maid's ministrations were crushed into her ribs.

'There.' The sincerity of Georgiana's smile brought tears to Mary's eyes. 'You look beautiful.'

Mary stared again at her reflection. She thought the tall headdress made her neck look scrawny, and she fancied she looked like nothing more than a frightened girl dressing up in her mother's best clothes. 'I hardly recognise myself.'

'So long as Lord Chatham does,' Georgiana said, and Mary choked down a flicker of anxiety at the prospect of facing John looking like this.

'I only hope he won't laugh.'

Lady Sydney put her powdered and feathered head through the doorway. 'May I come in?' She glanced at her second daughter, pursed her lips in approval, and held out her arm. 'Come to the drawing room. Your husband has arrived.'

The words "your husband" were still more than enough to send a rush of warmth through Mary's queasy stomach, but it was nothing compared to the feeling she got upon entering the drawing room. John wore his regimentals – scarlet with blue facings edged in glittering gold lace. The moment his eyes found hers he gave a slow, uneven smile. A short while before Mary had been worried she looked like an overdressed frump; now she knew she was the most beautiful woman in London. Behind John his sister Harriot, dressed in a pink and taupe mantua, arched her eyebrows.

John leaned over and pressed his lips briefly and encouragingly to Mary's. 'There is no need to fret. The King will fall in love with you the moment he claps eyes on you.'

'I'm not fretting,' Mary lied, and John's lips jerked spasmodically.

'Neither am I.' Contrary to his assertion, however, Mary fancied her husband was as green as a country actor experiencing his first night at Covent Garden. It surprised her, but she was beginning to realise there was more beneath his mask of poise than he showed to the world. She wondered whether John knew himself how heavily the great title he carried bore upon him.

'Lord and Lady Courtown are just arrived,' Lord Sydney said, just as the door opened and Mary's aunt and uncle came into the room, followed by Georgiana in her silver gown. John bowed to them, then glanced around the room and frowned.

'Where's William?'

'He only got in from Brighthelmstone this morning,' Harriot said blandly.

'I told him to be here on time.'

'And he made the journey specially, John. Don't worry, everything will be perfect. William will be there.'

'He had better be. Lady Chatham, it is time to go.' Mary blushed at her title, and John brushed her fingers against his lips. 'The drawing room starts at noon and we cannot wait for my brother any longer.'

Mary stepped out of the house and gasped. Three carriages were drawn up in the street, and two sedan chairs carried by servants wearing the Chatham blue-and-silver livery. Mary threw a glance at John, who gave an embarrassed smile. 'Sedan chairs for your mother and Lady Courtown, and carriages for the rest of us.'

'We'll make a grand appearance,' Mary said, taking in the thoroughbreds pawing the dusty ground and the grooms clinging to the back of the upholstered compartments.

'I certainly hope so.'

Mary started to reply, then looked more carefully at John's own carriage at the head of the procession. Her vision clouded.

'Ah, so you noticed I had the panels painted,' John said. 'See here?' He took her hand and ran it over the shiny new crest on the yellow door. Three yellow spots on a black background on the right; three blue scallop shells on the left, surmounted by an earl's coronet. Mary's fingers traced the outline and felt her heart beat faster. John leaned so close she could smell the scent in his hair powder. 'Our crest, Mary, yours and mine. Does it not look handsome?'

'It's perfect,' Mary said, finding her voice at last.

'I'm glad you think so.' He wrapped his arms around her and gave her a brief squeeze, then opened the door of the coach. 'Now let us show it off at St James's.'

The drawing room had not yet begun when Mary and John and their entourage arrived. Mary blinked at the sight of the crowds that met her eyes. The King's dislike of the Duke of Portland's ministry was well known, as was his hatred of Lord North and Charles Fox, the Home and Foreign Secretaries of State. Because of this, the government did its best to whip in support to court events. Men who had hardly attended a single drawing room throughout the American war were conspicuous in their best finery. Lord North's rotund figure moved genially through the crowds, Charles Fox by his side.

The windows had been thrown open to relieve the heat from the press of bodies clad in heavy silks and brocades. Ladies retreated to the edge of the room and waved their fans in a desperate attempt to shift the turgid air. Mary was surprised at how many ladies there were, for the Queen was in daily expectation of the birth of her fifteenth child and had not left Windsor Castle for weeks.

She felt John's anxious gaze on her and she stopped fiddling with her fan to smile at him. Instantly the corners of his eyes crinkled in response. She blew him a kiss and he choked on a ragged breath of air.

'Careful,' he murmured. 'If you do that again I will not be held responsible for my actions.'

'Are you threatening me, my lord?' Mary murmured back.

'No, but I believe you are trying to seduce me.'

'I hope I do not have to *try*.'

She saw his pupils dilate and she wondered if he would embrace her then and there, but then he pulled away with an expression of annoyance. 'William!'

The former Chancellor of the Exchequer moved towards them, flushed and sweaty in his dark blue coat. He pumped John briefly by the hand, then grinned at Mary. 'If it isn't my favourite sister-in-law!'

'She's your only sister-in-law,' John pointed out, adding, with an edge, 'You're nearly late. Where have you been?'

'Brighthelmstone, as you well know, since you sent me that note threatening me with instant death if I didn't hurry back to London to assist in your peacock-like display of rank and privilege. Lady Chatham, you look lovely.' William ignored John's thunderous expression and kissed Mary on each cheek. 'I apologise for my brother. He's always morose when he thinks he might be mocked. I am sure, however, you will give me credit for my sincerity when I say you have never looked so beautiful.'

'Stop making love to my wife,' John said, nudging William with his elbow. William nudged him back.

'I only state facts as I see them.'

At that moment there was a sharp knock and a cry of 'the King, the King' from the pages at the door. Suddenly all Mary could think of was the tightness in her stomach and the sweat beading her brow. The laughter and conversation that had filled the chamber from plush carpet to moulded ceiling gave way to a flurry of panic as the crowd tried to form a wide enough circle for everyone to be accessible to His Majesty.

The King, dressed in a plain plum-coloured coat and breeches, moved around the room counter-clockwise. He seemed in a hurry to get away. He spoke to everybody as he always did, but his questions were as brief as possible within the boundaries of politeness. It did not take him long to come level with John and Mary. Through a whistling in her ears Mary heard Lord Hertford, the Lord Chamberlain, intone, 'The Earl and Countess of Chatham.'

Across the room, Mary saw her parents beaming at her, Georgiana and Harriot close behind. Beside her John bent effortlessly into a bow, his left foot sliding forwards. Mary tried to ignore the sweat beading her forehead and sank into a deep curtsey.

The King had hardly stopped long enough to allow anyone time to kiss his hand, but now he halted. Instantly a hundred or so necks craned to see what was going on.

'Lord Chatham,' the King said. 'This must be your new Countess.' Beneath her gown, Mary's knees trembled. She hoped her ostrich feathers were not bobbing up and down to reflect it. She felt the King's hand under her chin, gently bringing her face up. She fought the urge to meet his protuberant blue eyes; it did not do to look at the King. 'I well remember your presentation as Miss Mary Townshend. You were not quite 17, I believe, and one of the prettiest young women at the drawing room. I'd say that was still the case, eh, Lord Chatham?'

'I most heartily agree, Your Majesty,' John said, and flashed Mary a swift smile. Mary returned it shyly. From the corner of her eyes she saw the King's lips twitch. He helped her out of her curtsey and she stifled a gasp of relief. Her hip was none too steady, but her ordeal was nearly over.

'You are lucky, Lady Chatham, to join such a celebrated family,' the King said. Mary wobbled back into a curtsey, and was about to rise out of it when she realised the King had not moved on. 'Lord Chatham.' He nodded at John, who bowed again after a momentary hesitation. 'Mr Pitt.' William bowed too, even though the Lord Chamberlain had not yet announced him. 'It is a pleasure to see two of my most faithful subjects here today.'

Until recently the King had always shown a marked frostiness when dealing with the sons of the hated Chatham. William, however, seemed to have expected no less. He said, 'Your Majesty knows my brother and I are ever his humble servants.'

John's head turned towards William a fraction. Despite court etiquette a low murmur arose from all corners of the room. Mary wondered how many here were now concluding that they should pay court to this young man who had only just turned 24, rather than His Majesty's present ministers.

Nor was the King yet finished. 'I trust, Mr Pitt, you recall how your father devoted the best years of his life to the struggle against political faction.'

Mary saw her brother-in-law's eyes flicker to resist returning the King's searching gaze. 'I will do my duty, sir.'

The King resumed his hasty circuit of the room. He did not speak to anyone else nearly as much as he had done to the Pitts; he barely spoke to Lord and Lady Sydney, even though he had made such a point of distinguishing their daughter. Less than half an hour later the King left, and the chamber burst into excited chatter.

Lord and Lady Sydney came over. Sydney's face was a picture of curiosity. 'Now what was all that about?'

'His Majesty was just being polite, I suppose,' William said.

'More polite than he's ever been to us before.' John looked like he wanted to say more, but Sydney forestalled him, placing his hands on Mary's shoulders.

'Now let us return to Albemarle Street. We have a court presentation to celebrate.'

Mary smiled at her father then looked back at her husband. John did not seem to be thinking about the King's behaviour towards William any more, but she suspected he had not forgotten about it any more than she had.

October 1783

John dismounted just as dusk was falling. One of his servants was outside lighting the lamps; the four windows on the first floor blazed with light. His was the only house in the square that had any sign of life. The meeting of Parliament was still a month away, and Berkeley Square's aristocratic residents would remain in the country as long as possible.

Mary had tried to dissuade John from going to town, of course. She had clung to his reins and kept him riding out of Hayes stables. 'Send Wood to run your errands, and stay here, with me.'

'Wood is a fine servant, but he is only barely literate. I hope to put Hayes on the market in the new year, and Mr Johnson wishes to show me the latest valuations.'

'Must you go?' Mary insisted, and John grinned.

'Are you nervous about running Hayes by yourself for the first time?'

'No,' Mary said, so promptly he knew he was right. He laughed and her scowl transformed reluctantly into a smile. 'I do not enjoy being apart from you. My place is by your side.'

He leaned over further and she stood on tiptoe so he could kiss her. 'I promise I will return as soon as my business is finished.'

So here he was, stepping up from the street into his London house, still musty and cold despite the efforts of his household to make it presentable. Mary was only a dozen miles away but she might as well have been in a different country. John stripped off his gloves and stood in front of the library fire. He felt cold, and not just because of the autumn chill. Only Mary's embrace could warm him.

He slept restlessly in the camp bed that had been set up for him, because the great four-posters were still dismantled for cleaning. Halfway through a breakfast of coffee and toast he was interrupted by the sound of the bell. One of the footmen entered the breakfast room. 'My lord, Mr Dundas has arrived for Mr Pitt. Shall I inform him Mr Pitt is not here?'

John laid his toast on the side of his plate. 'Mr Dundas?' John vaguely knew Dundas as a middle-aged, hard-drinking Scotsman with an uncouth tongue, but he was not well acquainted with the men who had long followed Lord North. 'But my brother is in France.'

'Shall I send Mr Dundas away, sir?'

'No, send him up. I am curious to find out why he is here.'

John was still wiping away the crumbs from breakfast when he came into the drawing room a few minutes later and found Dundas waiting. The erstwhile Lord Advocate and Treasurer of the Navy looked astonished to see John, as though it were a wonder for a man to live in his own house. John could tell he was not the man Dundas had hoped to see, nor was he to be trusted. He set his lips. The sentiment was mutual.

'Mr Dundas,' he said. 'An unexpected pleasure.'

'Many thanks for coming to me,' Dundas said with a bow, in the thick accent John remembered hearing at Lord Shelburne's meetings or at Westminster. 'Your Lordship must be aware, however, that I am here for Mr Pitt. I saw lights in this house last night.'

John kept his voice cold and neutral. 'My brother is in France, and has been since the middle of September, but any message you may have for him may, I assure you, be left with me.'

'With respect, my lord, what I have to say to him is in confidence. I expect him to return any day.'

'I am afraid I must disabuse you. Mr Pitt is not expected home till the beginning of November. You are at least ten days too soon.'

'Nevertheless, I have received word—' Dundas began, but John interrupted.

'What gives you the right to suppose Mr Pitt would prefer communicating with men of your stamp to his own brother?' Dundas said nothing, but raised his eyebrows. John gazed at him in dislike. He remembered William once referring to Dundas as a 'notorious turncoat', and certainly Dundas's political record – serving seamlessly under North, Rockingham and Shelburne, clinging to his place until finally dislodged by the Coalition – was hardly one to admire. 'I am certain Mr Pitt will inform you of his return, *when* he returns. In the meantime, good day.'

John did not have time to think again of Dundas's visit, or its significance, until he returned to Berkeley Square after four. He was so preoccupied with wondering whether he still stood a chance of riding back to Hayes and Mary before nightfall that he did not at first see the trunks and boxes stacked in the stairwell. Only when he heard a familiar voice coming from the parlour did he realise he was no longer alone.

John pushed the parlour door open. William, still wearing his travelling cloak, was giving instructions to the steward. At the sound of John's approach, he turned and beamed. 'John! I must admit I was not expecting to find you in residence already.'

'I was not expecting to see you here for some days either.' All the suspicions of his morning's meeting with Dundas rushed back in on John at once. He did not like the feeling that his own home was becoming the headquarters of secret political intrigue. He clutched the latch and forced a smile. 'Welcome back to England, William. You've been much in demand.'

Chapter Seven

November 1783

'This had better be good, Chatham.' The Duke of Rutland wore an extravagantly embroidered velvet coat and an anxious expression under his blue-powdered wig. 'I wasn't planning to leave Belvoir for another week, but your brother positively insisted I come up now. Has he received another offer to form a government?'

John was glad to hear his own suspicions voiced aloud by another. He clasped Rutland by the hand. 'That is possible, although I fail to see why circumstances are more propitious now than they were in February. But I daresay William intends to enlighten us tonight – at least,' he added grimly, 'I certainly hope so.'

Mary had discreetly disappeared to visit her parents at Albemarle Street, and Berkeley Square was overrun with William's young friends. Apart from Rutland, Lord Mahon and Eliot, who were virtually family, John knew very few of them, at least until the ringing of the bell preceded the arrival of John's cousins Lord Temple and his brother William Grenville.

George Grenville, Earl Temple since the death of his uncle Richard four years previously, had all the hallmarks of the Grenville line – the up-tilted nose, the dimpled chin, and the heavy-lidded eyes – but already at 30 he was unattractively plump, and his manner was abrasive. He ignored John completely and strode up to William. 'I apologise for the delay, cousin, but I have just come from Lord Thurlow. Am I late?'

'Not at all,' William said. 'You are most timely.'

Temple nodded and sat down. William Grenville looked abashed at his brother's rudeness. He was about William's age, short and plump with an overlarge head, but his large brown eyes were full of intelligence and he gave John an apologetic smile to show he at least knew who was master of the house. 'Lord Chatham.'

John smiled back, but tensely. He was wondering why the two men were here, for they had never been especially close to their Pitt cousins.

It was as though Temple's arrival was a signal William had been awaiting. He rose and rapped at the table with a spoon. 'Gentlemen ...' his voice, so accustomed to filling the chamber of the House of Commons, echoed effortlessly round the dining room, '... I am sorry I have had to curtail your holidays, but I have something very important, and very particular, to tell you.' He held each man's gaze in turn. 'Mr Fox has offered me a Cabinet post.'

That was the last thing John had been expecting, and he saw his astonishment reflected in nearly every face around him. He said, 'Fox has offered you office? Did you accept?'

Temple gave a harsh burst of laughter. William gave his cousin a quelling look. 'No. I will never serve in government with Lord North. Fox and I might, once, have worked together, but by his alliance with North he has rendered a junction impossible.'

'Then why offer?' Dudley Ryder asked. 'Fox must have known you would refuse.'

'Why does any man seek to make coalitions? Because Fox is desperate. He knows his government will need an accession of strength to survive the new parliamentary season. He intends to introduce a bill to reform the governance of India – a bill that may well bring down the Coalition.'

All around the table William's guests exchanged glances. John threw a knowing look across the table at Rutland, who arched his eyebrows. It was Rutland who said, 'How can you be certain the bill will provide a weapon against government? We do not even know the terms of it yet, and Fox and North are not secure enough in the King's good graces to risk controversy.'

'Do you not see, Your Grace?' Temple rose from his chair. 'It is precisely because Fox does not enjoy the King's confidence that he has been so secretive with this Bill. Mr Fox knows it has the power to destroy him.'

'If Fox succeeds he will guarantee the continuance of his ministry for years to come,' William agreed grimly. 'He proposes to set up an India Board consisting of 16 commissioners. Seven will be nominated by the government for a term of four years.' John was struck dumb by the audacity of the suggestion that the government might appropriate the King's prerogative to nominate his own servants. 'I am told Portland will nominate Fox's cousin Colonel Fitzpatrick and Lord North's own son, amongst other loyal adherents.'

'Needless to say,' Temple observed, 'His Majesty is not best pleased.'

'How do you know all this, if the government has been so secretive?' Rutland asked. 'Surely Fox did not tell you?'

'No, he did not,' William admitted. 'But at the same time that Mr Fox came to me, Lord North tried to recruit Lord Thurlow's support, and told him all.' He gave a thin smile. 'Unfortunately for North, Lord Thurlow had already approached me on the King's behalf.'

A murmur of astonishment filled the room. So William had received another offer of the Treasury after all. John had half-expected it ever since William had begun consorting with notorious court men like Dundas, but he was surprised at the strength of his own dismay. Nine months ago, William had been offered the premiership after the government's collapse. Now, Fox and North would have to be forced from office to provide an opening for a new ministry. John looked at his brother's flushed, eager face and wondered whether William saw the difference between the two situations as well as he did.

'Lord Thurlow is very much the King's man,' Temple said, 'but rest assured Mr Pitt and I have weighed that fact carefully against the desirability of forming a viable ministry. Should the India Bill be rejected by Parliament, government must necessarily fall; and with the Crown active on our behalf the Coalition will soon be broken.'

John felt his uneasiness deepen with every word Temple said. His voice sounded unnaturally loud in the silence. 'What if the bill is not rejected?'

'We must ensure that does not happen,' Temple said, his words chilling in their simplicity.

The meeting broke up with Temple's promise that he would transmit new information at the first opportunity. John and William found themselves alone. Through the large windows overlooking the square the night was black, as silent and mysterious as the plot to which John was now party. William kicked back his chair and nursed a glass of port. John wondered how William could look so relaxed after that night's revelations, then remembered his brother had already had several months to get used to it.

William set down his glass, his eyes bright. 'Well, John, I told you in February it would not be long before I returned to Downing Street.'

'Have I been such a poor host that you are in such haste to leave?' John said. William's expression wavered, but his triumphant smile remained.

'You must remember trying to persuade me to take office nine months ago. I did not take your advice then, for the time was not ripe, but now …'

'Now it is?' John's shock and betrayal nearly choked him. He jabbed at the fire with the poker. 'In case you had not noticed, Will, the India Bill has not yet even been proposed in Parliament, let alone defeated. What will you do if it passes? What then?'

'Once the King makes his opposition known, the bill must fail.'

'The King cannot oppose a government measure,' John said. 'To do so would be unconstitutional.'

'By forcing themselves on the King after Lord Shelburne fell, the Coalition have altered the rules. What might be termed "unconstitutional" in other circumstances cannot be deemed such now.'

'So one unconstitutional act excuses another?' John could barely believe what he was hearing. He threw the poker into the basket so hard a cloud of coal dust fell onto the carpet. 'You mentioned Lord Shelburne. What does he have to say about the King's offer?'

'Lord Shelburne?' William repeated, stunned, as though John had suggested the Emperor of China might have an opinion.

'Yes, Lord Shelburne. Shelburne, who brought you into his Cabinet. Shelburne, who suggested you as First Lord of the Treasury in February. Shelburne, who adheres to Papa's political principles.' William said nothing, but folded his long legs under his chair and sat forwards. 'You have not spoken with him, have you?'

'I told you in February I disliked his influence,' William said curtly.

'At least in February you would have headed a government of Papa's friends. What do you think Papa would say, to see you sell yourself to the Crown now, all for the opportunity of heading a ministry independent of Lord Shelburne?'

'You have no right to tell me what I can and cannot do,' William bristled, and John felt the fury he had been trying to keep under control rushing over him like a wave.

'You are wrong. How you choose to destroy yourself is none of my business, but it is not merely yourself you will destroy. You will drag our family's name – Papa's name – through the mire. You may be the statesman, William, but I am the head of the family. It is my duty to inform you that you have gone too far. It is yours to listen.'

'I wish to make the name William Pitt great again,' William said, his voice dangerously quiet. 'You cannot resent me for that.'

'What I resent,' John shouted, 'is that you have spent the past five months plotting under my roof, sharing my table, without breathing a word of it to me. I've told you before nothing hurts more than knowing you cannot confide in me. I will support you because I am your brother, but you are *my* brother too. You owe me better than this and you know it.'

'John—' William began, but John raised his hands and turned away.

'No, Will. You have nothing further to say that I wish to hear.'

****

Contrary to William's optimism the India Bill did not fail immediately, but passed all three Commons readings with large majorities. Aware of the strong opposition at court, Fox was driving his measure through Parliament faster than was usual.

'Now what?' Lord Mahon asked at one of the meetings William now held regularly at Berkeley Square. 'We cannot allow the India Bill to pass the House of Lords.'

John crossed his arms and waited for William's response, knowing all along what it would be and dreading it. At the head of the table William glanced at Lord Temple, who turned to Lord Thurlow. North's former Lord Chancellor replied, his eyes hard beneath the dark eyebrows that gave him his famed saturnine appearance. 'Lord Mahon is right. Should the bill become law, even the King will become powerless to choose his own ministers. Such a state of affairs is unconstitutional; in my opinion, strong measures are justified to ensure it does not come about.'

'Everyone knows His Majesty is opposed to a measure that was not explained to him adequately before being brought before Parliament,' Temple said, 'but he cannot be seen openly to frustrate his own ministers. Lord Thurlow and I have written to the King and informed him of the need to ensure that the Lords reject the bill. He has given us permission to use his name in … *persuading* their Lordships to cast their votes in the desired direction.'

'I'm not sure I like what I hear,' Rutland grumbled to the lacquered lid of his snuffbox. Thurlow glared at him.

'We have the King's approval, Your Grace, and that is all that matters.'

John could stand it no longer. He knew his exit would be remarked upon, but he wanted to get as far away from this grubbiness as possible. He pushed his chair back hard and strode out.

Mary was in the drawing room, writing letters, while Georgiana embroidered by the fire. Both looked up when John came in. The cold and damp of winter was never friendly to Mary, and she limped perceptibly as she crossed the room to take her husband's hands. 'What is the matter?'

'I'm sending you to Frognal to stay with your mother,' John snapped. Mary blanched.

'To Frognal? But my place is here, with you.'

'If you refuse I will send you all the way to Somerset to stay with my mother.' She stared at him, and he saw she did not know whether to test his threat or submit to it. His heart wrenched; he had never intended to take out his frustration on her. He took her in his arms. Mary's body was rigid with injured dignity, but she embraced him back.

'I am not leaving,' she muttered into his shoulder. 'Nor can you make me.'

'I cannot but be involved in any stupidities my brother may henceforth commit; but I want you to have no part in it.'

'I am your wife, John.' She looked up at him, her eyes bright with sincerity. 'I cannot help having a part in your life, even if you send me away.'

Warmth swept through his heart, chipping away at the bitterness. He knew he would never be able to send her away, even if she agreed to it. Her fingers pressed into his shoulders as though to anchor herself to him, and he pulled her closer. He needed her, now more than ever. She was a fixed point in a world that was steadily becoming more and more unbalanced. 'I only wish William had trusted me enough to tell me what he was doing.'

'He knew you would try to stop him,' Mary said, simply.

'And so I would.' John's anger returned; he drew a long, uneven breath. 'He will make himself a laughing stock... and us with him.'

****

With Temple and Thurlow so active in spreading the word of the King's opposition to his own ministry, the India Bill could not but fail. It did so in a crowded House of Lords on 17 December by 19 votes.

Just over 24 hours later, the household at Berkeley Square was roused long before dawn by a loud banging on the front door. John emerged from his room to see cousin Temple skipping up the stairs two at a time, hooded eyes darting left and right. 'Where's Pitt?'

John pulled his bed-gown about him and stifled a yawn. 'Sleeping.' He added, reproachfully, 'As was I.'

'Well then, wake him. I come on important business from the King.'

William was a deep sleeper and it took his servant several attempts to wake him. When he finally entered the library he was still bleary-eyed. Temple took one look at him in his cap and gown and snapped, 'Get dressed. We're going to the Queen's House. It's done.'

William's eyes widened. 'So soon? How—?'

'Never mind how,' Temple interrupted. 'Fox and North have been required to turn in their seals tonight. By morning the ministry will be no more.' He grasped William's arm and guided him out. As they passed John Temple said, 'Go back to bed, Chatham. This is none of your concern.'

Going to bed was the last thing John wanted to do. He shaved and dressed and waited for his brother to return. It was nearly the shortest day of the year and dawn had not yet broken when William reappeared, dressed in court wear, a powdered wig on his head and ceremonial sword at his side. His manner held a gravitas that had not been there when he had left. Perhaps William had simply woken up; perhaps it was something more, a reflection of the importance of the position he now held.

'I take it I am addressing His Majesty's new First Lord of the Treasury?' John said, stepping into William's line of sight at the stair-head. William smiled, but nervously, as though not sure how John would react.

'And Chancellor of the Exchequer.'

So, it was done. Whatever happened now, William was minister. His friends and family were bound up in the fate of a 24-year-old boy's government. The prospect made John feel dizzy, a little sick, and totally powerless.

Chapter Eight

December 1783

John caught sight of the three other carriages as his own drew up alongside his house in Berkeley Square. A choking, icy fog had prevented seeing them sooner. One belonged to Earl Camden, one to Earl Gower, and one to the Duke of Richmond, and they spoke eloquently of the inter-party alliances John's brother was trying to cobble together. Camden's credentials as a follower of the first Earl of Chatham were well established, but Gower had served under Lord North and Richmond was Fox's uncle.

Not that William had much choice but to rely on such a motley. His appointment to the premiership had been received by the Commons with a shout of laughter. An attempt to block an adjournment till the following Monday was rejected without a division, Fox and North's huge majority carrying all before them. Over the next three days 55 office-holders resigned at all levels of administration. A clearer statement of no confidence in the new premier could not have been made; and even existing supporters were proving unreliable. Only the previous day Lord Temple, one of the four lone members of the new Cabinet, had resigned, throwing all into chaos.

As he stepped down onto the pavement John caught sight of a group standing by a street lamp, rubbing their gloved hands, stamping their feet and pulling their coats closer against the fog. They peered at him keenly as he strode towards his front door. 'Is that him?'

'Could be. His coach has the family crest.'

'That's an earl's coronet. Young Pitt's taller, and his hair's lighter.'

'Just the brother then.' They turned away to peer into the fog in case anyone more interesting appeared.

Newspaper hacks, flocking to the headquarters of the flagging ministry like jackals attracted by the scent of blood. John set his lips, swept past them and entered the house.

John knew William would expect him to attend the meeting, but he wanted to steady himself before doing so and in any case had a letter to write before the post went out. He went up to his study and drew some paper towards him. His mother would want to know he was keeping his February promise. No doubt she had guessed from his recent, stilted letters that his heart was not entirely in it.

'My dear Mother, you will have so far seen by my last letter that my mind was not perfectly at ease on the subject of my brother, and that my congratulations on the situation he had reached were not written with the exultation you might have had cause to expect. I had but too much reason for it, as was confirmed by Lord Temple's finding it necessary to resign his seals. My brother felt he was obliged to go through with it and has remained.'

He ran the shaft of his pen against his lip and finished grimly:

'In what hopes of success we stand I know not, but as we now stand on the most unquestionable ground, whether we go on or are beat, we can risk no loss of character in making a stand for King and Constitution.'

Once he had finished John made his way reluctantly downstairs to the library. William sat at a large table. The youthful First Lord of the Treasury was dressed in a blue suit with only a tuft of lace at his throat and wrists to contrast with the darkness. His hair had been dressed and powdered and he held himself straight and proud, but he still looked like the 24-year-old boy he was.

William's eyes flicked briefly towards his brother and John knew his tardy entrance had been noticed by the strain in his brother's voice. 'As I was saying, the situation of the ministry following the resignation of Lord Temple is grave. His Lordship held the seals of office as Secretary of State for both departments, which makes his loss the more regrettable.'

'Do we yet know why his Lordship resigned?' William's friend Tom Steele asked. The awkwardness in the room intensified immediately. Even Steele, not the most politically astute of men, seemed to realise he had blundered. 'I merely wondered … his actions are, after all, open to the strangest interpretations.'

It was not William who replied but Temple's brother Will Grenville, his soft, quiet voice cutting easily through the thick silence. 'My brother recognises the difficulty in which the government is placed by his resignation, but his role in unseating the Coalition has rendered him notorious. He feels he can be of more use to Mr Pitt out of office than in.'

John caught the tail-end of Lord Thurlow's smirk. William nodded at Grenville as though to thank him for addressing a troublesome issue. 'Indeed, it was most noble of His Lordship to sacrifice himself for the sake of the government. In any case our situation is by no means desperate. My Lord Thurlow remains Lord Chancellor, and Lord Gower President of the Council. The Duke of Rutland has accepted the Privy Seal.' From the glazed look in Rutland's eyes John guessed the new Lord Privy Seal had been celebrating his appointment, or drowning his sorrows, all evening. 'My Lords Camden and Sydney, and His Grace of Richmond, are to join us in the new year; and Lord Carmarthen has agreed to take the seals of the Foreign Department.'

The fact that William had filled many of his Cabinet posts was good news, but John did not think the news was as good as William made it sound. Sydney was bound to William by ancient political loyalty, as was Camden, an old friend of the first Lord Chatham. Richmond was more of a surprise, but he was notoriously prickly.

William went on, determinedly optimistic. 'We have also filled several subordinate posts. Mr Dundas is joining us in an official capacity. Mr Steele will partner Mr Rose as Secretary to the Treasury, and Mr Eliot is to join the same department. Mr Arden will be Solicitor General. I have hopes we will be able to make a strong impression in both Houses when Parliament reconvenes in January.' That was a startling statement given that Fox and North had mustered majorities of over a hundred only a few days previously. William ignored the glances being swapped around the room. 'We have not yet tried a division in the House of Commons, but Mr Robinson ...' a chilly nod in the direction of North's former Secretary to the Treasury, who bowed back, '... assures me we might acquire a majority of 20 or 30 by the usual means if we dissolve immediately.'

He did not elaborate on the concept of "usual means", nor did he need to go into the arsenal of peerages, pensions and bribes the King had at his disposal. Men like Eliot and Wilberforce looked unmoved at the prospect of an election, but those who were more in tune with the way Parliament worked furrowed their brow. Arden spoke for many when he said, 'Is that truly wise, Pitt? There are certain measures that must be passed in the new year. The Mutiny Act, for example. If that fails, we have no army. And if the Supplies are not voted by March we will have no funds.'

'We may be able to complete the election before then,' William said, at which Lord Camden spoke up.

'Fox and North will fight the election as hard as they can, and we cannot rely on it taking the usual course. It may be four or five months before all constituencies have cast their votes.'

'Besides, there's always a chance we'll lose,' Steele said glumly.

'But Fox and North might use their majority to block any measures we bring in,' Wilberforce pointed out. 'Can we rely on passing the Mutiny Act and the Supplies before an election?'

'They would not dare obstruct the King's government so blatantly,' Mahon scoffed, but Camden shook his head.

'The situation is highly irregular.'

There was a long silence as everyone reflected on the truth of Camden's words. John glanced up at his brother. William's muscles were taut, his face glistening with the effort to retain an air of authority. John knew well how swiftly William's natural optimism could crumble. He felt his heart sink even further, something he had thought impossible.

The others left shortly afterwards. Each of them shook William's hand as though bidding farewell to a condemned man on the gallows. The sound of the carriages leaving Berkeley Square one by one cut between the Pitt brothers like the hiss of the wind.

John yawned ostentatiously, plucked a book off a nearby shelf, and pretended to read. He had stared at the page for hardly a minute before William said, 'Are you going to cut me out all night?'

'Not at all,' John replied without looking up. 'I simply felt the need for a little light reading.'

'Then for God's sake talk to me. Do not think I did not see you come late to the meeting.'

John snapped the book shut and looked up haughtily. 'Are you going to take me to task for it? His Majesty may have chosen you as his minister, but that does not mean I must bow before you as my master. If you must know, I was at Greenland's. I'm cancelling the sale of Hayes.'

'Cancelling it?' William said, startled. 'Why?'

'I haven't the time to deal with it now.' John's gaze hardened. 'Nor can I imagine any man wishing to purchase an estate so closely connected to a name that causes hilarity whenever it is mentioned.'

William's face filled instantly with anger. 'I told you before: this is my chance to form a ministry that is truly my own.'

'William, you are four and twenty. There is no man alive who believes the King means it to be truly your own.'

'I will make it my own,' William retorted. 'I could not do that with Lord Shelburne serving with me.'

'But you can serving with Thurlow and Dundas? They must have their own ambitions for *your* ministry. Have you thought about that? No, I expect you have, and that is why you have been filling up all the minor posts with your own friends. Eliot at the Treasury Board? Arden Solicitor General? My own father-in-law in the Cabinet? Dear God, it reads like a paean to nepotism. That, or it makes you look desperate.'

'I want a union of parties,' William said, white with anger. 'That means not just my father's friends, but all Whigs united under one banner.'

'Your friends will stand by you, and Camden and Sydney will remember their loyalty to our father, but what is to be made of the rest? Richmond, Gower, Thurlow – impressive names, I grant you, but desperate outcasts all. Can they work with you, let alone with each other?'

'I am ready to work with anyone who will work with me,' William said and John turned to look him directly in the face.

'And if they will not? How long before they flee the sinking ship? We've already lost Temple, and he was your own cousin!'

'I admit that Lord Temple's resignation was unexpected—'

'No,' John stopped him. 'Unfortunate, yes; ill-timed, absolutely; disastrous, no question; but unexpected – no, no, Will, it was never that. Someone had to pay the price for your foolhardiness, and you should be grateful it wasn't you – yet.'

'You really believe I have made a mistake, do you not?' William said at last.

'The biggest of your life,' John agreed grimly.

'You do not understand.'

'In faith, I do not.'

'Once an election has been held my government will have a majority in the Commons. I will not be captaining a 'sinking ship' then.'

John took a deep breath to steady his nerves. 'A dissolution will look like cowardice, as though you are trying to get other men to fight your battles. You know as well as I do the real reason Temple resigned is because he agrees with me on this. You must face Fox and show the world you were right to overturn his unconstitutional government. If you dissolve, people will assume you are no better than Temple, Thurlow, Robinson and Dundas – the men you are now associated with.'

'I am First Lord of the Treasury and Chancellor of the Exchequer,' William said, coldly. 'I am capable of making my own decisions.'

John stared at William incredulously, then rose. 'I can easily believe you have weightier issues to contend with than the loss of my goodwill.'

'For once in your life you are right,' William said with heavy sarcasm.

He drew some letters towards him and broke the first seal. John opened his mouth to call William a stubborn fool but shut it again. Trading insults would do no good, and he would do better to dissipate his frustration in a game of billiards at White's.

As he put his hand on the doorknob he became aware of a difference in mood. He turned. William gazed emptily at a letter laid out on the desk in front of him.

'Bad news?' John said. William looked as though he dearly wanted to ignore the question, but nodded. 'Who has refused to help you this time?'

'Grafton.' The Duke of Grafton had succeeded Lord Chatham as First Lord of the Treasury 15 years previously. He controlled several boroughs and wielded influence over several Commons members. 'He regrets but he cannot accept of office under me.'

It was a big blow. John watched William file Grafton's letter into a big leather portfolio, already bulging with similar letters from other equally important members of the upper house. Only a few moments before John had thought he did not care if William stood or fell; now he wanted nothing more than to put his arms round him as though they were children again, and tell him all would be well. The words, had they come, would in any case have been a lie.

January 1784

Early in the new year William finally received word of his re-election for Appleby. He determined to take his seat as First Lord and Chancellor of the Exchequer on the first day Parliament met after Christmas recess. John therefore found himself riding to Westminster in a coach with William, the Duke of Rutland, and three large red despatch boxes that sat between the brothers like a barrier.

They travelled in silence. Rutland's plump face was white and puffy, his eyes rimmed with the red of too much drink and too little sleep. William, digging through a despatch box, looked calm enough, but he must have been dreading the mauling he could expect from Fox and North in the House. It was all John could do to remind himself that William's predicament was of his own making.

A light snow was falling as the carriage drew up in Old Palace Yard. Inevitably, the arrival of the youthful premier attracted a large crowd. By the time the three men reached the Commons lobby the room was filling fast. Some faces expressed deep curiosity, others hostility; very few seemed in any way compassionate.

William's wide grey eyes had a hunted look in them, an expression John had seen many times in the eyes of a deer as the hunting-dogs laid into it. 'Good luck, Will.' John stretched out his hand instinctively and, after a moment, William took it.

'Be easy,' he said. 'It won't be as bad as you think.'

John tried to return his brother's smile. 'I heartily pray not.'

They stood clasped together for a second that lasted an age, then William's face rearranged itself into an expression of cold indifference. He strode towards the doors of the House, held open for him by two porters.

Rutland arched his brows at John. 'Well?'

'He seems cheerful.'

'He's always cheerful. Shall we go in?'

They had to jostle for space behind the Bar with other Lords and gentlemen who had not been able to find a seat. Lord Sydney was there, long-faced and anxious, and Thurlow and Gower. Robinson sat unobtrusively in a corner, waiting to see if his calculations would be borne out by the day's vote. His last estimate had predicted a majority for

William of over 30 votes following vigorous government activity over the Christmas recess. John hoped with every fibre of his being Robinson was right, but looking at the thinness of the government benches he had to doubt.

Rutland leaned over and whispered, 'Look at Fox.'

John obeyed and felt dismay course through him. The determined expression on the former Secretary of State's mobile face chilled him. Whatever William might think, the battle had not yet been won. It had not even begun.

When the Speaker announced the resumption of the debate William rose to read a message to the Commons from the King. His getting onto his feet was clearly the signal Fox had been waiting for to open hostilities. Before the Speaker called for the Chancellor of the Exchequer, Fox also stood up.

The low mutter that had echoed round the chamber upon William's taking his place on the Treasury Bench petered into a sepulchral silence. Fox should have ceded the floor to William, a government minister; but he did not. John, watching with rapidly rising horror, could see Fox knew exactly what he was doing. Fox kept his eyes fixed on his opponent, thick black eyebrows drawn in a line.

The Speaker announced, 'Mr Fox has the floor.'

'God damn it,' Rutland breathed, as the Commons exploded with noise.

Fox's supporters chanted his name aloud with great glee. Someone on the government side started calling out 'Pitt! Pitt! Pitt!' and several people caught up the refrain, but it was a pale riposte to the shouts of 'Fox! Fox! Fox!' echoing off the stone pillars and low wooden ceiling. William clung to the despatch box like a drowning man. He kept his eyes fixed on the Speaker as though he hoped he might change his mind.

'Mr Fox has the floor,' the Speaker repeated, adding sternly, 'Mr Pitt, you must give way.'

William's shoulders tensed, but just as it seemed the Speaker would have to call upon the Serjeant-at-Arms he sat down, very slowly. The opposition benches broke out in a roar of jubilant applause.

William's face was flushed, his eyes feverish. Dundas leaned over, touched his arm and whispered something, but William was not listening.

He was looking at Fox, and John saw something in his brother's eyes he had never seen there before, and shuddered.

Fox moved that the House go into a committee to discuss the state of the nation – effectively a vote of no confidence – and launched into a stinging attack on the integrity of the new minister. Contrary to Robinson's estimates, Fox's motion passed by a majority of 39 votes. An attempt by Dundas to adjourn was defeated by 54.

John and Rutland stood through it all without a word. William's ministry seemed doomed; John watched the opposition lay into it as though enchanted by some ghastly, terrible magic. With every resolution passed against government he looked at his brother's set face and willed him to fight: *Come on, Will. Do something.* At last, William stood to defend himself against Fox's accusations of corruption.

'I came up no backstairs,' he declared, haughtily, staring at Fox as though defying him to prove otherwise. 'I know of no secret influence. The integrity of my heart, and the probity of my public and private principles, shall always be my sources of action. Never will I be responsible for measures not my own, in which my heart and judgment do not cordially acquiesce.'

They were brave words, and John himself was nearly taken in by them. But they were not enough. A cry went up from the opposition benches: 'Will there be a dissolution?'

'Answer the question!'

'Answer!'

'Order in the House,' the Speaker interposed, but John could see he was as curious as everyone else to hear what William would do.

What William did was to put his hat firmly on his head and turn away, as steadily and calmly as though he was not being attacked and insulted, while the opposition continued to howl 'Answer! Answer!' at his retreating back.

****

There was no House the next day, to give everyone the chance to rest after the long debate – everyone except those closest to the government, of course. William spent much of the day in conference with his colleagues and John did not see him until the evening, when William summoned an emergency meeting at the Duke of Rutland's house in Arlington Street.

'I suppose you think I deserve everything that has occurred,' William said, his voice hoarse from over-use, the moment John entered the room. 'You must feel I have no-one to blame but myself.'

'I would never say such a thing,' John murmured.

'Maybe not, but I know you have thought it, many times.' John could not deny it; he said nothing and slid into his seat.

The smell of defeat hung heavily over the room. Richmond's bald scalp glowed under the candle-light; Camden chewed on a thumbnail; Rutland swilled the wine round the bowl of his glass of madeira, looking flushed. Dundas spoke. Like William's, his voice was croaky with fatigue; he, too, had shouldered much of the oratorical burden the previous night. 'We must decide what to do should Fox bring in another motion of censure against government.'

'Nothing,' Thurlow said promptly. 'His Majesty will reject all addresses for our removal.'

'How long can we go on like this, ignoring the voice of the House of Commons?' Sydney asked. 'How long can we maintain our position against Fox's onslaught?'

'Indefinitely, I would suppose,' Thurlow replied with a glare across the table at William, 'so long as Mr Pitt remains firm in his purpose against him.'

John looked at William. The deep rings under his brother's eyes spoke for themselves. Dundas said, anxiously, 'Do not forget, sir, that we have the support of the country. His Majesty has already received several dozen petitions in your favour.'

'Sir.' It was Camden who spoke up, with all the authority of his role as one of the first Lord Chatham's most faithful followers. 'When you formed your government, Mr Robinson presented you with estimates predicting a majority in the event of a general election. Mr Dundas is right: the nation is on your side. I entreat you to give up all notions of foolish pride and do what you must. Dissolve Parliament, sir, and call an election.'

'I disagree with Lord Camden,' Thurlow growled as soon as Camden had finished speaking. 'The quality of Mr Robinson's estimates may be most accurately gauged by his prediction that, yesterday, you would find yourself in the majority. All you must do, sir, is hold firm. Mr Fox may bluster all he wishes; but his words have no power so long as you retain His Majesty's confidence.'

John suspected that was easier for Thurlow to say than for William to believe, fresh from a drubbing at Fox's hands. John's gaze met Rutland's. Charles rolled his eyes and reached for the decanter again.

William stared at the table top with empty eyes. John wondered whether his brother would end up agreeing with Camden. At that moment, remembering as he did the previous night's debate, John would not have blamed him.

Thurlow seemed to have come to the same conclusion. When William did not respond, he snorted, pushed his chair back from the table and fumbled in his pocket for pipe and tobacco.

The screech of chair legs on the polished floor roused William. He glanced across at his brother, to John's astonishment. Worried that William would try to engage him in a discussion in which he had no place, John also rose from the table and went to pour himself a glass of brandy.

As he grasped the neck of the decanter he heard William speak. 'You say we have the country with us?'

Dundas said, 'Aye. Many of the petitions His Majesty has received in your favour come from the largest, most representative boroughs. With the aid of the King's influence we may find you a majority sufficient to defeat Fox and North.'

John bit his lip and sipped his brandy. Next to him Thurlow faced the window and puffed aggressively on his pipe, black brows drawn together in disapproval. At length William spoke. His voice was still exhausted, but there was a spark of contrariness in his tone that made John turn. 'If we have the country with us, then my way forward is clear. There will be no election.'

Thurlow choked on his smoke. His coughing was masked by an explosion of agitation from the table. Lord Carmarthen waved a manicured hand. 'What is this folly? If you do not dissolve we are all lost!'

'Look at yourself,' Lord Sydney said. 'You can hardly stand. Fox will have you on your knees in a fortnight.'

'The Opposition expects me to dissolve,' William explained. 'Mr Fox will accuse me of planning a corrupt election to bolster my government.

Each day that passes without one will rob his argument of its power. A delay will allow more petitions in favour of my government to arrive from the country, and allow His Majesty to exert his influence on my behalf.'

Dundas looked worried. 'If you go to the polls now you will not lose in standing, for all will acknowledge you have tried your best.'

'My decision stands. We still have business to secure – the Mutiny Act, the Supplies. They must be passed or government cannot go on.'

'Fox and North will never let you pass those measures and you know it,' Sydney warned.

'They may try to stop me,' William said, and with those six quiet words John again felt the chill he had experienced when he had seen his brother face Fox in the Commons for the first time.

That evening John and William stayed to dine with Rutland. They ate in silence, each wrapped in his own thoughts. When the servants came to take away the tablecloth for dessert William was summoned outside by a message from the King, leaving John and Rutland alone.

Rutland had started drinking at some point in the afternoon and had not yet stopped. John watched his old friend pour himself an unsteady glass of claret; if Rutland's hand was shaking, then he must have drunk more than any normal man could bear.

Rutland replaced the decanter. His eyes were pouched and red-rimmed and the expression in them did not match his smile. 'Has William told you the good news?'

'What good news?' John wondered whether Rutland was mocking him, for there had been precious little good news recently. Rutland reached for some grapes, and found the bowl on the third attempt.

'We shall shortly be parting company. I'm being sent to Ireland.'

For a moment the words did not quite penetrate. 'Ireland? What do you mean?'

'Lord Northington has sent in his resignation,' Rutland said. 'Not unexpectedly, as he was Portland's Lord Lieutenant, but it left a vacancy. Pitt judged I was the man to fill it.'

Rutland's news settled in the depths of John's mind like ice congealing on wintry ground. For William to send the affable, pleasure-loving Rutland away to Ireland …! Ireland, which only two years ago had threatened to burst into rebellion, where Catholic and Protestant were constantly at loggerheads, abject poverty was widespread, and absentee landowners controlled a Parliament as riddled with corruption as could be imagined!

Rutland saw his expression and interpreted it correctly. John fancied there were tears pricking Rutland's eyes before he closed them and drained his glass. 'I know. I would guess my days of ease are over.'

'When—' John's voice cracked. He took a sip of wine and started again. 'When do you leave?'

'By the end of February. Maybe the start of March.' Rutland raised his eyes to John with a rueful smile. 'My father always wanted me to make something of myself. I suppose I should be grateful to William for giving me the chance.'

John could think of nothing to say. Rutland was his closest, dearest friend. The thought of losing him was a hollowness he could barely acknowledge. He looked at Rutland's wine-saturated face and thought, with sudden certainty: *He cannot do it.* But Rutland would do it, for William, who wanted a friend in an office as important as that of Ireland's Lord Lieutenant; William, who had chosen the most loyal, but least strong, man for the task.

At that moment, William returned. He did not seem to notice the tone of the silence between John and Rutland, but resumed his seat without a word. He reached out for a handful of raisins and chewed thoughtfully, then said, 'John …' John had been trying to avoid his brother's gaze, but at this summons could no longer do so. William's eyes were wide and dark; he spoke like a child seeking the confirmation of an adult. 'Did I make the right decision in postponing a dissolution?'

'Naturally you did,' John snapped. He had no desire to reopen this discussion and focused his attention on the business of reducing some empty nutshells to crumbs. Rutland drunkenly proffered the claret jug and William held out his glass to be filled. For a moment or two the only sound in the room was of wine running richly against crystal.

William sipped his wine and said, 'I can count on your support, can I not?'

'Of course you can,' Rutland replied at once, but John knew the question had been mostly directed at him. He could feel the despair in William's searching gaze; angry though he still was at the situation William had placed them all in, he could not conquer his instinctive urge to help. William was too committed. He had to see the struggle through, to victory or defeat. Shakespeare's lines came to John's mind:

If he fall in, good night! or sink or swim:
Send danger from the east unto the west,
So honour cross it from the north to south,
And let them grapple.

And yet he did not know how to form the words. He did not know whether William would believe him if he told him all would come right in the end, for John barely believed it himself.

He saw William's eyes widen with the lengthening silence and said, hurriedly, 'I hope you know you can always rely on me.'

'I do,' William replied, but the pause that preceded his words told John much more than the half-murmured tone in which they were spoken.

Chapter Nine

February 1784

John had to admit William's gamble not to dissolve rapidly paid off. Every day Fox drew out the Commons debate until the small hours of the morning, trying to wear William down with insults and accusations, but every day that passed without an election robbed Fox's fulminations of their power. The trickle of pro-government petitions sent to the King in favour of his plucky young premier rapidly became a flood. Meanwhile, behind the scenes, the full influence of the Crown was brought to bear on parliamentary waverers. The Coalition majority, once over a hundred, now hovered uneasily close to single figures.

At the end of February the Aldermen of London voted William the freedom of the City. To mark the occasion there was to be a grand procession from John's house to the ceremonial dinner at Grocer's Hall, and William asked John and their brother-in-law Lord Mahon to accompany him.

By the time the Aldermen arrived in their scarlet cloaks and jewelled collars the crowd of spectators in Berkeley Square had swelled to such proportions that the dignitaries had to push through them to reach the front door. Mary was spending the evening with her parents in Albemarle Street, and the moment he saw the size of the crowds John was glad she was out of the way. He, William and Lord Mahon had difficulty pushing their way to the carriage, and when they got in a group of burly men unhitched the horses and hoisted the wooden struts onto their shoulders. They took an hour and a half to reach the Poultry, followed by a trail of Aldermen, Marshals, Constables, standards carried by young boys in white and pink cockades, and an entire orchestra of trumpets, clarinets and kettle drums.

'I don't think we should linger,' John murmured to William as they entered Grocer's Hall. The fact that the more respectable shopkeepers, artisans and merchants seemed outnumbered three to one worried him. William, however, was unconcerned.

'They're just curious, John. They will all be gone by the time we return.'

But if anything the crowds swelled still further over the next few hours. John had enjoyed the rich food and drunk deeply of the Grocers' wine, but he sobered up the instant he, William and Mahon emerged to face what was now more like a mob overflowing out of Grocer's Hall Court. They were already unhitching the horses from John's carriage before the three men had time to sit down.

The air smelled of cheap wine and spirits. Some of the crowd had stolen torches from link-boys, and the white facades of the City's guild-houses acquired a grim orange glow. John spotted some men in greasy leather overalls and large hats whispering together before dispersing. The sight of them made his skin prickle. Political feelings were especially volatile at the moment; these were not ordinary times.

'Papa always said the mob and the people of England were one,' William observed. He was half-drunk on alcohol and acclaim; John could smell the wine on his brother's breath from across the carriage. 'He would not have been afraid.'

'I am not afraid!' John snapped.

'In that case try to enjoy yourself. We will be home soon.'

After an hour, however, even William had gone pale and quiet. Without the horses, the three young men were utterly at the mercy of their mob. The cheers of 'Pitt for ever' had long ago been lost in random whoops of inebriated joy. A small child was nearly run down under the wheels, and William had to make more than one appearance to calm the crowds and cajole them, with difficulty, into changing direction.

'Where are we?' William asked for the tenth time in as many minutes. He had his back to the horses to be less easily seen, but his own view was thereby restricted. John looked out of the window and tried to recognise any landmarks. All he could see were large brick buildings, the odd bay window, and hundreds of people running alongside him, banging on doors, rattling windows and calling for lights. He slanted a sarcastic look in his brother's direction.

'At least you know you're popular, Will. This is the price of your success.'

The great dome of St Paul's finally hove into sight, shadowy against the night sky, and the crowd moved down Fleet Street to the Strand.

They passed the sprawling bulk of Somerset House just visible behind its pillared entrance. The carriage shuddered slowly by the King's mews and the statue of Charles I at Charing Cross, skirted the empty pillory on Cockspur Street, and turned down Pall Mall.

Just as John started to think they would soon be home, the mob stopped.

'Carlton House,' Mahon reported, peering through the window.

'Oh dear God,' John breathed. Carlton House was the private residence of the Prince of Wales, a notorious Foxite. The house's porticoed frontage was plunged into darkness; the Prince, mercifully, was not at home. Had he been, he would have heard hissing as the crowd pressed up to the gates.

'Down with Fox!'

'Down with the Prince!'

'We'll break his windows till he lights up for the minister!'

'Lights! Lights! Lights!'

'In Heaven's name, Will, do something!' John urged.

His brother gave him a frightened look then opened the carriage door. A cry of delight rent the air as he was spotted. John could almost hear William gritting his teeth as he acknowledged the cheers with a bow. 'Gentlemen! We have no business here. I commend you all for your enthusiasm, but I should like very much to get home.'

After a tense moment, the carriage once more began to move. John's relief did not last long. They had not progressed more than 50 yards before the mob stopped again. A dreadful combination of hissing, shouting and cursing reverberated off the stuccoed frontages of the houses.

'To St James's Place! Break Fox's windows!'

'Will …' John murmured, but his brother was already leaning out of the coach.

'Gentlemen! To Berkeley Square, I beg you!'

This time it took more effort on William's part before the crowd lurched off again, hauling the carriage with its helpless occupants. John gazed out of the window, teeth clenched. He had not seen the leather-clad men in shadowing hats since passing Carlton House, and it bothered him. At least they were nearly home: John fancied he could almost see his house on Berkeley Square rising in the distance.

But the real danger had not yet begun.

They had just passed St James's Place when the carriage stopped amid a sudden and terrible silence. John clung to the leather strap hanging from the carriage roof and peered out of the window. The men surrounding his carriage were looking, wide-eyed, at something ahead. Some of the nimbler ones turned and ran as though in fear of their lives.

'What is going on?' William said.

John craned his neck, but whatever was happening was directly in front of them. 'I do not know.'

'Open the window.'

'Are you insane?'

'I'll do it then.' William made to pull the glass pane down, but John slapped his hand away.

'Don't be a fool. Lie low.'

He eased down the glass. A couple more of the mob ran past as he did so. John turned his head to see what they were running from and felt his chest constrict.

They had stopped outside Brooks's, the Foxite club. A double line of porters and sedan-chairmen was blocking the street outside the club's main entrance. All of them were tall and broad-shouldered and all had stripped to their shirtsleeves, although it was a cold night. Each held a weapon. Some had broken sedan chair-poles. Some had stubby coshes with smooth, rounded ends. John thought he saw one with a knife.

The memory of the leather-clad men in their broad-brimmed hats rose in John's mind. Had they disappeared to warn Brooks's of the crowd's approach? Or had they been urging the mob on? John stared at the men blockading the street and knew with terrible certainty this had all been planned. By whom he could not say, but he did not suppose it would be long before he found out.

John caught William's gaze across the compartment. His brother had shrunk into the shadows, his eyes bright with apprehension.

One of the porters called out, 'We know you have come to break our windows. We will not allow it.'

One of the crowd spoke up in response, one of the better sort of men who had tried to restrain the crowd in its earlier stages. 'We merely want to take Mr Pitt and his brother home. We promise you will not be molested.'

'We know what value to place on Mr Pitt's promises,' one of the Brooks's men growled.

'Sirs, be reasonable. Let us by peaceably or there will be consequences on the morrow.'

'Oh, there will be consequences,' the reply came. 'But not on the morrow, we promise you that.'

John groaned and pulled up the window. He was hunting for the latch to open the carriage door when he heard a dull thump, followed by a cry. In an instant the trickle of people running away from the double line of porters became a flood.

William leaned forwards but John held him back. 'Do not show your face! If they see you, they will rip you apart.'

Mahon peeped through the glass on his side of the carriage. His tall forehead wrinkled. 'Others are coming out of Brooks's now.'

'Carrying sticks?' Mahon nodded and John cursed. He knocked against the boards of the roof to call the driver's attention. 'Can you get us away from here?'

'My lord, we have no horses,' came the reply.

The true peril of their situation sank in then. John could hear the cries from outside, interspersed with yelps of pain and the crack of sticks making contact with backs and skulls. The street was full of running figures, bumping into each other and trampling the fallen to get away.

William said, very quietly, 'Can the footmen draw the coach?'

'We'd need at least ten men to shift it with any speed, I would imagine,' Mahon replied, so promptly he must have been wondering the same thing.

William had stopped asking what was going on; the terrible sounds from outside spoke for themselves. His fearful expression was that of a soldier encountering his first bloodshed. The cries brought back unpleasant memories of John's own blooding, and his hand instinctively moved towards the place at his waist where his sword had once been. He knocked again to attract the driver's attention. 'How many of the footmen are armed?'

'We have one blunderbuss,' the driver said. 'It's not loaded.'

The coachman's answer deepened John's sense of impotence. The despair turned to alarm moments later when the carriage rocked ominously on its wheels.

'We could try getting into Brooks's and asking for help,' Mahon suggested. 'The gentlemen would have nothing to do with this, I am certain.'

John was not so sure. Faces at the club's windows gazed out languidly at the fleeing crowds and made not so much as a gesture to stop the violence. Up on the first floor the balcony thronged with shadowy forms. One or two men even threw missiles –bread rolls, candle stubs and dice. The others cheered every time one hit a fleeing man.

Suddenly a face peered into the carriage from the other side of the glass: a cultivated face, with powdered hair hanging in sweat-soaked tendrils. The man wore a half-mask of the kind worn while gambling at cards but John did not need to see all his features to recognise him. It was James Hare, one of Fox's staunchest friends, and a man with whom John himself had played many a rubber of whist.

John snapped out of his shock with effort. He pulled down the glass, put his hand in Hare's face and pushed him away, but it was too late: Hare had picked out William. 'It's him!'

A deathly 'View-Halloa' reverberated around the street. Apart from Hare, John recognised John Crewe and thought he might have seen Fox's cousin Colonel Fitzpatrick, though he could not be sure. All of them were men he had mixed with socially in the past.

A porter tried to break down Mahon's door. He managed to wrench it open a few inches but Mahon pulled it closed. A blow from a broken chair-pole shattered John's window, showering the three men with glass. John was dimly aware that he had cut his hands but he had no time to take stock of his injuries. Someone was aiming blows at William through the broken window and it was all he could do to shield his brother.

'White's.' William spoke through clenched lips. 'We should get to White's.'

'Are you mad? It's at the other end of the street!' John shouted.

'Have you got a better idea?'

There was a cry from the back of the coach. The three footmen had beaten the attackers off successfully with their fists, but they were no match for the mass of armed porters. A blue-and-silver-liveried body was thrown onto the cobbled pavement and set upon by men with sticks. A howl from the front of the coach signalled that the coachman had been overcome.

Someone broke in Mahon's door and ripped it off the hinges. Mahon kicked off the intruder with his long legs but John was having less luck on his side, from where the attackers could see William more clearly and tried harder to get at him. John pushed a man out of the way and shouted, 'William is right. We must get to White's before they rip the carriage apart. Have you got your canes?' Mahon nodded but William shook his head. John gritted his teeth, gripped his own stick and said, 'Stay close to me and keep your head down.'

He pushed his door open. The impact knocked down another attacker who had just climbed onto the step. John ploughed forwards, dragging William behind him, Mahon bringing up the rear. For a moment they had the element of surprise and John managed several steps before a cry from the club balcony alerted the porters to the fact their prizes were escaping. John staggered under a blow, then grabbed his attacker by the lapels and shoved him into the path of another man brandishing a broken chair-pole. He did not wait to see whether the two collided, but grabbed William's arm and ran for his life.

Most of the houses had darkened windows, their owners either away or pretending not to hear the fuss, but further off John could see lights. He remembered his cousin Temple's house on Pall Mall had been lit up when they had passed only a short while before. He grabbed his brother-in-law's arm. 'Mahon. Can you get to Temple's house?'

'I think so.'

'Go and get help. And quickly.'

Mahon sped away, dodging a couple of desultory blows, but the attackers were not interested in him. They were closing in on William, the real prey. John took his cane in both hands and pushed it against a chairman's breast to push him aside, but so many blows rained down on him and his brother from so many directions that he hardly had time to brace himself before the next one came. He shielded William as best he could but they were outnumbered, and it was a miracle they got as far as they did before someone grabbed John from behind.

For a tantalising moment he and William managed to maintain a connection; then William's fingers slipped away. John collapsed. His stick clattered onto the cobbles and rolled out of reach.

John pushed himself onto his knees. 'Will!'

Several men pounded past him towards his brother. At first John thought they were reinforcements from Brooks's, but then his eyes cleared and he felt a thrill of hope at the realisation that they were not from Brooks's but from White's. The Brooks's men forgot their original purpose and began trading blows with their rivals. Moments later Mahon appeared, followed by half a dozen men wearing Temple's livery. The gentlemen who had taken part in the struggle disappeared into the darkness. John did not even see them go.

Mahon knelt by John's side. 'Temple's sent for the Bow Street men. Where's William?'

'I don't know,' John replied, then struggled to his feet when he saw his brother coming towards him on the arm of one of Temple's servants.

'Are you injured?' Mahon asked. John gave his brother an appraising look. William's breath came in ragged gasps, he had lost his wig and his coat was torn, but he seemed unhurt.

'Can you run?' William's eyes rolled to meet John's. He nodded, and John took his arm. 'Then do so.'

The street-fight was over. By the time the Bow Street men arrived, if they ever did, they would find little but a ruined carriage and a handful of casualties, most of whom were being helped off the thoroughfare to be plied with brandy in the kitchens of White's. A White's porter, pale and trembling, held the door open for John, William and Mahon as they came in, then shut it behind them as though afraid of what might follow. John's hands shook and his ears rang, but they were safe at last.

The calm of White's barrel-roofed subscription rooms contrasted with the chaos the brothers had endured outside. Despite the late hour there were a few people there: Edward Eliot, Pepper Arden and Steele, among others. They watched in stunned silence as William was taken to a couch to sit down. It was not a moment too soon for John thought his brother's shaking legs were about to give out on him. He himself was suddenly aware of the bruises across his shoulders, arms and legs and of the stinging cuts all over his hands from the broken carriage window.

Someone forced a glass into his hands. He expected the wine to invigorate him but it didn't. All he felt was a numbness that deepened whenever he glanced across the room at William's ashen face.

The door flew open to admit Lord Sydney and his son John Townshend, both red-faced and out of breath. Sydney glanced at

William, who was wiping away the blood on his hands with the aid of a napkin dipped in a bowl of warm water, then rushed to his son-in-law's side. 'What the devil happened, John?'

'We heard the commotion from Lord Temple's house,' John Townshend explained. 'Papa and I were at dinner with him when Mahon came calling for help.'

'Are you hurt?' Sydney said.

'Merely bruised. William too.'

At the sound of his name William said, in a strange voice, 'Which is more than I can say for your carriage, John. They tore it to pieces, I think.' He gave a high, desperate laugh.

Sydney looked at William with anger in his eyes. 'Who did this? Fox?'

'I do not think Fox was involved,' John said. 'But I saw others: Crewe; Hare; Fitzpatrick. And they had accomplices. Strange-looking men in cocked hats. I saw them at Grocer's Hall, and they followed us all the way up to Pall Mall, where they disappeared.'

'An ambush?' Mahon frowned.

'Our attackers were prepared. They were ready for us, Charles.'

'It's a serious accusation,' Sydney said, looking worried. 'They might have killed you.'

'I do not think they wanted to kill us. Punish us, perhaps, and they certainly intended to injure us. But there were too many gentlemen involved.'

Mahon snorted but said nothing. John knew he was thinking how ungentlemanly it was to ambush a man and beat him to within an inch of his life, and he agreed. He was, however, highly aware of the delicacy of the situation. William was gaining public support, but the wrong response to tonight's activities might change everything. Blaming men whom John could not even be sure he had seen participating – although he was certain about Hare and Crewe – would get William nowhere. The attackers would get away with it.

John looked at William's bent head, Mahon's torn coat, and the concern on the faces of all around, and felt something tautened to impossible lengths break inside him. His numbness abruptly gave way to searing fury, and he gladly gave himself up to it. He stood and ran out of the room.

He heard William call, 'John!' but he pretended not to hear. His anger made him single-minded, his thoughts focused on the target of his frustration as surely as a compass needle was drawn to the north.

John burst out into the street. The carriage he and William had travelled in lay smashed on the cobblestones, and several chair-poles and bloodied coshes had been abandoned by the fleeing Brooks's men. The last of the wounded had been helped indoors and a few White's porters were cleaning up. John paid them no heed. He kept his eyes fixed on the pedimented front of Brooks's across the street.

He hammered on the door with all his might. He did not expect it to open but it helped alleviate the frustration. Someone touched his arm and he turned to see his brother-in-law and Lord Sydney.

'What do you think you are doing?' Mahon asked.

'I need to get in.'

'And what will you do if you succeed?'

'I'll find some answers.'

'Come away, John,' Sydney urged, but John ignored him. He gave the door a resounding kick.

'This is folly,' Mahon said. John rounded on him and pushed his brother-in-law so hard he almost fell down the front steps.

'You were there! You saw what happened!' He pointed at the crusted blood on Mahon's sleeve. 'I have to know why!'

For a moment John thought Mahon would try and stop him. Then Mahon stepped up and put his shoulder to the door. When John did not react, he said, 'On three.'

The weight of both men was enough to break the door on its hinges. They hurtled into the front hall of the club surrounded by dust and plaster. A Brooks's porter came halfway down the staircase, saw John dusting off his throbbing shoulder, and launched back up again shouting for help. By the time the man's shouts attracted assistance John had run up the stairs and into the subscription room.

Long velvet curtains had been drawn against the darkness outside. John tugged them back. The balconied area, which only half an hour previously had thronged with jeering Brooks's members, was empty and shrouded in night. The huge chandelier hanging from the vaulted ceiling had been extinguished, but recently, because the room still smelled of candle smoke. A few wall sconces cast a dim light across the empty leather chairs and card tables. Newspapers casually flung about the coffee room and half-empty glasses testified to recent activity.

John turned. A gaggle of Brooks's porters had followed him and watched warily, waiting for him to give them a reason to attack. Mahon and Sydney stood by, Sydney fearful, Mahon's eyes hooded.

'Where are they?' John snarled. The porters shrank back. One of them had a smear of blood on his cheek, another had torn clothes. They had been in the fight. John felt his hand curling into a fist even as a cool voice replied: 'Where are who?'

It was Mr Griffiths, the proprietor of Brooks's. He had obviously not participated in the night's activities for his black velvet suit and powdered wig were immaculate, but his expression of hostility rekindled John's fury.

'The members!'

'My dear Lord Chatham,' Griffiths said, as though John were a child, 'it is four o'clock in the morning.'

'They were here not half an hour ago!' John moved towards the library but found his way blocked. Behind him Griffiths said, 'They are not here now.'

Before anyone could stop John, he crossed the six or seven steps which separated him from the club manager. Griffiths was the heavier man, but John had the advantage of fury and surprise. He grabbed Griffiths by the lapels and shoved him against the wall.

Griffiths' face was an inch away, sheened with sweat. His mocking gaze seemed to ask John what he meant to do next, and indeed John did not know. He knew he must present a strange figure in his torn coat, his cut lip still bleeding; but he could not take his revenge out on Griffiths, however much he wanted to. Griffiths had condoned the attack, which was bad enough, but he was not responsible for it. John saw a porter move towards him out of the corner of his eye. He realised how impulsive and foolish he had been to rush into the bastion of the enemy, panting for revenge and laying himself so completely open to another attack.

He dropped his hands. Griffiths rubbed the back of his head and muttered, 'If you or your hell-born brother ever come in here again, I will send orders to have you thrown into the street.'

'Be easy,' John ground out. 'Neither my brother nor I intend to give you the pleasure.'

William awaited him in the hall of White's. His face was still bloodless but it was obvious that no physical harm had been done. John said, bitterly, 'The birds had flown.'

'What did you expect to achieve? You don't have to prove yourself to me. I saw what you did for me this night.' John said nothing. William's bruised mouth twitched into an uncertain smile. 'I know it means little to you now, but I hope this will mean more.'

He stretched his hand out. John looked down at it; he did not know what he was expected to do. 'I couldn't protect you,' he said, suddenly broken. The last of the numbness had left him and he could feel where the chair-poles had struck him, where he had absorbed the worst of the blows that had been meant for William.

'You saved my life.'

'Don't be a fool,' John scoffed, but William shook his head.

'I'm not. I could have been torn to pieces. And so could you.'

Mahon and Sydney hung back awkwardly, then passed the brothers and climbed the stairs to the subscription room. John started to follow them but William caught him back.

'John, why will you not take my hand? Are you angry with me?'

'Of course not!' Suddenly it was all too much. It was nearly five o'clock in the morning, John's muscles ached and his head buzzed with all the emotions of the past few hours. He said haltingly, 'It is only that when you held out your hand to me just now, it was as though what I had done – what you said I had done – seemed, almost … to surprise you.'

William blinked. 'After all that has happened to us both—' He stopped. His expression sharpened with understanding. 'But that is the point, is it not? After all that has passed of late, you thought I might have come to doubt you.'

'It had crossed my mind,' John admitted. The answer, when it came, was prompt and sincere.

'You are wrong. What you did for me tonight was more than I expect of any man; but I am not surprised you stood by me. I know we have our differences, John, but I trust you more than anyone else in the world, and I did so even before tonight. Can you accept that?'

John was ashamed to feel tears pricking his eyes. He willed his voice steady. 'Yes.'

'Then take my hand.'

This time John did.

****

The two brothers returned to Berkeley Square shortly after seven o'clock, but the moment John entered his room all thoughts of sleep flew completely out of his mind.

Mary stood at the bottom of the bed. He guessed from her expression how dishevelled he must look after the night's activities, but the love that flooded her face at the sight of him matched the sensation squeezing his own heart until he could barely breathe.

Mary took one of his hands and ran her thumb over his cut, bloodied knuckles, then touched the faint bruise a porter's cosh had left on the side of his jaw. Her eyes filled with anger. He caught her hand and kissed her palm. 'I thought you would still be in Albemarle Street.'

'My father told me what happened,' Mary said. He could tell she was trying to keep her voice steady. 'I thought you needed me to watch over you.'

'You were right.' John lifted her chin. He could see the tears trembling on her lashes, tears of fury, fear and love. 'I do need you, very much.'

She reached up for him at the same time that he lowered his lips to hers. For a short time, John forgot about William, the last night's attack, the state of the ministry, forgot everything except for his beautiful wife.

Chapter Ten

April 1784

John leapt out of his carriage and raced up the front stairs of his brother's Downing Street house. The rain was coming down in earnest now; in the brief interval between ringing the bell and the porter opening the door John got completely soaked. To judge by the muddy mess obscuring the chequered floor, he was far from being the first to arrive.

The whole house was flooded in candlelight. Every room John passed was full of people. Liveried messengers hammered up and down the stairs. A group of diplomats stood talking in French in one of the drawing rooms. Servants moved from room to room carrying wine, water and wafers.

George Rose and Tom Steele, the Secretaries to the Treasury, sat in the library poring over election returns. Steele glanced up as John passed and smiled in welcome.

'Lord Chatham! I am willing to wager that your presence turns your brother's good night into an excellent one.'

'I take it the news continues good?'

Steele beamed and pointed at a map mounted on a board, bristling with red ribbons pinned to every constituency won by a government candidate. 'Sixty Coalition men have been toppled already since the election started. Robinson can't believe it. He says we may be headed for a majority of over a 150.'

John caught his breath. 'Last I heard, Robinson thought we might buy our way up to 70.'

'Nobody could have foreseen this,' Steele said. 'Fox himself may lose his seat for Westminster. He's trailing a poor third behind Lord Hood and Sir Cecil Wray.'

'Where is my brother?'

'He got back from Cambridge yesterday. It is uncommon hard to find him alone nowadays, but I'm sure he will not mind your looking in.'

As Steele had suggested, John's face was well known and the footman guarding the door to William's study let him in. William was at his desk.

John Robinson leaned over to point out some figures, his arms full of papers. They looked up when John came in and William's eyes lit up with unfeigned joy.

As soon as the door closed behind Robinson, William rushed around the desk to embrace his brother. 'I cannot believe how long it has been since we last met!'

'It's only been two and a half weeks since you moved out of Berkeley Square,' John grinned. 'But in that short space of time you have turned the whole world on its head. Congratulations on your election for Cambridge University, Will. Well done.'

'I do not think the voters would have dared reject me,' William said breezily, but John knew better. William had stood for one of the University of Cambridge's two parliamentary seats at the beginning of his political career and come bottom of the poll; even now, with his high profile, his election for the notoriously independent constituency had never been a foregone conclusion. He and his friend Lord Euston had nevertheless headed the poll with their Foxite rivals far behind them.

William poured two glasses of wine from the decanters on the sideboard. He handed one to John, who studied his brother over the rim of his glass. William's eyes were ringed from lack of sleep and there were grooves on either side of his mouth that had not been there six months ago. 'When did you last get a full night's sleep, Will?'

'I will not conceal from you that I would love to slip into undisturbed slumber even for a handful of hours, but I cannot complain. All the good news does more for me than a week of sleep – and what news!' William's face glowed. 'Our friends are all in, most without contest. I received word from Eliot yesterday that he has been returned for Liskeard. And Wilberforce – when he went North I assumed he was going to stand for his old borough of Hull, but without telling me, he fought for the county of Yorkshire instead.'

'Yorkshire?' John was astonished. 'Hasn't that been held by a Rockingham candidate for years?'

'Yes! And Wilberforce won!' William cried. 'He won! The Foxite candidate withdrew without forcing a poll!'

William's exuberance was contagious. John set down his wineglass. 'I may be able to add to your stock of good news, Will, if you can bear it.'

'I think I am stout enough. Be warned that if it is news of a result at the polls, Robinson has probably told me already.'

'It's nothing like that.' John licked his lips. 'Mary is – she thinks – she is almost certain she is with child.'

Surprise, and genuine joy, filled William's face. 'Oh, John, that is wonderful news! When is the child due?'

'Christmas, most likely. Mary thinks she is only a few weeks gone. She said it was only fitting to tell you first, since this year has also seen the birth of your ministry.'

The rain buffeting the windows sounded loud in the silence. William fingered the twisted stem of his glass then said, suddenly serious, 'I still remember what you said all those months ago, the day after Lord Temple resigned. You said I could not depend on my colleagues; that I had filled my departments with friends and followers of North; that I had made the biggest mistake of my life.'

'Four months ago it did seem as though you had made a terrible error,' John stammered. 'But—'

William cut him off. 'I nearly resigned three times in January, after the first debates, when Fox and North were at full strength and I had nothing. I did not resign, because I knew if I could but hold firm I could not lose, not with His Majesty's support behind me.' He looked John firmly in the eye. 'What troubled me most was that my own brother did not comprehend why I took the Treasury.'

John felt his blush deepen. He glanced self-consciously around the room, at the fitted bookcases with their leather-bound volumes, the classical busts, Downing Street's elderly flock wallpaper. William paused then continued. 'When I was first asked to form a government last year, I would have been a puppet minister with Shelburne pulling the strings. When Lord Thurlow came to me again a few months later he made it clear Lord Shelburne was not involved. The offer came directly from the King. It was exactly what I wanted, and might never be offered again. I had to accept it, John.' A note of uncertainty entered his voice. 'Do you see?'

William's grey eyes were anxious. He looked so young, his powdered hair and dark clothing failing to add much authority to his appearance. A sudden urge to protect his brother overwhelmed John; he suppressed it, for he knew William would have been offended by it.

A knock on the door interrupted them. Their short time alone was drawing to a close. John looked at William's worried face and said, 'Why did you not tell me this before?'

'Because I did not think you would believe me.'

There was another, more insistent knock at the door. John rose, but he had one more question. 'What has changed?'

At that William's pale, tired face split into an enormous grin. He spread his arms as though to embrace the room in which they sat, the building that surrounded them, and the atmosphere of victory that increased with every breath they drew. 'Everything!'

Chapter Eleven

May 1784

Mary surfaced at intervals. Most of the time she felt like a vessel foundering in a sea of pain. Her hands were as translucent as the finest, whitest paper, and everything around her seemed permeated with the metallic stench of blood.

She was aware of little beyond the fragile world of her own body, although she knew she had lost the baby; an aching emptiness had replaced the warmth of growing life. She was so tired, and she longed to close her eyes and escape the agony of loss in welcoming darkness. She was falling away, the waters closing over the prow of her sinking ship, shutting off all sound and sensation.

Except one thing kept her tethered: a hand rubbing hers as though to massage back the life she felt draining away. At first it was little more than an irritation, like a fly buzzing around her head in her sleep, but it needled at her, drawing her back to the light. The hand was attached to a shadow, which resolved itself slowly into a face that reflected her pain as though absorbing it through the touch of his fingers.

John.

His touch alone kept her from disappearing. She knew she could not leave him, not now, not like this. Mary reached out from the shadows for him with all the strength she had remaining. She could see his love and his need for her shining in his face like flame, and for it – for him – she would do anything.

Chapter Twelve

July 1786

Breakfast at the Lord Lieutenant's hunting lodge in the Phoenix Park was always served sumptuously for guests. There were three different kinds of cold meat, salads, bread, wafers and cakes, all laid out on fine china plates. As had happened nearly every day since John's arrival in Dublin, the Lord Lieutenant's place was empty. Only the Duchess of Rutland waited for him at table, dressed in a plain linen morning dress, a cap covering most of her chestnut curls. Her eyes were fixed on the plate of fruit in front of her, but she glanced up when John took a chair opposite.

'Is the Duke not breakfasting?' John asked, reaching for a slice of bread. 'Has he got business at the Castle?'

'I presume so,' the Duchess replied, and John winced at the bitterness of her tone.

They breakfasted in silence. The Duchess picked at the fruit on her plate but nothing passed her lips. John chewed mechanically on a slice of cold chicken and studied Mary Rutland from the corner of his eye. He had once fancied himself half in love with Rutland's beautiful Duchess, and hardly knew what to make of the silent shadow sitting across from him. It was as though the two years Mary Rutland had spent in Ireland since her husband's appointment as Lord Lieutenant had transformed her into a different person.

The door crashed open and the Duke of Rutland stumbled in. The Duchess jumped at the abruptness of his entry but her face was emotionless when Rutland kissed her cheek. John could not help noticing she held her rigid body away from her husband.

'Sorry I am late, Chatham,' Rutland said, waving away a plate proffered by a footman and reaching instead for the decanter. 'I did not get in from my dinner with the city burgesses until past 11 last night. I apologise, too, that I cannot stay. I am to receive a petition from Dublin's cotton merchants in an hour.'

'I came here to visit you,' John quipped to cover his uneasiness. 'I had no idea I would only catch glimpses of you every other Tuesday.'

'My father was just as busy when he was in politics. It's the way of things, Chatham; it is the price we politicians must pay for our places. I am the King's representative in Ireland, with heavy responsibilities, it is true, but I would not have you report back to your brother that I am not meeting them.' Rutland drained his wineglass and refilled it. John winced.

'Rutland, you are my closest friend, and I have not seen you in two years. I hope you do not think my brother sent me here to spy on you?'

'You know how much your friendship means to me, and to Mary,' Rutland said, adding his wife's name as an afterthought, 'and I am delighted you made the journey to this godforsaken island to visit us.'

'But?' John hazarded. Rutland wiped his mouth and pushed himself unsteadily to his feet.

'For heaven's sake, Chatham, am I such a poor host you feel I have made you unwelcome?' He poured himself a third glass.

John said, a little too brightly, 'Will you not eat before you go?'

'I have no time for that. London's St Giles's and the Seven Dials have nothing on the stews backing onto Dublin Castle.' Rutland pointed at the slice of bread on John's dish. 'To take that bread from you, most of Dublin's inhabitants would slice your throat without hesitation. Think on that, and tell your brother I said it.'

Rutland gave his wife another kiss. Mary Rutland's eyelids flickered as her husband's wine-laced breath washed over her. He straightened with difficulty, gave John a shallow bow, and left.

John let his breath out. He looked at the slice of bread before him and felt suddenly sick. He pushed his plate away, excused himself to the Duchess and rose for some fresh air.

He stepped out onto the balcony. The Lord Lieutenant's lodge was small and plain to look at with its old-fashioned brick facade, but its location in the middle of the thousand acres of parkland was beautiful in an untamed way. A chilly breeze brought the scent of damp heather with it. There was a hint of thunder in the clouds hanging low over the purple band of the Black Rock Hills, and John glimpsed a fork of lightning on the horizon.

He was two weeks into his visit to Dublin, and his shock at Rutland's condition had yet to ebb. He had heard stories, of course, and received innumerable blotted, rambling letters from Rutland written in the small hours of the morning, but nothing had prepared him for the reality. Rutland lurched through Privy Council meetings, public audiences and military reviews in a barely-concealed alcoholic stupor. His was a punishing schedule in a post that brought him little love from either Irish or British politicians, but John barely recognised his dear friend in the swollen-faced drunk who hosted him.

John heard a slippered footfall behind him and turned. The Duchess stepped onto the balcony, pulling her gauze scarf around her shoulders. She leaned against the balustrade with her long-fingered hands clasped in front of her.

For a long while they remained silent. Every time John laid eyes on his friend's beautiful Duchess he thought of his own Mary, far away across St George's Channel. The distance between them only deepened his love for his quiet, shy wife. In contrast, Charles and Mary Rutland's marriage was an arid desert. Rutland was openly visiting whorehouses now, carousing for hours while his soldiers stood very public guard all night long. He and his wife were no longer lovers, and John wondered whether they even remained friends.

As though she knew what he was thinking about and wanted to change the subject, the Duchess said, 'How is your sister? I understand she and Mr Eliot are married.'

'They were wed last September,' John said. He had had to sell Hayes to provide Harriot with a dowry sufficient to placate Eliot's miserly father, but he left that bit out. 'My sister has been married nearly a year now, and is the happiest woman in Christendom.' Afraid that Mary Rutland might see this reference to another's marital bliss as crass, John added quickly, 'She is expecting her first child, and due to lie in shortly after my return to London.'

'Your mother must be delighted at the prospect of a grandchild.' John flinched, and he saw awkwardness chase across Mary Rutland's expression. He clearly did not need to tell her Mary's miscarriage still tore at his heart. The Duchess murmured, 'What a pity Lady Chatham could not accompany you to Ireland. The past two years must have been hard for you.'

'Yes,' John said quietly. 'They were.'

He did not elaborate, for he did not want to think of the misery since Mary's miscarriage. Losing the child had exacerbated the rheumatism in her hip, and she had spent over a year unable to move without the aid of a wheeled chair. Now her health was beginning to return and John no longer dreaded what each day might bring, but he would never forget her cries of pain whenever she had tried to cross the room, or how every day, every minute had been a milestone to be counted down until Mary could walk again. Sometimes, in the early hours, John still woke with a gasp from nightmares of Mary's yellow-lipped face, her body haemorrhaging blood beyond his ability to staunch it.

To change the subject, he said, 'The weather is so changeable here. I should go for a ride in the Park while it is still fine.'

'I'm sorry,' Mary Rutland murmured.

'Whatever for?'

'Because Charles was right. We have made you feel unwelcome. Do not pretend you did not notice Charles was drunk this morning.'

'He has a hard task,' John said, uncomfortably. 'The country is divided between rich Protestants and poor Catholics. I can easily believe it is difficult being the King's representative in a country that bears the English little love. But Rutland seems popular, for a Lord Lieutenant anyway. He's doing splendidly.'

'Is that what you will tell Mr Pitt?' Mary Rutland said and John blushed.

'My dear Duchess, I am here to visit you. Upon my honour, I have no other reason.'

'I believe you,' the Duchess said. 'But you must realise that your presence here adds considerably to my husband's troubles.'

The birds had stopped singing and there was a profound heaviness in the air. A growl of thunder broke the silence. John licked his dry lips. 'How so?'

'Last year your brother proposed a complete reformation of the commercial relations between England and Ireland. I need not remind you how his failure stirred up hostility against my husband in Dublin. What are the merchants supposed to think now the Earl of Chatham, Mr Pitt's brother, is come to spend the summer with the Duke of Rutland?'

'They are mistaken if they think I am my brother's instrument here,' John said. 'In any case, you and the Duke know differently.'

'I am not sure my husband does,' Mary said. 'He knows you and Mr Pitt are close. What will you tell your brother, Lord Chatham? That my husband works so hard to conciliate all Ireland's interests he hardly has time to eat? That he stays at table well into the night, and starts drinking the moment he rises in the morning? He is "doing splendidly", indeed.'

John did not know what to say. 'I am sorry you feel like this.'

The Duchess picked at a loose thread on her glove. 'All Charles wants is to prove himself worthy of his father. You of all men must comprehend the importance of that.'

'I do,' John admitted.

'Then you must know it is not your fault my husband is too good a man to be Lord Lieutenant.'

There was a great deal left unsaid in that sentence. John stared at Mary Rutland's profile, as hard as flint. 'It is not my brother's either,' he said at last.

'Of course not,' she said, but John did not believe her.

August 1786

John arrived back in London the first week of August after a long and turbulent journey. After he had peeled off his travelling clothes and overseen the unloading of his trunks John asked after his wife and discovered Mary had gone out. He suppressed a pang of disappointment, for he had been eagerly anticipating their reunion, but rather than wait aimlessly for her return he decided to visit William.

William's Downing Street house was at its quietest at the end of August, when most politicians and men of business were away terrorising the fowl on their country estates, but John had never yet managed to come upon his brother alone. William's secretary was carrying a towering pile of despatch boxes from the entrance hall to the study when John entered. 'He's in the library, with the Marquis of Carmarthen. Shall I have you announced?'

John was shown into the green drawing room, overlooking Horse Guards. A few minutes later his brother came to find him. William carried a packet of papers and looked preoccupied. The ministry was much better established than it had been two years ago, but the amount of work William had to do to keep his head above the water was staggering. He seemed to thrive on it, but John sometimes felt as though affairs of state had raised his attention above the level of ordinary mortals, and that his friends, family and connections constantly slipped beneath his notice.

William gave John an absent smile, as though his thoughts were still deeply engaged in discussing foreign affairs with Carmarthen. 'Good to see you back. How was your journey?'

'Poor. We were 24 hours sailing from Dublin to Holyhead. I've never been so sick in my life.'

'I thought you were hardly ever seasick.'

'Which comment proves you have never sailed from Dublin to Holyhead.'

'Lady Chatham is well? She has had no return of her complaint?'

'I have not seen her. She may have gone to Mr Partington's. He has a machine that creates electrical pulses, which he channels into her hip with glass rods.'

'Does it work?' William asked, his scientific interest piqued. John shrugged; he did not want to think about the animal terror with which Mary faced her weekly visits to Mr Partington, or the brittle, unconvincing cheerfulness with which she insisted, afterwards, that she felt so much better for them. In any case, William had already moved on.

'I am eager to hear of your visit to Ireland. How was it?' William opened the portfolio he was carrying and flicked through it. 'I trust all is well?'

John had been rehearsing what he would say about Rutland for days. He knew it was vital for his friend's sake that he make William aware of Rutland's situation, but he knew from long experience that William would not listen unless his attention was fully engaged, and clearly this was not the case. Even so, he had to try. 'Well enough. The country seems quiet. Will, about the Duke of Rutland—'

'That's good news,' William remarked, without raising his eyes from the papers in his hand. John fought the anger that rose in his breast, but what he had to say was too important.

'I need to speak to you about Rutland. He is doing excellent work as Lord Lieutenant, but I—'

This time the doorbell interrupted him. William's next visitor had arrived; John was reminded that his brother's time was no longer his own, and that William's own family had no greater claim over him than anyone else. John took one look at William's face and knew his opportunity was gone. For now at least, William was not paying enough attention for John to persuade him of Rutland's danger.

A footman opened the door and announced: 'The French Ambassador, sir.'

'I'm sorry, John,' William said, 'but as you see I am very busy. I have just left Lord Carmarthen, who was telling me about the latest correspondence from Paris. If Mr Eden can secure us a favourable commercial treaty with France, we shall meet the next parliamentary session in great strength.'

'I really must talk to you about Rutland,' John urged.

'Come to dinner on Friday. Steele and Long will be there. We can talk about it then.'

'Very well,' John said, knowing full well he would not be able to talk freely about Rutland if William's friends were present, but William already had his hand on the latch.

'Till Friday then. My love to Lady Chatham.'

The door closed behind him. John knew William had not intended to be dismissive, and that he would listen on Friday with all the alertness he had not had time to give today, but John could remember the days when he had not needed an appointment for his brother's attention.

****

Mary had returned by the time John came home. She was just untying the ribbons of her straw bonnet when the front door opened and John came in, chewing his bottom lip as he often did when preoccupied. When he caught sight of his wife warmth flooded his face; Mary's vision fogged. Aching hip forgotten, she picked up her skirts and flung herself into his arms.

They had been apart for six weeks. Once alone in their bedchamber John embraced her with still more ardour. Mary had not realised how much she had missed him until she felt the familiarity of his arms around her. She could feel his need, too, in the tightness of his hands on her shoulders.

For a long while there was no time for talking. At length, tired of kissing, they propped each other up on a chaise-longue, wallowing in their proximity after such a long time apart.

'You are plumper than when I last saw you,' John said with approval. He stroked her cheek. 'That dress suits you.'

Mary twitched her long grey walking dress. 'It's just a smock.'

'I think you should wear it more often.'

'Georgiana is always telling me I need to wear dresses that are less drab.' She plucked at the velvet lapel of John's elegantly tailored coat. 'She says I look like a mouse married to a peacock.'

'Your sister said I was a peacock?' John said, raising his eyebrow. Mary pushed him back against the pillows of the chaise-longue.

'Are you going to deny it? You learned fashion at the feet of your foppish friend Rutland.' She leaned over to kiss him and felt him tense in her arms. 'What is troubling you? I can tell something is wrong.'

For a moment, she thought he was going to resist her, but then he sighed in resignation and closed his eyes. 'You are, as usual, very perceptive.'

The agony of affection glistened on his face as he told her about his visit to Ireland and his fears for the Lord Lieutenant. He did not go into detail, but Mary recognised the seriousness of the situation in the trembling of his voice. She listened in silence, her head against his shoulder.

'What do you think will happen if the Duke remains in Dublin?' she asked when he had finished.

'I do not know, in truth I do not. Rutland does not have the frame of mind for hard business. I do not blame my brother for appointing him Lord Lieutenant, for God knows William needs a man he can trust in Ireland, but I do not think William took Rutland's frailties into account.'

'Have you spoken with William about this?'

'No.'

'You should,' Mary said, but she had caught the hesitation in that single syllable. She pushed her hair over her ears and sat up. 'John, you have not told me all. Something else is troubling you. What is it?'

'Nothing,' he said. Mary did not believe him. She studied his taut profile, waiting for the words to come, and at length they did. 'I only wish I could be certain William will listen to me.'

'Why should he not? You are his brother.'

'Do you think that is enough? William is at the head of government – a government in which I have no part. Every time I see him I feel he begrudges the time he has to give to me.'

'I am certain he will want to know your thoughts about Ireland.'

'And that is just the thing,' John said, gritting his teeth. 'No-one in Dublin imagined I had simply come to pay Rutland a friendly visit. They all thought I would report back to my brother. Even Rutland said so.'

'He was probably drunk.'

'He was definitely drunk, but that's not the point. I am William's brother, and they all naturally assumed I have his ear, his trust. Could it be any more ironic?' His lips curved downwards. 'Rutland should never have gone to Ireland in the first place. William made a mistake. But who am I to tell him? I have no official capacity; I have no value beyond our family connection, and that is not enough. All I can do is vote where my brother tells me to, and wait for him to bestow a few crumbs of attention on me, like a common backbencher.'

'You are being too harsh on William, and yourself.'

'Before he left, Rutland told me he was grateful to William for the chance to prove himself worthy of his father. The Marquis of Granby was nearly as celebrated as mine, you know. What if William never trusts me enough to give me the same chance?'

'He knows what you are capable of. You are his only brother, John. He trusts you.'

'Does he?' John said, and now he no longer even pretended to hide the pain in his voice. 'He did not let me into the secret when he first took the seals, and he was living under my roof. I thought things had changed, after I—' He broke off. 'I know he owes me nothing. But to continue as we are, on such unequal ground ...'

'Is it office, then, that you want?' Mary asked when he tailed off. In her private opinion, John was as temperamentally unfit for the rigours of office as Rutland was, but she said nothing, knowing it was not what he needed to hear. John pulled a face and bent his head over his clasped hands.

'I have always admired William's brilliance; I have never doubted he was destined for great things. But what if he has accustomed himself to my silence? What if he will not listen to me when it truly matters?'

Mary looked down at the top of his head. She had always admired John's aristocratic elegance, his quiet charm, but beneath it all she had long recognised an endearing vulnerability. Faced with a direct question about his ambitions he had hedged without answering, and Mary did not suppose he was even aware he had done so. John was so accustomed to coming second, he had stopped questioning it long ago. She wondered if William was aware how lucky he was to have such a self-effacing brother. She put her hands on John's cheeks and kissed him.

'It takes more strength to stand in the shadow than bask in the light,' she said. 'You are the best, most devoted man I know, and I love you for it, truly I do.'

The glow of affection on his face was her reward. John pulled her to him and buried his face in her hair. She pressed against him, desperate to absorb his pain and doubt, longing to lose the world around her in the brightness of his love.

****

At the end of the summer John took Mary to visit her parents at their country house of Frognal. He returned to Berkeley Square a few days later, and was just stepping out of his carriage when he caught sight of his brother's valet, Williams, riding up from Berkeley Street on a broad-backed shire-horse. The servant was dressed from head to foot in black woollen mourning.

John's throat constricted immediately. Heedless of onlookers, he ran across the road and grabbed Williams' reins. 'My mother?'

Williams looked older than his 60 years, his brown eyes rimmed with red. He had been in John's father's service for many years, and had seen all the Pitt children grow up. Now he dismounted and stood with bowed head, crushed by the news he had to bring. 'Your mother is well as far as we know, Your Lordship.' He handed John a letter in William's handwriting, sealed with a black wax wafer. John stared at it, hardly daring to touch it, as though until he did so the news the letter contained could not possibly be true. 'But I'm afraid I have mighty bad news regarding your sister Lady Harriot.'

October 1786

Every room in the Dowager Countess of Chatham's house at Burton Pynsent was covered in black crape. The thin October light barely penetrated, as though grief had sapped it away. When Mary and John had arrived a few days before, the Dowager Countess had been almost unable to leave her room, crippled by the loss of her daughter. A week later she was finally able to get as far as the small drawing room. Here she sat huddled in her mourning, weeping on and off while Mary held her hand helplessly and John stood by the window cuffing at his own eyes when he thought no-one was looking.

Just as the sprawling, crumbling old house seemed to be returning to something like a daily routine, the carriage they had all been expecting from London rattled down the gravel-strewn driveway from the Curry road. Mary stood by her husband in the portico to greet it. Behind them the sun was setting behind Troy Hill, setting off the monument John's father had erected in a blaze of scarlet glory. The pillar cast a long shadow across the green, fertile farmlands below. Mary glanced briefly at it, then turned back to the vehicle drawing up in front of the house, its cheerful yellow panels boarded over with mourning black.

Her husband's jaw was tight, the muscles standing out like cords in his neck. As Mary's eyes brushed over him he swallowed convulsively as though trying not to give in to tears. Mary discreetly squeezed his hand, and the uneven pressure of his fingers in response told her more eloquently of his pain than any words. She had dreaded William's arrival, certain it would unblock the emotional dam John had set up against his grief for his mother's sake, but she knew John needed the release.

The footman jumped off the plate and opened the carriage door. Mary released John's hand, and he stepped forwards to meet his brother.

William looked worse than John did. Mary did not think his hair had been powdered for some time, and his normally youthful face looked older than his years. But the change in him was nothing compared to the change in the man who emerged from the compartment after him. Mary had never known Edward Eliot to be anything but a happy, smiling young man, relaxed in his own wealth and good humour. This was a man in anguish, crushed beneath the weight of a pain beyond healing.

John, too, seemed frozen to the spot. Then he clasped Eliot by the hand. 'My dear Eliot, I cannot tell you how sorry I am. At least God has spared you your daughter.'

'My daughter.' Eliot did not look like he had found John's words comforting, and Mary had no doubt Eliot felt God had left him the wrong one. 'Yes, it is true, I still have Harriot Hester.' His voice broke on the name. His glassy expression acquired a desperate sheen. 'I trust you will excuse me.'

He pushed past John and entered the house. John looked after him in helpless silence, then turned back to William. The autumnal breeze cut between the two brothers, the only two remaining from the first Lord Chatham's fine brood. It twitched at the black velvet of John's collar and flung a lock of William's lank, unpowdered hair into his face. Nothing could be heard but the sound of sheep bleating distantly and the tolling of the church bell in the village.

John was the first to move. He stepped forwards and put a hand on William's shoulder. Not a word was said, but Mary could almost see the strength of the shared pain passing through that touch, and the air around them seemed to turn thick. William's mouth twisted. John's face did not move, but a tear carved its way down his cheek and trembled on his chin. At last William broke away from John and held a hand out to Mary. She wrapped her arms around his shoulders. He smelled of stale powder and misery.

'Where is our niece?' John asked.

'We left her nursing at Langport. I do not suppose it will be long before she arrives. How is Mama?'

'Suffering, as you would expect. But she is bearing up, despite the severity of the blow. You will see for yourself.'

'Thank God you were able to come to her so quickly,' William said. 'I would have come down sooner, but Eliot …'

He tailed off. John reached out again and squeezed his brother's shoulder.

'Eliot has us to look after him.'

And you have each other, Mary thought, although she did not speak the words aloud. John was still holding his grief in like a blocked fountain, but somehow William's presence had given him strength, as if the knowledge that he was not alone had taken the edge off his pain. Time would be needed to heal the wounds, if indeed they could ever fully be healed; but if they could be, Mary felt the process had begun here, on Burton's portico.

****

Eliot was not well enough to support the ordeal of seeing the Dowager Countess, and stayed in his room all evening. When the two brothers retired to the library to discuss little Harriot Hester's future, Mary stayed with her mother-in-law. She and John had been cooperating to make sure

Lady Chatham was alone as little as possible. Most of their time together was spent in silence, for physical proximity was what Lady Chatham needed more than conversation.

Mary took up her station by the fire and drew her workbox close. Lady Chatham watched as she selected a skein of coloured thread and continued working at the tambour frame. She was making a tiny gown for her new niece, decorated with pink and white roses to symbolise new life and youth. Her needle flashed in and out of the fabric, catching the firelight with tiny bursts of flame.

Mary did not know how long she sat there in silence, the turmoil in her mind easing with every stitch, before Lady Chatham placed a black-gloved hand on her arm and stilled her needle.

'I remember you when you were a little girl,' she said.

Mary looked up. Her mother-in-law's face was partially hidden behind the lace of her mourning veil, but her heavy-lidded grey eyes, so like those of her eldest son, were full of affection. Mary smiled. 'That was a long time ago.'

'No, it was not. Your mother brought you with her on a visit to Hayes. You must have been seven or eight. Four years younger than my poor Harriot.'

Lady Chatham stopped talking. Mary said hastily, 'Only speak of her if you wish to. I am happy sewing if you find you prefer silence.'

'It is not of her I wish to speak,' Lady Chatham said with a shake of her head. 'Or of my poor Hetty, already gone so long. I wish to speak of my *third* daughter, the one I first met all those years ago.'

Mary said nothing, choked with emotion. She could feel a heat in her cheeks that had nothing to do with being so close to the fire.

'I recall it so well,' Lady Chatham went on. 'You wore a yellow dress, with white flowers in your hair. You were so pretty, and so well-behaved, and I remember thinking even then you would make a man very, very lucky.' Her hand on Mary's arm tightened. 'I was so pleased when John chose you for his bride. I knew you would be good for him; but even then, I had no idea how right I was.'

'I do not think he is so lucky,' Mary said uncomfortably. She could not help adding, with a push of pain, 'If I truly made him lucky, I would be able to give him an heir.'

The agony of that failure throbbed inside her the more intensely because, only two months previously, she and John had once more had cause to hope she might be expecting a child at last. She could still taste her disappointment, like ashes, bitter and dry. But Lady Chatham shook her head.

'Nonsense. Do you think any of us think the less of you for that? I have four grand-daughters. I love them all dearly, but they cost both my daughters their lives.' Mary did not trust herself to speak. Lady Chatham wiped her eyes and finished, 'Do not lose yourself in what might have been. John would not recover if he lost you. Never doubt that.' She leaned over and planted a kiss on her daughter-in-law's cheek. 'You are his jewel. That is why he is so lucky to have you.'

'As am I to have him,' Mary said, perhaps a little defensively. Lady Chatham took her hand.

'We are all lucky to find someone who brings out the best in us, to stand by us when we have most need of their strength and love.'

****

After supper Mary went up to the second floor. The upper servants slept here; the ceilings were lower, the floors uncarpeted, and the walls painted a uniform shade of cream. She entered the room that had been transformed into a makeshift nursery for little Harriot Hester. The chamber had been cleared of all furniture save for an elegantly carved cradle, a small truckle-bed, and a chair for the wet-nurse, who stood and curtseyed when Mary entered.

Mary tiptoed over to the cradle. Harriot Hester had arrived at Burton an hour or so after her uncle and father. John's three-week-old niece lay on her side, swaddled tightly, her tiny round head covered in wispy dark hair. She was asleep, her eyes tightly closed, and as Mary watched her little pink tongue darted out once or twice as though to taste milk in her dream.

Mary felt a swell of warmth inside her, but also a tug deep inside she could not suppress. She had told the truth to Lady Chatham; she regretted not being able to give her husband an heir. She had ached with envy for Harriot Eliot's good fortune in falling pregnant so quickly. In her darkest moments, Mary's black fancies had painted images in her mind she was ashamed, even horrified, to acknowledge: Harriot miscarrying, bringing forth a dead child, suffering in her labour. Yet even though she knew very well the dangers of childbed, Mary had never imagined Harriot giving up her life.

The baby screwed her face up as though about to cry. Mary reached out a hand, then pulled it back, suddenly unsure.

'You won't wake her, your ladyship,' the nurse said. Mary tentatively touched her fingers to the little girl's cheek. It was covered with a velvety down and surprisingly warm.

'She's so small,' Mary said.

'She will grow, madam,' the wet-nurse replied. 'She has a fine appetite.'

The wet-nurse left the room to fetch some linen. Mary's hand lingered over the baby's silky head. She, a mother without a child, gazed down upon this child without a mother, and felt her heart ache.

A hand fell on her shoulder. Mary turned to see her husband. John's long face was cast in shadow; a sprinkling of powder lay stark against the black collar of his coat. He looked lost, and tears leapt to her eyes. He wiped them away, then cupped her face in his hand. She could feel his grief in the trembling of his fingers as he lowered his mouth to hers.

'I had a feeling I would find you here,' John murmured. Mary tightened her arms around him. He clung to her.

'How is Mr Eliot?'

'Mr Woodforde has prescribed an opiate so he can get some rest after the journey.' John did not go into any more detail, and Mary did not press for it. He shifted restlessly. 'We will need to decide what to do with our poor niece. Eliot is in no state to look after her, at least for now. She may have to remain here, with my mother, until he recovers.'

If he recovers, Mary thought instinctively, but she said, 'Will she go to his parents in Cornwall?'

'No doubt they will have her occasionally, but William said Eliot particularly wanted the little girl to stay with Mama.' A pause. 'He thought it was what Harriot would have wanted.'

Mary nodded. She remained silent, happy just to be near him. Then something John had said struck her and she frowned. 'You said you had known you would find me here. Why?' He did not respond immediately. Mary turned and looked up at him. 'Why, John? Tell me.'

'My mother said you were sorry you had not been able to give me a child.' He kissed her again. 'I hope you know that means nothing to me.'

'I know,' Mary said. John pulled her closer and buried his head in her hair. He spoke so quietly she barely heard him.

'I cannot lose you, Mary.'

Next to them, little Harriot Hester gave a small sigh and wriggled in her swaddling. John glanced down at her and Mary saw his lips twitch. She reached up and pressed her lips to his. There was tension in his jaw under her fingers, but it relaxed as she deepened the embrace.

'You will not lose me,' she said. 'I promise.'

Chapter Thirteen

October 1787

'John …'

The servant who had been undoing John's coat buttons glanced up and immediately retired. Mary stood in the doorway to her husband's dressing room. She was wrapped in a dressing gown; his eyes sought the clock on the mantelpiece. It was nearly midnight.

'What is it, Mary?' Her furrowed brow worried him. 'What has happened?'

'Your brother sent up just now.' Mary hesitated. 'There is news from Dublin.'

'From Dublin?' John's mouth went dry. 'The Duke – Charles …?'

He had been expecting this for days, ever since hearing that Rutland was dangerously ill with a fever; and yet the shock he felt when Mary nodded rendered him incapable of further speech. Surely the morning would bring one of his rambling, blotted letters admitting it was all a joke, informing John he was well, and coming home at last.

But there would be no homecoming for Rutland. John had known there would not be since the reports of Rutland's indisposition had first trickled in three weeks ago. He had known ever since he had visited Rutland and seen his friend's yellowed face, prematurely scored with strain.

His greatest friend was dead. The reality of the news broke in upon him then and tore through the numbness. John was not sure what hurt more: knowing he would never see Rutland again, or knowing he might have saved him had he only spoken up.

****

The funeral procession reached Bottesford shortly after noon. A thin rain had begun falling shortly after the cavalcade left Rutland's seat at Belvoir Castle, and by the time it had reached the valley the church's tall steeple could only just be picked out from the mist.

Rutland's largesse to the people who lived on his land was legendary, and a gratifyingly large crowd had formed to watch their lord laid to rest.

Many of them were well-to-do artisans, prosperously dressed in sombre linen, but John, riding behind the hearse, saw several men and women in ragged clothes and bare feet. Nobody spoke; even the children watched in silence as Rutland's coffin passed.

The chancel of Bottesford Church was so full of monuments the coffin had to be carried very carefully past them to be laid before the altar. The blank-eyed alabaster statues of Rutland's ancestors gazed on as Reverend Crabbe, Rutland's old chaplain, gave the service. It seemed to John as though the statues were participating in the mourning, their hands clasped in prayer for Rutland's soul.

Once the coffin, covered with its velvet pall, had been lowered into the family vault, John accompanied the procession back up to Belvoir. The climb up to the castle, with its commanding view over the Leicestershire hills, was painful. John had spent so many happy hours here, hunting, drinking and making merry with his friend. Those days were gone, and Rutland was no more. The Duke of Rutland now was a boy a month from his tenth birthday, slim, dark-haired, and struggling against his emotions. John watched the boy he had always known as Lord Granby wiping his eyes and trying to look older than he was. His heart tightened at the sight. He remembered all too well the disorientation of coming to terms with losing a father and gaining a title in the same moment.

Reverend Crabbe gave a lengthy eulogy to Rutland in Belvoir's family chapel. 'To a good disposition he joined those sentiments and ideas which are more particularly expected in the eminent and great: a dignity of mind, a frankness of manners, a largeness of heart. He thought nobly, he spoke liberally, he lived honourably.' The minister looked grave. 'Now he is dead, it is not a family alone, it is a nation that weeps for him.'

And his friend. John could feel the tears he had been suppressing all day breaking through despite his best efforts. He placed one hand over his eyes to hide them. Mary laced her fingers through those of his disengaged hand and squeezed them. He squeezed back, grateful beyond words for her presence beside him.

After the service, John and Mary paid their respects to the Duchess of Rutland. She had changed since John had last seen her in Ireland; she looked much thinner, and older, with great black marks under her beautiful brown eyes. She was not wearing make-up, and John realised with a shock he had never seen her bare-faced, not once in all the years he had known her. The strength of her grief at losing Rutland had shocked everyone, for she had been living apart from him at Belvoir for some time. John wondered if she felt guilty for having left her husband in Ireland, for not having been with him when he died.

Mary kissed the Duchess on the cheek. John took her hand. He could barely find the words, but he had to say something, anything, and hope it would carry the sincerity he truly felt but could not articulate. 'My dear Duchess.' What could he say? No words could convey his pain. 'I am so sorry.'

'I know,' Mary Rutland said. 'You loved him nearly as much as I did.'

After the vigil, John took his wife back up to their guest rooms. They walked along the castle's stone-flagged corridors in silence. All John could think of was of how often his friend had spoken to him of his wish to rebuild his castle into a home, to bring it back to life. He had bought so many paintings while Lord Lieutenant, most of which were still crated up in the art gallery. Rutland would never get to transform Belvoir into a family home. He would never get to see his precious paintings on the walls. He would never hold his wife and children ever again.

The personal nature of the loss sliced deeper still. Rutland had been the only man he knew who had truly understood what it was to bear the burden of a great name. It was something even William did not seem to comprehend – that a man might wish for the anonymity of mediocrity, if only to relieve the pressure of his inherited responsibilities. Rutland had paid the price of that lack of understanding.

'It's not your fault,' Mary said quietly. She seemed, as always, to have read his thoughts. John closed his eyes.

'I cannot help wondering what would have happened had Rutland not gone to Ireland … or if I had been able to persuade William to call him back.'

'You are not responsible for your brother's decisions.'

He smiled sadly at her. 'You are right, of course.' But he suspected she knew it did not make him feel any better.

Chapter Fourteen

June 1788

'When will you be back, my love?'

'Rather late, I imagine. Do not wait with supper if I am not home by midnight.' John bent over to kiss Mary on the cheek. 'After a whole day traipsing through the streets of Westminster you will be famished.'

'In this heat? I doubt it.' Mary laid down her pen and caught John back for another kiss. 'Enjoy your play.'

'And good luck to you,' John said. He started to move away but Mary pulled his lips down to hers yet again.

'I think I need a little more luck.'

He left with a grin. Mary turned back to her letter writing, and picked up her ivory-handled penknife to sharpen her quill. She and her sister were campaigning for Lord Hood, the government MP for Westminster, who was doing poorly against the Foxite candidate in a by-election. Conscious that the opposition had glamorous ladies like the Duchess of Devonshire campaigning actively, Mary had stepped forwards to bolster Hood's cause. Making small talk with artisans did not always come easily to her, but it was pleasant to see how grateful men were for the privilege of a word with the Minister's sister-in-law.

Mary was about to apply her pen back to the page and finish her letter when the commotion began. First she heard shouting, then neighing and a horse's hooves striking the road in an irregular tattoo. The shouting grew louder.

Mary looked out of the window and gasped. Her husband's carriage stood in the street, the door hanging open. Both horses attached to the traces reared and plunged in a desperate attempt to break free. The coachman and postilion clung to the reins, John alongside them in his Covent Garden finery. Two other servants raced out of the house to help.

At that moment one of the horses gave a sharp kick and knocked John backwards. Mary stood, her skirts knocking her étui and several sheets of foolscap to the floor.

She had no memory of leaving the room or going downstairs. The first thing she was aware of was running across the pavement and sinking beside her husband in a flurry of silk skirts. Some passers-by hurried over, two liveried footmen and a gentleman in a brown coat. Mary was vaguely aware of them, and of the horses still plunging and foaming on the road, but mostly her attention was focused on John's bloodless face and rigid jaw, and his leg. The blow had knocked his knee-buckle deeply into his flesh; the silk stockings were red with blood, and the skin she could see through the torn fabric was mottled and swollen. Her stomach lurched; she forced herself to look away. 'What happened?'

His breathing came in shallow, irregular gasps, but he managed to reply. 'Not sure … a bee sting, perhaps. One horse reared, then the other. I got too close.'

'What is going on? Mary?' Mary looked up at the sound of her name. It was Georgiana, her eyes wide. For a moment, Mary wondered what her sister was doing here, then remembered she and Georgiana had meant to go canvassing. All that seemed a world away now, and completely unimportant. She did not rise or let go of John's hand but said, 'George, go home. There will be no canvass today.' A sudden epiphany struck Mary. 'On second thoughts go and tell Wood to send for Dr Warren.'

'We need a surgeon,' the groom muttered. Georgiana groaned and Mary felt her skin burst out in sweat, but she forced her voice to remain calm.

'A surgeon, then. Just go.'

Georgiana pulled up her skirts and sprinted into the house. In the street, the coachman had finally managed to quieten the horses. Their legs trembled while the coachman crooned softly to them. Mary's eyes kept being drawn to John's limb. She knew without having to be told that it was broken. Only the surgeon would be able to tell her how badly.

****

Wood sent for the King's own surgeon, John Hunter. He was approaching 60, stooped and flat-faced, his drooping eyelids accustomed to hiding thoughts and emotions from his patients. With him came two large, thick-set young men in leather overalls carrying a long canvas bag. Mary tried not to look at it.

John had been carried to an easy chair in the drawing room. Hunter squinted through round spectacles at the bruised swelling just below John's knee. He shook his head over the buckle wound, then announced, 'I am fairly certain, my lord, we are dealing with an oblique tibial fracture.'

'What does that mean?' John asked, his voice strained from the effort of keeping it steady.

'Essentially, it means you have broken your shin.' Even though she had known the leg was broken, Mary's mouth still went dry. 'The leg must be set at once. Have you any old linen about the house, my lady? Tablecloths or bedsheets perhaps?'

'Of course,' Mary said. 'But why—'

'For bandages. Send one of your footmen to cut three or four old sheets into strips and roll them round a stick. Make sure he douses them in vinegar and water first, to help them bind better.' Mary rose and gave the order. When the footman returned with the bandages Hunter said, 'My lady, you may wish to leave the room.'

Mary had steeled herself to obey any order from the surgeon, but this brought her up short. 'That is out of the question.'

'I prefer to operate without women present.' Hunter's expression did not change but his voice tightened. 'I find it inconvenient when they faint.'

'I will not faint,' Mary said. She risked a glance at her husband; John's lips were thin with pain. 'I will stay with my lord.'

Hunter shrugged as though he had only meant to make a suggestion. He unfolded himself slowly, flexing his fingers. 'In that case, Madam, would you be so kind as to pour your husband a glass of brandy?'

John looked like the last thing he wanted was to let anything pass his lips. He took a tiny sip and gagged, and Mary wondered briefly whether he might vomit.

Hunter looked dissatisfied. 'You should drink a little faster, my lord.'

'My dear sir, you are trying to make me drunk,' John managed, with a faint smile.

Hunter's jaw clenched. 'It is to save time,' he said, unconvincingly, and Mary blanched. *He* is *trying to get John drunk*. There could be only one reason for that. She gripped John's hand tightly, as though she would be the one to feel the pain.

The thick-set assistant had quietly taken up station behind John's chair. The other stood by Hunter, who ran his broad-fingered hands up John's bruised leg with surprising gentleness, much like Mary had seen the coachman checking the fetlocks of the carriage horses after a long journey. He gave a grunt of triumph and nodded at his assistants. Mary barely saw them move. The man behind John grasped him under the armpits and pinned him to the chair. The other assistant held John firmly around the thigh. Hunter grasped John's calf and, to Mary's horror, gave it a sharp twist.

John stiffened and gave a cry. 'What do you think you are doing?' Mary blurted out, more in shock than anger, but Hunter ignored her. He spoke to the footman, who stood by the door, frozen in dismay.

'The bandages! Quickly now!'

The footman thrust an uneven roll of torn bedsheets at Hunter. A strong stench of vinegar filled Mary's nostrils, turning her stomach. Hunter swiftly wound the bandages around the middle of John's leg, up over the knee, back down to the ankles and round the foot, leaving the heel and toes uncovered.

'Splints,' Hunter said. The assistant who had been steadying John's thigh reached into Hunter's bag and withdrew four thin flat wooden rods. Hunter continued binding John's leg with practised hands, up and down, overlapping each strip.

'It feels tight,' John said. It was the first time he had spoken for some time.

'Good,' Hunter replied without looking up, an expression of concentration on his frog-like face. 'If the bandages are too loose the fracture will not set properly.' He fastened the last strip of linen with a pin then stood with a groan. 'Well then, my lord, I reckon you have earned yourself another glass of brandy.'

Mary watched as the footmen settled her husband with his leg elevated on a chair, a glass of brandy in his hands. John gave her a lopsided smile.

'You were meant to be off canvassing,' he said.

Mary glanced down at her gloved hands and green and white striped gown, mildly surprised to find herself still wearing her finery. 'I did not really want to go anyway.'

'I entertained you much better, did I not?' John murmured. He seemed to be falling asleep; Mary wondered if it was the brandy or the shock. She blinked back tears and leaned over to kiss him.

'Hush, John. Don't talk nonsense.'

****

Hunter recommended complete rest to ensure the leg healed, and John was quite happy to remain on his couch. Mary cancelled her social engagements and sat with him, administering his doses of laudanum and reading to him to pass the time.

By the third day she felt happy enough to return to the canvass for Lord Hood. She and Georgiana rode through the hot, dusty streets of Westminster, stopping to speak to anyone who might be interested in the contest, from gentlemen of quality down to joiners, tailors and shoemakers. She saw the Duchess of Devonshire out canvassing also, wearing a scarf fashioned out of fox-tails. The two of them exchanged frigid nods.

At the day's end Mary wanted nothing more than a bath to wash off the dirt from the city streets. She could not be sure which ached more, her head or her hip. The minute her carriage turned into Berkeley Square, however, she laid a hand on Georgiana's arm.

'What is it?' her sister said.

'Dr Warren's carriage,' Mary replied, with an icy twist of dread.

She ran into the house and mounted the stairs without removing her hat, shawl or gloves. The doctor was in her husband's bedroom. He turned to her with a solemn expression, but she did not need to hear him speak to know what had happened. One look at John's waxen face against the bolster was enough.

Warren sent for Hunter, who examined the wound on John's leg in silence. Mary, standing on the other side of the room with her hands clasped as though in prayer, caught only a glimpse of the angry redness of the skin fringed with yellow. Then Hunter barked, 'Fetch my bag. I must make a plaster.'

Mary was vaguely aware of Hunter pressing a hot, watered-down, wax-like mixture to the injured leg, and of Warren taking a basinful of blood from John's arm. She did not ask why: she simply sat by John's bedside, holding his hand and bathing his brow. She had to do something to help him, otherwise she felt she might go mad with frustration and worry.

For most of the next day the three of them fought to keep John's fever down. Warren tried everything, from blistering to bark. Mary laid compress after compress on her husband's head. John's lack of response worried her. He had been either unconscious or delirious ever since Mary's return from the canvass. Neither Hunter's poking, nor Warren's ministrations, drew so much as a moan from him. None of it had any effect whatever.

At nine in the morning after a sleepless night Georgiana finally persuaded her sister to take a rest. Mary had time only to dash off a quick note to her brother-in-law in Downing Street, who had been sending up to Berkeley Square all day for news, before collapsing on her bed and giving in to a nightmare-disturbed sleep.

She was awakened just after noon to see her sister gazing down at her with eyes round with hope. 'Mary, listen to me. The fever has broken.'

For a moment Mary did not know what she meant. Then the words rearranged themselves in her mind and she gasped. 'How?'

'I do not know, but Warren is more cheerful now. Come and see for yourself.'

Mary could see the change in him immediately. John was lucid for the first time in 24 hours, propped up in bed with his injured leg elevated on a pillow. His lips were white from blood loss and chapped from fever but he managed a smile when he saw his wife. She lost him then in the tears that blurred her vision; she had only an impression of sweat-streaked skin as she leaned over and kissed him.

'How do you fare?' she said, and nearly laughed at herself because of the stupidity of the question. John squeezed her hand as strongly as he could.

'Much better for seeing you.'

'I have barely left your side,' she said, and John lifted her hand to his lips.

'I know. Warren told me.'

Warren gave him a sleeping draught and Mary held John's hand until he drifted into calm, feverless rest. Once he was settled, and Warren had left, she sat down at her writing desk to write another letter to William. Messengers had been dashing between Berkeley Square and Downing Street all day, but she wanted her brother-in-law – who was also her husband's heir – to know John was out of danger.

The moment she drew paper towards her, however, the full import of what had nearly happened finally caught up with her. The words chased themselves round her head without making sense. She laid the pen down and pressed her hands together to stop them trembling, then got up and paced to the window. She leaned heavily against the sash window-frame and drew in great heaves of breath to steady herself.

Warren and Hunter had both said they believed her husband would recover, but she had seen, all too clearly, the reality of John's mortality written on their faces. She had once told John he would not lose her; until now she had never properly faced the prospect of losing him. She gazed out of the window at the sun-drenched Square, drew her fichu closer round her shoulders and shuddered.

Chapter Fifteen

July 1788

John lay against the pillows of the sofa and focused his gaze on the moulded cornice above him. He had been staring at it for above half an hour now. He had picked out every golden glitter, every chip, every peel of plaster. It was stupendously dull, but it was preferable to listening to Georgiana and Lady Sydney's conversation.

'... and Lady Courtown said to the Queen, "Feverfew and ginger are sovereign for gout, did you not know?" whereupon Her Majesty called for some to administer to the King. I gather he felt much better for it afterwards.'

'Aunt Courtown knows this well, for poor Lord Courtown suffers terribly from gout ...'

The doorbell tinkled distantly. John shifted on his couch. Mary was out canvassing again and, on the misguided supposition that John wanted constant company while chained to his sofa, she had asked her mother and Georgiana to sit with him. John was fond of his mother- and sister-in-law, but he was having trouble suppressing the increasingly desperate urge to gag them.

'... Frances is just turned 16, so next year will be her first season, and— oh!'

Georgiana dropped her sewing, and she and her mother stumbled to their feet. John cried out in relief. 'William!'

'Still on your sofa?' Every time he came to visit William seemed to be enjoying affrontingly good health. He looked fresh and cheerful, his high cheeks flushed with colour. 'You mustn't take advantage of us, John. Your leg must be as sound as ever by now.'

'If you ever have the misfortune to break your leg, I'll remind you of that.'

'Fear not! I'm not such a fool as to stand within kicking range of a rearing horse.'

Lady Sydney and Georgiana left the brothers alone. John waited till the door closed behind them before saying, with absolute sincerity, 'I cannot tell you how grateful I am for your appearance just now.'

William's lips twitched. 'Townshends talking you to death?'

'You could say that.'

'Look upon it as penance for giving us such a fright.'

Despite the flippancy of William's remark, his concern was plain to see. Three weeks had passed since John's severe illness but the break ached terribly, the wound remained inflamed, and John had not yet rid himself of a low, persistent fever. William caught John's gaze and the humour dropped from his face.

'I thought we'd lost you, Johnny,' he said in a muffled voice, and John swallowed hard to ease the lump in his throat. William had not called him "Johnny" for years.

'Has the Minister not got better things to do than visit his sick brother's bedside?' John asked, to break the tension.

'This and that.'

'"This and that?"' John repeated, with a raised eyebrow. William looked sheepish.

'Let us just say I have nothing more pressing to do at present.'

Until now William had only had time for fleeting visits to John's sickbed; even those must have cost him, for John well knew how busy his brother was. John pushed himself up against the pillows. 'I feel there is something you want to say to me.'

'Is it too much to believe that I simply want to spend time with you?' William protested, and laughed when John tilted his head back and turned his incredulous gaze to the ceiling. 'Apparently I am far too transparent, although seeing you so much better gives me more pleasure than poring over Foreign Office reports or chairing Treasury committees. I have news for you, John, which will hasten your convalescence.'

John's mind raced through the possible options. 'You're reducing taxes for gentlemen with fractured shins?'

'Lord Howe has left the Admiralty,' William said, ignoring John's comment. 'He and the Navy Board did not agree on the way the Admiralty is run. He has submitted his resignation and the King has accepted it.' Not knowing what kind of answer William was looking for,

John contented himself with a noncommittal grunt. William looked proud. 'We shall therefore require a replacement for Lord Howe.'

'I'm ecstatic,' John said flatly. 'Why are you telling me this?'

'Because I hope very much you will take Lord Howe's place.'

John took a moment to arrange the words in his head so that they made sense. The room felt suddenly very hot. 'First Lord ...' His voice cracked. 'First Lord of the Admiralty?'

'What do you say to it?' William crossed his legs, for all the world as though he had just offered John a game of chess.

'I'm a soldier,' John managed at last. 'You need a sailor.'

'In my opinion sailors are the least fitted men to head the Admiralty. A man who is not bred to the sea will be more likely to think generally about the needs of the service. Lord Howe has shown me I need a man I can trust in charge of our naval forces.'

'But I have no experience. No knowledge.'

'The Navy Board will supply that. You'll manage.'

'I'm no orator.'

William twitched an eyebrow. 'Leave the oratory to me.' He reached across and laid a hand over John's. His eyes glistened with sincerity. 'I nearly lost you in the past few weeks. All I could think of was that I never told you how much I value you. You are my brother, you are my friend, and I trust you with my life. I believe you have already saved it on one occasion.'

The raw feeling in William's voice robbed John of the ability to speak. Gratitude overwhelmed him, but at the same time the prospect of Cabinet office – and such an office – terrified him. He knew nothing of ships or sailors, nothing. 'There must be a better man.'

'There is no man I would rather have than you,' William replied.

There was nothing John could say to that. He closed his eyes and tried to believe the spinning of his head was entirely due to his fever. 'In that case, I accept.'

William's face cleared instantly. 'You will not regret it. Although obviously you must prepare.' William crossed to the bell-pull and gave it a tug. 'The Comptroller of the Navy has sent some books, which you will wish to peruse before taking up your duties. I took the liberty of bringing them today.' Two footmen laid a large wooden crate next to John's sofa. William pulled up the lid to reveal at least a dozen thick octavos and several bulging leather folders tied with silk cord. 'You will no doubt find it heavy going, but I imagine you have some time on your hands.'

John stared at the contents of the box. 'You said this would help me feel better.'

'Could it be worse than Miss Townshend's prattle?' William asked. John blinked, then gave a slow grin.

'*Nothing* could be worse than Miss Townshend's prattle.'

The door opened and Mary came in, pulling off her gloves, her straw hat hanging off one arm. She froze when she saw William; John supposed she had been expecting to find him still in the company of her mother and sister. William kissed her on each cheek.

'My dear Lady Chatham,' he said, 'you will soon be moving into new lodgings.'

'New lodgings?' Mary repeated. William took her hands and spun her round.

'Yes, and we shall practically be neighbours. Admiralty House!'

Mary fired an incredulous glance at John. John beamed back. *First Lord of the Admiralty*! A new day – a new opportunity – was just beginning. He knew Mary would agree.

****

Later that evening Mary came into John's drawing room while the footmen unfolded a table for them and laid it out with a light supper of fresh rolls, cold meats and dried fruit. She poured John a glass of claret and carried it to him. John barely looked up as she sank onto the edge of his sofa. His injured leg rested on a cushion; his sound one was bent at the knee to form a rudimentary bookrest for an enormous leather-bound volume bristling with roughly-cut pages and bookmarks.

Mary stroked his powdered hair back over the top of his ear. 'Do you not think you have read enough?'

He jumped as though he had not noticed her enter the room. 'I have at least eight more volumes of this to work through.'

John had unfolded a cross-section of a large ship of the line, with various observations and mathematical calculations scribbled into the margin. Mary stretched out a hand and folded the sheet back into the book. 'You need to eat your supper.'

She helped him off the sofa and supported him across the room to the supper table. Mary could feel him leaning heavily on her arm; she could feel, too, how hot his hand was on hers. At least his appetite was returning: even a week ago, John could not have sat down to supper without complaining of queasiness, but now he ate two buttered rolls and some cheese with every appearance of enjoyment. Mary picked at her food and listened to him talk.

'William tells me there are unlikely to be many Cabinet meetings until I am better, but there may be some dockyard inspections to undertake, since there are several ships building. Admiralty House will not be ready for us for a few months: Lord Howe was having it fitted up for himself, but it is not yet ready. We might visit it, however, if you like.'

Mary nodded. John was talking about visits to dockyards and touring new houses as though he had not just needed her help to walk across the room. She bent her head over her roll and concentrated on buttering it.

'I understand the salary of the First Lord is generous, so we shall have no trouble procuring more servants, for Admiralty House is larger than Berkeley Square.'

'You will have to work for it,' Mary said, before she could stop herself. John peered at her over the rim of his wineglass.

'I beg your pardon?'

'The salary.' Mary laid her roll back on the plate, untouched. 'You will have to earn it.'

'Well, yes,' John said, his brow creasing between his eyes. 'Naturally, there will be work to do.'

Did he know how much? Mary glanced across at the open chest of books, the volume John had been reading – one of eight – lying on the pillow of his sofa. Visits to dockyards, ship launches, inspections … All that was very well, but what of Board meetings, and Cabinets, and court levees and drawing rooms? What if there was war? Could John stand being roused by despatches in the small hours of the morning? Could he make decisions on which the fate of nations might depend? Was he strong enough to take responsibility when things went wrong?

She looked at him from under her eyelashes. He looked so happy. John had always wanted the opportunity to show his worth; she suspected he needed convincing of it as much as the rest of the world. Why, then, was she not more pleased for him?

He looked anxiously at her. 'Mary? Are you well?'

She loved him too much: that was the problem. She wanted him to succeed, but she did not want to think of what might happen if William's gift became a burden to him. 'Just surprised, my love, that is all. I still cannot believe it.'

'Neither can I,' John said, and his grin was Mary's reward. She pressed a kiss to his cheek, filling it with all the hope and love in her heart. He was a Pitt, the Earl of Chatham no less. Politics was in his blood. So long as he and William kept together, all would be well.

Chapter Sixteen

February 1793

Mary awoke to the sound of marching. She gazed up at the diamond pattern inlaid on the wooden bed canopy and wondered whether the echo of booted feet against gravel came from dream or reality. Then she remembered: today the Foot Guards marched to Greenwich to embark for Holland.

She pushed off the coverlet and slipped out of bed. John was a sound sleeper, but he stirred and reached across for her. When his arms encountered nothing but empty air he opened his eyes and murmured, 'Mary?'

Mary padded to the window. A burst of chill air met her as she parted the curtains. 'I am supposed to be at Greenwich in a few hours. Will you come?'

'To Greenwich?' John spoke as though Mary had suggested a jaunt to Africa. 'I suppose that involves getting out of bed?'

Outside Admiralty House, on Horse Guards Parade, Mary could just about make out the shadows of hundreds of men moving in formation. A dense fog prevented her seeing much, but the trembling glow of oil lamps glanced off white cross-belts and silvery musket-barrels. 'Go back to sleep, John,' she muttered, but her husband had already turned over, pulled the blanket over his ears and started snoring.

Mary looked at him in exasperation, but tried to make allowances for the difficulty of the circumstances. Just over a month had passed since France had executed her King in the throes of revolution, three weeks since she had declared war on Britain. The Duke of York was being sent to Helvoetsluys with 2,000 Foot Guards to join with the allied Austrian and Prussian army under the Prince of Coburg. Nine men-of-war waited at Greenwich to receive them, and Mary supposed John was entitled to sleep off the strain of the lengthy, late-night meetings and inter-departmental discussions required to get everything ready.

Mary's maid dressed her in a pink silk gown with the old-fashioned and impractical hoop dictated by court etiquette. She would happily have foregone the pleasure of going to Greenwich to see the troops embark, but the Queen had insisted. So it was that at seven, just as the Foot Guards began their march through Storey's Gate, Mary came down Admiralty House's elliptical staircase in her fur-lined tippet and muff, passed through the marble entrance hallway and stepped into the cobbled courtyard. She could barely see the top of the Admiralty's tall pillars through the fog. The Admiralty's cipher, an anchor wrapped around with rope, was completely lost to view.

Lady Sydney's carriage waited in the street. Her mother and sister lay half-asleep against the cushions, shrouded in furs and resting their feet on the charcoal brazier. They also wore court hoops, so there was not much room to spare once Mary wedged herself in.

'When will the Queen arrive?' Georgiana yawned as the carriage rattled off.

'She leaves Buckingham House at eight. We should be at the Governor's house by then.'

'Is Sir Hugh expecting Her Majesty?' Mary's mother asked.

'His Majesty asked her to keep her arrival as secret as possible.' The brazier under Mary's seat seemed to be having very little effect; her teeth chattered and she could barely feel her toes. 'That is why Her Majesty invited us to watch the embarkation. She expects us to, ah … *prepare* Sir Hugh for the honour he is about to be paid.'

Mary, Georgiana and Lady Sydney arrived at Greenwich Hospital shortly after eight o'clock. Sir Christopher Wren's twin cupolas loomed out of the mist. The skeletal masts of the great ships waiting to transport the troops to Holland could just about be discerned on the river beyond. A long line of horses, carts and baggage waggons stood on the dockside waiting for the flat-bottomed boats to ferry them to the vessels. The shrill call of a boatswain's whistle cut through the cold, thin air.

Sir Hugh Palliser's wide-set brown eyes widened when he found Mary in the Painted Hall gazing up at the high ceiling with its colourfully depicted allegories of British naval power. 'Lady Chatham. You are here to watch the troops embark?'

'Her Majesty commanded our presence here to receive her and the Princesses. They wish to bid farewell to the Duke of York as he embarks on his first continental command.'

'The Queen? All – all six Princesses?' Palliser was too well versed in the shocks and reverses of battle to be thrown by receiving half the Royal Family at the shortest possible notice. Even so, Mary saw the old man grip the pommel of his dress sword until his knuckles stood white. 'We were expecting His Majesty and the Prince of Wales, but the Queen …'

'If you wish, my mother and sister and I might make the arrangements,' Mary suggested, taking pity on him. 'We know what Her Majesty best likes.'

Sir Hugh all too happily delegated responsibility for the preparations and hurried off, probably to drink a fortifying brandy before the arrival of the unexpected royal party. Lady Sydney and Georgiana went downstairs to the kitchens to order refreshments, while Mary went upstairs with the steward. She quickly found the best rooms, large and airy with tall sash windows that looked out onto the square towards the river. The Hospital's servants bustled about under Mary's orders, moving furniture, dusting the gold eaves until they gleamed, and arranging enormous plates of sandwiches and cold meats in the adjoining room.

Mary was wiping perspiration from her brow when she heard hooves striking the cobbles of the Hospital courtyard. Five elegant, lightly-sprung coaches driven by grooms in red and gold royal livery drew up by the Governor's door, followed by several gentlemen on horseback and the smaller carriages of Her Majesty's attendants.

Queen Charlotte's long, flat face was grey from lack of sleep, the rings under her eyes barely concealed with powder and paste. Mary curtseyed low and wondered what it must be like to send a loved one off to war. Her palms went slick with sweat at the thought, and she was glad John had no intention of renewing his military career while he remained First Lord of the Admiralty.

'Sir Hugh,' the Queen said, allowing Palliser to kiss her hand. Thirty years after coming to England her German accent remained thick. Behind her stood the six Princesses, from the 26-year-old Princess Royal to 10-year-old Princess Amelia, in matching white and gold muslin dresses. 'I trust we do not impose upon you.'

'Not at all, Your Majesty,' Palliser said. 'It is an honour.'

Mary led the royal party upstairs to the rooms which had been specially prepared. The Queen and Princesses looked upon the cold collation with distant approval but did not attempt to eat. The Queen looked like food was the last thing on her mind, and the Princesses looked strained. Princess Elizabeth was pale and distracted, and little Amelia seemed constantly on the verge of tears.

The fog was lifting at last. The warehouses on the north bank could now clearly be seen, as could the nine enormous warships lying at anchor in the middle of the river, sails tightly furled. They bobbed up and down gently on the tide, while herring gulls whirled around them, screaming.

Crowds had been gathering on the quay and along the roads for hours, and it was their cheering that warned Mary the Foot Guards were approaching at last. The Queen sat a little straighter in her chair and stopped talking to her ladies.

A band played a jaunty march: flutes whistled; horns sounded; drums beat. The King appeared, on a white charger, his portly form encased in the scarlet of a general's uniform. The Duke of York rode behind, his round, youthful face bright with excitement. Next to him was the Prince of Wales, in the dark uniform of the 10th Light Dragoons, of which he was colonel. Behind them marched the Foot Guards. Their boots struck dust from the road as they marched to the stately beat of ordinary time.

The King and his sons the turned this way and that to acknowledge the acclaim. When they caught sight of the Queen and Princesses waving their handkerchiefs from the window of the Governor's house they removed their hats and bowed. Strains of "God Save the King" wafted through the cheering crowd.

'The Duke looks so handsome,' Georgiana whispered to Mary. Mary nodded, but kept her eye on the 15-year-old Princess Sophia. At the sight of her father and brothers the poor girl had gone white and started to teeter. Mary was certain the Princess was about to faint. Her gaze crossed with that of Princess Mary. Some message must have passed between them, for the Princess stepped forwards and took her sister's arm.

The soldiers began to enter the flat-bottomed boats. They behaved as though they were on holiday, waving at the crowds and joining in with the patriotic songs. To Mary's eye they were not quite sober, many moving in a markedly sinuous fashion. One or two stumbled out of line and were beaten back by their outraged sergeant.

'Why are those men not marching in a straight line?' Princess Amelia said, loudly.

The Queen's fan stopped whirring through the air. The Princess Royal, holding her younger sister's hand, froze. Mary thought quickly and said, hurriedly, 'They are overcome with the honour of Your Royal Highness' presence.'

Amelia looked satisfied and turned her large blue eyes back to the spectacle outside. Mary saw the relief cross the Queen's face before the muscles tightened back into a neutral expression. Princess Augusta, on the other hand, looked across at Mary with a twitch that looked perilously like the beginning of a grin.

The last men were embarking now. Only the Duke of York remained ashore. Mary watched the young general in his gold braid, the scarlet of his coat stark against the white road. He looked like a boy about to go on an adventure. When his turn came to board the transport he waved one last time at the crowds. The "huzzas" launched in response were deafening.

'Isn't it marvellous?' Georgiana whispered again. 'So moving.'

Mary said nothing. Fifteen hundred of England's best troops had just embarked amidst a show of loyal fervour.

'*O Lord our God, arise,*

Scatter his enemies

And make them fall …'

All outside was holiday, the sun high in a blue winter's sky, yet Mary shivered as though a shadow had fallen across her. The soldiers on the transport decks blurred into one indistinguishable mass, their coats red as blood. She felt that her fate was somehow bound up with them, as though if they fell they would take her with them.

Behind her, Princess Sophia groaned and collapsed in a dead faint.

Chapter Seventeen

November 1793

'I apologise, my lord, but I cannot have heard correctly. *How* many men?'

John shifted in his leather armchair. He glanced up briefly at the beautiful concentric patterns on the Admiralty Board Room's ceiling, plunged in the gloom of a November evening, and repeated, 'There are just under 5,000 men in Toulon.'

Admiral Gardner's expression did not change, but the muscles of his weather-beaten face tightened ever so slightly. 'I thought Mr Pitt promised Lord Hood an army of 60,000.'

'He did.' John rubbed his chin and stifled a yawn. He had been up late the previous night poring over naval charts; he did not think he was likely to get to bed any sooner tonight.

To his relief, Gardner did not ask where the 55,000 missing men were. John liked Gardner, who could be blunt to the point of rudeness but, unlike many, recognised the First Lord of the Admiralty's efforts to learn about his role and the navy under his command.

Along with most naval men, however, Gardner could hardly restrain his indignation at the way government was squandering the greatest strategic ace Britain had acquired since the start of the French war. Supporters of the French monarchy had petitioned the British navy in the Mediterranean, under Lord Hood, to protect Toulon against the republicans. The town could provide a base for launching an attack on France's heart from the south, but so far little had been done to fortify it. 'The Austrian force?'

'Has not yet arrived.' The other members of the Admiralty Board looked grave. Charles Perceval tapped at the table-top with the metal sheath of his pencil. The elderly Admiral Affleck crossed his arms. Like John, they knew the Austrians were only interested in the war in the north, in Flanders, where they currently had 60,000 men in the field.

'I understand the counter-revolutionaries in Marseilles and Lyons have already been suppressed by republican forces.' Gardner's blue eyes, clear and piercing, held John's. 'Louis XVII's supporters placed Toulon in our hands in trust. So long as we remain there we control half the French navy. Should Toulon fall—'

'Toulon will not fall,' John said, quietly. Gardner sighed.

'I certainly hope it will not, my lord, for should Toulon become a second Dunkirk ...'

The silence in the Board Room was complete. Barely two months had passed since the Duke of York's terrible defeat at Dunkirk. The 1,500 men that had sailed from Greenwich in February had been reinforced to 7,000 and joined by 30,000 Austrians, Dutch and Hanoverians, but it had not been enough to defeat the 45,000-strong French army; 10,000 men had died and the survivors forced into a humiliating retreat, all because the Duke had not received supplies and equipment in time – equipment carried by ships in John's navy; ships that had sailed too late, and missed the crucial tide that might have saved York and his army.

Toulon could not be allowed to fall. For John, saving Toulon now meant saving his reputation. The one was bound up with the other.

****

Mary was dozing by the library fire, some neglected embroidery in her lap, when John came back from the meeting. She started awake when he leaned over, kissed her gently on the cheek and said, 'I told you not to wait for me.'

'And I told you I would.' She rubbed at her eyes and glanced at the clock: it was well past midnight. 'These Board meetings are getting longer and longer, my love. I cannot recall the last time you came to me before ten.'

'Yes,' John said, his face suddenly tight. 'Although apparently my late nights are due to my getting drunk and sitting up at card tables until the small hours of the morning. The only gambling I have done since summer is with men's lives, and my own career.'

Mary stretched her aching limbs, wincing as her hip twinged in protest. 'John, what is the matter? Did the Board ...?'

'Nobody on the Board would dare throw the rumours in my face,' John said, through clenched teeth. 'But they are all aware of them. Since Dunkirk the rumours have got worse.'

'But you did what you were ordered to do.' Mary rose and placed her hands on John's shoulders. His muscles were taut as a bow-string. 'It is not your fault the decision to besiege Dunkirk was taken at the last minute.'

'It is not just Dunkirk,' John muttered. 'News came this afternoon. Another merchant vessel has been captured. There was a full convoy, of course, but the fool of a master did not want to wait for its protection. Not that inconvenient facts will stop my enemies shedding my blood.'

'William will defend you.'

'He will,' John agreed, with a bitter smile. 'But others may choose not to.'

He threw himself in a chair, stretched his legs towards the fire and laid his head against the embroidered back-rest. The gold plaster mouldings of Admiralty House's elegant ceilings glittered in the candlelight. The flames glanced off the tall pier glasses between the windows and played dark tricks on John's brooding face. The treacherous thought that perhaps losing his office might be the best thing for his health occurred to Mary; she quashed it with difficulty. Forced retirement might relieve John's immediate stress, but the humiliation of it would destroy him.

To stop herself feeling completely useless she crossed to the decanters and poured him a glass. While he drank, she stood behind his chair and brushed her hand against the taut muscles of his cheek, willing her love to heal his wounds. 'You said others may choose not to defend you. Did you mean the Duke of Richmond?'

Richmond, the Master General of the Ordnance, also shared responsibility for the late arrival of the siege equipment at Dunkirk. The Duke was a notoriously difficult colleague, and Mary would not have been surprised if he had tried to throw his share of the blame on John, but her husband shook his head. 'Even if Richmond were to cause trouble my brother would not listen. But there are others who may seek to protect themselves at my expense. Dundas, for example.'

'Dundas?' Mary wrinkled her nose instinctively. Her little social contact with William's Secretary of State for Home Affairs had not attracted her to him. She found his Scottish accent hard to understand, and his wine-reddened face and blunt-fingered hands with their bitten nails revolted her. Yet she knew William valued Dundas's advice highly, and that he had more impact on war policy than any other man.

'Once, many years ago, William agreed with me about Dundas. He agreed with me on so many things.' John kicked violently at the ashes in the grate, sending up a great cloud of sparks. 'How times have changed.'

'Surely your brother will not choose Dundas over you?'

'I wish I agreed,' John said, and Mary dropped her hand away at the despair in his voice, a despair she was powerless to stem.

****

The précis of the latest despatches circulated the Cabinet table in silence. John knew much of the information already, for his department had compiled half the document, but he read it again anyway, poking at the wound as though exacerbating the pain might help it pass more quickly: 3,000 sick at Toulon; the French closing in fast; the Austrians defeated at Wattignies, freeing up more Frenchmen to march south against Hood in Toulon.

William waited until the paper had gone round the table. 'As you see, gentlemen, the situation is grave.'

John glanced round the table. The Duke of Richmond, still smarting from the attacks launched at him after Dunkirk, was turned away, his lined face full of anger.

'I trust we are all agreed the Duke of York must be recalled from Flanders,' Dundas said. His deep-set eyes roamed round the table, seeking out challenge. None came.

William's taut face relaxed a little. 'Withdrawing our men from northern Europe will provide us with disposable manpower for the first time in a long while. We must decide where best to apply that force.'

'The men will need to recover,' the Duke of Richmond growled. 'By all accounts half are sick with marsh fever.'

Neither William nor Dundas reacted, accustomed to ignoring Richmond's protests. John was inclined to think Richmond spoke sensibly, but the prospect of sending reinforcements to Toulon was not one he could let pass. He nerved himself to speak. 'Whatever their condition, the troops will be greatly appreciated by Lord Hood. The revolutionary forces in the south will soon be reinforced. It will not be long before an attempt is made to eject us from Toulon.'

His words fell into a profound silence. William and Dundas exchanged a look. It was too brief for John to make much of it, but something warned him his brother and the Home Secretary already had plans for York's troops.

'You do intend to reinforce Lord Hood, do you not?' John stammered, aware none of the other Cabinet members had so much as nodded either.

'Of course we do,' William said, soothingly. 'Provision for him will be made in the army estimates.'

John was stunned. 'The army estimates? In March? That's four months away!'

Lord Grenville, John and William's cousin, now ennobled and William's Foreign Secretary, spoke up. 'Our ambassador in Vienna has been instructed to emphasise the importance of sending men to Toulon as soon as possible. I have no reason to believe—'

'The Austrians?' Now John was convinced his colleagues were playing him for a fool. 'They are in full retreat! What can we expect from them?'

'Perhaps nothing,' Dundas interposed, with a quelling look at Grenville. 'However, there is a more pressing claim on our resources. Word has arrived from the West Indies that Guadeloupe has fallen to the French, and that we have failed to retake Martinique. We cannot allow the enemy to keep the islands; our sugar trade must be secured. Eight regiments will sail under the command of Sir Charles Grey.'

For a moment, John was speechless. 'Eight regiments?'

'Yes, my lord,' Dundas replied, as though speaking to a child. 'Eight.'

'I suppose they will require transports? Where will we obtain them?'

'You are First Lord of the Admiralty,' Dundas said thinly. 'You tell me.'

'I do not think I need to tell you where our ships are to be found!' John realised he was on the edge of losing his temper. He lowered his voice. 'Sir, please consider. We have ships in the Atlantic, and in the Mediterranean. We have every single French Channel port blockaded. We must provide convoys for our mercantile shipping. I beg of you, do not waste resources on the West Indies. Toulon and the French fleet are in our hands. We hold them like a knife to the heart of the revolution. If we must send our men anywhere, let it be where it can make the most difference. Let it be Toulon.'

William braced a finger against his top lip, his eyes fixed on Dundas. The Scotsman's head was pitched to one side as though straining to listen. John felt his heart shrivel from the cold in the older man's gaze.

'The formation of military strategy falls under my remit as Secretary of State,' Dundas said. 'I would thank you, my lord, to mind your own business.'

'I think you will find this *is* my business,' John replied instantly. 'Any matters pertaining to naval strategy must perforce—'

'Naval strategy is but a part of the broader war effort!' Dundas snapped. 'The main actions of the war have taken place on land. The needs of the navy must bow to the requirements of our army and our trade.'

John could not believe what he was hearing. 'If we do not fight for Toulon, we will lose it.'

Dundas took a deep breath, and in that moment John knew the Home Secretary had already given Toulon up for lost. 'You are persistent, my lord. Had you been so determined about sending ships to Flanders, the Duke of York might even now be marching on Paris.'

'Gentlemen.' William raised his hands to stop any further exchange. 'Lord Chatham, I am grateful for your advice, knowing it comes from your knowledge of the resources at your command. As a military man, however, you must recognise the need for flexibility. We cannot allow the French to profit from the West Indies. We must trust to our continental alliances to provide for Lord Hood and look to our own interests.'

'Do you mean to exclude our men in Toulon from that tally?' John retorted.

'You are out of order, sir,' Dundas protested.

'That is for Mr Pitt to decide.' Anger made John bold. He met William's cold gaze. 'I have not yet had a reply to my question.'

'In war, difficult choices must be made,' William said, woodenly.

'At the expense of good men? You know I have served in the West Indies. I can tell you better than Mr Dundas's despatches how disease will kill more of our men than the French will.' William raised his chin. Aware that he was not making progress, John used the last weapon in his arsenal. 'William, our own brother died in the West Indies.'

William's eyes dilated in shock. Dundas thumped the table. 'Enough! With the navy in such hands I do not wonder we have yet to defeat the French at sea, and that our trade convoys are swallowed up by enemy privateers.'

John's vision blurred. He stood, his chair-legs screaming against the wooden floor. 'If you, sir, took advice from military men once in a while, you might discover war is more complicated than calculating columns of figures or fighting battles on paper.'

John's vision cleared enough to see Dundas's expression of triumph. His ears caught up with his tongue and he winced. Everyone knew war strategy was decided by three men: Dundas, Grenville and William. John had aimed his insult too clumsily.

'I think the matter has been discussed enough,' William snapped. 'Lord Chatham, I appreciate your concerns, but the decision stands. Eight regiments will go to the West Indies, and the Admiralty will find sufficient transports.'

John could say nothing in the face of a direct order. 'Of course, sir.'

The Cabinet broke up soon after. John was knotting the cords round his leather folder embossed with the Admiralty anchor when he felt William's hand on his upper arm. 'A word with you, Lord Chatham.'

The use of his title warned John he could expect nothing good, but he followed his brother into William's study with its windows overlooking the garden and St James's Park. William's secretaries, Joe Smith and John Carthew, were working at a great table on one side of the room. When they saw William's expression they hastily took their leave.

William stalked over to his desk. Spread over its surface, hedged in by several books bristling with bookmarks, was an avalanche of papers and letters, red and green seals winking in the candlelight. William dragged a large folio out of the chaos and banged it down on the secretaries' table.

'There.' He dragged John over and pointed. John looked down reluctantly: it was a map of Martinique and Guadeloupe. 'That is where the ships are to be sent. Can you fix it in your mind? You will not send the transports elsewhere in a fit of pique?'

'I would do no such thing and you know it,' John said, bristling at the implication. William slammed the atlas closed. Several unopened letters slid to the floor.

'What did you imagine you would achieve by attacking Dundas in that manner?'

'He provoked me.'

'I do not care!' William shouted. 'I will not allow you to reduce a Cabinet meeting to the level of a petty rivalry. If you have nothing sensible to contribute, I advise you to keep your mouth shut.'

The unfairness of the attack horrified John. 'I think I have a right to defend myself against a personal assault on my ability to—'

'Perhaps you ought to consider whether that assault has any basis in fact?' John stared at his brother. William braced himself against the table and pinched the bridge of his nose. 'I am sorry, John. I know you are not the only minister to have attracted blame for what has passed.' He looked up, and John felt the steel in his brother's gaze pierce him like a blade. 'But blame has attached, and I think you ought to be very careful in what you do and say, for the government cannot afford any more disasters.'

The words fell into John's mind, coldly and evenly. He stayed silent, not sure what response to make to something that had sounded very much like a threat.

William's gaze sharpened. 'Have I made myself clear?'

John bit his lip and tasted blood. 'Quite clear.'

Chapter Eighteen

June 1794

The carriage drew up before the Opera House on the Haymarket. Dusk was just falling after a warm June day, and enormous flambeaux had been lit beneath the Doric pediments at either end of the theatre's street frontage. From inside came the faint strains of an orchestra, and the trill of a female voice singing an aria.

Mary gave John her hand and stepped down onto the pavement. The air was sticky with humidity, and the silk of her high-waisted dress stuck to her back. Beside her Georgiana ran a finger discreetly behind her crimson sash, the ostrich feathers in her hair bouncing in the wind from her fan.

'Tell me how it goes,' John murmured. He dropped a kiss on Mary's cheek and grasped the strap to re-enter the vehicle. Mary stopped him.

'Will you not come in with us?'

The flickering flambeaux dwelled on the dents below the bridge of John's nose, the line between his eyes, the downward curve of his pursed lips. 'Tonight is your triumph, my love.'

'But it's not.' Mary and John had discussed the matter so many times, but now, faced with the immediate prospect of going in alone, Mary tried again. 'Lord Howe's naval victory is in no way mine, John. Six prizes taken, the French fleet broken … The triumph is yours.'

'Do you not think Lord Howe might disagree?'

'You know what I mean. Lord Howe may have won the battle, but he did so with resources provided by *your* Admiralty.' She hesitated over the words "Dunkirk" and "Toulon", wondering whether she should express her conviction that Howe's victory off Ushant totally offset those defeats, but decided against casting blemish on the glorious news. She spoke firmly. 'John, listen to me. Lord Howe's victory is your justification. You have something Mr Dundas does not have: success.' John's face hardened at the mention of the Secretary of State. Mary pressed her lips to his. 'Can you not see you are safe now?'

He wrapped his arms tightly around her. For a moment, Mary thought she might have convinced him, but then he pulled away and climbed into the carriage. 'I hope you are correct, Mary. Truly I do.'

Mary watched the carriage turn down Cockspur Street until it disappeared, then turned to Georgiana. Now that John was gone, the knowledge of what she still had to do filled her heart with dread. 'Shall we go in?'

The vestibule and grand stone staircase were empty of all save liveried porters. John's box was halfway round the left-hand side of the theatre's horseshoe shape on the first floor. Mary pushed open the heavy oak door and she and Georgiana slipped into the crimson upholstered seats.

The theatre was full. The stalls thronged; nearly every box was occupied; and even the gods were crowded. On the stage the latest Italian sensation, La Morichelli, was in the middle of her aria, hands clasped before her ample bosom as she rose effortlessly to the highest notes.

Every instinct told her just to listen to the music, but Mary had come to the opera for a purpose. She waited for the aria to finish and the applause to die down, then stood.

Georgiana squeezed her hand. 'Good luck.'

Mary grinned at her over the banging of her heart against her ribs, then leaned on the carved wooden balustrade and raised her voice. 'My lords and ladies! Gentlemen!'

A hush fell across the crowded theatre. Down in the orchestra pit the musicians turned to peer up at Mary. La Morichelli blinked up into the light of the great chandelier.

Mary's name echoed about the theatre. She quailed under the scrutiny, but the thought of John emboldened her. Emotion choked her so much she had to force out her announcement: 'Victory!'

The company dissolved into delighted acclamation; the orchestra began spontaneously to play "God Save the King". Mary listened to the cheering and wished John could have stayed to witness the jubilation. Lord Howe's victory had saved John's Admiralty. Why could John not allow himself to relax?

****

Perspiration ran between Mary's breasts and soaked into her stays. The heat from the sun was overwhelming and her side ached terribly, but she dared not complain for fear of upsetting John. She glanced at her husband's pale face, then looked out across the cream canvas of the royal canopy towards the great ship sitting on the stocks. The ship's black and gold paint glistened in the sun and her height dwarfed everything. The four flags she carried instead of masts – the Royal Standard, the Portsmouth and Admiralty flags, and the British Jack – danced against the clear sky.

Three days into the royal gala at Portsmouth to celebrate Lord Howe's victory, very little was going to plan. A storm had broken at almost the precise moment the King boarded Lord Howe's flagship, the *Queen Charlotte*, drenching everyone; by some oversight the anti-monarchical slogans daubed all over the captain's quarters of the captured ship *Pompée* had not been removed before the King's visit to the vessel; and the frigate carrying the royal party around the Isle of Wight had accidentally run aground, stranding the King and Queen for several hours until the tide came in. Now the *Prince of Wales* was about to launch, and Mary realised she was waiting for something else to go awry. Perhaps the ropes would break too soon, or the ship would be swallowed by the waves the moment it entered the water.

Around them every house with a decent view onto the dockyard had heads poking out of open windows. Between the harbour and the Isle of Wight stood dozens of fishing boats and pleasure-barges, all filled with spectators. Beyond them were the hulking forms of the victorious ships, Britain's hearts of oak. Several still bore their battle scars in the form of mangled sails or broken masts; some had hastily repaired hulls, plain brown boards patched over their jauntily-painted flanks.

The Master of the Dockyards began a seemingly interminable speech about the honour of naming the vessel after the heir to the throne, even though the Prince of Wales had chosen to remain at Brighthelmstone with his mistress rather than attend the launch. John shifted and wiped his brow with his handkerchief. Mary placed a hand discreetly on his knee. 'What is the matter?'

'Nothing.' He brushed her away. Mary folded her hands in her lap and fought down her concern. The fatigue of attending the King from six in the morning to ten at night had brought on a bilious fever, and John had been nauseous since breakfast. Mary could tell by the grey sheen of his skin that the heat was not helping. 'Is William here yet?'

Mary peered towards the royal canopy. The King and Queen were surrounded by court attendants and several of their children, the princes in miniature Windsor uniforms, the princesses in white dresses with gold sashes. Mary saw Admiral Howe (the diamond hilt of the sword he had received in recognition of his victory glinting at his waist), the governor of Portsmouth, and officials from the Admiralty and Navy Boards, but of William there was no sign. 'No,' she said, and John sighed. Mary did not know exactly why, but William's continued absence was worrying her husband.

The Master of the Dockyards sat down at last and the Governor of Portsmouth began another speech. Mary snapped out her fan just as John stood and pushed past the gentlemen and ladies surrounding him. Astonished at the breach of etiquette, Mary followed.

She caught up with him beside a pile of barrels stacked outside a warehouse. From here the bowsprit of the new ship with its effigy of the Prince of Wales in his garter robes was partly concealed by the surrounding buildings. Mary tugged her husband's arm. 'John, honestly, what is amiss? Please return to your seat before someone notices you are gone.'

John ignored her, drawing in deep breaths. Suddenly he leaned against one of the barrels and retched.

For a moment Mary was too startled to react, but then instinct took over. She put her arm round John's shoulders to shield him from sight. He did not vomit, but she could tell he was putting all his effort into holding back the urge. At length, he straightened and wiped his mouth. Mary stood back with her arms crossed till his breathing steadied. 'Better?' He nodded and tucked his handkerchief away. 'Do you think you can return to your seat?'

John opened his mouth to answer, but shut it when someone called out: 'Lord Chatham!'

Henry Dundas emerged from one of the dockside houses. His face was reddened from three days of following the royal party round the dockyards. 'Not seasick, my lord? Or should I say land-sick?'

He chuckled at his own joke. Mary took a defensive step closer to her husband. John swallowed convulsively; tension radiated from him like heat from a brazier. 'What are you doing here? Why are you not with the King?'

'I think I should go back,' Mary muttered, but John seized her by the wrist. He did not look at her, but she sensed he needed her support in the presence of his enemy.

'I wanted to make sure the blacksmith was ready to receive Their Majesties later this afternoon, when the royal party visits the smithy to see the new ship coppered. And yourself?' Dundas added, as though he had not just seen John trying desperately not to vomit. John's face had gone grey again, and Mary wondered whether he might be sick after all, but he managed to compose himself.

'Stretching my legs.' Dundas raised his sandy eyebrows but said nothing. He started to walk away; to Mary's astonishment John called him back. 'Have you seen my brother?'

'Mr Pitt? No. Parliament must have claimed him.'

'At the end of June? You know better than I how thin the Commons is this close to the recess. Something must have kept him.' Dundas shrugged. Mary listened tensely. John's voice was low and hurried; she had to strain to hear him. 'When I left London, I heard all sorts of rumours about how my brother intends to consolidate his government. Are those rumours true? Is my brother about to coalesce with the Duke of Portland?'

The Duke of Portland was Fox's former political leader, but the two had separated after the French revolution. Portland and his sizeable parliamentary following had been operating independently for some time. 'I think you had best ask Mr Pitt yourself.'

'Dundas, I beg of you. I know my brother makes no decision without your advice, and I am your colleague in Cabinet. I have a right to know whether I am likely to continue in that capacity.'

Behind them the crowd cheered. For a long moment, any response Dundas might have made would have been lost in the huzzas ringing out from the dockyards. When at last he could make himself heard Dundas said, with an ironic twist that made the hairs rise at the nape of Mary's neck, 'Do not fret, my lord. Your brother will not let you go just yet.'

'So there *is* to be a coalition?' John pressed.

'I am not saying that is what has kept Mr Pitt in London, but I suppose there is no harm in telling you that yes, Mr Pitt hopes the Duke of Portland and his friends will join us.'

John looked like his worst fears had been realised. 'I presume my brother will have to be generous in the disposition of offices.'

'Mr Pitt would not abandon his friends,' Dundas said, with a curl of his lips.

'Normally I would agree with you, but I know several of the Duke's friends have been spreading rumours about my … my … *unfitness* for office.' Dundas was silent. 'I know how strong this coalition will make us in Parliament. No doubt Portland and his friends know it too. What if they decide to make me the test of my brother's sincerity?'

Another cheer went up. Dundas glanced towards the dockyards, then rested his eyes contemptuously on John. 'My lord, I give you my word there is no talk of a change at the Admiralty. You have Mr Pitt's full confidence, although I am damned if I know why.'

John narrowed his eyes but said nothing. Dundas gave a low bow and walked away.

Mary released her breath. She never enjoyed being in Dundas's company, but at least now she knew why John had been so anxious when Howe's victory should have chased away all his fears.

She took his hands. 'My love, listen to me. Mr Dundas' opinion does not matter, but he is right about one thing. You are William's brother. He will not sacrifice you for the sake of the Duke of Portland.'

John's cold gaze was fixed on Dundas's back. 'Perhaps not for Portland,' he murmured, and Mary shuddered at his tone. There was nothing John hated more than to be held in contempt. She did not think she would ever forget the mocking tone of Dundas's voice, or the murderous look on her husband's face.

Chapter Nineteen

November 1794

Despite the November chill, a large crowd had gathered outside Burlington House to boo at ministers as they arrived for Cabinet. The radical John Thelwall was being tried for high treason for daring to suggest Britain's Parliament ought to be reformed. Two other men, Thomas Hardy and John Horne Tooke, had just been acquitted of the same crime. The mob clearly felt all three men had been unjustly maligned. They pressed forwards around John's carriage and hissed.

John peered out of the window. Among the men with open-toed shoes and the women with stained aprons and greasy bonnets he could make out a few silver buttons, even the glint of a shoe-buckle. The artisans and shopkeepers, the wealthier disenfranchised, were openly opposing government now. The last two summers had been dry, the winters harsh. If the seasons did not become more temperate there would be famine to add to heavy war taxes and rising prices. Two years into the war there was little to show but broken alliances and an enemy who now threatened an invasion of Britain's own shores.

Someone recognised the crest on the carriage door; John heard his name. 'Lord Chatham!'

'The minister's brother!'

'What say you to Hardy's acquittal, Your Lordship?'

'Let's see if we can make the minister's brother cheer.'

The coachman shifted on the block. His voice came through the slats. 'What shall I do, my lord?'

'Take your time.' John waved a gloved hand. 'Only do not run any of them down.'

Darkness was falling by the time John's carriage passed through the archway into Burlington House's icy cobbled courtyard. Several carriages stood here already and John knew he was probably one of the last to arrive. Even so, he took his time climbing the grand staircase. He was in no hurry for this Cabinet meeting, his first since returning to

London after a lengthy holiday to shake off a recurring stomach complaint.

He could feel the unease in the air as he pushed open the door to the Duke of Portland's oval library. William had finalised his coalition with the Duke and his followers over the summer, but ten years of bitter opposition died hard. Had John been an impartial observer he would have laughed at the way the old hands –William, Grenville and Dundas – huddled together on one side of the room, while Portland and his adherents clustered opposite.

'Lord Chatham.' The Duke of Portland bowed; he was a handsome middle-aged man whose bearing breathed aristocracy and breeding. 'I trust the mob did not molest you? Your health is improved? Mr Pitt tells me you have been ill.'

'I am much better for some country air,' John said, woodenly. Portland took the hint and resumed his seat. Across the table, Lord Spencer, Lord Fitzwilliam and William Windham watched John carefully. These men had spent much of the last year spreading tales of his getting drunk, sleeping late and neglecting his office. John knew it, and could tell they knew he did.

The Cabinet opened with a discussion of the state of the war. Windham had spent some weeks shadowing the forces in Holland, Britain's second attempt to send military aid to the continent under the Duke of York. The Austrians and Prussians had been pushed back by the French beyond the Rhine, leaving York's men trapped behind the frozen river Waal. Windham described the poor state of the men – badly clothed and low on ammunition, forced to live off the land and the slender generosity of the locals. 'One thing is abundantly clear. Our forces can do no good where they are, as they are, under such a commander.'

Silence greeted Windham's assessment. William drummed his fingers on the table-top. The treason trial acquittals and a string of continental disasters had deepened the shadows under his eyes and hardened his expression. His cheeks were full of colour, more due to wine than health. 'I think we are all of one mind. The troops must be recalled.'

'The King will not be pleased,' Grenville observed. John was not certain whether he meant it as an objection or as a statement of fact. William inclined his head.

'As much as it may pain His Majesty, we have no other option. All that remains is to arrange for ships to bring His Royal Highness home. My Lord Chatham?'

John had hoped to remain unnoticed, but William gave him no choice but to respond. 'Of course, sir, transports will be sent as soon as possible, although given the lateness of the season I cannot guarantee when that will be.'

Dundas drew a deep breath and growled, 'There are such things as tide charts. I suggest Your Lordship consults them.'

John stiffened. William, alert to the change in mood, stepped in promptly. 'I have every confidence in the Admiralty Board.'

'Just so long as they learn from past mistakes,' Dundas said, and John felt the blood drain away from his face at this pointed insult.

But John had not forgotten the dressing down he had received from William after his outburst the previous year over Toulon. His fears for the French port had proven well founded, but John did not think that fact would help him if he became embroiled in another argument. 'The Board will do its best, assuming all other departments work with us.'

In his desperate effort to keep his temper he had forgotten how half the criticisms surrounding the Dunkirk campaign had fastened on the inability of the Ordnance and Admiralty to cooperate. The Duke of Richmond looked furious. 'I take it that hint was for me?'

'No, not at all,' John protested, aghast. 'I meant only that transporting troops puts pressure on several different departments, which must work harmoniously to ensure success. This has not always been the case; but the blame in no way falls upon Your Grace.'

Richmond subsided, half-mollified, but to John's horror Dundas leapt into the breach, his Scots accent thickened with anger. 'Who, then, did you intend to mark out with your comment? Perhaps you intended it for my department?'

'You misunderstand!' John snapped. Suddenly he would much rather be outside in his carriage, surrounded by a hissing mob, than here in Portland's elegant library, unfairly assaulted by his colleagues. 'I merely passed comment on a lack of cohesion in matters where cooperation is of the greatest importance—'

'Where is this lack of cohesion?' Dundas cut in.

'Mr Dundas,' William said, warningly. Dundas pointed at the Duke of Portland.

'I trust you cast no aspersions upon our new allies? It is unfair to attack men who have followed their principles and joined with us, particularly when you have made no effort to acquaint yourself with them.'

'I said nothing of the s—' John began, then bit off his own sentence. 'Your meaning, sir?'

'I meant,' Dundas said balefully, 'that you have spent most of the autumn away from London. But then it has always been so. The minute Parliament rises, off you go to avail yourself of country sport.'

The unjustness of that half-staggered John, who had been virtually the only Cabinet minister to remain in town the previous year. 'This from the man who spent last summer potting partridges while the Duke of York's men died!'

'So it was I, then, you meant to single out?'

'Mr Dundas!' William interposed, more loudly this time. John, aware now of the thinness of the ice beneath his feet, said nothing.

Dundas ignored William. 'Say it.' His words hung in the air, whisper-thin, like a deadly spider's web. 'Say it, my lord.'

'Gentlemen,' William said, urgently. 'We must move on.'

John's eyes flicked over his colleagues. Portland looked nervous. Grenville had his hand over his mouth and peered at John in concern. William's steely gaze was desperate. John could see his own undoing in it, if he chose to rise to Dundas's bait. Yet his pride would not permit Dundas to have the last word. He placed his palm deliberately on the table-top and raised his voice.

'What do you wish me to say? That you are an upstart turncoat Scotsman with all the grasp of military affairs to be expected from a pettifogging attorney?'

Dundas's eyes snapped open. He stood, but William was faster. He threw out a hand and caught Dundas around the wrist. The Scotsman sat back down and glared across the short distance that separated him from John.

William's lips were thin, his shoulders pulled back so sharply his neck seemed to lengthen. 'The Cabinet is over,' he said tightly. 'Gentlemen, good night.'

****

173

The letter came next morning while John was at an Admiralty Board meeting. He had just given orders for the *Circe* to sail to Helvoetsluys to fetch the Duke of York when a footman laid a despatch box at the top of the table.

John opened the box while Sir Charles Middleton detailed the latest reports from Vice Admiral Cotton at Plymouth. The moment he saw his brother's neat handwriting and the words "Most Private" a shiver ran through him.

After the Board broke up John carried the box to his study in Admiralty House, locked the door and broke the seal with shaking hands.

'*My dear Brother*, he read. *I do not write to you till after a very painful struggle in my mind. After what passed between us last year I flattered myself there was an end of the embarrassment we had experienced, but I cannot disguise from you that from various circumstances, and especially from what occurred at Cabinet yesterday, I foresee too evidently the utter impossibility that business can permanently go on between you and those with whom in your present department you must have continual intercourse.*

I trust you will think I consult my affection to you as much as what I owe to public considerations in telling you fairly, though reluctantly, my conviction that the time is come when it will be best if you will exchange your present situation for one of a different description.

I have no doubt the King will agree to bestow the position of Lord Privy Seal upon you, should you choose to take it.

I have preferred telling this to you by letter to a conversation, which must be unnecessarily distressing to us both.'

John raised his eyes from the letter and focused them on a point a few inches in front of his face. The letter-filled compartments of his desk, the standish and pens, the map of the principal ports and dockyards of England affixed to the wall above, all became blurred and indistinct. In contrast, the noises around him seemed much sharper. He could hear the clicking of a maid's pattens on the marble floor downstairs, the distant clang of the bells at Horse Guards, the grinding of gravel on the Parade under the boots of a passer-by. His wife's clear, musical laugh echoed from another room.

"A painful struggle … absolutely required … unnecessarily distressing to us both."

John laid the letter down on the leather surface of his desk. He rose, unlocked the door and strode out.

His wife came out of the library at almost the same moment with her sister Georgiana. They were still laughing together at some joke. John wished they would not; he felt as though he would never laugh at anything ever again. Mary caught his eye and the humour drained from her face. 'John, what is the matter? What is wrong?'

What was wrong? Did she not know? Surely he did not have to tell his own wife he was demoted, disgraced, destroyed? The bleakness in his heart swelled and nearly choked him. 'I need to go outside. I must walk.'

'I'll come with you,' she said promptly, but he whipped his arm out of hers.

'Alone!'

To his relief, she did not follow him.

The skies were leaden and heavy with snow. Horse Guards Parade, a grey gravel expanse surrounded by stuccoed buildings, looked washed out against a stone-coloured sky. The entrance to Downing Street was blocked off by a troop of horse fencibles, volunteers raised to defend the country against invasion and French principles. They had been here for a few weeks now, expecting reprisals following the end of the treason trials, but they parted to let John through unchallenged. They were used to seeing the Minister's brother, who was, after all, a member of the Cabinet. John ground his teeth at the thought.

Downing Street's spacious anterooms were generally filled with liveried messengers, travel-weary military men with despatches wrapped in oilskin, secretaries carrying reports from parliamentary committees, even the occasional French émigré in threadbare brocade. John could tell immediately from the lack of bustle that his brother was not in. He had not expected him to be, but his disappointment when Joe Smith confirmed it was still acute.

'Where has he gone?' John asked. The secretary shrugged.

'His country house, I suppose. He often goes for the weekend when Parliament is up.'

'But it's Monday.' Smith shrugged again, awkwardly. John looked keenly at him. 'Is he alone?'

'He will be back soon,' Smith said, but John shook his head.

'I asked you a question. Did my brother go alone?'

The secretary's expression was full of a pity that suggested he knew why John was asking. 'No.'

John did not need to ask who was with him. In any case, it hardly mattered. William was not in; but he was the Minister. He could not stay away indefinitely.

****

William returned to London the next day. John waited as long as he dared for his brother to send an explanation. When none came, he deluded himself for a while that William was too busy to write, but he soon realised the silence was much too complete.

After the Admiralty Board meeting he retired to his study and dipped his pen in ink.

'My dear Brother, I am impatient to see you, as I cannot but feel great anxiety on an occasion which involves in it every consideration that ought to be most dear to me. If you let me know when is convenient, I will either call upon you or shall be glad to see you here, as you please.'

The reply arrived promptly, borne to the Admiralty by one of William's junior footmen, his shoes white with dust from the gravel surface of Horse Guards Parade. John tore open the wrapper.

'I really can see no possibility that explanation or discussion can be of any advantage. I hoped I had said enough to show you that my opinion was formed on grounds which will not admit of its being changed, and in times like these I must act on that opinion, even with the sacrifice of the personal considerations which are nearest my heart.'

John winced. Either William was made of stone or he truly did not understand the difficulty, the uncertainty of his brother's position. John pulled another sheet of paper towards him and wrote again.

'I will not attempt to describe the pain which your letter has given me. I should be very sorry to urge anything that could be unpleasant to you, but I hope I am not unreasonable in earnestly desiring to see you, when

you recollect that I must continue to meet my colleagues in office and attend the King. Without something further passing between us I stand in a very perplexing situation.'

The response was just as prompt as the last.

'I will call upon you soon after 12 tomorrow. I trust your decision will have been such as to relieve me from the most anxious of all situations. My own opinion remains and must remain the same, and I can hardly bear to think to how painful an extremity I am necessarily driven if you cannot bring yourself to agree to what has been proposed.'

John screwed the letter into a ball and hurled it at the wall. "*12 o'clock!*" Did William not know the Admiralty Board met every day at 11? But of course William knew, just as John knew William would manage to be mysteriously unavailable at any other hour he should propose. And "*painful extremity*" – what did that mean? If John refused to step down from the Admiralty, would William dismiss him from the Cabinet altogether? Ask the King to order him out in disgrace? Abandon him to parliamentary censure? John was certain the threat was an empty one, and he resented it the more because he knew William was trying to frighten him.

Still, the talk of "painful extremities" gave him an idea. The thought of carrying out his plan made the bile rise in John's throat, but William, it seemed, left him no choice.

****

The last of the light had long fled, and Mary ordered a branch of candles to be lit so she could continue her work. Idleness made her thoughts whir round her head, and for the last few days John's mood had been so poor she could think of nothing good. She bit through a thread, picked out another colour in her workbox and squinted at the eye of her needle. Even though John had not confided in her about what was agitating him, she had a very good idea what it might be.

Even Georgiana had noticed John's short temper. 'What has happened to your husband, Mary? He is normally so calm. Has bad news arrived from the continent?'

Mary pulled the silk embroidery thread through the tautened fabric in her lap. She did not answer Georgiana's question directly. 'I confess I worry for him, George. He has not been himself for some time.'

'Not for months, I agree.' Georgiana sewed a little in silence. 'Ever since the news of Lord Howe's victory came in, I would say. Odd, is it not? The Admiralty received so much praise.'

'He's been ill,' Mary said noncommittally.

'But he is safe in office now. I should not suppose Mr Pitt could remove him from the Admiralty even if he wanted to. A year ago, perhaps, it would have made sense. But now ... Now, both Mr Pitt and Lord Chatham would look like fools.'

Mary hid her discomfort by pretending to hunt in her workbox for another skein of thread. Georgiana was right: John's losing his post now, six months after a tremendous victory, before the start of a parliamentary session, would not reflect well upon him at all. For any man, to lose their post under such circumstances would be crushing. For John, whose status and position meant so much to him, Mary could think of nothing worse.

At that moment John came in. He wore a pea-green velvet suit lined with pink silk, his wigless hair frizzed, powdered and drawn back into a queue. At the sight of him Mary felt her heart beat more quickly, and not just because he looked handsome. The determination in his eyes sent a chill through her.

He kissed her in a cloud of bergamot pomade. She reached up and placed a hand on his smoothly shaven cheek. 'Where are you going?'

'To the Cabinet dinner.'

'Lord Mansfield's dinner? But you said you had no intention of going.'

'I changed my mind,' he said. She twisted round to face him. The candlelight flickered across the tightness of his jaw. 'I need to speak with my brother.'

Mary could not decide whether to feel relief or concern at that, but she sensed John wanted nothing more than her support. 'I wish you luck.'

She watched him leave, then laid her embroidery down and pressed trembling hands to her cheeks. On balance, she decided she was more concerned than relieved. She had been married to John for 11 years now, more than long enough to recognise his need for constants in a life where everything was subject to comparison. She did not want to guess at what might happen if John were forced to choose between his brother and his reputation.

****

Lord Mansfield lived in the newest and most fashionable sector of town, Portland Place. His house was only a few doors away from the open fields that marked the end of urban development.

There were no guarantees John's plan would work, but the omens were good. William's carriage had already arrived; his footman was about to jump back onto the footplate. John called him over and gave him an order. John and William's servants were accustomed to taking orders from either brother; whenever they needed more staff, for a large dinner or a ball, the brothers often borrowed each other's best men. The footman passed on the message to the coachman, who whipped up the horses and drove off. The first part of John's plan was underway. Now he had to get through the ordeal of the dinner.

It was the first time he had appeared before his colleagues since his quarrel with Dundas. William mastered his surprise at John's unexpected appearance well enough, but John fancied there was anxiety in his brother's eyes, as though William were worried John might tackle him over the dinner table. John nearly bit his tongue at the thought. Windham and Spencer would have been agog, and John had no intention of gratifying Dundas with any sign of distress.

John was moving around the table to his seat when Windham cried out: 'My Lord Chatham! I wish to congratulate you on your new office.'

The hum of conversation around the table quietened. John curled his hand around his chair. He had wondered whether his colleagues knew of William's plans for him. Now he knew the answer.

'I wished you joy as Privy Seal,' Windham said, amiably enough, his large, dark eyes shining with something unfathomable. 'I understand you are to have it when you leave the Admiralty.'

John's eyes flicked to Lord Spencer, the current Privy Seal. Spencer's freckled skin flushed to the roots of his powdered red hair. 'I have not yet made up my mind to take it.'

'That is your choice, my lord.'

It was perfectly clear that Windham believed it was not his choice. John's mouth tightened grimly but he slipped into his seat without another word. A few minutes later the conversations around the table resumed.

John passed most of the evening watching William, waiting for the signal, and at length it came. He had not expected his brother to remain long in company that was not entirely congenial to him, and before the tablecloth was removed for dessert William threw down his napkin and made his excuses. John waited until his brother had left the room before rising in turn. He turned to Lord Mansfield. 'I must apologise, my lord, but I have business.'

'Need sleep, more like,' came a mutter from the other end of the table and a choked-off laugh in response. Mansfield's gimlet-like eyes sought for the offender, but if Windham had spoken he was engrossed in mopping up the sauce on his plate with a mouthful of bread. Mansfield turned back to John.

'As you wish, Lord Chatham.'

John caught up with William in the entrance hall. His brother had his greatcoat on and remonstrated with the porter. 'What do you mean, it is not here? It must be here.'

'Sir, I have not seen your carriage all evening.'

'I gave orders to my man to wait at the door at half past nine. What am I to do? Take a hackney carriage?'

John took a deep breath and stepped out of the shadows. 'That is unnecessary, brother. Travel with me.'

William's freckled cheeks had been flushed with frustration, but the moment he laid eyes on John they drained of colour. 'You are not staying for the third service?'

'I thought you might need assistance getting home.'

John gave William a direct look. William looked confused, but then John's words registered and anger chased across his face. 'I would not put you to the inconvenience.'

'It will take my coachman all of 20 minutes to take you to Downing Street. It will be no inconvenience whatever. Unless, of course, you had rather walk?'

For a moment, John thought he might actually do it, but although William had drunk deeply of Mansfield's excellent wine he had not completely lost his good sense. For the Prime Minister to walk unattended around London at a time when popular hatred of him was high would be positively foolhardy. William said nothing, but gathered his greatcoat about him defensively and stood aside to allow John access to the threshold.

John's coachman had been walking the horses back and forth all evening. On John's appearance, the footman jumped down, opened the door and pulled down the steps. William stared at the compartment as though it were a cart taking him to Tyburn, then grabbed the strap and pulled himself in. John took the opposite bench and the coachman whipped up the horses.

It was raining, a thick, sleety mix hurled against the glass panes of the carriage by bursts of wind. The braziers were full of embers and John could feel their heat at his heels, but from the knees up he was frozen. Now that he had William in the carriage John became aware his head was aching. The words he had been rehearsing all evening abandoned him.

The glass-fronted lamp swinging in the compartment threw strange shadows across William's tense face. Anger quivered behind every word. 'What, pray, have you done with my carriage?'

'I told your coachman you were coming home with me.'

'How prescient of you,' William said. 'You said yourself it will take 20 minutes to drive to Downing Street. Is that enough time for you to say your piece?'

'I am no fool, Will. I've given my man instructions to drive us up and down until we are finished.'

William gave John a disbelieving glare and looked out of the window. The fury and alarm on his face when he saw they were indeed travelling away from Downing Street gave John pause, but it was too late. William forced out between clenched teeth, 'Well then, I have been well and truly kidnapped by my own brother.'

For a short while nothing but the rattle of carriage wheels and the clip of horses' hooves disturbed the silence. John's headache was growing worse. He closed his eyes and rubbed his temples. William said, more softly, 'I hope you are not about to experience a return of your complaint.'

John took a deep breath and plunged in. 'I admit I have felt materially worse in myself since receiving your letter dismissing me from the Admiralty.'

A frostiness fell instantly, as though John had pulled down the glass and brought the weather inside. 'A discussion of my decision can only distress us both, and change nothing.'

'Do you not see I need more from you than that? What you have decided may well lead to my complete public disgrace.'

'What more do you want?' William snapped. 'You will retain a seat in Cabinet. Is that not enough?'

'No,' John said quietly. 'It is not.'

'Then what in God's name *do* you want? Yes, the Privy Seal will mean a small reduction in your salary, but your Cabinet standing will be higher.'

John shook his head. 'The Privy Seal is a glorified sinecure. The Admiralty is not a sinecure. It is a real office, with real responsibility, and no-one will believe you have taken it from me for any reason but that you feel I am unfit for the office.'

'Nobody said you were unfit for it.'

'Is that so?' John said. He crossed his arms. 'In that case, there is something you are not telling me. Something you do not want me to know.'

'I told you in my letter.' William's voice was strained: here was a man who was trying, very hard, not to tell the whole truth, and it was painfully obvious to one who knew him. 'You are mistaken if you suppose I have any particular circumstance to state which has caused your removal. I must have the best government fitted to fight a desperate war; and our new arrangements, our new colleagues—'

'His Grace of Portland and his friends, yes.' John had wondered how long it would take William to mention the coalition. 'Lord Spencer currently holds the Privy Seal, which you would have me take. Will he succeed me at the Admiralty?'

The sound of wheels turning and horses walking filled the silence.

'I have not yet devoted much thought to that,' William hedged. 'I—'

'Who is to succeed me?' John insisted. When William did not immediately reply, he added, 'Come, brother, in all your avowed ruminations on my removal, you must have fixed on my replacement. What would it say about your feelings for me if you had not?'

For a moment John wondered whether his brother would simply refuse to answer, but at length William gave up. 'Very well. Yes. You and Lord Spencer are to exchange offices.'

At least that explained Windham's glee and Spencer's awkwardness that evening. John experienced a flash of anger, but he could not deny he had expected the news. There was more behind William's reticence that John was determined to tease out. 'I trust you know what you are doing, giving such men control of Britain's navy. I say nothing of Portland – he seems decent enough. I speak of men like Mansfield, who loves you little, and of Windham, who loves you not at all.'

'I trust I am equal to whatever lies ahead,' William said frostily. 'Dundas and Grenville remain in the Cabinet, as will you, even as Privy Seal.'

John sat back in triumph. 'I am glad to hear you say so, William. Very glad.'

'I do not understand.'

'No? Very well, I shall speak plainly. You have talked much of our new colleagues. But only now have you mentioned our old ones.' John smiled mirthlessly. 'You took Dundas with you out of town, did you not? After my quarrel with him in Cabinet. I'm willing to bet that subject came up at least once.'

'You will have to speak plainer than that,' William snapped.

'I do not think so, but if you wish … Did Dundas make me the price of his continuance in office?' For the first time John got the impression William was truly afraid to answer. Dread shifted in his stomach but he ignored it: he needed to know. 'Will, answer me. Did Dundas threaten resignation if you did not remove me from the Admiralty?'

The sound of the carriage wheels turning over the cobbles filled the compartment again. William closed his eyes and nodded.

The confirmation of John's fears hurt more than he had anticipated. He said, coldly, 'So, forced to choose between Dundas and me, you chose the Scottish turncoat? My blood, my name, my reputation sacrificed to keep a driveller in office a little longer?' Inside John something burst and filled him with venom. He spat out the bitterness, each word a dart aimed at William's heart. 'I know the value you place on Dundas's abilities, but even *Judas* would not do such a thing to his own brother.'

'John …' William's voice trembled. 'John, listen—'

But John was beyond listening. He knew, of course, that Dundas was William's main ally in the Commons, that he had even more weight in Cabinet now Portland's followers formed so large a faction there. It was the way William had treated John as a pawn on a chessboard with no weight, no voice, no opinion, that hurt the most.

'Ask me to lay down my life and I will do so without demur, if it would buy you even a moment's respite.' Anger and humiliation choked John's voice to a gasp. 'But do not ask me to disgrace myself for the convenience of Henry Dundas.'

'It was necessary for the good of the country,' William protested, white-faced. It was the usual platitude and it offered John even less consolation than before.

'No, Will. You have done this for the good of yourself.'

Outside the sleet had turned to snow. It fell in silent, feathery flakes, coating the frozen cobbles in a thin white layer. The oil lamps plunged half William's face into shadow and exaggerated the thinness of his lips, the icy glint in his eyes. 'I do not take your meaning.'

John smiled sardonically. 'You talk of duty and heartache, and how much it pains you to subject me to this. Do not expect me to share your self-pity. You have made no sacrifice. You remain, in office, untouched – despite all your blunders.'

'I have justified myself enough to Parliament over the past two years. I do not intend to go over it all again now.'

'Nor do you need to. I have always stood by you; I have always supported you. And how have you repaid me? All I hear are rumours of my incompetence, spread by our new allies, spread by Dundas, for whom you expect me to destroy myself.'

'I hope you do not think I believe such rumours?'

'Even if you do not, these rumours must have influenced your decision. It must be so much easier to cut me loose than to give me a chance to prove them wrong.'

'You're mad,' William said flatly.

'Then grant me an inquiry into my conduct.'

'You *are* mad!'

'Why?' John launched. 'Because I wish to defend myself? You know as well as I do my dismissal will be debated the moment Parliament reconvenes. The opposition will want to know why I have been removed. In God's name, let me tell them.'

'No!' William gasped. He took a moment to control himself, then continued. 'I know how this will look and I am sorry for it, but *please* believe that *I have no choice*.'

'You did have a choice,' John said, quietly. 'The fact is, Will, you did not choose me.'

'I told you there would be no benefit in our debating this.' William rapped against the slats to communicate with the coachman. 'Stop the carriage.'

The carriage rumbled to a halt at Charing Cross, at the foot of the empty stocks. William wrenched open the door. His leather-soled shoes skidded on the icy pavement and he only stopped himself from falling by grabbing hold of the footman who had approached to help him down. Even at this hour the area thronged with crowds of the lower sort. John shouted, 'Have a care, William, you'll have your throat cut.'

'I'll take my chances.'

William launched off towards Whitehall. John caught up with him opposite the equestrian statue of Charles I and pulled him back. 'When have I ever given you reason to doubt me? You brought me into your Cabinet because you trusted me. You even told me once that I saved your life.'

William stopped so abruptly he nearly slipped over again. John hardly recognised his brother's deep-toned voice in the emotional hiss that came out of his mouth. 'I have had enough of your selfishness. Every time we argue you reel off the same catalogue of good deeds like some Catholic running through his Hail Marys, as though they somehow atone for your past actions.'

For a moment John felt as though the world had collapsed beneath him, leaving him teetering on the brink of a precipice. His horror seemed likely to pull him in and drown him; then anger flooded his veins and buoyed him up as the full weight of William's words registered. William saw the fury sweep across John's face. His hard, white expression changed instantly to fear. He held out the hand he had just wrenched out of his brother's grip as though John had leprosy. 'Upon my word, I am sorry, I did not mean—'

'Atonement?' John cut in. 'What for?'

'I spoke too hurriedly. I did not intend—'

'What have I to atone for, William?' John interrupted. 'When have I ever failed you? When have I ever given you reason to suppose me unreliable?'

William's eyes were round, his teeth clenched. He looked at John as though begging him to stop. And then it hit John, with great force. "*Unreliable*". He was plunged back 16 years to the library of Hayes Place, his father lying dead upstairs. "*It has always been that way, has it not? Always late, always unreliable. You never think of how others might feel.*"

He took a step forwards. William took a corresponding one backwards. John saw pain in his brother's eyes and went for the vulnerability like a hound scenting blood. 'Good God, Will, is that what you believe? That everything I have done for you I have done, not because I am your brother, but because of a fundamental deficiency in our relations?'

'I said nothing of the sort,' William protested, without much spirit.

'Is this meant to be my penance?'

'I beg your pardon?'

'The Privy Seal,' John ground out. 'Did you think I would rush to cover myself in ridicule to offset past mistakes?' The words tore themselves out of him, drenched in bitterness. 'You must think I am nothing but a sentimental fool.'

A group of onlookers had gathered behind the statue of Charles I to witness their quarrel, with all a crowd's unerring attraction to high drama. William clearly knew it would not be long before they were recognised and their argument became copy for the next day's newspapers. He spoke hurriedly. 'John, listen. As far as concerns your office my hands are tied, more than I think you realise. Regarding what happened in the past, we cannot allow it to come between us.'

'Then you should have let it lie,' John snapped. 'But since you insist on re-opening old wounds, let me tell you how I felt when Papa died and I joined my regiment in Gibraltar. I felt grief, anger, guilt – enough of each to wash away the sin of my leaving you ten times over. But it wasn't a sin, Will. It was a mistake, and if you think it has guided my conduct for the past 16 years then you do not deserve to call yourself my brother.'

A stricken look came onto William's face; then there was only anger. His fingers dug into John's arm like blades. 'How can you talk about it as though it doesn't signify? I had just lost my father!'

'So had I,' John said. William flinched and struck back.

'You left me at my most vulnerable moment, without a thought for anyone but yourself. I knew then what I could expect from you. I learned I could never rely on you when it truly mattered. Never.'

The words were those John had always most dreaded to hear, and yet they came almost as a relief. 'If what I did at my worst moment means more to you than the sacrifices I made for you at my best, then I pity you.'

William did not try to follow him any further; this last sally seemed to have nailed him to the frozen cobbles. John did not dare look at William's face. It took all his strength to take those steps away from his brother, across the road, and out of sight and sound.

****

Mary was just drifting off to sleep, huddled under the blankets, when she heard footsteps. She sat up, her heart pounding. 'Georgiana?'

The floorboards creaked and a shadow appeared through the gap between the door and the floor. Her husband's voice reached her. 'Go to sleep, Mary.'

She pushed off the covers and shoved back the bed curtains, ignoring the chill air needling her skin through her nightgown. John was halfway to the library by the time she wrenched open the door. 'Did you speak with William?'

A few candles still burned in their mirrored sconces. They glinted off the silver buttons on his elegant green coat, the same coat that had made him look so handsome earlier that evening. He did not look handsome now. His face, half-plunged in shadow, was hard; cold fury blazed from him like an aura. Not once in their 11 years of marriage had John given her cause to fear him, but Mary found herself shrinking back and clutching for the support of the latch.

'Yes, I did,' he said.

Mary's breath caught. So he *had* lost the Admiralty. Everything about him screamed at her to drop the subject, but she knew too well what was at stake. She ran to him and took his hand. It felt dry and cold. 'Did you argue?'

Close up she could see the exhaustion under his anger, and the vulnerability in the downward twist of his lips wrenched her heart. 'You could say that.'

'Will you speak with him again?'

'I do not think there is much point,' John said, with a sneer. Mary's alarm deepened.

'William needs you, John.' *And you need William*. But her words were wasted. A lifetime of bitterness poured into John's response: 'He does not.'

She dropped his hand as though it had caught fire. Another chill coursed down her spine, and she had to remind herself that this anger was not focused at her, that she merely happened to be in the way of it, catching the brunt of its acid sweep through his heart.

****

John did not reappear all night. Mary lay alone in their great bed, remembering how terrified she had been when he had first taken office – terrified he would be swallowed whole in the vicissitudes of public life. Now that her fears were becoming reality, she refused to see him cast aside without fighting. She stared into the darkness as the hours crawled past and felt her despair solidify into determination.

At dawn she dressed and choked down a cupful of coffee. She stopped outside the library, but not a sound came from inside. She knew better than to suppose John was asleep.

She and her maid walked swiftly to Downing Street. She had never approached her brother-in-law on her own account before, and even accompanied by a servant she did not know whether it was strictly proper, but she had to try. Seeing John in such distress filled her heart with bleakness.

It was still early, but Mary was relieved to see lights burning on all floors of Downing Street, and to hear the bustle of activity from the enormous kitchens. William's secretary was too astonished to protest when she asked for him to send his master to the drawing room. Minutes later William himself came in.

Mary stopped tugging nervously at her gloves. The mixture of relief and anger at the sight of him almost overpowered her. Relief, because he was going to give her a chance to say her piece; anger, because he had always had the power to hurt her husband more than anyone in the world, and last night had used that power.

'Lady Chatham.' William bent over her hand. Mary was pleased to see he had deep rings under his eyes. She had never been able to read her enigmatic brother-in-law's thoughts, but love for John made her bold; she swallowed, and lifted her chin.

'Mr Pitt. I must ask a favour.'

The coldness in his eyes intensified, but he smiled. He was getting over his surprise at finding her in his house, and re-establishing control over himself. 'Of course, dear Lady Chatham. Anything for you and yours.'

Mary's hands tightened into fists. If William thought he was going to sweep her aside as a woman petitioning for her family he would soon find the stakes had risen too high. 'I do not know what happened between you and my husband last night. I am not certain I wish to find out. But I do know you have his reputation, his very self, in your hands.'

'If you wish me to keep your husband at the Admiralty, you must know nothing would give me more pleasure, but it is impossible.'

'I realise there have been engagements made.' She forced herself to meet William's steely gaze. 'But to dismiss him now, without a defeat or scandal, without any apparent reason, is too cruel.'

'The arrangement will be so discreet that—' William began, but Mary was ready for him.

'Your discretion will look like avoiding confrontation. My husband has been attacked for over a year now. You know how much he values his dignity and reputation.' William looked at her. There was nothing for it; she would have to plead. She closed her eyes and threw all her love into the task. 'I ask only that you wait, William. Three months; six. No more than that. But to remove him now, with no chance to defend himself, will destroy him.'

He blinked at the use of his Christian name, but otherwise Mary felt she was talking to a statue. He said, in a strained voice, 'Lady Chatham, I cannot.'

William's gaze was level and piercing, but there was something distant in it, something she could not touch. She realised she had her hands clasped before her as though begging. She unlinked them.

Mary had known John and William since childhood. She had always felt John, shackled to the Earldom, was less certain of his identity, whereas William had always known who and what he was. And yet, as much as they quarrelled, the brothers complemented each other perfectly. Mary did not fully comprehend their bond, but she respected it.

This went beyond a quarrel. This was a dagger in the heart of their brotherhood. She refused to believe William did not see it; she refused to believe his heart was so much cast into stone he did not care.

She stepped forwards and saw a flicker of doubt in her brother-in-law's grey eyes. 'What I most love in my husband is his ability to set himself aside, to think only of his duty to others. But in this, Mr Pitt, you have thought only of yourself, and for that I will never forgive you.'

She turned from him and left before the trembling of her hands gave her away.

****

The Admiralty clock chimed three in the morning, and for the third night running John was wide awake to hear it. He brought the candelabrum closer and glared at the half-empty decanter before him until it blurred.

He could hear the snapping of the threads tying him and his brother together, feel the distance widening between them. This deep, wrenching wound, freshly inflicted and bubbling with blood, was one he could not easily forgive. William's words had transformed all the companionship and affection between them into a lie. He had spoken of atonement for a mistake John had made in his youth; but John did not know if William would ever make up for his own error.

At four John moved into the study to write. He covered several expensive, gold-edged sheets of paper with abortive sentences before, finally, finding the right words. He rubbed his hand through his hair, causing a shower of powder to fall onto the page, and wrote:

'My dear brother, I have not been able to compose myself sufficiently since our conversation to put pen to paper. But what makes me wish to write you these few lines, is that I am aware I have said nothing of my personal feelings towards you, which I can assure you arose only from finding myself unequal to doing it. The recollection of the affection which has uninterruptedly subsisted between us from our earliest days makes me feel the present circumstances doubly painful; but whatever may be my fate in life, I shall sincerely wish for your honour and prosperity.

Believe me, very affectionately yours, Chatham.'

190

John stared at the letter, dry-eyed and dry-mouthed, until the maid-of-all-work came to sweep the grate and lay a new fire. He gritted his teeth and made a firm decision. He sprinkled pounce over the sheet even though the words had long dried; folded it four times into an envelope; melted a gob of wax onto the flap; and sealed it, firmly, with the ring on his right hand.

He hesitated on the threshold, but only for a moment. Then he closed the door and left with a heavy step.

Chapter Twenty

June 1795

John gazed out of the carriage window and dreaded seeing his mother. Although he had not breathed a syllable of his rift with William in his letters to her, others would have had no such reticence. He had never forgotten how she had pleaded with him to support his brother all those years ago when William had first been offered the Treasury. What if Mama felt he had, finally, broken his promise?

He did not think he could stand any more judgment. As John had predicted, his transfer to the Privy Seal had attracted ridicule from all quarters. When John first appeared in Parliament in his new capacity he had to run a gauntlet of abuse:

'If it isn't the *late* First Lord of the Admiralty!'

'The august keeper of the King's Privy Seal!'

'I trust your new duties are not too *onerous*, my lord?'

These were the thoughts that needled him every day, every moment, poisoning his humour and souring his mood. He and William could not avoid each other completely, of course; they had to meet occasionally at cabinets and levees, but so far they had limited themselves to greeting each other coldly. John had resolved not to be the one to make the first move towards reconciliation, but the longer it took for William to approach him, the more bitter John became. Six months had now passed since their quarrel and John was still waiting.

John glanced across at his wife. Mary's eyes were fixed on the passing landscape. She had always been perfectly attuned to her husband's attitudes and desires, but now that he no longer knew where he stood with himself, let alone anyone else, Mary also seemed to have become as rudderless as a storm-stricken ship.

The carriage climbed out of Langport and John felt his heart constrict. Travelling through the familiar landscape of his childhood always brought back memories, and the little village of Curry Rivel with its square-towered church, cottages and hay-strewn lanes had hardly changed. But as the carriage drew up outside Burton Pynsent he had to make a conscious effort to compose himself. A welcoming committee had formed beneath the portico. Mrs Stapleton, his mother's companion, clutched a shawl against the bitter wind. Beside her was John's brother-in-law Edward Eliot, his face prematurely aged by a grief that had only grown since Harriot's death. His hands rested on the shoulders of his daughter, eight-year-old Harriot Hester. Before them all was John's mother, leaning heavily on her cane with swollen-knuckled hands.

Little Harriot Hester wriggled out of her father's embrace, ran down the steps with her pink silk sash trailing behind her and launched herself into Mary's arms. 'Aunt Chatham! Uncle Chatham!'

Mary smiled and bent to accept the embrace. John stroked the little girl's head fondly, but kept his eyes on his mother. The expression on Hester Chatham's strong-boned face was worse than the judgment he had half-expected to find. She looked sad and uncomfortable, as though someone had died and she hardly knew how to offer condolences.

'Oh, Johnny,' she murmured, and his resolution to maintain a dignified aloofness crumbled. He closed his eyes against the tears. His mother came down the steps and clasped him to her tightly, just as she had done when he had woken from nightmares as a child, floating free in the darkness, disorientated, lost.

****

After dinner Mrs Stapleton took out her embroidery, and Eliot and the little girl sat down to a game of backgammon. Mary hung over Harriot Hester's shoulder and gave her assistance. John found himself by the window with Mama. Since their emotional meeting neither of them had breathed a word of what had happened over the past six months. John could see Lady Chatham was working up to it. She sat in her padded chair wrapped in shawls, her arthritic hands clasped. Her eyes rested on Harriot Hester.

'My niece is much grown,' John observed.

Lady Chatham studied her eldest son for a moment. 'She has outgrown all her clothes. Mrs Capper has had to find another seamstress in Langport, because the one in Curry cannot keep up.'

John watched Mary whisper into Harriot's ear. The little girl moved one of her backgammon pieces, and Mary whispered something else. Little Harriot giggled. Something about the scene fed John's sense of loss and obsolescence. He rose from his chair. A rustle and the click of a cane on the floorboards told him his mother followed.

'John …' she began, but tailed off. She could not alter what had happened and they both knew it. John was aware he had clothed himself in righteous humiliation as though it were armour. He knew many judged him for it, but so long as it repelled unwanted pity or dismay, he did not much care.

'I suppose,' he said, stiffly, 'you are going to take me to task?'

'Whatever for? You have done nothing wrong.'

The bitter taste in John's mouth intensified. 'My brother disagrees. You'll have to ask him why.'

'I do not need to ask him anything. He tells me all.' John snorted so hard the window misted in front of his face. Lady Chatham placed a hand on his arm. He could feel her fingers trembling through his fine woollen coat. 'I worry for you, my son.'

'I am astonished to hear that,' John said. His anger took himself by surprise. 'You have always been more likely to worry about my brother.'

'I worry for both of you.'

'Which is why you are about to tell me I must stand by my brother, are you not?'

'William,' Lady Chatham murmured. 'Your brother's name is William.'

'Is it really?' John said. 'I had forgotten.'

Lady Chatham tugged at her shawl. 'You are William's only remaining sibling. You must know your assistance is more valuable to him than ever. Please speak with him.'

'Give me one reason why I should!' John shouted, and his mother shrank back as though he had struck her.

At the backgammon table Mary straightened, but Eliot stood and whispered a few words in her ear. Mary shot John an expression of doubt, then slowly sank into Eliot's place at the backgammon board.

Eliot came over and took John's arm. 'Harriot is still young, but she has her mother's brains. I find I cannot play backgammon with her without developing a headache. Will you take a turn with me in the saloon?'

Eliot was already guiding John out; John recognised he was not being given a choice. The last person he wanted to talk to was his brother's closest friend, but neither did he want to remain here with Mama. The headache Eliot had used as a pretext was growing very much a reality for John, and he did not have the strength to fight.

The saloon was on the ground floor, with a view across the terrace towards Sedgemoor. The sky was the colour of lead and the burgundy-painted walls covered with Italianate paintings looked dark and depressing. The black of Eliot's coat and breeches contrasted with the paleness of his face. He leaned against one of the chairs lining the wall but did not sit. John took up a reluctant station opposite.

'I wanted to thank you and Lady Chatham for allowing Harriot Hester to spend the winter with you in London,' Eliot began after a pause. 'She still talks about it now, and asks when she can return.'

Gratitude and affection pierced John's defensiveness. 'We were happy to have her. Mary much wishes for a daughter of her own.' He left that hanging for a moment, then decided he could not possibly make the conversation any more awkward by adding, 'And she reminds us of my sister.'

Mentioning Harriot was always a gamble, for Eliot had never really emerged from the black fog of mourning her unexpected death. Eliot's face went waxy, but he said only, 'She is very like her mother.'

John had always thought the red-haired, snub-nosed Harriot Hester looked more like her father than anyone, but he said nothing. A memory flashed into John's mind of the time, long ago, when he had come upon Eliot and his sister cosily ensconced together in Vauxhall Gardens. Time had polished away much of the detail, but he would never forget the way Harriot's hand had floated close to Eliot's on the table-top, or the fondness glistening in Eliot's eyes as she talked. The young, fresh-faced boy who had surrendered his heart to Harriot all those years ago was now a gaunt-cheeked, prematurely aged man who was still in love with a ghost.

Yet John knew Eliot would now scold him for remaining overly attached to the past. He dreaded it; although he wore his hurt like a badge for all to see, it came from something intensely private, and he had no wish to share it with anyone.

At length, it came. Eliot uncrossed his arms. 'You were unfair on your mother.'

'I do not think so.'

'You would force her to take sides,' Eliot said quietly. 'You cannot do it. She loves you, Chatham, but she loves Pitt just as much. If she thinks Pitt has wronged you, I am certain she believes you have wronged Pitt.' John snorted. Eliot asked the question John was tired of hearing from all quarters. 'Have you spoken with your brother?'

'No, I have not,' John said, so harshly Eliot's white face infused with colour. 'I should have known you would line up to hurl abuse at me. You've always been his friend rather than mine.'

'Far from it. Were I not your friend, I would not have intervened when you attacked your mother earlier.'

'I did not attack—'

'No,' Eliot agreed. 'You did not. But you would have done, had I not stepped in.' John was silent. Eliot was right: William's betrayal lanced through him like a throbbing wound, and anyone who touched it received the brunt of his agony, no matter who they were. 'As your friend, then, I ask you to listen. I do not pretend I have earned the right to your trust, but I am your brother as much as I am Pitt's.'

The sun was setting. Shadows grew longer and the burgundy of the walls deepened to the shade of blood. John drew one of the chairs away from the wall and sank into it. 'I do trust you.'

The sharpness on Eliot's face softened in relief. He, too, drew a chair and leaned over his knees. 'I suppose you know Pitt has been indisposed?'

William's fits of gout were a regular occurrence now. John, like William himself, had got used to them. 'Of course I know. I am still a member of the Cabinet.'

'You know, then, that he still drinks.'

From the drawing room came the sound of cheering. John guessed Mary had allowed Harriot Hester to win the backgammon game. He shifted in his chair; talk of William's escalated drinking unsettled him. He tried to tell himself it was none of his concern, but he could not get the Duke of Rutland out of his mind. He had seen Rutland reach determinedly for the decanter much as William had been doing ever since the war had begun to go badly.

'I have spent the last eight years living in Pitt's house,' Eliot said, adding shakily, 'The house Harriot died in. At first I remained because I was afraid I might abandon a part of *her* if I left. But latterly I have remained because I know Pitt needs me to stay.' Eliot paused. 'People used to say Pitt and I were like brothers, even before I married Harriot. But you truly *are* his brother, Chatham. You know him better than anyone, certainly better than I. That is why you must speak with him. We are all he has left. Pitt has nobody but us.'

'He has plenty of friends. Dundas.' John spat the name with distaste. 'Our cousin Grenville.'

'I say nothing of Dundas, but Grenville is turning away from Pitt more and more. He is vehemently against any peace with the Republicans, whereas Pitt is warming to the idea out of necessity. He and Grenville are, I fear, parting ways, and I do not think Pitt can afford to lose another friendship.'

A sour taste came into John's mouth. 'It won't affect him more than losing mine.'

'My dear Chatham,' Eliot said. 'It is killing him.'

The simplicity of that statement brought John up short. He gave a nervous laugh. 'What do you mean?'

'Have you not noticed? I suppose you have not been living with him. You have not seen the marks of exhaustion on his face.'

'It is the war,' John said, adding bitterly, 'I have given him time enough to come to me; he has not done so. He may regret Grenville's friendship, but I can only conclude he has little regard for mine.'

John's anger with his brother surged again, and with it the bitterness and frustration of his situation. He rose restlessly and paced back to the tall windows. Dusk was drawing in, great fingers of darkness reaching up the flagstones of the terrace. For a while both men said nothing. John was trying very hard not to think of anything; Eliot must have been putting his thoughts in order.

Eliot spoke at length. 'How can you say such a thing?'

'I think my brother's treatment of me speaks for itself,' John ground out.

'Chatham, please think. Pitt needs you.'

'He may need *you*.'

'He needs both of us,' Eliot insisted. 'My ties to Pitt are strong, I grant you; but the ties of blood are stronger. You are right to fault Pitt for his behaviour, but he is no ordinary man.'

'I know,' John said, with poison in his voice. 'I have heard nothing else all my life.'

'You do not understand. Power changes a man, no matter how good, no matter how brave. Pitt is surrounded by flatterers, men who have known him only as Minister. He has become accustomed to his every wish being carried out in an instant: men come to him, not he to them. He cannot see what has happened to him, but we, his friends, must accept it is what he has become. He tells us half-truths, he dissembles, but he still needs us, and when his manner drives us away, he crumbles.'

John shook his head. 'I don't feel it.'

'It's his way,' Eliot said, mildly. 'The Minister in him sees every selfless act on our part as his due. We that love him must take him as he is.'

John was touched that his brother might have such a friend, but he knew his brother-in-law was very religious, and suspected his willingness to give William the benefit of a doubt came more from Christian charity than true conviction. John could not think of William in such terms, not yet; the prospect that he might still owe something to his brother was one he was not yet ready to face.

'So what should I do?' he said at last, bleakly. 'Should I forgive him?' Eliot nodded and John felt despair welling inside. 'I do not know that I can.'

'It may be that you have to go further, and find forgiveness for yourself.'

'I have nothing to reproach myself for,' John said immediately, and coldly. 'I have no need to beg my brother's pardon.'

'That is not what I meant,' Eliot murmured.

Chapter Twenty-one

September 1795

The wind flung icy drizzle into John's face as he rode out from his mother's dower-house. The haze and the low clouds, trapped by the Sedgemoor hills, prevented a view even as far as Burton Pynsent itself.

St Aubin, his valet, had been surprised at his resolve to go out, but John had been adamant. He rarely made more than one visit a year to his mother, but even though he had had no intention of being at Burton Pynsent while his brother was visiting, he knew this might be his only chance to talk with William away from the distractions of London. He was determined to put his flying visit to good use.

John tethered his horse to a stile near the monumental pillar his father had erected on Troy Hill, struggling to secure the leather straps with hands slick with rain. He squinted at the lantern-shaped viewing platform at the top of the pillar, framed against the ash-coloured sky. Nobody was there. He drew out his watch to check the time, but his hands were half-numbed with cold and the fob caught against the band of his leather riding breeches. One of his seals flew off into the long grass. John cursed. Losing his seal was an ill omen, but he had no time to look for it now.

The steps up to the viewing platform were covered with moss and slippery with damp. John and his siblings had often climbed the tower as children, but no-one had been here for many years. Grass grew through cracks in the stones. A single pigeon eyed John in a startled manner before flying off in a burst of feathers. The view across Sedgemoor was truncated by the bad weather, but the feeling of being enveloped in fog, cut off from the rest of the world, seemed fitting under the circumstances. John wiped bat droppings off the surface of the stone bench, sat down, and waited.

Little time passed before he heard hoof-beats. John thrust out his booted legs and concentrated on making grooves in the moss with his spurs. Footsteps echoed up the monument's winding staircase. They seemed to John to be slower than necessary. A few moments later

William appeared. He sat opposite John with a sigh and began mopping the rain off his face with his handkerchief.

John tried to keep his expression neutral, which was not easy. He experienced, again, the alarm he had felt upon seeing William for the first time the day before. William was only 36 but he might have been a decade years older. Gout had plagued him on and off since March, and a catalogue of woes weighed heavily on his shoulders: domestic bread riots; Prussia's separate peace; still more continental disasters. The exertion of climbing the hundred steps to the top of the tower had robbed him of breath. John was damned, however, if he would let his concern show. This meeting had been called on his terms, and that was how it would be carried out.

William folded the handkerchief back into his pocket, pressed a hand to his forehead and said, 'If I did not know you better, I would say you called me up here in the hopes that I might die making the effort to climb those stairs.'

John looked coldly at him. William's eyes lost some of their humorous sparkle and his expression became more circumspect. He glanced down at his crossed arms.

The wind whistled through the pillars of the viewing platform. John sat stiff-backed, listening to the soft sound of the rain striking the stone column. He avoided his brother's gazes. After a space, William spoke. 'Brrr, it's cold. Why are we sitting out here when we could be playing a round of cards with Mama and our little niece?'

'We can talk better here,' John said, curtly, trying to ignore the chattering of his teeth. He felt safer here, on neutral ground.

'You might have spoken to me at any time since your arrival yesterday.' William picked grass burrs off the tails of his coat. 'Since you are staying only a few days, and you were only here three months ago, I take it you made the journey to see me – so what on earth have you to say that you cannot tell me indoors, in the warmth?'

'You know perfectly well what I want to talk about.' William flinched. John bit off the instinct to continue, for it would not do to lose his temper this early in the conversation. He had promised himself to see this through, for his own peace of mind. He softened his tone. 'I hear you've been ill.'

'Not very,' William replied, impenetrably. It was so short a response that John could do very little with it. He struggled for a moment, then gave up.

'Glad to hear it.'

Silence again. William inspected his gloves. He must have been just as alarmed as John was to find that they could not even have an inconsequential talk without shadows hanging over them. 'How long are you here?'

'Not long. Mary is with her parents at Frognal. I plan to join her there for a week or two before we return to town.'

Awkward silence again. John's mind raced desperately for a way to keep his brother talking. He could think of nothing but politics, which always brought out the side of William he found most difficult to relate to, but in view of the alternatives it was the safest option. 'I hear our friend young Camden is to go to Ireland?'

He could see at once that he had lit upon the perfect subject. William's face cleared. 'Yes, it seems likely. It will please me much to have an ally in Dublin again.'

'Ireland will need careful handling,' John acknowledged, trying not to remember that the last time his brother had sent a friend, Rutland, to Ireland, the results had been tragic. 'Camden is the perfect choice. He has a conciliatory manner. I recall what Ireland was like when I went there in '86; there is much poverty and misery there.'

'I had forgotten you went to Ireland.' William had only been out of England once, to France for six weeks before becoming Minister. John had been round the world, to Canada and the West Indies, and fought for the Crown; William had hardly seen anything at all save for the University of Cambridge and the clubs of London. And yet it was William, not John, who planned the campaigns; William, who had no idea what Holland was like, or Toulon, or Corsica, or any other place that had made the news recently. John felt a prick of injustice; he fought it. This was not the time or the place.

He said, instead, 'Camden must beware not to follow the path of conciliation too far. Past Lord Lieutenants have been too willing to listen to Ireland's Catholics. In peacetime, I'd say nothing of it, but we are at war and the French will take advantage of any Catholic disaffection. Camden must stamp it out, with force if necessary.'

William had been following John's words eagerly enough; now John was aware of a chill that had nothing to do with the weather. 'You think Camden ought to ally himself with the Protestants against the Catholics?'

John could not quite believe his brother disagreed. 'The Catholics will be poison in the system for years to come. If control is to be re-established, it will be with the help of the Protestant interest, who have always been our friends.'

William said nothing, but gave John a look that combined irritation and suspicion with a surprising amount of affection. That glint of amused exasperation in his brother's eyes disconcerted John. It was as though seeing something that had been so much a part of their closeness, after so long an estrangement, undermined the seriousness of their quarrel.

There had been a time, and not so long ago either, when he and William could have spoken on any topic in complete cordiality. For the first time John began seriously to doubt whether they could ever conquer their awkwardness.

Defeated, he was reduced to talking of the weather. He rose from the stone bench and leaned against the stone balustrade of the viewing platform. The long grass of Troy Hill sloped sharply down into a void of cloud and mist; Sedgemoor and the glimpses of Burton Pynsent through his father's oak trees were lost to him. 'If the weather does not improve soon, they say the harvest will be ruined for a third time.'

'I know,' William said. He took off his cocked hat and examined the silk ribbon along the brim of it with long, probing fingers. 'There is already talk of a scarcity.'

'What will we do if we cannot import enough grain?' John asked, despairingly. 'Will the people starve? Will there be a revolution, as there was in France? Will we have to declare martial law here, as we have done in Ireland?'

'I do not know.' Those simple words spoke more eloquently of William's despair and vulnerability than the longest, most eloquent of his speeches, coming as they did from an incurable optimist. It was a hand stretched into the gloom and John reached for it.

'Will matters ever go back to the way they were?'

'I do not know that either,' William replied, lifting his eyes to John's. 'I heartily hope we may.'

John was not sure they were talking about the state of the country any more. He looked at William's pale, puffy face and took a deep breath. If he did not say his piece now, perhaps he never would. 'Will ... I know you are busy, but when we are back in town, Mary and I would be obliged if you would dine with us.' William said nothing. John wondered if he had been too abrupt, but their conversation had proceeded so awkwardly he did not know if he had the heart for more small talk. He added, desperately, 'We have not seen you for so long.'

For a moment, John thought his brother might try to remind him just why that was. He was needlessly worried; William's severe expression broke into a disbelieving smile. 'I would be delighted.'

John was so relieved he could think of nothing to say but, 'Good.'

They grinned at each other for a space in awkward silence. John was just nerving himself to say something else when William heaved himself off the bench and thrust out his hand. 'John ... thank you.'

John stared blankly at his brother's hand, and then the bitterness was back, so suddenly he had no time to raise the defences against it. By thanking John for putting an end to the quarrel William appeared to set himself apart from it, happy to accept its resolution as no more than John's duty. John stepped away and snapped, 'I am doing this for Mama, Will. Not for you.'

It was not strictly the truth, and he was immediately sorry when he saw pain sweep across William's face. John thought he might have undone all the good work of the previous half hour, but then William shrugged and said, 'Then let us go and tell her.'

They entered their mother's dressing room together an hour later. Lady Chatham's pale, lined face lit up in happiness at the sight of her sons arm in arm. While William bent to kiss his mother, Eliot whispered into John's ear: 'Well done, you've made him the happiest he's been in a long while.'

John smiled half-heartedly. Being told this by Eliot was tantamount to being told so by William himself, and yet John would much rather have heard the words from William's own mouth. Some recognition of his own fault, some reference to the hurt done to John's pride, anything would have done; but all John had received were thanks for the fact that he had, as usual, made all the sacrifices.

He could feel it slipping out of his hands, running through his fingers as finely as silk thread blown away by the wind. The feeling of entrapment was so strong and stifling he almost choked. Still, mindful of Eliot's advice and his own instincts, he forced himself to join the family group as though nothing had happened.

Chapter Twenty-two

November 1796

'My dear Lady Chatham! Congratulations!'

Lady Macclesfield crossed the throne room of St James's Palace and kissed Mary on both cheeks. Mary blushed, wondering whether her friend had spotted something she was not yet willing to reveal, but then she realised what Lady Macclesfield meant and gave a quiet sigh of relief. 'The congratulations are due to my husband, not me.'

'Indeed, Chatham.' Lord Macclesfield came to stand by his wife. 'Congratulations on your appointment as Lord President. I can see how pleased you are.'

'I am,' John nodded. 'Very much pleased.'

Mary watched her husband conversing with Macclesfield and thought John's pleasure was not quite reflected in his expression. The Lord Presidency of the Privy Council was a significant honour. It was a better paid and more responsible post than the Privy Seal, and William had intended the promotion as an olive branch, but Mary and her husband both knew it was not the Presidency of the Council that would restore John's public reputation.

The thing most responsible for the recent improvement in John's humour was not his new Cabinet post. Even while Lord and Lady Macclesfield plied John with good wishes Mary could see his attention was elsewhere. He was looking at her, his eyes full of hope and anxiety. Frustrated affection bubbled inside her. A month past his fortieth birthday, he was as transparent as a schoolboy.

While Lord and Lady Macclesfield greeted the arrival of Lord Mornington, Mary whispered into John's ear, 'Don't look at me like that, as though I am made of glass. Everyone will guess.'

'I can't help it.' John slipped his arm around her waist above her court hoop. His touch was tender, but also protective. 'I keep thinking something might happen to you … to the child.' He kissed her neck. 'I do not want this pregnancy to end like the others.'

'It won't,' Mary said, more robustly than she felt, but she knew this was what John needed to hear.

'Vaughan said you should rest.'

'Vaughan also says I must remain cheerful. How am I meant to do that, shut up for months until this child arrives?'

He opened his mouth, then closed it again because Lord and Lady Macclesfield were approaching. Macclesfield glanced round at the other courtiers in their finery, the men in their heavily embroidered waistcoats, the women with their long silk trains. 'Where is Pitt? He rarely misses drawing rooms.'

'I imagine he is busy with Lord Grenville,' John said. 'Lord Malmesbury arrived in Paris a week ago. My brother will be trying to gauge from his despatches what chances we have of making an honourable peace.'

'I trust a good one, now that we are bereft of allies in Europe. The war has gone on too long, and we cannot afford to fight the French alone now both Prussia and Austria have made terms.'

'Well, Lord Chatham,' Lady Macclesfield said brightly, in an obvious attempt to lighten the mood. 'Now that you are Lord President of the Council, what will become of the Privy Seal?'

'Why?' Mary joked. 'Do you want it for your husband?'

'Everyone will be wondering who is next to be raised to the Cabinet.'

John gave a sardonic smile. 'You are right, and that is why my brother intends to put the Privy Seal into commission.'

'I read in *The Times* it was to go to Lord Liverpool,' Lord Macclesfield said.

'Liverpool?' John snorted. 'He has the Duchy of Lancaster. I do not think he can hold both posts, and Lancaster is more valuable by £400 a year.'

'But the Privy Seal is a much higher-ranking position within the Privy Council. You know how much Lord Liverpool values his standing.'

At that moment, the doors to the throne room opened to admit the Countess of Liverpool herself in a yellow silk gown, fanning her broad, ruddy-cheeked face. 'Why, here is Lady Liverpool now,' Mary said. 'We can ask her.'

'Do you not think we ought to find out—' John began, but Mary barely heard him. She was too full of happiness and determined to share it. She crossed the room and tapped Lady Liverpool on the arm with her fan.

'My dear Lady Liverpool, Lord Macclesfield tells me I am to wish you and your husband joy.'

Lady Liverpool's plump face turned to Mary's in suspicion. 'Joy? Whatever for?'

A hand fastened round Mary's arm. It was John. 'Mary …'

'For the Privy Seal,' Mary said, starting to doubt in the face of Lady Liverpool's scowl, but too committed to withdraw. 'I understand it is to be his.'

Lady Liverpool's eyes flicked from Mary to John, and Mary saw the colour rise in her jowly cheeks. She was only now realising she had made a terrible error, but it was too late. Lady Liverpool raised her voice. 'The Privy Seal? Hah! Unlike *your* husband, *mine* will not allow Mr Pitt to make a fool of him so easily.'

Silence fell instantly across the room. All eyes turned to Lady Liverpool and to Mary; then, as one, they turned onto John. Mary felt the heat rising in her face. She did not dare look at her husband.

John hand tightened around her arm. 'Mary, come away, please.'

Mary longed to repay Lady Liverpool's rudeness in kind, but she knew she had already done damage enough. She raised her chin and gave Lady Liverpool a shaky but defiant look. 'You are of course entitled to your opinion.'

The room began to hum with conversation again, but Mary felt as though everyone was still staring at her and her husband. John shooed her to a more secluded position, his face red with embarrassment.

'Well then,' Macclesfield said, uncomfortably. 'That seems categorical enough. Liverpool is not minded to take the Privy Seal.'

'Whatever possessed you to step up to Lady Liverpool like that?' John snapped at Mary under his breath. Mary's eyes flickered, but she tried not to react to the injustice of his words. John softened his voice. 'Look, I know you meant well, but you should have waited until the rumour was confirmed.'

'I meant no malice,' Mary said. She raised her eyes to meet John's and said, deliberately, 'The Privy Seal is an honourable post, after all.'

John swallowed and gave a wan smile. 'Yes, it is.'

He kissed her hand, but Mary could tell his thoughts were elsewhere. She fought down the lump in her throat. Honourable the Privy Seal might be, but it was no more than that. Many considered it a catch-all post for Cabinet members unfit for serious business. Lady Liverpool was shrewish enough to have said so to John's face; but how many others had thought the words she had dared speak aloud?

****

By the time John and Mary returned to Berkeley Square John's embarrassment had ebbed. The King had been particularly gracious, which would mean much: His Majesty, at least, clearly believed John worthy of his new office. Mary could only hope John would find the strength to turn from the past and face the future with determination.

The future, indeed, was much on her mind. They spent a good while embracing after retiring to bed, as the candle guttered down to its last inch. Once they had sated themselves with kisses John stroked out her long dark hair. He kissed the corner of her mouth, her neck, her breasts, and then, after a long hesitation, her belly, firm and flat under her linen nightdress. In the semi-darkness he looked full of shy wonder, and much younger than his years. 'I still cannot believe it.'

'Neither can I,' Mary murmured. She put her hand over his, as though to protect it.

'If it is a son, do you think William will finally allow me to re-join the army?'

'Perhaps, once our son comes between him and the earldom.' The phrase "our son" seemed altogether too strange for Mary to credit, and chased all other words out of her head. John caught the tone of her pause; anxiety flashed back into his face.

'I still think you should not have gone to court today.'

'How many times do I have to say it? I am with child, not ill.' But she could hardly blame him for not daring to believe in their good fortune after all the long years of waiting and hoping and, finally, despairing. Luck was not usually on John's side.

He brushed his lips against hers. She could see he was aware his inability to become attached to this pregnancy hurt her more than she would admit. 'I am sorry. Only I do not want to … to … I could not withstand another disappointment.'

'Plenty of women have their first child at 34,' Mary said. 'Your mother was older.'

He shifted uncomfortably. 'It's not that. It's— Mary, I can barely even think about what it is. After all these years, to get what I have wanted so much, for so long …'

He tailed off into silence, but Mary understood. This child was more than the long-awaited heir to the earldom. It was John's fulfilment and absolution. It was a way into the future, a path away from all the unpleasantness of the past.

'This time it will happen.' She held his gaze, willing him to partake of her determination. 'I promise.'

She tried not to think of all the times it had not happened, and her body had betrayed her best hopes. She was all too aware that her own happiness was a fragile bridge laid across a deep quagmire of fear. So far she had not lost her footing, but she hardly dared look down for what she might see. John, however, had given himself entirely to those black thoughts. His eyes were wide and dark, his mouth twisted with the pain of doubt.

'I cannot lose you,' he said.

That simple phrase brought her too close to the abyss of terror she was trying so desperately to avoid: the pain of her miscarriages, the fate of her sister-in-law Harriot Eliot. For his sake, however, she forced the hope into her voice. 'You will not.'

He snuffed the candle. Mary lay for a long time in his arms, eyes open, staring up towards the bed canopy and painting her dreams and fears in the darkness.

****

Something woke her early in the morning. At first she was not sure what it was; the sun had not yet completely risen, and she had to blink to adjust her eyes to the grey half-light of dawn.

Shadows loomed around her: the curtain hanging round the bed; the velvet canopy above, fastened to the bedframe with mahogany studs; the great red stain sticking her nightdress to her thighs.

Only then did she feel the pain, lancing between her hips like hot steel. She doubled over with a gasp. 'John!' She pressed her hands to her belly as though to hold herself together. They came away scarlet. 'John, wake up. Please wake up!'

His eyes fluttered open. Realisation settled over his features like a film. His face was grey and his expression filled with a desolation that spoke of broken hearts and lost hopes.

****

John had no desire to leave the house, but he had promised William he would attend Cabinet and Mary persuaded him he had to go. He knew his lateness would only pander to the prejudices of his colleagues who wished him no good, but he did not care. His thoughts remained half a mile away in Berkeley Square.

The moment he opened the door to the Cabinet room all faces turned towards him, reflecting various degrees of disapproval. Windham arched an eyebrow and muttered, 'Well, if it isn't the *late* Lord Chatham.'

William, at least, gave John a broad smile. Since John's acceptance of the Presidency of the Council William had been almost pathetically friendly, as though the promotion had ended all awkwardness between them. 'My lord! You are just in time. Lord Grenville is about to read the latest despatches from Lord Malmesbury in Paris.' His face changed. 'Brother, are you well?'

'Never better,' John snapped. He could see William was not deceived any more than the others, but to his relief his brother simply gave him a worried look and said, 'I'm glad to hear it. Take a seat and Grenville will continue.'

How John got through that hour he did not know. He listened in a daze as Grenville went over the peace terms Malmesbury had received from the French Directory. He watched the Cabinet discussions as though seeing through the eyes of another man, hearing with someone else's ears. All he could think of was Mary, and those bloodstained sheets. Nothing else was real.

The Cabinet broke up. One by one the members rose, bowed, and left. John pushed his chair back and got to his feet. William had been putting his papers away at the top of the table. He said, 'John, stay a moment.'

'I ought to be getting home.' The last thing John wanted to do was be detained here, when Mary needed him. He did not have the energy to make conversation with William, always an exhausting experience since their quarrel.

'I'm worried about you,' William said. 'You look like death. Are you certain you are well? I received rather the opposite impression.'

'I am perfectly well.' John had intended to tell William everything but now, faced with the prospect, he found he could not do it.

William nodded, but looked unsatisfied. 'What is the matter then? Is it Mary?' John blinked rapidly. William closed his eyes. 'Is it a return of her rheumatism? I can arrange for her to see Sir Walter Farquhar if you wish.'

'Thank you,' John said, steadily. 'But we will do very well with Dr Vaughan.'

Why did he not just tell William about the miscarriage? For the same reason, perhaps, that he had not told William of Mary's pregnancy in the first place – it was a private matter between him and his wife. But that was not strictly true, because so long as John remained without a son, William was the heir to the Earldom.

The futility of his situation rose in him like a choking, poisonous cloud. He had failed again, utterly and irreversibly. He balled his hands into fists and dug his nails into his palm until it hurt. 'William ...'

'Yes?'

'Give me a command.'

'What did you say?' William hugged the despatch box as though it were a shield.

'Give me a command, Will. Send me to India if you like. Just give me a command.'

'John,' William said, as though to a child, 'it is out of the question. You cannot waste your life in battle.'

It was what he had known William would say, but John felt deflated nonetheless, as though his last hope had been snatched from him. 'I understand.'

William smiled and closed the door behind him. As the latch clicked into place John felt his legs give way beneath him. He collapsed back into his chair and buried his head in his hands, as though this final blow had sapped the last of his strength.

****

Mary lay on a chaise-longue in her dressing room when John came home. His heart wrenched at the misery on her face. He gave her a gentle kiss on the cheek and she closed her eyes and pressed his hand hard, but said nothing.

Dr Vaughan turned away until he was certain John had finished greeting his wife, then rose and bowed. He was a young man of about 30, competent and trustworthy. John drew him away to the other side of the room. 'Well, Vaughan?'

'Her ladyship is comfortable, Your Lordship. She has lost a great deal of blood, but I think I have stopped the flow with an anodyne draught and a wad of linen soaked in vinegar.'

'Thank God,' John said. The haemorrhage that had followed Mary's first miscarriage had nearly killed her.

'I have left a vial of digitalis with her ladyship's maid. A few drops may be given if the bleeding shows any signs of recurring. Otherwise tincture of opium will possibly help her sleep, which is the best thing in these circumstances.'

John nodded, his mouth dry. 'And the child?'

Vaughan looked grave. 'If only her ladyship had consented to remain abed, as I had counselled – although I confess I doubt it would have made any difference.'

John had expected nothing less, but Vaughan's words struck him like a blow. It was as though he was witnessing, again, Mary's anguish and bleeding early that morning. He turned away, knowing if he did not Vaughan would see tears in his eyes. 'If my wife has further need of your services I will send for you.'

Once Vaughan had left John turned back to the couch. The window stood open; cold November air spilled into the room, but despite this Mary was covered only in a thin woollen blanket. Cold, John remembered, was considered one of the best ways to halt the bleeding of a miscarriage. He shivered, despite the sweat beading his brow and upper lip. These were unpleasant memories; memories he had deliberately pushed to the back of his mind; memories he was now reliving.

The weak winter sunlight cast unflattering shadows across Mary's face, lingering on the harsh contour of her cheekbones, the drained whiteness of her lips, the hollows under her eyes. They had lost their colour; the pupils had swallowed up the iris, so dilated were they. The gaze she gave him was empty of everything save pain – pain and guilt. John was transfixed by it, nailed to the spot by an agony he could barely acknowledge, let alone relieve. When he remained staring at her, unmoving, tears spilled over her lashes and traced tracks down her cheeks.

'Don't weep,' John said, surprised at the gruffness of his own voice. 'Don't.'

'I am so sorry, John … You were right. I did too much.'

'Vaughan says there was nothing you could have done.'

Her mouth twisted, and at last John found the strength to move. He knelt next to the couch and reached out to push the hair back from her forehead. There was suddenly a lot more grey in it than he remembered.

They sat together in silence, healing their wounds through the companionship of intertwined hands. Then Mary said, 'Did you tell William?'

John set his lips. 'No.'

'You should, John. He has a right to know.'

'It's none of his business,' John said vehemently.

'He's your heir, John. Of course it is his business.' She added, uncertainly, 'Even if he were not, he is also your brother.'

'I will tell him. Only give me time to come to terms with it.' Her hand in his felt heavy, as though she did not have the strength to lift it. 'When I saw William I asked him for a command.'

She pushed herself up on one elbow. 'A command? Whatever for?'

'I only wanted to see what he would say.' John set his teeth together, hard. 'He said no, of course.'

Mary stared at him for a moment then said, 'Is this because of what Lady Liverpool said?'

'No, no, not at all.'

'John,' Mary said, and he knew she did not believe him. 'John, listen. It matters not what people say. You are worth so much more than the Privy Seal, even the Presidency of the Council. William knows it too.'

John listened in silence. Mary looked at him and he could see she was wondering if he had heard her words. He had heard every one, but he was not sure they mattered any more. He felt hollow, as though the last of his hopes had fled or died. 'You are right. It does not matter what people think. It stopped mattering long ago. Whatever I do, whatever I say, nobody sees and nobody hears. *He* has my destiny in his hands, and *he* may do what he wills with it.'

'No, John, no, that is not what I meant.'

'I know.' John was perilously close to tears now. He had wanted a glorious title, an estate unencumbered by debt; his father's extravagance had denied it to him. He had wanted to remain at the Admiralty; William had taken it away. He desired an heir to carry his name to the next generation, but it was not to be. He shook his head. He would not admit defeat, not on that. 'We will try again, Mary. We have to try again.'

'Try again?' she repeated. John nodded, unable to meet her eyes.

'When you are better, we will take you to Bath, or Buxton. You will drink the waters and regain your strength. Then we will try again, and next time all will be well.'

Mary finally guessed his meaning. She drew a long, ragged breath. 'John …' She took his hand back into hers, her touch full of regret. 'There will never be another chance.'

Still John could not look at her. To do so would be to admit defeat. 'Did Vaughan tell you that?'

'He did not need to tell me. I know.'

John raised his eyes to hers at last. He had started out as the comforter, but now it was Mary who drew him close and held him, as a mother might to do a child, while the tears he had kept back for so long – tears for Mary, for the child that would never be, and for himself – finally began to flow.

Chapter Twenty-three

September 1799

'Battalion!' John's voice echoed across the parade ground on Barham Downs, and the captains of the companies picked up the refrain. 'Form square!'

For a short, busy space the warm September air was filled with sound as the 4th Regiment of Foot carried out their colonel's order. 'Quick march! Halt! Dress!' The hasty tramp of feet, the metallic rattling of shouldered muskets, the slapping of leather cartridge boxes against wool-covered thighs created a militaristic symphony as the men formed their square in perfect time.

Most of them had been recruited from the militia, and almost all still wore their militia uniforms rather than the 4th's blue facings, but after a month of intensive drilling they were starting to move like proper regulars. John was especially proud because today they were in august company: the Prince of Wales had come to give the battalion its new colours, and John's brother and Dundas were here to watch.

'Present arms!' John cried. The battalion's musicians stepped out, followed by two ensigns carrying the Colours. On the right was the Royal Colour – the Union flag with the royal insignia surrounded by the Garter; on the left the Regimental Colour – deep blue with the royal insignia and three lions surrounded by tiny purple roses. The musicians led the Colours around the square then stopped in front. The flutes and trumpets ceased to play; the drummers held their drumsticks level. The enormous silk flags snapped in the breeze.

The Prince of Wales moved forwards on his black charger. The heir to the throne had responded to the occasion with theatrical gusto: he wore the extravagant black uniform smothered in silver lace of the 10th Prince of Wales's Light Dragoons, cut to flatter his portly figure. 'Lord Chatham, tell your men to stand easy,' he said in his soft, high-pitched voice.

John gave the order. The men stood with arms curled around their muskets, hands clasped, right foot slightly behind them. The Prince removed his feathered busby. 'Men of the 4th! It affords me the highest satisfaction to present this gallant and distinguished corps with their Colours. Nothing but a blameless accident could have deprived you of those you possessed before.' A few years previously the officers of the 4th had been captured at sea by a French privateer. The Colours had been dropped overboard to prevent them being taken. 'I now replace them, certain there is not a regiment in His Majesty's service that will ever support and defend its Colours with more valour.'

'Three cheers for His Royal Highness!' The Prince of Wales bowed to John as the men called out three ringing huzzas.

The battalion paraded before the Prince before returning to the encampment spread across the grassy expanse of Barham Downs. As far as John could see were tents, canvas flecks against the green of the fields, arranged in rows by regiment and company. John's brigade consisted of 3,000 4th and 1,000 men of the 31st; together they formed just under half of the troops waiting here for orders to sail to Holland.

Sixteen thousand British troops were already marching south from the northernmost Dutch point of Helder. Twenty thousand Russian troops were to join them, and John's men, too, would soon sail across the sea. An allied force of nearly 45,000 men would march on Amsterdam, the heart of Holland, restore the exiled House of Orange, and flush the French out of the so-called "Batavian Republic".

John dismounted by the large fly tent overlooking the camp. The new Colours had been placed on either side of it and flapped in the breeze. A table had been laid out with refreshments, and some of the senior officers stood conversing with the Prince of Wales and his entourage. At John's approach the Prince of Wales turned to him with a smile on his boyish face. 'Well, Lord Chatham, d'you suppose your men will be pleased with their new Colours?'

John bowed deeply. 'Your Royal Highness, my men are sensible of the honour you have done in presenting the new Colours in person. They will fight a hundred times more fiercely in defence of them.'

'You do your men an injustice. They seemed keen enough even before my paltry little speech.'

John knew the Prince well enough to catch the hint in that last sentence. The courtier in him rose to the challenge. 'Sir, I would hardly call it paltry. Your speech was eloquent and apposite.'

The Prince smiled at the flattery and handed John a glass of claret. 'I am glad to see you wearing your scarlet again, Chatham. It has been too long.'

John replied noncommittally, 'I am happy for the opportunity to serve, sir.'

'You know I would join you were I permitted to do so,' the Prince said with a sideways glance, and John supposed if any man might understand his frustration at being kept by his brother from serving so long, then it was the Prince of Wales, who had repeatedly been refused permission to fight abroad.

The Prince began talking to someone else and John steeled himself to join his brother and Dundas. They must have been on their fifth or even sixth glass of madeira, and their faces had acquired a ruddy hue not entirely attributable to the heat. They turned, unsteadily, at John's approach. John and Dundas exchanged frigid bows, but William's smile of welcome was genuine. 'Why, here is the brave soldier himself. I was telling Dundas how you once saved a ship carrying you from the West Indies.'

'I would not say I *saved* it exactly,' John protested. William clapped him on the shoulder and pressed a glass into his hand.

'You said you spent several nights bailing water from the lower decks.'

'I and the other 11 officers on board, yes. Not to mention the captain and crew. I can hardly claim sole responsibility.'

'So it is true?' Dundas peered at John with new respect. 'You had a lucky escape, my lord.'

'As did I,' William laughed. 'Had my brother drowned I would have been Earl of Chatham at 20 and never set foot in the House of Commons!' John stiffened at this reminder of the obligation he was under to his brother and heir apparent, but William was oblivious. 'You see, Dundas, my brother is quite the hero. With men like him in command, how can we fail? To the capture of Amsterdam!'

John, suddenly superstitious, placed his glass down without tasting it. 'Is that toast not a little premature?'

'I for one am allowing myself to hope,' William said. He handed his glass to a servant to be refilled. 'With French forces tied up by Marshal Suvorov in Italy, and the Dutch people bound to rise in favour of the House of Orange, you cannot but succeed.'

Dundas was collared by an officer and moved away, leaving John and William alone. As always when they found themselves tête-à-tête, a hint of awkwardness arose between them. It wasn't that John disliked being with William, but he was out of practice with the brotherly banter that had once been so much a part of their relationship. He fell back on straightforward honesty. 'Thank you, Will.'

William looked up, startled. 'Whatever for?'

'For this.' John indicated his red coat with its blue facings and gold lace. He did not know why William had changed his mind about allowing him to serve again, but he wanted William to know he was grateful, the more so because he did not think William would ever truly understand why. 'For giving me a chance.'

William looked embarrassed, but then his long face broke into a smile. 'If you want to thank me, come home safe and covered in glory.'

'That's a tall order,' John said dryly, and William's smile dropped away.

'Then just come home safe. That will suffice.'

He turned away as though his show of emotion discomfited him. John was himself amazed, touched and saddened by it, for William's naked display of emotion reminded him too much of their closeness of old.

But John was not the kind of man to make that most futile of wishes, to turn back time and start anew. In a month he would be 43; this was his chance to step out of William's shadow at last. Henceforth John would be his own man, Major-General the Lord Chatham and not William Pitt's older brother. He intended to make the most of the opportunity.

****

John returned to his billet, Bifrons House, a little after six. He was in a hurry, for the house also hosted the Prince of Wales and it did not do to keep the heir to the throne waiting.

Bifrons was an elegant country house with an unusual double-fronted design, tucked away in a hollow of the Downs. It belonged to the older brother of Major Herbert Taylor, the Duke of York's principal aide-de-camp. Edward Taylor had offered his residence for the use of the commanding officers of the brigades waiting to sail to Holland, but only John had taken up the offer, at least until the Prince of Wales had appeared.

Only that morning Bifrons had been a bustle of activity, with gentlemen begging audiences, red-coated equerries ordering the household staff about, and the Prince holding court as though he were in his salon at Carlton House. Now, as John rode into the stable-yard, he was astonished to discover an empty building.

Mary waited in the drawing room. She had insisted on travelling with her husband as far as Canterbury and John had no wish to dissuade her on the eve of his departure. He took her hands. 'Where is the Prince? Has he recollected another dinner engagement?'

'He's gone,' Mary said.

'Gone? Where?'

'Into Canterbury. John ...' Mary jerked her head towards the other end of the room. John followed her gesture and straightened. Edward Taylor stood by the fireplace, and beside him, in his mud-stained regimentals, was his brother Major Herbert Taylor.

'Lord Chatham.' Major Taylor handed John a letter. 'His Royal Highness the Duke of York requires an immediate acknowledgment of these orders. If you will consent to write him a line, I will carry it to him tonight.'

John broke the seal and read the words he had expected to read. In her chair, Mary hugged herself and gazed at the empty fireplace. John looked up at Major Taylor. 'We march tomorrow?'

'The wind is favourable, and the Duke wishes to sail before it changes.'

John felt anticipation and fear settle upon him. He turned to Edward Taylor. 'Might I request pen, ink and paper?'

A small writing table and writing materials were brought in. John dashed off a couple of lines and sealed them with the fob at his waist. He handed it to Major Taylor. 'You may tell the Duke my men and I will be on the road first thing tomorrow.'

Major Taylor bowed and left at once with his brother. John looked at his wife. Mary's expression was hidden behind a fold of her lace cap. 'I should find St Aubin and give him instructions to pack.'

'I've already done it,' Mary replied. 'Your valises are in the parlour.'

'How did you know?'

'A messenger waited for the Prince of Wales when he returned from the ceremony this afternoon. He left immediately. He wrote you this.'

She handed John a letter. He read, in the Prince's neat copperplate:

'Dear Lord Chatham, I have this moment heard your brigade is under orders of march tomorrow morning. In all probability you as well as Lady Chatham will wish to be rid of me. I hope in God Lady Chatham's fortitude and good sense will support her through this severe trial. My good wishes attend you always my dear Lord, and I am ever with great truth, your very sincere friend, George P.'

'That's the Prince for you,' John said, with a shaky laugh. 'Ever the romantic.'

Mary watched him for a space, her eyes dark with apprehension, then said in a small voice, 'I do not suppose there is any point in my asking you to stay?'

Before John could reply the door opened to admit two servants bearing a cold supper of roast chicken. They laid it on the same table on which John had written his letter to the Duke of York and bowed themselves out. Upon their departure John's aide, Captain Graham, appeared. Mary fiddled with her sleeves while John gave Graham instructions for the colonels of the 4th and 31st.

As soon as Graham had left Mary kissed John's hands. 'Sweetheart, don't go. I don't want you to go.'

'I have my orders,' John said. 'Even if I did not, I cannot let this opportunity pass.'

He did not have to elaborate; Mary had often said his eyes were plates of glass through which she could discern the workings of his mind. He knew she wanted him to succeed in his military career, but he understood her fears. This was the first time they would be separated by war, the first time in fact since John's visit to Ireland in 1786 that they would be apart for more than a few days.

She forced a trembling smile. 'I know, but I had to try.'

'I wish I could take you with me,' John murmured. He cupped her face and her eyes closed.

'All you have to do is ask.'

'Oh, Mary …' It was impossible. Even if officers' wives were occasionally tolerated, Mary's health would not stand it. There was something, however, in her eyes that spoke of strength sourced from deep within, and for a moment John considered the thrilling possibility that she might not take no for an answer. The hope crumbled into the bleak knowledge that, on the morrow, he would leave her behind, perhaps forever.

The same bleakness flooded into Mary's eyes as they moved towards each other. Their embrace shielded them from the reality of their imminent separation and their lips met hungrily.

The supper grew stale on the table. At some point they abandoned the drawing room for their guest apartments. The servants remained discreetly absent, so Mary pushed John's red coat off his shoulders while John fumbled with the pins that held together the bodice of her gown. After 16 years of married life their love-making was more affectionate than spontaneous, but tonight there was naked need in the way they discarded their layers of clothing in an erratic path to the bed.

Night was falling by the time they had finished. Reluctant to break the charm of their intimacy by calling a servant, John padded across the floor to the mantelpiece and found the tinderbox behind the clock. Mary watched, curled among the crumpled bedsheets, as John struggled to kindle a flame with unpractised fingers. Eventually he managed to light a candle and climbed back into bed. She pressed up to him and he curled his fingers in her hair, trying to imprint her softness, her sensation, her smell on his memory. Dear God, he was going to miss this. He was not sure what he would do, who he would be, without her at his side.

Mary stroked John's chest in circles. He placed his hand over hers. 'I wonder when we will meet again. If we succeed in driving the French out of Holland, we may remain on the continent some months.' Mary's hand under his clenched. John kissed her. 'I know. I want to return as swiftly as possible, but I want to return victorious.'

'John,' Mary protested, her voice muffled. 'This is our last night together, for goodness knows how long. Can we forget, just for a moment, that you will be leaving me soon? Can we enjoy what we have here, now? Please?'

'You want our campaign to succeed, do you not?' John teased. In the light of the candle Mary's eyes glistened with strange intensity.

'The only thing I want is this. Come home to me, whole and healthy. Come home with both your arms, and both your legs, and everything else.' She pressed her lips to each limb, then ran a trail of kisses up to his mouth.

'I promise,' John murmured with a slow smile. Mary did not return it.

'Do not make promises you may not be able to keep.'

Chapter Twenty-four

October 1799

The sun shone for the first time in weeks. It shimmered in the rainwater pooled in the hollows of the landscape and glared off the steep, scrubby face of the sand hills rising nearly 200 feet behind the village of Schoorl. A strong seaward wind carried gun-smoke into the plains in skeins, along with cries and the reek of powder and blood.

John wiped his brow and peered up at the twisted birch trees clinging to the heather-fringed hilltops. Out of sight behind the forests fringing the flatter, landward side of Schoorl, was the day's prize: the town of Bergen. John and his brigade were meant to be covering a Russian advance, sweeping the enemy out of the dunes that separated them from the rest of the Allied force, and joining with General Ralph Abercromby for a final push on enemy lines. Two hours earlier the sand hills had been alive with French and Dutch raining musket-shot on the British and Russians assaulting Schoorl. Not far off men still fought and died, but here in the plains nothing now moved apart from the torn, shot-peppered sails of Schoorl's great windmill flapping in the wind.

'What's going on?' John muttered, and mopped another thin line of sweat from under his bicorne hat.

Approaching hoofbeats attracted his attention. Captain John Chetham rode up, his black hair plastered to his forehead with perspiration. 'My lord!'

Chetham was not John's aide-de-camp. Captain Graham held that honour, but ever since John had landed in Holland three weeks previously Graham had been laid up with fever. Chetham had been recommended to John as a young man ambitious for advancement. With the Duke of York's approbation, he had been promoted to the rank of captain and attached to his brigade commander, and so far, John had no reason to complain. 'Mr Chetham. What have you discovered?'

'Nothing worth telling, my lord.' On Chetham's approach, John's colonels – Hodgson, Twisden, Dickson and Cholmondeley, of the 4th, and Hepburn and McMurdo of the 31st – had approached to listen. 'Nobody has heard from General Dundas for some time.'

'Generals Coote and Burrard?'

'General Burrard is on the northern edge of the dunes. But General Coote's brigade was last seen entering the heights to pursue the enemy.' Chetham hesitated and looked uncomfortable. 'I can, however, confirm that General Essen remains in Schoorl.'

'What the devil sort of game is Essen playing?' John exclaimed. 'We are meant to be covering his advance on Bergen!'

'I was told he awaits further orders from General Dundas, my lord.'

'But nobody knows where General Dundas is.'

'I daresay Essen has no intention of repeating the experience of the 19th September,' Colonel Hodgson sneered.

Two weeks previously the Russians had led an assault on the enemy at Alkmaar. Through a combination of foolhardiness and poor communication the Russians had been ambushed and suffered huge losses. Their commander-in-chief, Hermann, had been captured, and many Russians – including Essen – felt their British allies could have done more to assist. John kneaded his horse's reins between his fingers and swallowed a burst of irritation. He and his men had seen no action on the 19th; the Russians' over-eagerness had cut their part of the battle short before they had had a chance to fight. Now it seemed Russian over-caution would have the same result. John was not sure what he feared most: that he and his men would soon join the fray – or that they would not.

The 4,000 men of his brigade were arrayed with ordered arms on the flatlands behind him. John supposed he was a fitting commander for this miscellaneous group of untried boys, very few of whom had experienced anything more of battle than the manoeuvres of a militia field-day. At least John had his colonels to rely on. He turned back to them and tried not to sound too much at a loss. 'Gentlemen?'

'We must return to Schoorl,' Colonel McMurdo said promptly. 'We must await further information, and the 31st is perilously low on water.'

'The 4th too,' Hodgson added. 'Some of the men have already emptied their canteens. We may not be employed today, but if we are we will need water or we will lose men to the heat.'

'You are right,' John said quietly, yet he could not help feeling that returning to Schoorl would be a retreat. He had already marched the men out and back again to no good purpose on the 19th; he did not want to do it again.

Just then a movement on top of the sand hills, amongst the scrawny birch-trees, caught John's eye. Beside him, Chetham had seen the same thing. The youthful aide anticipated his superior's order; John had not opened his mouth before Chetham reached into his haversack and brought out a telescope. John trained it on the group of figures above. For a heart-stopping moment he thought they were enemy troops, but then he adjusted the focus and recognised the red coat and gold lace of a British officer. An aide-de-camp and three soldiers, zig-zagging cautiously down the steep, sandy hillside.

'My Lord Chatham!' The officer was in such a hurry to deliver his message he began speaking as soon as he was within earshot. 'General Dundas begs leave to request that, if your men are not otherwise engaged, you are to bring your brigade to the aid of General Coote!'

John drew a deep breath. His desire for action was about to be fulfilled. With effort he ignored the queasy twist in his stomach. 'Where are we required?'

'General Coote has been drawn by the fleeing enemy into an exposed position on the right, my lord. The 85th is being molested by enemy riflemen. Without assistance, General Dundas fears they will be overcome.'

'Surely Colonel MacDonald's Reserve must be closer?'

'If Your Lordship knows where Colonel MacDonald is to be found, you know more than General Dundas. The Reserve was last seen entering the dunes at Campe at ten o'clock, and we have heard nothing of them since.'

'Then we must be General Coote's Reserve.' John suppressed another burst of nervous excitement and unsheathed his sword. Sunlight glistened off the blade. 'Gentlemen, we must march to the aide of General Coote. If you would be so good as to give the order?'

'My lord,' Hodgson said after a hesitation, 'I must remind you that the men have not been able to replenish their water. If we are to march—'

'I am afraid we have no time. If we complete our task in good order, we may find more water within the next few hours.' Hodgson was too much of a soldier to argue, but an expression of doubt crossed his face. It was an expression John had seen more than once on the face of his immediate subordinates, as though they wondered whether the Minister's untried brother would prove an ineffective or, worse, inept commander. He gritted his teeth. 'Mr Hodgson?'

'My lord.' Hodgson turned his horse around and cantered back to his men. The brigade was suddenly all activity. Cries of 'Form up!' and 'Shoulder arms!' and 'Dress!' cut through the air. Drumbeats overlay each other in a chaotic jumble and fifes whistled a jaunty rendition of *The Girl I left Behind Me*. The ensigns lifted the Colours higher. The huge silk squares – dark blue for the 4th, buff-coloured for the 31st – unfurled and danced against the cloudless sky.

The men moved into columns. Even though the paths up the sand hills were well-trodden by cattle and held together by clumps of heather, the sand was soft enough to give way underfoot. Thankfully the heights were clear of enemy troops, for the climb was steep and progress was slow. John's horse was struggling, its hooves sinking into the sand with every step. The men's faces glistened with the effort of keeping rank, and some companies gave the order to support arms.

At last they reached the top. From here John had a clear view across the flatlands of the peninsula, thinly veined with dark canals and interrupted by bulbous church towers and small settlements. On the horizon, he could just see the thin blue line of the Zuyder Zee. There was no time, however, to enjoy the view. John led his men into the dense birch-land. Sunlight dappled the white sand with shadows through the leaves of the gnarled, bent trees, the undulating sand now also crisscrossed with naked tree roots.

All of a sudden John came out onto an open ridge, and for the first time got a full view of the battlefield. He gave a low whistle. 'Good God.'

The dunes lay before him like a bunched-up quilt, tufted with scrubby bushes. Gun-smoke lay across the landscape like a fog. Far to the right, British troops was being fired on from above by sharpshooters hidden in a coppice. Not far away from these men, but out of sight to them behind a lip of scrub-covered sand, was the rest of General Coote's brigade. They were close enough to John for him to pick out the flags of the 2nd, 27th and 29th regiments waving desperately as the men scrambled over the slippery terrain. The enemy was arrayed across the road to Bergen.

Tree trunks, broken carts and farmyard furniture had been stacked into temporary barricades, and more sharpshooters were at work from the trees flanking them.

'The 85th.' Chetham trained his telescope on the unit that had been separated from Coote's brigade. 'They're under direct attack.'

'Go to Colonels Hepburne and McMurdo and tell them to march over at once. If they can extend the 85th's line, they may be able to turn the enemy flank and allow the 85th to re-join their brigade.'

Chetham sped off, and a few minutes later the 31st marched into the dunes. John tried to think as quickly as he could, aware even as he pondered that the French and Dutch troops had become aware of his brigade's presence and started firing at them. He called Chetham back.

'We must extend General Coote's line and re-join the 31st and 85th. If we can, we will present a most formidable front to the enemy. Give the order for the 4th to march.'

'We will be exposed to enemy fire,' Chetham pointed out.

'We shall mostly be covered by the sand hills. We may be exposed for a short while, but we must aid General Coote.'

Chetham rode off again, and John offered a quick prayer that he was right. His brigade and Coote's together would form a long line from the edge of the dunes all the way beyond the Bergen road. General Abercromby's division ought to be on the south side of Bergen and was hopefully making good progress. Somewhere inland General Pulteney was waiting with another division to join an attack on Bergen. Even if the Russians refused to leave Schoorl, a triple-fronted attempt might still be successful. John's heartbeat quickened and he fought down a burst of nausea. 'Brigade! March!'

The bitter smell of gunpowder and blood mixed with the salt of the sea. John saw the enemy line dividing and struggling round on the soft sand to face his men's approach. Despite the treacherous ground, they acted with tremendous speed; the 4th was only halfway across open ground before the enemy volley echoed off the dunes like thunder. John heard cries of 'Close up!' from behind and knew some of his men had fallen, but he resisted the urge to turn and assess the damage.

A battalion of the enemy crested the hill just as John's men came off their ridge, aiming to cut them off in their approach to Coote, but they were too late. The enemy discharged another volley just as John's men passed into the shelter of the dunes, but most of the shot lodged ineffectively in the sand. The thudding of John's heart transformed into relief. He could see the left flank of Coote's brigade now, the men of the 27th's powder-blackened faces cracking into grins as they realised they were being reinforced.

General Sir Eyre Coote and his officers approached. 'Lord Chatham! Your appearance is timely!'

'My men and I are yours to command.' John stood in his stirrups and peered over the heads of his men as the 4th wheeled and dressed up to the 27th. 'Did you know the 85th is just over that ridge?'

'Is it, by God?' Coote turned his protuberant eyes in the direction John indicated. 'If we move forwards we may be able to communicate with them through that channel.'

The two brigades advanced, breaking into divisions to filter through the terrain. At first the enemy fell back, but as the British approached the forest fringing the dunes another enemy battalion appeared and fired. Colonel Cholmondeley gave the order to wheel but a couple of companies hesitated, betrayed by the 4th's militia background. The line trembled in confusion. The men eventually pulled round, but not before the enemy loosed another volley and felled several more men. John could see the fear catching from face to face as the soldiers stared down at their fallen colleagues. He turned to Colonel Maitland of the 27th, who was within hailing distance. 'Sir! The enemy – the trees!'

Maitland saluted and barked out some orders. The 27th wheeled, fired off two volleys with mechanical precision, then charged bayonets up the ridge until the enemy dispersed into the woods. The 27th were seasoned troops who had just shown the raw militiamen of the 4th how soldiers ought to behave under fire. 'Well done – you've done more than my whole brigade!' John called out to Maitland as the men returned to their position.

Clouds were gathering by the time John and Coote's brigades made unexpected contact with Macdonald's Reserve shortly after four o'clock. Twenty minutes later the 85th and 31st re-joined the left of the line. The French and Dutch troops continued firing as they fell back, and a half-mile towards Bergen John discovered two guns erected on one of the steeper sand-dunes, but even the artillery was no match for the combined brigades. The enemy's retreat heartened John's weary men, and as they marched steadily up the ridge even the artillery fell silent. By the time John and his men reached them the gunners were long gone, the two cannons spiked and useless.

By now the wind was blowing hard, bringing the smell of salt and approaching rain. The setting sun smeared long, bloody shadows across the white sand of the dunes, but as clouds filled the sky the shadows faded into darkness.

Gunfire still echoed from somewhere in the distance, but here the fight was over. The 4th and 31st, reunited at last, fell out. The men collapsed, exhausted, on the sand. Most of them had not had a mouthful to drink since noon, and John himself had a scratchy throat and pounding head from lack of water.

Chetham rode up followed by General Coote and the senior officers of John's brigade. Hodgson spoke first, his voice hoarse and cracked, his uniform crusted with sand, sweat and gunpowder just as John supposed his must be. 'Do we move on Bergen, my lord?'

'We must await orders,' John said. 'Nothing can be done without the Russians.'

'Then nothing will be done.' Coote grimaced. 'General Essen would not leave Schoorl without direct orders from the Duke of York. For all I know he remains there.'

'What if General Abercromby gives us orders to march? He may well have taken Egmont by now.'

But even as John spoke, the first drops of rain began to fall. At first they patted into the sand one at a time, then gathered strength until the heavens opened and the rain came down in torrents. Coote scowled at the darkening clouds. 'It will have to wait. Tonight, we shall have to find what shelter we can in the hills.'

It was the same heavy rain that had plagued the British and Russian force since mid-September, but for once the men were glad of it. Many held out their hats to catch the falling rain; some stood with their mouths open as the water ran white tracks through the dirt on their faces.

John wiped moisture from his eyes and turned to see his aide, Chetham, holding out a blanket and a flask. He grinned in gratitude, took a lengthy swig of cold, bitter rainwater from the flask, and wrapped the blanket around his head. 'My thanks. You're a gem.' John handed the flask to Chetham who, after a hesitation, drank thirstily. 'Are you certain you have never been an aide-de-camp before?'

'Never had the chance, sir. Two weeks ago, I was merely a lieutenant.'

'I suppose with a name like Jack Chetham you and I were fated to make a pairing,' John joked. For a moment Chetham's round, youthful face looked blank, then he caught John's meaning and grinned.

'Oh yes, my lord, I suppose we were!'

Chetham went off to check the men were settled. John drew his blanket closer and shivered. Darkness was falling now in earnest, and he could see nothing but the black rise and fall of the dunes surrounding him, hear nothing but the whistle of the wind and the pattering of rain on sand. An aching tiredness infused his bones and he felt he could close his eyes and sleep for a month, rain or not.

But then Chetham was back, rain dripping from his spiky black hair. John saw the letter in his hands with the Duke of York's seal and knew the day's ordeal was not yet over.

****

Night had fallen completely by the time John arrived at the Allied headquarters at Schagerbrug. The tiny village, little more than a handful of brick houses clustered around a small church and the bridge that gave it its name, was plunged into darkness. Chetham's lantern did little to pierce the rain-sodden gloom, but the windows of the Duke of York's quarters blazed with light and John reluctantly made for the glow.

He was stiff and aching from the day's events, but that was not the only reason he took his time dismounting. Even from the street he could hear raised voices, and he was in no hurry to discover who was doing the shouting and why.

A pair of Russian officers sat by the parlour fire when John and Chetham passed through. They presented a fierce, larger-than-life appearance with their long-tailed green uniforms, enormous silver gorgets and thick curled moustaches; even after three weeks of fighting together with them Chetham was clearly trying hard not to stare. The Russians ignored the two British men, but John knew they had not gone unnoticed because the officers switched from French into Russian dialect. As John climbed the stairs, however, they switched back into French, evidently intending to be heard and understood: 'Ever since the action of the 19th the British have brought us bad luck.'

'And bad weather!'

They laughed, and switched back into Russian. John ignored them.

Captain Fitzgerald, one of the Duke of York's aides, opened the door to him. The Duke sat at the head of a large deal table, a decanter and a glass at his elbow, his right hand clenched on the table-top. Arrayed round him were his lieutenants-general, Abercromby, Dundas, Pulteney and Hulse, all wearing sand-caked uniforms and wooden expressions. The Russian generals, Essen and Sedmoratski, sat opposite. Sedmoratski had his hand over his mouth and gazed up at the extravagantly painted wooden beams above his head. Essen was shouting and striking the table with his fist. With each blow the wine in the Duke of York's decanter shivered and sparkled red like blood.

'… cannot hold us responsible for the failure of the campaign!' Essen cried in French, rolling his R's even more extravagantly than usual. 'If Your Royal Highness had seen fit to send us your instructions—'

'General Essen,' the Duke cut in with a wave of his plump white hand. He, too, spoke in heavily-accented French. 'I fully understand your reluctance to leave Schoorl without instructions, after the unfortunate affair of the 19th, but your Emperor placed you and your men under my command. The aim of today's action was the capture of Bergen. Had you bestirred yourselves, we might have held this council there this very night.'

'Bestir ourselves!' Essen roared, his high-boned face suffused with scarlet. 'Had Your Royal Highness's officers bestirred *themselves* on the 19th, today's caution would have been unnecessary. Then again, why am I so surprised? None of your generals seemed to know where your brigades might be found. From men who cannot communicate even between each other, what can be expected? You cannot even make sound judgments from the evidence at your disposal.'

'I do not understand,' York said coldly.

'The people of this country! You assured us they would rise to support us. If the Dutch favour anyone at all, it is the French.'

Sedmoratski brought his gaze down and spotted John. He sat up, twitched Essen's coat tail, and whispered something in hasty Russian. John guessed the Russian general had just accused him of being his brother's spy. He was, after all, the only major-general on a Council of War that ought to consist only of the most senior officers.

Essen's eyes narrowed, but took the hint. The Duke of York looked relieved at John's interruption of Essen's tirade. He, too, looked exhausted, his face raw from exposure to sun and sand, his bulbous blue eyes bloodshot. 'Lord Chatham. Take a seat.'

'Your Lordship is, as usual, the last to arrive,' Essen observed, pointedly. John took a deep breath, and said, in his best French for the benefit of the Russians,

'I must apologise to Your Royal Highness, but your messenger got lost in the dunes and did not find me until after seven o'clock.'

'You have no need to make any excuses to me, Chatham,' the Duke said. 'General Dundas tells me your prompt and judicious actions today saved General Coote from disaster.'

John glanced across the table at David Dundas. The old man's lined face relaxed into a half-smile. 'Indeed, my lord, General Coote was very full in his praise.'

'I did no more than my duty,' John muttered. The other generals watched him benevolently but coolly; Sedmoratski and Essen were not the only men who harboured suspicions about John's role on the council.

'Sirs,' the Duke announced, when John had taken his seat. 'My thanks for today's victory. Our scouts report the road to Bergen is clear, so that we might take possession of it tomorrow. I propose to move our headquarters to Alkmaar. But we must move swiftly, for our scouts also report the enemy is now entrenching between Beverwijk and Wijk-op-Zee. More alarming still, prisoners taken today confirm that General Brune expects 5,000 men in reinforcements.'

'The enemy has protected his right flank by flooding the dykes,' Abercromby added. 'The left flank, however, remains vulnerable. If we can flush the French and Dutch out of Beverwijk and the villages of Limmen, Bakkum and Akersloot, they will have no recourse but to fall back in confusion.'

'If we can take Beverwijk,' the Duke concluded proudly, 'then Amsterdam – and Holland – will be ours by the middle of the month.'

John shifted in his seat, only partly to ease his aching muscles. He had lost count of the number of times he had been told the campaign would be over before the end of September, yet here they were, in October, discussing the reduction of a town that was still ten miles from Amsterdam.

Abercromby spoke. He was an elderly man with a reputation for over-caution, and John was not surprised to hear his words. 'Sir, I agree that Beverwijk must be taken, but I may not have impressed upon you the full extent of the damage wrought by today's battle. Our men have been fighting since daybreak and are unlikely to get much rest in the dunes. Many of my men went all yesterday without nourishment; today they were only provisioned when the waggons came in at four o'clock. If we do not allow them a day's rest, we will break them.'

Dundas sucked at his lips as though he had a bitter taste in his mouth, and Pulteney drew a deep breath. York scratched his balding head and said, 'The longer we wait, the more time the enemy has to entrench, and to be reinforced.'

'It will take no more than a day. Once we take possession of Alkmaar and Egmont-op-Zee we will have access to the provisions of the towns. We might make our strike on the 4th, or the 5th at the latest.'

'I would urge against delay,' Pulteney said gruffly. 'The men have performed wonderfully today and will do so again tomorrow, should we ask it of them.'

'I agree,' Hulse nodded. 'Marsh fever has begun to spread. We may be courting disaster if we remain here in the wetlands.'

'What is your opinion, Lord Chatham?' Essen cut in suddenly.

'My opinion?' John repeated, glancing from one face to another in some confusion. Essen's dark, dangerous gaze hardened.

'I am interested to hear what Mr Pitt's brother has to say. How else are we to know what the English Cabinet wishes us to do?'

'I have no instructions from Mr Pitt on military strategy,' John said, firmly.

'You must have an opinion, unless the stories I have heard are correct, and you are little more than a fool burdened with a great name.'

'General Essen!' the Duke remonstrated, belatedly. Essen subsided, but looked triumphant. John had no choice now but to respond to Essen's challenge and York knew it. 'Lord Chatham, what *do* you think? I should very much like to hear your views.'

Tiredness ran through John's veins like lead. The last thing he wanted to do was weigh in on a topic that divided the council so thoroughly. 'I fully appreciate the difficulties stated by General Abercromby, but I also see the necessity of proceeding swiftly to Beverwijk. I can vouch for the resilience of my brigade, and their devotion to Your Royal Highness. I am perhaps the least fitted man here to give Your Royal Highness advice, but since you have asked for it, I say if we are to strike, let it be now.'

He glanced at Essen, and could see his words had not displeased the Russian general. For all his sarcasm Essen clearly agreed that Abercromby was being too cautious. And yet Abercromby was the senior general at the table, commander of the troops in all but name, for the Duke of York had been appointed commander-in-chief only as a sop to the Russians who had demanded nothing less than to be commanded by a Prince of the Blood.

The Duke scratched his head again. 'A sound opinion, and I thank you for your honesty. I tend to agree, but General Abercromby has made good points. Perhaps the solution is not to engage for Beverwijk on the first day, but to clear the enemy's advance posts in Akersloot, Limmen and Bakkum once the weather has improved. We might then re-assess the situation in view of our advanced position.'

Solomon could not have been prouder of such a judgment. Dundas and Pulteney looked displeased, but the commander-in-chief had spoken. The Council of War broke up. Abercromby, Pulteney and Hulse left first, shrugging into their redingotes in anticipation of the rain that still fell heavily. John was calling for Chetham when he heard his name. General Dundas appeared at his elbow.

'I meant what I said to the Duke,' he said, his slate-coloured eyes glinting under his white brows. 'Your assistance today was important. General Coote owes you thanks, as do I.'

'I only hope I may be of further assistance in any upcoming action.'

'General Abercromby's opinion notwithstanding, I suspect your wish will be granted. We cannot remain long where we are, and the Russians are growing restless. Have you heard the rumour?'

'What rumour?'

'The prisoners taken today inform us of a victory over General Suvorov by Marshal Massena at Zurich. They say the Russian campaign in Switzerland is over. Of course, it may be a lie, but General Essen has taken it to heart. He feels our government might have done more to assist Russia, rather than wasting resources on Holland.'

That explained Essen's bad mood. John blew out his cheeks. 'Surely he knows this expedition was intended in part to distract the French from Switzerland?'

'If rumours of this defeat at Zurich prove well founded, we may shortly find ourselves the enemy's sole focus.' A chill that had nothing to do with the damp ran through John. Dundas gave a grim smile. 'I think you had better re-join your brigade before the roads are flooded.'

John found Chetham half-asleep in the parlour. Just as they were bracing themselves to step into the rain, however, John heard his name called again. '*Milord* Chatham!'

John heaved a sigh. 'General Essen.'

The lamplight glinted off Essen's gorget and the gold lace that frilled the green of his uniform. His large dark eyes remained cold, but there was a respect in his face that had not been there earlier. 'I was pleased to find you so much of my mind in the council chamber. You are a sensible man.'

'You seem surprised,' John remarked icily.

'Let us say your eagerness to press on to Amsterdam does not accord with your reputation; but I would not have you report back to your brother that I have been uncivil to you, or insubordinate to His Royal Highness of York.'

'I am not a spy.'

'I just said you were a sensible man, and a sensible man would believe otherwise.' John said nothing. Essen's lips twitched. 'Whatever your role, my lord, I am pleased to find there are gentlemen in His Britannic Majesty's army. I only hope there are men of action as well as men of honour.'

It was a rather back-handed compliment but John knew it was intended as an apology of sorts. He gave a stiff bow. 'I trust we will rise to your expectations.'

'I hope so,' Essen said darkly. 'And that before long, or General Brune will make another Zurich of us.'

****

Abercromby got his way, but only because the weather, rather than improving, got worse. John and his troops spent two nights encamped on the sand dunes surrounding Egmont-op-Zee, wet, cold and utterly wretched, until they were ordered to march into the town and join with

General Abercromby's division. Egmont, on the sea-front, offered little protection from the driving rain or the wind slicing off the waves like a salty blade; but at least John could finally change into dry clothes, shave off his three-day-accumulation of stubble, and enjoy some of the benefits of civilisation.

Sunday 6th October dawned dry but misty. News arrived after breakfast from the Duke of York's new headquarters at Alkmaar that General Coote was ordered to take Limmen, General d'Oyly to take Ackersloot, and Essen's Russians to take Bakkum. Abercromby's division, however – and John's brigade – would not be wanted until the next move had been decided, and Abercromby's aide informed John there would probably be another military council after the three small towns had been taken.

The tolling of the church bells calling the people of Egmont to worship was soon drowned out by the rattle of musketry and the booming of cannons. Towards noon, news arrived that all three towns had fallen, the enemy falling back on Castricum and Beverwijk. It was not a moment too soon, for a crash of thunder preceded a torrent of rain so dense it was impossible even to see the towering dunes fringing the village to the landward side.

The gunfire, however, proceeded uninterrupted. Shortly after one o'clock John was sitting down to luncheon when Captain Chetham burst breathlessly into his quarters. 'My lord, General Abercromby has sent word. The Russians require your assistance at Castricum.'

John was already strapping on his sword, but at Chetham's words he looked up in astonishment. 'Castricum? What in God's name is Essen doing out there?'

Coote, d'Oyly and Essen had been given strict instructions to await further orders after taking Limmen, Ackersloot and Bakkum; assuming the others had obeyed orders, Essen would be miles from the nearest reinforcements. John shook his head. A few days ago, Essen's reluctance to leave Schoorl had cost the British a decisive victory. Now his eagerness to press the enemy in their stronghold was going to put John and his men in danger.

John found his men arrayed a little way out of Egmont, just at the point where the dunes began their disorderly climb. The brigade had washed and shaved but their sodden uniforms were still caked with sand and mud. Many of them must have been thinking wistfully of their life as militiamen, quartered in the taverns and farmhouses of the county in which they had been born. John himself experienced a momentary vision, as though Mary were standing before him, the lace of her cap snatching in the wind. "*Come home to me.*" Her words echoed in his mind so clearly he glanced round, half-expecting to see her behind him, but Mary was in England and every mile between them ached like a wound. John dug his spurs into his horse's flank. 'Brigade! Prepare to march!'

It was seven miles from Egmont to the outskirts of Castricum. The brigade marched in column, mud spattering the men's black boots as they passed down the waterlogged roads. Nothing moved but the grey herons peering impassively at the rain-ringed surface of the water channels cutting through the landscape. They flew off in a silent, ungainly fashion at the brigade's approach. The men marched with their arms over their musket locks to keep them as dry as possible, but their cartridge boxes must have been soaked through and already livid patches of rust had begun to disfigure the burnished metal of the musket barrels.

On the outskirts of Binnen there was a thunder of hooves. Three Russian officers approached from the left. John recognised General Sedmoratski accompanied by two aides. The Russian general swept off his hat with a flourish that sent droplets of water flying into the air. '*Milord!* You are just in time!'

'General Sedmoratski!' John brought his mount closer to the Russian general. 'What has happened here? Why has General Essen attempted to assault Castricum?'

Sedmoratski was flushed and out of breath, and mopping ineffectually at his handsome, strong-boned face with a sodden handkerchief. 'It was a trap, *milord*. Some prisoners we took this morning at Bakkum gave us false information that General Brune had failed to complete his fortifications at Castricum. General Essen expected no resistance. We held Castricum for an hour this morning, but the enemy sent in reinforcements and chased us from the town.'

'Where is General Essen now?' John said. Sedmoratski gestured at the half-flooded farmlands separating Binnen from the coast. 'Have any other reinforcements arrived?'

'General Abercromby reached us an hour ago from Egmont. General d'Oyly and General Hutchinson have been sent to support us outside the town gates, but I do not know if they have managed to reach General Essen.'

'What do you wish us to do?' John asked.

'Continue to Castricum. Word is the French have sent their cavalry under General Brune himself.' Sedmoratski gave John a taut look, and finished, 'And hurry.'

The firing got louder and the mist got denser as they approached Castricum. What had been meant to be a simple manoeuvre pushing the British lines forwards had turned into a desperate battle in poor visibility. John and his men passed dozens of badly wounded men and several corpses. The grass here was flattened, the mud churned up by marching feet.

They made contact with General Hutchinson a half hour later. Hutchinson had been forced to retreat from the town and was regrouping when John found him. The young general's coat was spattered with earth and blood; he looked exhausted, but explained the situation to John as succinctly as possible. The British and Russians had forced the enemy back onto Castricum, but General Abercromby was having trouble re-entering the town. 'He's had to retreat to the heights above Egmont. From there he has kept the enemy at bay, but they have three batteries outside Castricum and all our assaults have been repulsed.' That explained the sound of heavy artillery John could hear over the constant fire of musketry. 'The General has just sent me a message ordering me to strengthen the Russians on the left of the town. Last reports were the Russians had been forced back again. I am certain your brigade will not be *de trop*.'

'Do we know where our allies are?' John asked, peering into the mist. Hutchinson raised his eyes to the low-hanging clouds.

'Be careful, my lord.'

So it was that John found himself once more leaving the flatland paths for the sodden sand that sucked at his horse's hooves and layered itself across everything in a thin film. The dunes here were shallower than the massive, forest-fringed sand hills at Schoorl, but they still formed an impressive network of hills and valleys edged with dense scrub, and John wanted to keep well away from them. He had lost Hutchinson's brigade to his left. They were close, but although it was only about four o'clock in the afternoon, the mist had already blotted out the sun, and it felt like dusk.

As the brigade approached the walls of Castricum the sound of firing grew louder. Reports brought back by the brigade's skirmishing party suggested the Russians were very close, and John ordered each battalion to form a line in the expectation of meeting the Allies at any moment. The men took a few minutes to complete the manoeuvre, tired from their march and unnerved by the booming of cannons and the rattling of musketry in the gloom. John's insides were in knots. He felt as though he was wearing a cold, wet blindfold, and every shadow looming out of the mist was a potential enemy.

The rain had eased, but the mist rising from the canals and the gun-smoke hanging over the fields combined so thickly that John did not see the Russians until they were a couple of hundred yards away. The green-coated troops were running in some disorder, their white breeches turned grey with mud. Hardly any of them carried muskets; some stumbled and fell, and were trampled by their colleagues following.

'What on earth...?' Colonel Cholmondeley muttered, moments before the Russians ran headlong into the 2nd Battalion of the 4th.

The confusion was instantaneous. John's men stood their ground, but the Russians desperately tried to break their way through, shouting something chilling in their guttural language that John could not understand.

'Damn you!' Hodgson's terrifying baritone rose above the chaos. He rode among the fleeing Russians, beating at them with the flat of his sword, but there were too many. 'Get back, you dogs! Get back!'

John could hear a dull rumble, like thunder preceding a storm. 'What has happened? Where is their commander?' he called out to Chetham, but the aide was staring at something beyond the furred caps of the Russian soldiers, his eyes round and his mouth hanging open. John followed Chetham's gaze, and saw for the first time what the Russians were running from.

A dark shadow moved across the field and resolved itself into a line of horses – hundreds of horses, the cuirasses of their riders winking as they hammered across the muddy soil. John could see the clumps of earth thrown up by the hooves; he heard an officer bark out an order in French,

239

then the rasp of metal against leather as hundreds of curved swords left their scabbards.

Cavalry.

His ears whistled. He pulled at his horse's reins so abruptly it staggered, and turned to shout at Cholmondeley, who was nearest. 'Brigade! *Form square!*'

The last time his men had performed that manoeuvre had been on Barham Down, before the Prince of Wales. The memory of that warm, blue-skied day raced through his mind – the smell of fresh grass, the bright yellow of the cowslips, the peace. They had had all the time in the world to form their square. Now, they had seconds at most – and even as John heard the frantic efforts of his men to follow his orders, he knew it was too late.

The French cavalry thundered into the flank of the militia-trained 4th with the force of an earthquake.

John heard Colonel McMurdo of the 31st shout, 'Give fire!'

Tiny bursts of light broke the gloom. Probably only about half the muskets went off in the damp, and the French cavalry were already among the 4th. Fear rose off the scarlet ranks like a tangible thing. The routed Russians had shaken them, and the sight of their colleagues being cut down by the enemy cavalry had destroyed any courage they had left.

'Keep the line!' Colonel Hodgson bellowed, throwing his horse forwards with a kick of his spurs, but panic was already spreading. The enemy broke easily through the thin ranks, bringing their swords down with fatal effect. They aimed for the officers: they knew what they were doing. Colonel Dickson, riding along the broken line trying to encourage his men, was sliced from his horse by an enemy sabre.

Even the most seasoned troops could not have withstood the power of the charge, but these were not seasoned troops. Many of them still wore their militia uniforms. As the bodies began to litter the ground, John knew many of them would never wear anything else.

'Brigade!' John shouted. 'Stand firm! *Stand firm!*'

It was useless. He could barely hear his own voice above the chaos.

'We must fall back, my lord,' Hodgson urged. The officer's face dripped with moisture from the rain; his eyes were round with fear, something John had never thought to see in the seasoned veteran's face. John exchanged a helpless look with Hodgson then raised his sword.

'Fall back!' he shouted, forcing his voice to carry until it cracked. 'Form square to the rear!' To Chetham: 'Go to General Hutchinson and get help. Quickly.'

Chetham sped off. The brigade moved more slowly than John would have liked, half-paralysed with terror. John followed the alarmingly unstable ranks as they moved to the rear, picking their way over the bodies of their fallen colleagues – so many bodies. John tried not to look at them.

'Form square!' Hodgson bellowed the refrain. 'Form square, good God, unless you want to die!'

The cavalry were coming for another charge, but the enemy infantry were also approaching. John could hear the tramp of their feet before he saw their columns piercing through the mist, silhouetted against Castricum's grey walls. Unlike his brigade, these were seasoned troops. He watched in horrified fascination as the great-coated figures fanned out into line in a fluid, organic movement, then gave fire. Flame burst through the mist in an explosion of noise, and then all John could hear was shouting – cries of fury from the French, screams of terror and pain as more of his men suffered and died.

'Prepare to give fire!' John cried.

The front ranks of the squares dropped to their knees and those standing behind fumbled with their muskets.

'Load!' John shouted into the darkness. 'Present and fire!'

A ragged volley answered him. Before his brigade managed to load another shot the enemy fired a second time. The 3rd Battalion of the 4th presented and fired, but the enemy responded and yet more of John's men dropped. John watched it all as though from a distance. He could see the fear on his men's faces, and taste their despair as their muskets misfired with powder that had grown damper and damper all day.

Where was everyone else? No help could be expected from the Russians, but flashes of fire all along the distant sand hills towards Egmont told John that the rest of Abercromby's division was not far off. More men had fallen; the ranks closed up over the dead and wounded. Just as John began to think he, too, would die on this strip of scrub-covered sand, trapped between barren fields and the sea, Chetham reappeared. He leaned over his horse's neck and gasped, unable to say anything but to point at a line of red-coated soldiers approaching from the left. They fired and the enemy paused, slowed for a moment in its onslaught.

'General Hutchinson,' Chetham managed. 'Lord Paget's cavalry coming.'

Relief flooded John's veins so fast he felt dizzy, but then the enemy fired again. A few yards away from him, Colonel Hodgson gasped and fell off his horse. John looked down at him in consternation, then raised his sword and shouted, 'Brigade! Prime and load!'

Fingers slippery with rain fumbled in cartridge boxes for sodden paper-wrapped charges. Ramrods flashed up and down barrels with a metallic whistling sound. John raised his sword. 'Make ready! Give fi—'

A rumble of enemy musketry interrupted him. John felt a shock to his shoulder as though he had been whipped. His sword flew out of his hand and his horse staggered back. Beside him Chetham started forwards with a cry. John wondered what Chetham was shouting about, until he saw his coat half-ripped from his shoulders and the blood seeping through his shirt. Only then did he feel the pain, surging down his arm as though his blood flowed full of knives.

Chapter Twenty-five

November 1799

'Fools!' Essen's staccato French echoed about the Horse Guards council chamber. He must have spoken loudly enough to be heard in the street, where London's citizens went up and down Whitehall about their business. 'Fools, all of you. The Austrians have betrayed us in Switzerland, and you have ruined us with your incompetence. God help Russia, for nobody else can!'

John rubbed his thumb over the stem of his wineglass. He glanced down the table at the other generals. This was the first meeting they had held since returning from Holland bereft of victory. General Pulteney was still in Holland, overseeing the evacuation of the army, but John had landed at Yarmouth at the end of October and made his way to London, where he and the other generals had been summoned immediately to council with the Duke of York. John had not had time to unpack; he had barely had a moment to see his wife. He wished heartily he were elsewhere, for the atmosphere of defeat was almost as stifling as Essen's bitterness.

'General Essen,' Abercromby said. 'The campaign in Switzerland was over before we struck a single blow in Holland. The outcome of our campaign would not have averted General Suvorov's defeat. You cannot hold the British Government responsible for what happened at Zurich.'

'Responsible!' Essen spluttered. 'What do you know of responsibility? Eight thousand Russian troops have been wasted – 8,000 troops that might have saved Suvorov! Now they will moulder away on your godforsaken islands of Jersey and Guernsey until your government decides what to do with them. Well, they are *your* responsibility now – prisoners in all but name!'

'You forget yourself!' Abercromby snapped. 'Had you followed orders on the 6th of October—'

'Had you marched to our aid on the 19th of September,' Essen interrupted, 'we would, perhaps, be celebrating the capture of

Amsterdam. As for your *orders*, I have always had to interpret them as best I could.'

Across the table the Duke of York poured himself another glass of claret. John, too, helped himself, wincing as his wounded arm throbbed with the effort. The shot he had received outside Castricum had proven to be nothing but a spent ball, but although the stitches had long ago been removed the wound remained tender, a pulsing reminder of the disappointment of the Dutch campaign.

The battle for Castricum had continued long into the night. Although the French and Dutch had retreated to Beverwijk, Abercromby decided not to pursue them in the face of worsening weather and increasingly stretched lines of supply. The day after the assault on Castricum the British and Russians had marched 30 miles back to their old positions behind the Zijpe canal. Lashed by wind and rain, trapped by the enemy, and with marsh fever spreading through the ranks, the only viable strategy had been to negotiate. General Brune had eventually permitted the entire Allied army to evacuate Holland unmolested, on condition that the British government release 8,000 French prisoners of war. The memory made John reach again for the decanter.

The Duke of York rose unsteadily. 'General Essen, the campaign in Holland did not fall entirely upon Russian shoulders. We British, too, took many casualties. We should all be glad most of our army has returned safely to fight on another occasion.'

The memory of Colonel Dickson being felled from his horse by an enemy sabre rose like a poisonous bubble in John's wine-addled mind; Colonel Cholmondeley, too, cut off from the rest of the brigade along with 300 of his men, all of whom were captured in the darkness and carried off as prisoners of war. The fact much of this had happened in the confusion after John had been carried off the field did not help. He could still hear the screaming, and the scent of blood and powder filled his nose. This was what defeat felt like; it felt like emptiness, discord and fear.

He hastily downed his glass and refilled it. He wanted oblivion, if only for one night or even one hour – anything to escape the knowledge that his military career might be over. William would never allow him to serve abroad again; the spent ball to John's shoulder had killed any chance of that.

****

John's carriage drove him the five-minute journey home. A footman had to support him in staggering down the compartment steps, drunk as John was on the commander-in-chief's wine. Although it was late, the oil lamps hanging outside his door still burned. The first-floor windows were ablaze with candlelight. The sound of voices and laughter drifted down as John hammered a sinuous route upstairs to the drawing room.

The room was full of people, his brother's friends mostly. Men like Lord Mulgrave, John Villiers, Tom Steele, George Rose. Dundas sat by the window, looking exhausted, but still finding it in him to laugh at a joke someone had made. Some of William's younger friends were here too, the new bloods recruited since the start of the French conflict: Lord Hawkesbury, thin and gangling, and George Canning, one of William's cleverest and deepest admirers.

In the middle of it all sat John's wife and brother. Mary was evidently enjoying her unfamiliar role as hostess. Her face had a youthful pinkness to it John had not seen for some time. She leaned forwards to touch William's arm gently with her fan, as though to draw a response to something she had said. William was laughing. Despite the military and diplomatic setbacks on the continent his legendary optimism apparently remained unshaken. He looked thin but healthier, and happier, than John could remember.

None of them noticed John's entrance, as though they were a thousand miles from the conflict tearing Europe apart. John bore the stink of that conflict from his boots to his powdered hair. He could still hear the shouts of the French cavalry and the screams of his men. The shapeless anger he had felt since landing at Yarmouth finally coalesced into something specific. How could they sit here, when 12,000 Allied soldiers had died? How could they laugh, when John's career, his independence, his reputation, had dissolved into nothing in the relentless Dutch rain?

He slammed the door. The impact of wood against wood snuffed several candles in their mirrored sconces. Mary turned, arching her eyebrows, and a look of caution crossed the faces of everyone but William, who took John's hand. 'My dear brother, you see we have formed a welcoming committee for you. Lady Chatham told me you would be home late but I wanted very much to take you by the hand again.' The tone of the silence registered at last. His smile faded. 'What is amiss?'

William's concerned face swam like a blur before John's eyes. John glanced over at his wife; Mary's gaze was stern and appraising. Only the thought of seeing her again had got him through the last few ignominious weeks of the campaign, but disappointment had tainted everything, even their reunion. 'I see you've taken the rabble in.'

There was a hiss of indrawn breath. The blood drained from Mary's face. 'John!'

'You're not well,' William frowned. He reached out to place a hand on John's injured right shoulder, and John recoiled with a cry of pain.

'Don't touch me!'

William held up his hands in a backing-off gesture. Mary hissed, 'John, for goodness' sake go to bed.'

'Mary is right,' William murmured. 'You must be exhausted. Your guests—'

'They are not my guests,' John interrupted, coldly. 'They are yours. But it matters little, for Major-General the Lord Chatham is home. I suppose you are longing to hear my stories of bloodshed and defeat.' Nobody moved. John's mouth curled. 'I assure you it makes a fine tale for a winter's evening.'

'I think we ought to leave,' Dundas said. Steele and Mulgrave rose, but John barred their way.

'No, stay a while. I long to hear what has been happening while I have been spilling my blood for my country.'

'And we are grateful,' William interposed, to deflect the flow of John's drunken ire. 'We are glad to see you safe.'

It was a singularly ill-judged statement in John's current mood. 'Well, that's never been much of a concern for you, has it?'

William looked as though John had kicked him in the stomach. 'What do you mean?'

'My well-being,' John snapped. 'Although I suppose you do have a right to be concerned about it. If I were to die, you would go to the Lords as Earl of Chatham and that would be the end of your ministry, would it not?' The horrified look on William's face made John laugh. 'It sometimes gives me great pleasure to know I have more power than Fox to bring down your government, simply by taking a knife and—'

'You're drunk,' William gasped. John leaned back and addressed the plaster mouldings on the ceiling.

'Hark at the pot calling the kettle black!'

'If you really meant what you said then it is long past time you got some rest.'

John moved closer to his brother until their faces were only inches apart. He could see the doubt in William's grey eyes, the freckles across the bridge of his nose, the smudge of brown hair at his temples beneath the powder. 'Maybe I am drunk, but I still know what has been going on. You, Dundas and Windham, sending good troops to Belle-Isle, Ferrol and Minorca. What did we get? A load of drunken militiamen, enough to stave off the reckoning for six weeks in Holland and no more.' Out of the corner of his eye John saw Dundas rise, a concerned look on his wine-reddened face. 'Perhaps you never meant me to return at all. Perhaps you sent me on a doomed campaign to dispose of your embarrassment of a brother. Tell me you were not disappointed when you heard that spent musket ball had not killed me.'

'If you wish to insult me,' William snarled, 'for God's sake be consistent.'

'If I wished to insult you,' John snapped back, 'I should point to that corner of the room …' at Canning and Hawkesbury, watching anxiously, '… and ask why you spend so much time in the company of pretty young men. Perhaps it is the same reason you and my wife were getting on so well just now?'

John's words echoed in the deep silence that greeted them. William went white. All of a sudden Mary pushed herself out of her chair, crossed the room in three long strides, and gave her husband a resounding slap. The sharp sound of flesh meeting flesh echoed like a whip-crack.

'Leave this room,' she said. 'Now.'

John's vision was fuzzy with wine, but the hard emotion on Mary's face shone through his drunken fog like a beacon. He put a hand to his smarting cheek and said nothing.

Mary's voice rose a pitch; a touch of colour infused her face. 'You have insulted me, and just about everyone else in this room, quite enough. Go!'

Behind Mary the others were arranged in various awkward poses, trying very hard not to be there. In the middle of the room, as bloodless as though he, not John, had been struck in the face, was William. His expression was full of hurt and astonishment, with a nascent hint of anger. John did not wait to see whether that anger would become anything more concrete. He gave Mary a lopsided look and turned to leave.

He paused in the doorway. His frustrated ambition still seared through his heart like acid and it was this, rather than drunken anger, that gave his words a new lucidity. 'Only now do I realise how much I have suffered from being your elder brother. Any other military man of my rank would have been employed in battle ten times over. Why not me? Because it took you that long to overcome your fear that I might die and throw you into the Lords. I am the cross you must bear every day, Will. I know now that you are mine.'

He climbed the stairs and staggered into his dressing room. St Aubin offered to take his coat as he went past but John ignored him. Sobriety was creeping up on him, cold, grey and unforgiving, drawing him into a black hole from which he did not know how to escape.

He went to the shaving mirror over the dresser. His long chin was unshaven, his heavy-lidded blue eyes rimmed with red. There were disappointed grooves on either side of his mouth and between his black eyebrows. The older he got the more he looked like his father. The thought did not please him in the least.

****

The guests left shortly after John's departure, each kissing Mary's hand in subdued farewell. Mary could not meet anyone's eye, least of all her brother-in-law's. He hesitated before taking his leave. 'Might I be of service?'

'Thank you, but no,' Mary said. 'John will be well enough after a night's rest.'

Why had she invited William and the others? She had truly thought she was doing the right thing, and William had been so keen to come. She had assumed John's return to the army would allow him to forget the past. She had hoped serving abroad would have given him a new confidence in himself. She should have known better.

She hesitated a moment outside her husband's dressing room, then knocked. There was no response. She waited a space then opened the door. John sat by the dresser. He still wore his regimentals; the gold braid winked in the light from the candles as he turned fractionally to glance over his shoulder.

'John,' she said. He did not reply. She came to stand behind him, close enough to smell the wine on his breath and hear his uneven breathing. His gloved hands were knotted in his lap and he seemed to be waiting for the recriminations to begin. Mary had fully intended to tell him what she thought of his shocking behaviour, but faced with the naked vulnerability in his hunched shoulders she found she could not do it. 'You should have a glass of water. There's a carafe by the bed.' When John did not move, Mary went to the bedchamber next door and poured him a glass herself. She pressed it into his hand. 'Here. Drink.'

He obeyed, keeping his eyes down. She moved a chair next to his, gathered her skirts and sat down in a rustle of silk. John cradled the empty glass in his hands; he seemed fascinated by the refraction of the candlelight in its smooth, curved surface. Mary spoke again, with a tremble of anguish.

'I have spent six weeks waiting for you, counting every day, every hour, every minute of our separation, knowing every one brought me closer to your return. Now you are home, and I find myself wishing you had stayed away longer.'

At last John raised his eyes to meet hers. The pain and disappointment in their blue depths tore through the remainder of her righteous indignation. Tears spilled down her cheeks and John raised a hand to wipe them away. She tensed at his touch, but the crushed expression on his face in response brought the last of her defences crashing down. She moved across onto his lap and laid her head against his chest. She heard his sigh of relief, and felt his fingers trembling as he raised them to stroke her hair.

'I am sorry,' he murmured, thickly.

'I truly hoped for victory.' Mary raised her head and looked at him. 'So did William.'

'Holland was meant to be my opportunity. It was nothing but the grave for several thousand men.'

His eyes stared, glassily, at something only he could see. The whiteness of his face took on a yellow, sickly sheen. Mary reached out a hand, then let it fall back into her lap. She had no idea what he was going through; she had not seen soldiers die; she had not been the one to give the orders that had led to their deaths.

The distance between them felt unbridgeable.

'You had a command,' was all she could think of to say. 'You were commended in the despatches.'

'I did not embarrass myself, if that is what you mean.' He hesitated, then said in a strained, uneven voice, 'All I wanted was a chance to prove myself worthy.'

Mary listened to him with a cold sense of dread. She had feared this self-consuming bitterness more than anything. 'William thinks highly of you, John.'

'Then he must have changed his mind since '94,' John said. Mary remained silent. There was nothing she could tell him that she had not tried to say before.

Chapter Twenty-six

October 1800

Dusk was falling when John arrived at Woodley after a long journey on Berkshire's pot-holed roads. His host met him on the steps of the house. Henry Addington was Speaker of the House of Commons and a childhood friend. John liked Addington very much: he was a handsome, modest man whose innate sense of fairness had allowed him to excel in the Speaker's Chair. 'Lord Chatham. I trust the journey was a good one?'

'My coachman nearly broke an axle near Woking, but we made good time once the horses were calmed.' The two men shook hands. 'I am afraid I cannot stay more than a night. My regiment has just arrived in Winchester and I must join them tomorrow.'

'And yet you took Woodley in your way? It is good to see you, but I take it you are not here on my account?'

'It is always a pleasure to spend time with you,' John protested, and Addington smiled.

'I knew you would be too polite to say so. Your brother is in the garden. I think you will find him vastly improved.'

'I'm glad to hear it,' John said. Before William had left London, he had told John how badly he was sleeping and how ill he felt. William was accustomed to remain at his desk long after ordinary mortals would have taken to their sickbed; for him to complain about his health was uncharacteristic and troubling.

The political situation did not help. After the failure of the Dutch campaign Austria and Russia had both broken alliance with Britain. At home the harvest had failed yet again; the price of bread spiked and panicked magistrates reported rumours of armed insurrections everywhere. Ireland had rebelled in 1798, and still smouldered sullenly. An Act of Union had been rushed through, but only corruption and bribery had ensured its passing and the Cabinet remained deeply divided over whether to include Ireland's Catholics in the political arrangements.

John followed Addington down to the ornamental lake, his boots crunching on the gravelled path. William sat on a bench beneath a willow tree. From behind all John could see was a tall, spare figure wearing a high-crowned hat and grey garrick.

Addington placed a hand on William's shoulder. 'Pitt, you have a visitor.'

'Who is it?' William sounded fractious, almost frightened. A treacherous memory sliced through John's mind of their father during one of his mental breakdowns, bursting into tears at the prospect of having to receive even the most innocuous of well-wishers.

He quashed the memory with difficulty, took a deep breath and stepped into William's line of sight. 'Well now, Will. I trust our friend Addington has been treating you well?'

William had lost the gauntness about the jawline that spoke so eloquently of countless missed meals, but his eyes were dull and his hands shook noticeably even lying idle in his lap. It was hard to tell from his distracted expression whether he was relieved or dismayed by his visitor's identity. 'I have no complaints. Apart, of course, from the fact he will not allow me more than a bottle of wine at dinner, and that shared with him.'

So someone had finally put a stop to William's over-indulgent use of wine. Addington looked awkward and said, as though to excuse an impoliteness, 'I gave Sir Walter Farquhar my word on the matter.'

'Sir Walter Farquhar is a meddlesome old fool,' William said, without rancour, but the effort of remaining light-hearted was too much. His chest heaved as though he struggled to breathe. 'And you? What brings you to Woodley? I hope you have not made the journey to see me?'

'I'm passing through on my way to Winchester to join the 4th.'

'Are you not tired to death of military life? You've spent the whole summer at Swinley marching your men up and down.'

John was sure William had not meant to speak dismissively, but "marching men up and down" rankled. He could not help but wonder – again – how a man who held the fate of nations in his hands could be so naive. Looking closer at his brother's pouched eyes and grey complexion, John wondered whether it was merely William's method of grappling with a situation that had spiralled beyond his ability to control or understand. The stab of pity John experienced at the thought unsettled him. He had never pitied his brother before.

Beneath his coat, William's body trembled like his hands. It could have been from cold but John did not think so. Just in case he said, 'Shall we go indoors? Darkness is drawing in.'

'Yes,' Addington agreed. 'I've had a fire laid in the library, and it is time for dinner. My cook has prepared a haunch of beef for us.'

William blanched at the mention of food, but he nodded and picked up his ivory-headed cane. John helped him to his feet and supported his arm as they walked uphill. By the time they got to the house William was out of breath again, and John found his pity turning, once more, to anxiety.

At dinner, however, William's demeanour changed. When Addington's wife Ursula greeted him, he straightened and forced a smile. He ate very little but he was cheerful enough, and if John had not seen William by the lake he would have believed him fully recovered. But it was a mask, and before dinner was over it started to slip. While Ursula spoke about the Addington boys' latest exploits at Winchester School, William apparently stopped listening to the conversation completely, and when Addington tried to reel him back in he had to have the past few comments repeated.

John was not surprised when William rose before the last service and said, 'I'm afraid I am poor company tonight. If you have no objections I shall turn in early.'

'Are you certain?' Addington said. 'Lord Chatham, after all, leaves tomorrow.'

William flicked his eyes over to his brother; John had the impression William was perfectly happy not to spend more time in his company. 'I know. I'm sorry.'

The servants removed the cloth, and Ursula retired to the parlour. In accordance with his promise to Sir Walter Farquhar, Addington had kept only one decanter of wine on the table. Now that William was gone he called for another. Addington turned to John while the footman filled their glasses. 'Well?'

He had no need to elaborate; his anxiety spoke eloquently enough. John drank thoughtfully and chose his words with care. 'You are right. He does seem better.'

Ten years of sitting in the Speaker's Chair listening to the verbal contortions of politicians had attuned Addington to nuances of speech. 'But?'

'But … I admit I had hoped to find him a little better in the … a little *brighter* than this.' John sighed and poured himself more wine. 'Parliament is due to meet soon. It's deucedly early, but we have no choice. He must know he must be well by then. Why, then, do I get the impression he is not even trying?'

'I wish he had gone to Bath,' Addington said. 'At least I was able to offer him my hospitality to recuperate. I'm certain he will rally. Your visit has done him good, I'm sure.'

John made an uncomfortable snorting noise. He did not think he could do William any good at all. On the contrary he had been glad when William left the dinner table early; dealing with William in this state was too exhausting. He changed the subject. 'Has he talked much about public matters?'

'No. I gave Sir Walter Farquhar my word I would not broach any political subject, nor have I.' Addington hesitated. 'Since Pitt is not here, I would like to ask you about Ireland and the union.'

John swilled the wine around in the bowl of his glass. 'I do not know how much I am at liberty to say.'

'I do not ask you to divulge any secrets. But you must know there are all sorts of rumours: that the Cabinet is divided, for example.'

John snorted again. 'That's not a rumour. That is a well-known fact.'

'I do not mean divisions over war strategy. I mean the disagreement over what to do with Ireland when the union comes into force.'

'You mean the Catholic question.' John sighed. 'Some of my colleagues believe the Catholics must be placated at any cost, to stop Ireland rebelling again; some believe it would be madness of the highest order; the rest do not seem to care either way. The whole business is a lamentable mess and my brother's ill-health could not have come at a worse time.'

Addington scooped some raisins from the bowl in the middle of the table. 'When I was at Weymouth a few weeks ago, attending the King, the talk of the court was that the Cabinet would soon allow Catholics to sit in Parliament and hold high office. There was even a letter, supposedly written by your brother and the Lord Lieutenant, promising the Catholics relief in return for supporting the Union. Have any such promises been made?'

John was horrified. 'I assure you we have had weightier issues to discuss. The Cabinet has discussed the Catholics only once, and there was such a division of opinion my brother did not press the issue.' A sudden chill entered his heart. 'Has the King … has he heard these rumours?' Addington looked at him and John felt the blood drain from his cheeks. The King was a staunch opponent of any relaxation of Britain's bar against Catholics serving in army or state. 'Good God. Does my brother know?'

'I told you. I have not brought the issue up and neither has he.' A pause. Addington threw a searching look at John. 'You said the Cabinet has discussed the Catholics. Is any measure to placate them in contemplation?'

'I cannot imagine my brother would go against the King's wishes,' John said slowly. 'I can see why he might want to win the Catholics over; if they are disgruntled they will be more likely to listen to French enticements. But as the war stands it would be madness to risk the survival of the ministry on such a question.'

'I see you and I agree on the matter.' Addington looked satisfied, but John looked down at his half-empty wine glass with a gnawing doubt in his chest. He had spoken the truth: a healthy, self-possessed William would not venture to propose a measure the King would certainly veto. But William was not healthy. Any self-possession remaining was fragile at best, and John was beginning to wonder whether he knew William well enough any more to guess what he might do.

February 1801

The first battalion of the 4th was on the parade ground, practising drill-book manoeuvres. John, standing outside the pillared frontage of the King's House barracks, watched proudly. Fifteen months had passed since the raw militia recruits of the 4th had faced their first battlefield. John did not know when they would serve abroad again, but when they did he knew they would perform well.

'By companies, on the left backwards wheel!' Colonel Hodgson called. 'Quick march!' Booted feet hammered against frozen ground as the men moved swiftly backwards, eyes fixed inwards towards the stationary pivot point. Each platoon halted, faced front, and dressed up to the platoon that formed the fixed point for the line. 'Wheel up! Form line! Dress!'

'Excellent work, Mr Hodgson,' John called as Hodgson lowered his sword. 'I think your men might fall out now.'

The men pulled on their gloves, twitched the collars of their coats and rubbed their arms, while indoors the womenfolk brewed enormous vats of tea. Hodgson came across the parade ground, his proud face flushed with cold and the effort of calling out orders. 'Well, my lord? Are they not a credit to the service?'

'They have come on wonderfully since Swinley Down last summer, and I thought they were a credit to it then.' Hodgson looked pleased. John had initially supposed his subordinate held his abilities in contempt, but since the Dutch expedition a distant but real respect had grown between them. John was grateful the wound Hodgson had received outside Castricum had not invalided him from the army.

They went inside. The King's House had, as the name suggested, once been a royal palace, intended by Charles II to rival the French Versailles, at least until he had run out of money. It was a grand, spacious building but its conversion into barracks had made it a maze of floors and mezzanines. John's offices as the 4th's colonel were up two winding flights of stairs. He poured Hodgson a glass of brandy and they drank at the window, watching the soldiers outside cradling their metal mugs.

'When do you return to London, sir?' Hodgson asked, after they had discussed plans for the mounting of the guard.

'Whenever business calls me.' John was in no hurry to return to town. He was content here in Winchester with his regiment, where his life revolved around a military schedule and the sinuous beauty of parade. 'I am, happily, not immediately required. The Privy Council can do without a Lord President for a while longer.'

He was interrupted by a knock at the door. It was Captain Chetham, carrying the morning's newspapers. He laid them on the desk, then handed John a slim packet. 'I beg your pardon, my lord, but this arrived by special messenger during parade.'

The packet was from William, marked "Most secret". Dread dropped into John's stomach like a weight. He had not heard from William for weeks. What was amiss? Had another ally made peace with France? The country had been quiet since the price of bread had dropped, but what if there had been more rioting – or worse, an insurrection?

'Is all well, my lord?' Hodgson frowned. John forced a smile.

'I am certain it is, Mr Hodgson, but would you object very much to my reading this letter now? I fear it may require an immediate answer.'

Hodgson retreated to the other side of the room and studied the volumes in John's bookcase. John moved to the window and broke his brother's seal. The fading light glinted off the gold edging of the thick-laid paper.

'My dear Brother, I have been wishing to write to you every day this week, but this busy time has left me not a moment to dispose of. We have both experienced enough times of difficulty to be prepared for anything, however unexpected. I am sure, therefore, that the best thing I can do is to put you at once in possession of the facts.

You left town before we had resumed Cabinet consideration of the Catholic Question. We have discussed it two or three times in the past weeks. As you seemed to have no decided bias in your mind, I did not propose to you to come up at a time when I knew it to be inconvenient. In any case the majority opinion seemed in favour of repealing the laws by which Catholics or Dissenters are excluded from office or Parliament.

At a recent Levee, however, the King's language was so strong and unqualified as to show that his mind was made up to go to any extremity rather than consent to such a measure. Intimations to the same effect from other quarters left me in no doubt of the imprudent degree to which the King's name was committed on a question not yet even regularly submitted to him.

Under these circumstances, with the opinion I had formed and after all that had passed, I had no option but to submit my resignation.'

An involuntary exclamation slipped from John's mouth. Hodgson looked up from the book in his hands. 'My lord? Is anything the matter?'

John ignored him. The paper creased under the pressure of his fingers. There were no blots, no corrections, not even any light inky finger-prints. He could only guess at how many drafts William must have gone through before sending this polished, bland, impersonal copy.

'No option but to submit my resignation.'

A buzzing filled John's ears. He stumbled to the desk, pulled out a chair and sat down. His confusion, bewilderment and shock slowly coalesced into a hard ball of anger. He pulled the brandy decanter towards him and drank a glass down. After a moment, he poured a second glass and gulped that down too. The anger solidified, and grew.

Hodgson shifted uncomfortably. 'Should I go, my lord?'

John had almost forgotten Hodgson was there. His hand tightened into a fist and he came to a decision. He had spent too long living in uncertainty, out of control of his own life. He owed it to himself to face William once and for all. John raised his head and Hodgson's eyes widened at the sight of his expression.

'It appears I was wrong,' John said. 'I am needed in London after all.'

****

The servant in Westminster livery threw open the doors to the Speaker's drawing room and announced, 'Lord Chatham.'

John found Henry Addington by the window overlooking the elegant riverside gardens. A hard frost had shrouded each bare branch in white, and a thin mist from the Thames gave the view an unworldly aspect. The new Prime Minister's handsome face bore deeper lines and his eyes were ringed from lack of sleep, but Addington was plainly resolved to meet his new responsibilities with determination, and John thought it would not be amiss to have a fresh, healthy hand at the helm for a change.

The moment Addington saw John he came over and took his hand. 'My lord! You have travelled swiftly to London.'

'I left the same day I wrote to you. My congratulations, Addington. I could not think of a better man to succeed my brother.'

'Many would disagree,' Addington said lightly. John said nothing. Addington might have been Speaker of the House of Commons for 11 years, but he was still a doctor's son and his sudden elevation to the Treasury and Chancellorship of the Exchequer – the posts William had held for 17 years – had provoked considerable derision. 'Many thanks for your kind letter, Chatham. I am pleased you have decided to remain in office under me. Too many of your colleagues have submitted their resignation.'

'I am no proponent of Catholic relief,' John said. 'There is no reason why I might not remain.'

'And much reason why you might. Pitt has repeatedly expressed his intention to lend my administration all the support that he can, but your remaining will give the doubters confidence in his intentions.' Addington laughed. 'After all, Pitt's own brother would hardly stay on without his approval!'

John smiled thinly and said nothing.

****

'I will not conceal from you that the last few weeks have been difficult. Thank God you came so quickly. It has been ...'

William stumbled into a quavering silence. John gazed rigidly at his plate, its elegant blue china design more than half-obscured by slices of venison, and waited for his brother to regain his composure. It was as though the mask of the Prime Minister was slipping, and William was as shocked as anyone else to discover what lay beneath.

William's confusion was eloquently reflected in the chaos that surrounded him. The brothers had found it difficult to sit down to dinner until the late hour of seven o'clock because of the constant coming and going of visitors. Downing Street was filled with crates, valises and suitcases being packed full of furniture, crockery and linen. Piles of folios stood stacked in the hallway, and John had seen William's two secretaries, Joe Smith and John Carthew, hastily stuffing papers into boxes. The last time John remembered seeing Downing Street in such chaos had been February 1783, when William had received his first offer of the Treasury. So much had happened, so much innocence lost, since then.

'It has been,' William finished at last, 'the hardest experience of my life. And it is not over. His Majesty has accepted my resignation, but he has not yet requested my seals.'

'If you still have your seals, you need not turn them in,' John said, managing with effort to remain dispassionate.

'The King has offered Addington my place, and Addington has accepted. I cannot ask Addington to step aside.'

William reached for more wine. Addington's prohibition of more than one decanter at dinner had not done any good, and the effect of William's escalated drinking was visible in the trembling of his hand as he poured. John watched him drink, then looked away. Once he might have passed comment, but he was long past caring. 'Many would argue Addington's kindly nature suits him better to the Speaker's Chair.'

'You know as well as I do Addington is perfectly fitted for his new office.'

'He is intelligent, he is capable and he has the King's support,' John said shortly, 'but to be frank, William, I cannot comprehend how Addington's fitness for office became a matter of public discussion in the first place.'

William said nothing for a space, concentrating on keeping his hand still to pour himself another glass. 'You must see the King's stand on the Catholic matter gave me no choice but to resign. I told you not to try to change my mind.'

John's fingers tightened around the silver handle of his knife. The Catholic matter! William seemed to think it answered all questions, whereas it merely gave birth to more. 'I am not trying to change your mind. I am merely telling you what everyone else has no doubt told you already, clearly to no avail: that in times of war, famine and unrest your government is more valuable than the remote possibility of relief for Ireland's Catholics. You owe the nation better than this. You owe the King better than this.'

'I deeply regret that His Majesty has anything to reproach me for,' William said, 'but I could have pursued no other course. If the French have any opportunity to inflame opinion against us in Ireland they will not hesitate. Another rebellion would ruin us.'

'And your resigning over a triviality will not?'

'The situation of the Irish Catholics is not trivial. I told you—'

But John was in no mood to discover what it was William had told him. He felt he was on a circular path, taking him round and round without progress. It was time to launch off into the unknown. 'Oh, have *done*, William! Save your breath. Even I can see this has nothing to do with the Irish Catholics.'

'Nothing to do with them?' William's deep voice trembled with anger. 'You think I am resigning because I want to?'

'I do not know why you are resigning,' John said. He wiped his lips with a napkin so hard his lips stung. 'I do not much wish to find out, even if you were to tell me –which I doubt you are capable of doing. You are out. Addington is in. The French are still winning the war, the people continue to starve, and you clearly do not care a whit.'

'John ... John, stop speaking. Be quiet!'

'Why? Because I'm telling the truth?' John did not know why he was speaking like this. Perhaps it was the wine, for William had always had a first-rate taste for alcohol. He did feel a bit inebriated, but only because he spoke directly from the heart. 'I owe you no lip-service. You are no longer my Minister.'

'I never asked for lip-service. I do not even ask for your understanding. I ask only for your support, and I thought when you came to town you had come to give it to me.'

John became suddenly aware of the servant standing behind William's chair and listening with every sign of eagerness. Knowing this was one conversation he wished to remain private John snapped, 'Take away the plates. We are finished.'

The man looked disappointed but gave him a stiff bow, balanced the plates carelessly on one arm, and left the room.

'You seem to think I have come here because of *you*,' John continued when they were alone. He stood. 'You have done nothing but tell me all evening why *you* have resigned; what *you* feel you owe to everyone in the current circumstances. I've no doubt you believe you are acting selflessly for the Irish Catholics, and for our friend Addington, but I don't want to talk about them any more. I have no intention of talking any more about *you* at all.'

'I do not understand.' William watched John warily. John curled a hand round his shield-backed chair.

'I had two reasons for coming to London. My first I fulfilled this morning. I called on Mr Addington and informed him I would remain in office under him.' It was a calculated blow, and it struck home. William's face drained of colour. John had expected the reaction, but the confirmation of his suspicions still infuriated him. 'You seem surprised. I do not know why, for I thought you had been encouraging all your followers to stay on under Addington. Did I misunderstand you? Is it possible you never imagined I would act on your instructions?'

William was fast recovering from the shock. Shaken his nerves might be, but he still had something of the dignity he had always shown in a crisis. 'That was your first reason. You have yet to tell me your second.'

'My second reason,' John said, 'is why I accepted your invitation to dine tonight. I wish to bid you farewell.'

William's haughty expression dropped from his face. His red-rimmed eyes burned with sudden intensity. 'Farewell? Are you going back to Winchester?'

'No,' John said. 'I am staying in London.'

'Then why …?'

'Because we have so little to say to each other I feel we ought to stop trying.'

William started back as though John had struck him, then fury filled his face. His response, when it came, was cold. 'I brought you to my Cabinet. I kept you in it against the advice of my closest friends. You may still blame me for taking you from the Admiralty, but I have nothing to reproach myself for. I made you what you are.'

'What you say is true,' John replied. 'And yet you still abandoned me to my enemies without a qualm.'

'What do you expect me to say?' William said. John closed his eyes.

'Nothing, Will. I expect you to say nothing, as you have done for the past six years.'

William set his lips, but the anger in his face melted into fear as John took a step towards the door. 'John, don't go.'

'You are no longer my Minister,' John said. 'You have no need for me.'

'I am still your brother.'

The burst of fury John felt at those words took him by surprise. He spun round and William flinched. 'No, you are not my brother. You have never been my brother. *I* have always been *yours*, and you have no conception of how hard it has been to bear that knowledge all my life.'

William sat open-mouthed, his eyes strangely dilated. John braced himself for the attack that never came. Instead William's face crumpled and he burst into convulsive tears.

John was too stunned to move. He had expected anger, coldness, perhaps even indifference, but not this clear evidence that his words had wounded William more than he had ever been wounded before. What made it so much worse was that even now John had to fight the instinct to lower his weapons, to offer assistance, to surrender. Even now, after everything, he felt guilty.

And then William made it a thousand times worse. He looked up at his brother and said, 'I am sorry, John. I'm sorry.'

Nothing in the world would induce John to admit these were the very words he had awaited during the whole period of their estrangement. Once they might have been enough, but John had spent six years stewing in unfulfilled bitterness. He set his lips and told a lie.

'I do not care.'

He tensed himself for William's next attempt to keep him from leaving the room. Somewhat to his surprise nothing came. John felt a pulse of disappointment, for William's unwillingness to try harder seemed to be confirmation of John's unworthiness. But when John turned he caught sight of William's lost, broken expression, the expression of a man who had received one blow too many. John suddenly remembered how alone his brother truly was, faced with the prospect of retirement after nearly half his life in office, surrounded by supporters who did not understand what he had done.

In that moment, John knew – felt, even, with every nerve in his body – that he had gone too far. In his haste to step out of William's shadow he had dealt William a worse blow than William had ever inflicted on him. The shock of the realisation came like a sabre-thrust to his stomach, cutting him in two.

He wrenched at the doorknob and fled. In later years when he looked back on that evening he always remembered everything in crisp detail. The plush red carpet under his feet. The smell of damp from the stairwell. John Carthew's exhausted voice remonstrating with a creditor in the parlour. The bite of the cold air on his cheek as he stepped into the street, and the wetness of snowflakes in his hair before he put on his hat. Yet at the time he was aware of nothing but the hollowness at his core. He took one last look at the building with its large sash windows, the soot-blackened exterior, the large front door with its fanlight and knocker in the shape of a roaring lion, all illuminated by the flickering of the oil-lamp.

Then he did what he had sworn 23 years ago he would never do again. He turned up his collar against the wind, stepped onto the icy pavement, and left William to face the future alone.

Chapter Twenty-seven

January 1806

'Now tell me again,' Mary said, kindly but firmly. 'What did you say his name was, and his profession?'

'His name is William Pringle, and he is a colonel in the army. I trust you have no quarrel with that, my lord *General*?' There were spots of colour on Harriot Hester's freckled cheeks and her blue eyes sparkled with defiance. John and Mary had taken her into their house in St James's Square after the death of John's mother three years previously. Edward Eliot, her father, was long gone; he had never got over the death of his wife, and mourned himself into the grave beside her. Now 19, Harriot Hester was undeniably the daughter of Lady Harriot Pitt, fiery and unpredictable.

John sighed. In the weak winter light Mary could count every one of his 49 years in the creases on his brow and round his eyes. 'I have no objection to his profession. I am concerned more particularly about his ability to provide for you.'

'My mother came poor to my father, yet they managed very well, and I am heiress to £10,000 pounds a year.'

'That is precisely why we are concerned—'

'William loves me!' Harriot Hester snapped. Mary flinched at her familiar use of Pringle's first name. 'He cares nothing for my fortune.'

Mary strongly doubted it. Neither she nor John knew much of William Pringle beyond the fact Harriot Hester had met him at a St James's drawing room, and that he was 15 years her senior. The words "fortune-hunter" hung like a spectre behind every heated conversation on the matter, but so far had remained unspoken.

'Miss Eliot, your parents waited to obtain your grandfather's permission before marrying. They were—'

'They were,' Harriot Hester interrupted again, 'under the protection of my *other* uncle, who persuaded my grandfather to give his blessing to a love-match.' John's mouth tightened. Harriot leapt to her feet. 'I wish I had gone to live with Uncle Pitt, along with my cousin Hester. What a pity you did not give me the chance.'

She left in a flurry of cotton muslin and braided auburn hair. John rose but Mary restrained him. 'Let her go. I will go to her.'

John sat back down in obvious relief. A middle-aged, childless man saddled with a headstrong girl could not be expected to have the same tolerance as a man surrounded by daughters. 'A bad business. A very bad business.'

'She's in love.'

'She *thinks* she is.' Mary said nothing. John hesitated. 'Do you suppose she really regrets coming to us?'

'She has been happy here until now.'

'No doubt she is jealous of her cousin Hester,' John said. Since William's return to the premiership just over a year ago, his eldest niece Lady Hester Stanhope had acted as his political hostess, attending the most glamorous functions and enjoying London's social and political life as one of the most important women in the capital after the Queen and Princesses.

'She might have gone to live with your brother. He is also her guardian.'

John snorted. 'William, offer the run of his house to two women? The world was shocked enough when he took in one! Nor did he need to take Hester in at all. My sister may be long dead, but Lord Stanhope is still alive.'

'You can hardly blame Hester for wanting to flee her father.'

'He has made unfortunate political decisions, true enough, and his endorsement of French republicanism makes him dangerous to know, but I cannot forget what Stanhope was when he was still Lord Mahon. I cannot forget he was once my brother-in-law and friend.'

'You are more forgiving of Lord Stanhope than of William,' Mary remarked softly.

John's head jerked up, and she immediately wished she had not spoken. She and John could speak of almost anything, but his quarrel with William was the one topic she had long ago realised she could not broach. Even over the past 18 months, during which he and William had served once more as colleagues in a wartime cabinet, John had taken care never to engage his emotions when speaking of his brother.

Mary would be the first to admit there was much to distract John from inspecting his feelings for his brother. William had wanted to succeed Addington with a strong ministry embracing all political factions, but circumstances had forced him into a narrow, precarious arrangement besieged by the excluded on all sides. Even his own cousin, Grenville, had coalesced with Charles Fox's opposition.

A series of disasters had exacerbated William's political weakness. Henry Dundas, now Lord Melville and the First Lord of the Admiralty, had been accused of embezzling funds while Treasurer of the Navy and would soon stand trial for it. On the continent, a new military coalition had been formed against France, but the defeat of Austria at Ulm and Russia at Austerlitz had destroyed all hope there. The only comforting news had been the victory over the French and Spanish fleets at Trafalgar, but Admiral Lord Nelson's death had overshadowed even that. There was a real chance William's government would not survive the upcoming parliamentary assault. William himself certainly knew it; he had only just returned from six weeks in Bath recouping his health ahead of a session that promised to be rigorous and decisive.

Love and forgiveness, life and death. Mary pressed her fingers to her aching temples. Beneath her hands, she saw her husband watching in concern. She knew she had not been fully present for some time now, and that John had noticed, as wrapped up as he was in public affairs and the prospect of losing his Cabinet post. But everything Mary had seen and heard pointed towards another, private danger on the horizon, one that would soon force her to breach the tacit prohibition that had existed for so long on William. Her husband would soon have more need for her support than, perhaps, he yet knew. She dropped her hands and said, 'You should speak with William about Harriot Hester.'

John's reaction was instant, as though she had suggested something distasteful. 'Why would I want to do that?'

Because once, you would have told him everything without qualm. Because I know you miss that openness more than you will ever say. But Mary said only, 'Because he is also her guardian.'

'I do think he might have more important matters to think about. Parliament meets next week, and William has just returned from Bath. As far as I know he remains at his house in Putney.'

'Are you not worried about William's remaining out of town so close to the sitting of Parliament?' Mary asked, but John either accidentally or deliberately misunderstood her.

'It's not as though he is still in Bath. You know William. He never stops working, even on holiday. I can go to him whenever I wish.'

Mary set her lips in frustration, but she had to insist. 'Come now, John, you've not seen him since the beginning of December.'

'Very well.' John gave an ungracious sigh. 'I will go to Putney tomorrow. In any case I have a letter to deliver to my brother from the King.'

'Good.' Mary closed her eyes in relief, and yet John's unconcerned tone of voice alarmed her. Did he truly not see how unusual it was for his brother to have remained in Bath so long? Could John be so distracted by the political situation that he had not heard the whispers? Or did he simply not want to see, or hear, or believe, the signs that William was more ill than he had ever been before?

But then Mary could hardly blame John for remaining oblivious when she was scarcely able to understand the significance of what was happening herself. She was all too aware that until John and William made their peace, John himself would find none.

****

Mary found Harriot Hester in her room, scowling into her dressing table mirror. Their eyes met in the reflection; Harriot Hester's lips tightened but she said nothing. No doubt John would have received a different reaction, but Harriot Hester had not yet reached the point of chasing her aunt from the room.

Mary drew up a chair and they sat in silence. Harriot Hester looked very young, with her auburn ringlets, her snub nose and her wide blue eyes. Mary could well see why Colonel Pringle might wish to court her, quite beyond her personal fortune. What she could not get past in her mind, however, was how little Harriot Hester looked like her mother. Mary could still remember how similar Lady Harriot Eliot's eyes had looked to John's, almond-shaped and flecked with amber. There was nothing of John at all in Harriot Hester.

'Should you not rest, Aunt Chatham?' Harriot Hester said eventually. 'You seem tired.'

'I am well enough.'

Harriot Hester nodded, unconvinced. She seemed to be waiting for Mary to resume the conversation. Mary supposed it was reasonable of her to do so; why would she have sought her niece out, unless to tell her something specific? And yet she had almost forgotten what she had wanted to say. Her thoughts flew about her head as though something had disturbed them.

At length Harriot Hester said, 'I am sorry about what I said downstairs. I did not mean it.' A pause, then with spirit, 'Apart from what I said about Colonel Pringle. I meant every word of that.'

'You truly wish to wed him?'

'He has asked me to be his wife, and I do not see why I should refuse him.' An expression Mary recognised well enough came into Harriot Hester's eyes. She smiled bashfully at her aunt. 'I love him.'

'Love counts for much,' Mary said. 'But it cannot perform miracles.'

Almost exactly 25 years had passed since she had first fallen in love with John on the terrace at Albemarle Street. Mary wondered if, in the early days of their courtship, she had looked as Harriot Hester did now, glowing with the pleasure of love. She caught a glimpse of herself in the long mirror: her cheeks were sallow, her hair streaked liberally with grey under her powder and cap. It was the face of a stranger. She jumped as Harriot Hester took her hands. Her niece looked anxious.

'Aunt Chatham, I do not think you *are* well.'

Mary opened her mouth to deny it, but something in the touch of Harriot Hester's hand released something that had been kept shut up for too long. She bent her head and choked out a sob.

Harriot Hester's hands tightened. 'Oh, Aunt, I am so sorry. Had I known how much pain I would cause you by my attachment to Colonel Pringle—'

'No, it is not that. It is … it is … I barely know what. I am worried about my husband.'

'Uncle Chatham? Because of the situation of the ministry?' Harriot Hester hazarded. 'Is Uncle Pitt in peril?'

Mary felt hollow, as though the tears had cried all feeling out of her, for now at least. 'I think he is.'

'Then don't worry.' Harriot Hester grinned unconvincingly. 'Uncle Pitt has survived far worse than this. He will surprise us all. He always does.'

That was not what Mary had meant, but she forced a smile, conscious that Harriot Hester needed reassurance as much as she did.

Chapter Twenty-eight

January 1806

The deserted streets were plunged into a winter's gloom when John's carriage left St James's Square for Putney. A strong wind whistled round the glass window and threatened to blow out John's travelling lamp as he crossed the simple wooden toll-bridge between Fulham and Wandsworth. He tried to distract himself with reading, but the movement of the coach made him feel ill and forced him to abandon his book. He gazed out of the window at the bare-branched trees, the frosty fields, and the passing houses, and thought.

This visit to Putney was a fool's errand. He had nothing to say to William that could not wait till his brother was in London. Why had Mary insisted on his going now? John frowned at his reflection in the carriage window. Somewhere beyond his worries about the fate of the ministry and the prospect of losing his Cabinet post, John was vaguely aware his wife was slipping away from him. He was finding it increasingly difficult to read her thoughts, as though she were afraid of what he might find if she let him in.

The pale bronze sky promised snow as the carriage turned off the Portsmouth road onto the gravel path leading to Bowling Green House. John peered at the approaching house's long, stuccoed frontage with some trepidation. Melville, Ulm, Austerlitz – would William shrug it all off, as he often did bad news? Would he need comfort? If so would John be capable of giving it to him?

These questions dropped out of his mind the moment he stepped across the threshold. John had expected William to have plenty of visitors, and had anticipated being one of many clamouring for a moment of his brother's time. And yet the house was quiet and empty. There were no liveried messengers, no clerks carrying bundles of papers, no backbenchers waiting for an audience, nobody at all except George Pretyman-Tomline, Bishop of Lincoln.

John clasped the Bishop's hand in greeting. 'My dear Bishop, what brings you here? And where is everyone else?'

He was a little rattled to find himself alone with the Bishop. Tomline had been William's college tutor at Cambridge and John knew him as an affable, if on occasion overly pious, man. He could not, however, for the life of him guess why William might have invited an old friend this close to an important parliamentary season.

Whatever the Bishop's business was, it was clearly a burden to him: he wore a weary, worried expression. 'The answers to your questions are connected. Mr Pitt has already seen Lord Mulgrave and Mr Rose, and is expecting Marquis Wellesley at four; but everyone else has been turned away so that Mr Pitt does not over-exert himself.'

'I see,' John said, feeling more confused than ever. William would have to be very ill indeed to submit to enforced rest less than a week before the meeting of Parliament. 'Where is he, by the way?'

'He is taking an airing in his carriage with Lady Hester Stanhope.'

'Well, I am glad he seems to be feeling better!' The Bishop smiled, but humourlessly, as though in spontaneous reaction to John's words. 'When can I see him?'

'It depends on the nature of your business.' John frowned; the practice of interrogating Cabinet ministers before allowing them into William's presence was nothing if not novel. The Bishop raised his hands. 'I do not ask for Cabinet secrets, my lord. It is merely that Mr Pitt invited me to Putney to transact his business until he is better recovered.'

John opened his mouth to say he had been misunderstood, then the full force of the Bishop's words struck him. 'I do not think I heard properly. Did you say *transact his business*?'

The Bishop looked sharply at John, as though searching for the answer to an unspoken question, then opened the door to the drawing room. 'I think, my lord, you had better take a seat.'

John stepped past the Bishop. Before it had been converted into lodgings, Bowling Green House had been an inn devoted to the illegal practice of cock-fighting, and several of the rooms still bore signs of their convivial past. This drawing room was vast enough to hold 50 people or more. At one end of the room stood an enormous stone-fronted fireplace, capable of providing heat to a large company of people. The Bishop drew up two chairs before the coal fire. John took one of them, his fists resting on his knees. The Bishop took the other.

Tomline seemed suddenly disinclined to speak, as though he had not thought properly ahead and did not know how to begin. His pouched brown eyes darted nervously about him at the ceiling, out of the window, then down at his clasped hands. At length, he said, 'You know, of course, that Mr Pitt returned from Bath three days ago, having found the waters ineffective.'

'I understand he intends to remain here until he has shaken off the gout.'

The Bishop hesitated, as though he wanted to make a correction to John's statement. 'When he arrived here, the first thing he did was consult with Sir Walter Farquhar. At Mr Pitt's request Sir Walter summoned two other physicians, Dr Baillie and Dr Reynolds, for another opinion. All three agree that Mr Pitt ought to rest as much as possible.'

'Rest!' John interrupted, aghast. 'How can he rest? Parliament meets in six days!'

'Since rest is what he needs,' the Bishop continued, ignoring John, 'rest is what he must get. If he cannot see you today, I will send a messenger to you tomorrow if he is better.'

John wondered for a moment if Tomline was trying to give himself an air of exaggerated importance, but he dismissed the suspicion immediately: the Bishop's drawn face suggested he did not relish his task. John narrowed his eyes. 'Do you mean to keep His Majesty's Minister uninformed of public affairs?'

'No. I wish to keep him from dwelling on subjects which are liable to distress him. I refer to the upcoming trial of Lord Melville, and the recent defeats on the continent.'

'Whether it causes him distress or not, he will have to know eventually.' The Bishop made the same convulsive smile he had given earlier when John had made his flippant remark about William's health, and John got the unpleasant feeling there was something he was not being told. 'If you must know, I have a letter to deliver to Mr Pitt from His Majesty, and a few words of a private nature to tell him. There should be no need to touch on politics at all.'

He was interrupted by the sound of a carriage coming to a halt on the gravelled area outside. John saw concern cross the Bishop's jowled face. 'If you will excuse me?'

'Of course.'

The Bishop closed the door behind him. John heard footsteps crunch across the gravel and several low voices. He heard his niece, Lady Hester Stanhope, saying, 'We had to turn back at the end of the common. A little too much perhaps.'

Another voice chimed in with a lowland Scots burr: Sir Walter Farquhar, William's physician. 'Perhaps we ought to fetch a chair.'

'No,' a third voice said, a hollow, exhausted voice John did not at first recognise as his brother's. 'I have enough strength remaining to assault the stairs.'

John leapt to his feet as the door reopened, but the Bishop closed it so quickly he saw nothing in the hallway but the tail of a coat and the flash of a white stocking. Tomline's face seemed more lined than it had been before he had left the room, but he forced out the same strange smile he had given several times already and said, 'Mr Pitt has returned, but I am afraid he is too tired for visitors. Perhaps it is best if I take your letter and give it to him myself.'

John had been expecting something like this from the moment the Bishop had shown him into the drawing room. Tomline's sanctimonious air was beginning to annoy him. He said, sharply, 'My dear Bishop, I have a private family matter to discuss with Mr Pitt. Withholding the information from him may produce the most serious consequences.'

Tomline looked worried for a moment, then said reluctantly, 'If you will wait a moment, I will ask upstairs.'

He left the room. John settled back in his chair and waited to be summoned. The clock showed that it was only three o'clock, but already the trees at the end of the garden were silhouetted against a coal-coloured sky. John listened for a while to the sounds from upstairs: creaking boards, muffled voices, the occasional hollow cough. A maid came in, curtseyed to John, and lit two branches of candles with a taper.

The Bishop did not reappear. John chose a well-thumbed book of Horace's poems off the bookshelf, drew up the candelabrum and sat down to read, but the longer it took for someone to come and fetch him the less he found himself capable of concentrating on the Latin text. He knew very well his business was not urgent, but he was damned if he was going to be kept waiting like some common back-bencher.

He snapped the book shut with an oath, glanced angrily at the clock, and went upstairs.

At the sound of his approach one of the doors opened instantly, and the Bishop of Lincoln's head appeared. At the sight of John, he opened his mouth indignantly. 'My lord, you promised—'

'So did you,' John replied, and pushed past.

The candles in the sconces bathed the small room in a warm glow. William's valet stood by the bed, holding a bowl and a towel. Sitting in a wicker chair was a grizzled, heavy-jowled man John knew to be Sir Walter Farquhar. He held a watch in one hand and took William's pulse with the other. William lay on a green striped chaise-longue, holding a cup of amber liquid. His coat, waistcoat and lace stock had been removed and three or four buttons at the top of his shirt undone.

Farquhar was speaking, insistently, as though coaxing a reluctant child. 'It is an egg mixed in brandy. You really must drink it, sir. It will give you strength.'

'I do not think I can.' William's voice was strained, as though his throat were constricted.

'You must drink,' Farquhar repeated, with all the emphasis of simplicity.

William forced the cup to his lips. The Bishop, who had entered the room after John, said in warning, 'Doctor ...'

Farquhar looked up from his patient and saw John. Fury crossed his face. 'What is the meaning of this?'

'I have come to see my brother,' John said, his eyes on William.

William's translucent, bruised eyelids fluttered open and focused on John with difficulty. 'Is it urgent?'

Two months had passed since John had last seen his brother. He knew William had not drawn much benefit from the Bath waters, knew it had taken him three days to travel to Putney, but nothing had prepared him for this. John had come expecting to find the Minister; he found himself face to face, unexpectedly, with his brother, his face radiating pain, his voice weak and insubstantial.

Shock robbed John momentarily of speech. He fished in his pocket and brought out the King's packet. 'I have a letter for you.'

'It can wait.'

'Perhaps,' John said, reluctant to give up his advantage now that he was in the room, 'but I also wish to speak with you.'

William closed his eyes, as though it was too much effort to keep them open. He seemed to concentrate on some inner turmoil for a moment. Farquhar said, 'My lord, I must ask you to leave.'

'Are you not even going to read your letter?' John pressed, ignoring the doctor. He knew perfectly well the King's note contained nothing vital, and yet it had become, suddenly, terribly important that William should read it. John's mind shied away from the implications of his apparent inability to do so. 'Are you afraid it will contain news of another Ulm, another Austerlitz?'

William's brow contracted. 'John, please ...'

'My lord,' the Bishop of Lincoln cut in, but John paid him no heed. Rage flooded his veins and he did not know how to account for it, or how to stem it.

'You cannot rest on that couch forever! How will any business get done?'

'I am trying,' William said, peevishly. 'Only give me time.'

'*You have no time*!' John shouted. 'Parliament opens in six days!' William shook his head weakly and turned away. Fury and fear lodged in John's throat; without thinking he grabbed William by the shoulders. '*Look at me*!'

Shock sliced through him the moment his fingers made contact. Through the fabric of his shirt William was skeletally thin. Even as that thought dropped into John's mind, William looked him in the eyes for the first time. John reeled from the pain and suffering he saw there. He recoiled from his brother as though stung.

'My Lord Chatham,' the Bishop of Lincoln said, breaking the ensuing silence. 'I really think you ought to come downstairs.'

Tomline's expression was solemn but there was no anger in it. John glanced back at William. His brother had put the glass of egg brandy to his lips again with much concentration and a heavily furrowed brow. His wrists were bony and his hands shook. Panic filled John's veins, suddenly, incomprehensibly.

The Bishop accompanied him to the drawing room and pressed a glass into John's hand. Hardly knowing what he was doing John took a sip; warmth rushed to his lips and down his throat, but still he felt numb. Somewhere on the fringe of his consciousness were the thoughts he knew he would eventually have to consider, but he was not yet ready for them. He turned to Tomline, who had resumed his seat by the fire. 'Why did you not tell me he was like this?'

'I thought Mr Pitt would not be able to see you,' Tomline said regretfully.

'So you thought I might leave and spare you the need to inform me of my brother's situation!' A pulse of anger ripped through John's numbness. He ran his hands through his hair. 'He was supposed to be getting better. Farquhar said the gout had gone—'

He was interrupted by the door crashing open. As though he had heard his name Sir Walter Farquhar stormed in, his long face grey with fury. 'What the devil were you trying to achieve with your grand entrance, sir?'

'I was not aware of my brother's situation,' John said, stiffly. 'If you had let me know sooner, perhaps I might have come prepared.'

Farquhar's blue eyes widened. 'Mr Pitt is a sick man, as you must have realised. It took all my effort to persuade him to go to Bath. If your antics have undone all my good work—'

'I am certain Lord Chatham meant no harm,' the Bishop intervened, unexpectedly, in John's favour. 'I believe he was simply shocked when he realised the severity of Mr Pitt's condition.'

John did not expect that to mollify Farquhar, but he was startled by the vehemence of the doctor's response. 'There is no reason for over-reaction! Mr Pitt has been very ill but he is getting better. There is nothing more to it, Bishop.'

The Bishop looked doubtful. 'I do not know if you—'

'You do not understand!' Sir Walter interrupted, and John suddenly saw the pallor of Farquhar's skin, the sheen of sweat on his upper lip: the doctor was terrified. 'I have told you over and over again. There is no organic damage, and you know as well as I do how quickly Mr Pitt can recover from the most serious illnesses.'

'You're mad,' Tomline said, shaking his head. 'There is no *need* for organic damage. Mr Pitt can keep nothing down. How is he to recover strength?'

'Mr Pitt has recovered in the past from worse attacks than this. What he needs more than anything else is rest and quiet.' Farquhar turned his burning gaze back onto John. 'So I would be obliged if Your Lordship would refrain from repeating your little performance.'

'I am sorry, I did not know—' John began, but Farquhar did not wait for him to finish. He turned on his heel and stalked out of the room.

The Bishop said nothing for a moment, visibly shaken. John drained his glass of brandy in silence. He was disturbed by the fear he had seen in Farquhar's face, and did not want to think too much about what it might portend.

He put the empty brandy glass down on the mantelpiece and wiped his clammy hands against his waistcoat. 'I am sorry. Truly sorry.'

'Do not fret overmuch,' the Bishop said, abruptly but not unkindly. 'I expect you did less damage to Mr Pitt than Lords Castlereagh and Hawkesbury did yesterday when they came to discuss the situation in Europe.'

The mention of the War and Home Secretaries gave John a sickening jolt. Ill though he was, William still headed a ministry that was due to face a hostile political assault in six days. 'Will my brother be well enough to attend Parliament?' The Bishop looked at him. John's mouth went dry. 'Will he have to resign?'

'We will think about that when the time comes.'

There was a great deal in that sentence left unsaid. John saw his unspoken thoughts reflected in the Bishop's drawn face, and felt the swell of cold fear.

The silence was broken by the sound of painful retching from upstairs. Clearly the egg in brandy would provide no nourishment. John saw Tomline's distress; his fear intensified. Only that morning he had been fretting about the possibility that his niece might elope with an unsuitable man. He would have given anything to have only that to worry about again.

Chapter Twenty-nine

January 1806

The day of the Queen's birthday, Saturday the 18th of January, dawned frosty and grey. John rose that morning and calmly dressed as though nothing was wrong. The newspapers were full of desponding accounts from Putney, but he drew normality about him like a cloak, trying to block out all acknowledgment that William might be in danger. It was easier that way – for now, at least.

'Is it appropriate for us to go?' Mary asked at breakfast, toying with her buttered toast listlessly without taking a bite. John paused midmouthful.

'Why should it not be?'

He held her gaze for a moment, daring her to say the words. Her eyelids flickered and she looked down at her plate. She did not look well and John felt a pang of guilt, but before he could apologise she had risen from the table and left the room.

A thin sleet was falling by the time John helped Mary negotiate her large hooped skirts out of the house. Despite the weather the city was in a state of celebration: all the public buildings and churches were hung with the union flag. As John walked through the crenellated red brick entrance of St James's Palace with Mary on his arm he could hear the loud report of artillery in St James's Park firing 61 blanks, one for each year of Queen Charlotte's life.

Court instructions were not to light candles for anything less than a ball, and it was difficult to make out the company in the winter gloom. The Grand Council Chamber was full of people. The Queen's birthday was one of the most important dates in the calendar of royal pageantry, but drawing rooms were never so crowded as at times when ministries were under threat.

John remarked on the number of oppositionists present, like vultures waiting for the kill. 'I do not think I have seen Richard Sheridan at court in nearly 20 years. As for our supporters, there are not as many as I would have expected.' He peered around, thinking of all the drawing rooms he and Mary had attended over the years. So many of the faces of William's first ministry were missing or gone. Mary's father was long dead, struck down by apoplexy six years ago. Thurlow and Richmond were too old and infirm to make a regular bow at court. Henry Dundas, Lord Melville could not appear whilst under the shadow of impeachment.

Time was moving on. The faces here were of the new generation; but there were some notable absences.

'Lady Hester Stanhope,' John said. His eyes still searched the throng, increasingly desperate. 'She is not here.'

Mary looked relieved that she would not to have to submit to Lady Hester's biting tongue, but John felt his anxiety rising. The minister's hostess could not miss the Queen's birthday drawing room, and he had hoped to acquire news from Putney from her.

'Perhaps she is late,' Mary said.

'Perhaps.' John craned his neck again, then drew back with a sharp breath. 'Oh, good God.'

'What is it?' Mary hissed, but John had already schooled his face into what he hoped was an impenetrable mask as his cousin pushed through the crowds towards them. Grenville was the last person John wanted to talk to, but it was too late to pretend he had not seen him. He steeled himself for the ordeal.

'Lord Grenville.'

'Lord Chatham. Lady Chatham.' William's former Foreign Secretary, now Fox's ally and head of the political opposition, bowed to John and kissed Mary's hand.

An awkward silence fell. John saw Mary looking up curiously at him, waiting for him to say something, but he was too busy trying to work out how to make the exchange as brief as possible without seeming rude. Grenville had changed since John had last seen him. He had always been a small man, but now he was getting plump, and what little hair he had left was streaked with grey. He looked as uncomfortable as John felt, and when he spoke his voice was strained. 'I wished, my dear cousin, to congratulate you on your appointment as commander of the Eastern District.'

Across the room, John's Cabinet colleagues, Lord Hawkesbury and Lord Castlereagh, had noticed John and Grenville together and began whispering to each other. John tried to ignore them. 'My thanks.'

'I hear,' Grenville went on, wretchedly, wringing his hands, 'that you will soon take up headquarters at Colchester?'

'I had planned to do so, but given the current state of public affairs I will remain in London for at least another month.' The shadow of the two men's relative political positions cast itself down hard upon John's words. Grenville's hand-wringing became more desperate. 'Besides, I do not feel it right to leave town until my brother's health has improved.'

His words seemed to relieve Grenville of a weight, as though he had wanted to introduce the subject of William and was glad it had been done for him. 'What news have you from Putney?' John pressed his lips firmly together. So that was what this was all about. He had suspected the congratulations on the military appointment had been nothing but an excuse to approach him. He fixed his eyes on Grenville, wondering how much he should say to this man who was, after all, the leader of the opposition. Grenville understood immediately what was passing through his mind and shook his head. 'I hope you understand I speak as your cousin, not as a politician. I know I have no reason to expect, or deserve, anything more from you, but...'

He tailed off, but he had no need to blunder on with his protestations. As reluctant as he was to give the opposition leader any information, John had no news to impart anyway. 'You should be asking my niece, Lady Hester Stanhope.'

'She is not here.'

That was true enough, and John tried not to think too hard about what her absence might mean. He deflected the uncomfortable thoughts with a stiff shrug. 'I'm afraid I know very little.' He added, sarcastically. 'Like you, I am not in the secret.'

He bowed, clearly intending to end the conversation, but instead of taking the hint Grenville blurted out, 'Wellesley told me you saw Pitt the same day he did.'

Lord Wellesley, a close friend of William's and an old university companion of Grenville's, had just come back from a long governor-generalship of India. Although he could not quite say why, a nagging doubt entered his mind. He spoke as blithely as he could. 'What did he tell you?'

It had been a simple request for information, but to John's astonishment Grenville's melancholy grey eyes widened and filled with tears. He mastered the emotion quickly enough, but for a man who had always been less disposed to showing his emotions in public than William it was a disturbing reaction. He parried John's question with another. 'How did you find him?'

'Wellesley? I left before he arrived—'

'Not Wellesley,' Grenville corrected. 'Pitt.'

Even after two years of political estrangement Grenville still referred to the Prime Minister by the familiar use of his last name. For the first time John felt a twinge of familiarity with his cousin, who, like him, found himself looking in on William's life from the outside. It was this feeling rather than any desire to talk about what had happened at Putney that prompted John to reply. 'He was clearly unwell, and I was only able to spend a short time with him. I spent most of my time with the Bishop of Lincoln.' He dwelt on that conversation a second or so, then pushed it roughly out of his mind: he was not ready to devote much thought to it yet. He finished, with a half-shrug, 'I admit he's weak, but he will rally soon. He always does.'

On the edge of his field of vision he saw Mary close her eyes and heard her exhale sharply, as though against a sweep of pain. Grenville, on the other hand, looked openly offended now. He said in a strained voice, 'You think I am spying for information.'

'Not at all,' John said hurriedly. Grenville's voice shook with emotion.

'Many things have passed between Pitt and me over the last few years, most of which I heartily regret, but if I thought there was even the slightest chance of being allowed to his bedside to beg forgiveness, I need not tell you how quickly I would go ... How severe is his danger?'

A chill raced through John at Grenville's words, as though someone had opened a door and let in a rush of frozen air. All he could think of was William's hoarse, exhausted voice, hollow eyes, and wasted body. The memory cut at him like a knife; he winced at the pain, staggering away from the blow. Beside him, Mary slid her hand round his and squeezed it. The pressure from her gloved hand brought him out of the past and back into the present. It took John only a moment to summon the anger required to bury the panic in his heart. 'I have told you all I know, my lord. What do you wish me to say? That my brother is dying?'

'Oh, John ...' Mary muttered.

Grenville stared at John. 'He is not?'

'Would I be here if he were?' John said coldly.

Grenville said nothing, but continued to look at John with the same mixture of astonishment, dismay and pity. It struck John that Grenville knew a lot more about William's situation than he was letting on. He experienced the same prick of cold fear he had felt in William's Putney drawing room, when the Bishop of Lincoln had given him a look like the one Grenville was giving him now. His anger evaporated as quickly as it had come. After years of offering impeccable service as an emotional shield, it had finally met its match in the cold reality that William might die.

The royal band in the anteroom struck up the birthday ode, announcing the arrival of the Queen. Grenville gave John a last, long scrutiny, then bowed and returned to the other side of the room.

John gave one last, desperate look around him. Castlereagh and Hawkesbury were still staring at him with little favour, but he was too shaken by what had just passed to pay them any heed. 'Lady Hester is still not here.'

'No,' Mary whispered back. 'She is not.'

The Queen rustled into the room, wearing a dark grey velvet gown with gold tassels in the shape of acorns. She took position leaning against a marble-topped table placed under a window to take full advantage of the fading light. The days when both the King and Queen had each made their own circuit around the assemblage were long gone. The King, incapacitated by his increasing blindness, rarely attended drawing rooms, and the Queen preferred the company to come to her. Each individual was announced by the chamberlain and then brought by their sponsors to kiss Her Majesty's hand.

Beside John, Mary caught her breath. She flung out a hand and clung to her husband's arm, her breath coming out in ragged gasps. Her face was the colour of fresh snow. John felt her leaning against him with all her weight. He remembered how off-colour she had seemed lately and his mouth went dry. 'Careful. Are you well?'

Across the room he could see heads turning in her direction. Some frowned, others whispered behind their hands. Mary, too, was aware they were in a public place. He could tell she was still in pain, but she raised her head and steadied her breathing under the curious eyes of the rest of the crowd. 'Don't fret. I merely slept badly last night.'

'You're so pale,' he said, unconvinced. She looked like wax in the thin winter light, and there were rings under her eyes. Through her gloves, John could feel the bones in her wrist; it occurred to him that it had been some time since he had seen her do anything beyond push her food half-heartedly around on her plate. 'You should go home.'

She shook her head bravely. 'The Queen is here. I'll rest later.'

John opened his mouth to protest, but then he saw something that wiped all other thoughts out of his mind. Even though it was bad etiquette to enter the council chamber after presentations had begun, two people had just slipped in: Lady Hester Stanhope, and her 17-year-old brother James.

The wave of relief that flooded through him was such that he only then realised how much their absence had fed his unacknowledged fears.

The presentations ended as the last of the winter light fled from the gilded council chamber. After the Queen had departed, the room burst into a hum of conversation. John took Mary's hand from his arm. 'Excuse me.'

'We should leave here before it becomes too dark to see our way out,' Mary said, but John smiled absently.

'In a minute.'

Mary followed his gaze. She saw Lady Hester then looked up at her husband with an expression he could not quite gauge; it was full of sadness and pity. He led her over to his niece. Lady Hester was already preparing to leave, even though she had arrived late. James Stanhope dealt with a string of people while his sister stood silently by the door waiting for a suitable gap in the departing crowds. She wore a high-waisted black and green velvet gown studded with rubies, her considerable height increased by a head-dress of feathers and diamonds, but she uncharacteristically shied away from attention, fiddling with her silk gloves and smiling coldly to deter anyone who approached.

He had expected Lady Hester to greet him coldly, but he had at least expected her to greet him. The moment she saw her uncle approach she set her carmined lips in a thin line and turned deliberately away.

Disbelief and fury filled John's veins. In his outrage, he forgot that he was supposed to wait for a lady to acknowledge him and called out, 'Lady Hester. A word, if I may.'

Lady Hester was chalky white under her rouge. Her eyes were ringed with sleeplessness and her voice was unsteady with fury and fear. 'You may not.'

John did not know what shocked him more, her words or the desolation in her eyes. Lady Hester took the opportunity of his speechlessness to turn away again, but John caught her back, cold fear slicing through him again. 'I only want to ask you how my brother is.'

'Ask him yourself,' Lady Hester snapped, so shrilly that several courtiers looked round with interest. John's hand tightened round Mary's.

'I only thought, since you were here—'

'You *thought*, no doubt,' Lady Hester interrupted, 'as little as you did last week, when you came to Putney and attacked my uncle on his sickbed. All you deserve to know is that he did not suffer for your foolishness.'

'John,' Mary murmured, but John was too angry and embarrassed to pay her any heed.

'I only want to know if he is improving. I did not think you would have come here if he were worse.'

Lady Hester flung him a hysterical look, but said nothing. This time John did not hold her back, and she slipped into the crowds picking their way blindly along the long, unlit hallway.

He turned to Mary and gave her a half-smile to hide how shaken he was by the exchange. 'Foolish child.' Mary just looked at him; John saw the trembling of the feathers in her head-dress and realised she was swaying slightly. Despite the coldness of the room, her forehead was sheened in sweat. He frowned. 'What is the matter?'

'Will you return to Putney?' It was the closest she had come to questioning his opinion of William's illness. He could see the effort the words cost her. John blinked. Time was moving too swiftly for his liking;

all was confusion, all was noise, his thoughts drowned out by the possibility that his brother might, after all, be dying.

And yet he had no reason to believe that. His fear had been stoked by the darkness and by the gloom. Had there been reason to be despondent, surely someone would have told him so, and as rude as Lady Hester had been, she had not said William was worse. Mary was right: the only way he could lay those ghosts to rest was by returning to Putney and seeing for himself. 'I suppose I should, probably, yes.'

Naked relief chased across her face. 'Will you go today?'

'Good lord, what's the rush? It will be dark in an hour. There will be plenty of time to visit William tomorrow, or the day after that.' Mary flinched, but she did not protest further. She looked as though she could barely stand. John bit his lip against his concern and put his arm around her shoulders. 'Come. Let us return to St James's Square. I think you need a rest.'

****

Parliament opened on the 21st of January under a pall. The floor of the House of Lords was crowded with strangers, waiting and hoping to see the opposition tear the ministry limb from limb. They were disappointed. Lord Grenville, even more strained and miserable than at the Queen's drawing room, announced his decision to postpone his attack until more favourable accounts should be received of the First Lord of the Treasury. Fox made the same announcement in the Commons. The sword of Damocles suspended over the ministry continued to hang by a thread.

John finally set out for Putney the morning after the opening of Parliament. The sky was still dark and there was a hard frost on the ground shrouding everything in white. He still clung to a vague hope that Farquhar had been right and William was merely weakened by gout, but the moment the porter opened the door John knew his brother's situation was serious. The porter was grey-faced and deeply upset. He barely seemed to recognise John, and made to close the door in his face. 'I am sorry, sir, but Sir Walter said no visitors.'

'But I am the Earl of Chatham,' John protested, his breath pooling desperately before him in clouds of steam. He added, unnecessarily, as though he had something to prove, 'Mr Pitt's brother.'

The porter looked wretched, as though weighing the consequences of disobeying Farquhar's orders against the consequences of locking out the brother of the Prime Minister. Eventually he compromised, and allowed John access to the drawing room while Sir Walter's judgment was sought.

William, ever the optimist, had always been very fond of green, and the colour of hope was everywhere. It was in the curtains, the fabric of the chairs and sofas, even in the heavy woollen rugs laid in front of the terrace doors. John wished he had chosen a different colour; its freshness and vigour in this house of sickness offended him. There was a constant thunder of footsteps going up and down stairs as servants bustled past carrying trays of medicines. John found himself straining for noises from the first floor, any sign at all that his brother might be able to see him.

After a few minutes the door opened and Sir Walter entered. He looked exhausted, but his face was hard and uncompromising. 'Lord Chatham. I wondered when you would darken this door again.'

John flinched at the hostility in Farquhar's tone. 'I wish to see my brother.'

'Mr Pitt is unable to receive visitors,' Farquhar replied, and slanted a hard glance down on John.

The look pierced John like a shard of ice. He had put off his visit as long as possible, but never once had he entertained the prospect that he might be turned away. He forced himself to speak civilly. 'I am pleased you are taking my brother's well-being so much in hand, but I trust you will make an exception for his brother.'

Sir Walter's lips tightened as though he thought John had sacrificed all entitlement to that claim. 'It would be irresponsible of me to admit you to Mr Pitt's bedside after what happened last week.'

For the second time John felt Farquhar had knocked the breath out of his body. Until now he had thought Farquhar was the chief obstacle standing between him and William; with a shock, he began to realise why the doctor was so hostile. 'I will not leave until I have seen him.'

'Then you will not leave,' Farquhar said, his voice rising angrily. At that moment, the door opened to admit the Bishop of Lincoln. Sir Walter turned to him in appeal. 'Sir, my Lord Chatham insists on seeing his brother.'

The Bishop placed a placatory hand on Sir Walter's shoulder. 'My dear doctor, you should not make such a noise. You can be heard above stairs.' The image of the sick man lying above them drove into John's mind like a dagger. Tomline smiled as though to say *Be easy. I will deal with this*, and said to Sir Walter, 'You should go to him. Pursler says it is time for his opiate.'

Sir Walter gave John one last glare then left the room. John breathed a sigh of relief and turned to Tomline, certain he had one ally in the house. 'Bishop, I must see my brother.'

Tomline said nothing, but sank heavily into a chair. The silence was so deep John thought he would be driven deaf by it. The Bishop raised his head and John looked him in the eyes for the first time. Another chill coursed down his spine. Tomline, it appeared, was no more minded than Farquhar to give John a chance to cause his brother harm.

'I do not have the authority to override Sir Walter in the sickroom,' Tomline said. 'If he says visitors cannot be admitted, I must uphold that prohibition, even if the King himself were to request an audience.'

John's mind raced so fast he could barely sort through his thoughts. He opted for the brazen approach; he was damned if he would leave without fighting. 'May I ask why I am to be denied access?'

'I am not denying you access.'

'Sir Walter is, and as you just told me, it amounts to the same thing.'

The Bishop said nothing for a moment, caught out. At length he said, 'To be honest, I am not displeased Sir Walter wishes Mr Pitt to remain undisturbed. I have been sitting with your brother this morning. He and I have been praying. Now he needs reflection, untroubled by worldly matters.'

The Bishop's brown eyes were bright, and held John's with a penetrating gaze. As soon as it became apparent he was not going to get a straight answer, John dropped his head. Tomline was too subtle to reproach him directly, but Farquhar had had no such qualms. It was only a week since John had burst into William's room and shouted at him to pull himself together. He did not feel any better knowing that, had he come to Putney earlier, he would have been turned away in the same manner.

A cold, desperate stillness came upon him, dousing the frantic urgency that had powered him until that moment. The anger he had focused on Farquhar and Tomline for obstructing him crumbled in his heart. He had no-one to blame but himself.

'You said he has prayed. Is he, then ... will he ...?'

He tailed off, but clearly saw the answer to his unspoken question in the Bishop's ashen face. The hollowness inside dug a little deeper.

He found his voice at last. 'Answer me one question. Did Wi— did my brother ask you to keep me away?'

'I give you my word he would greet you with open arms.'

Still John was not satisfied. He said, 'You know I will have to see him eventually.'

'And so you shall.' Tomline rose and walked to the door. He turned to John with one hand on the latch. 'Come back later, my lord. You can do nothing here at present. I will summon you when Sir Walter and I feel it would do Mr Pitt more good than harm to take you by the hand.'

John looked at Tomline, then at the open doorway. He knew a dismissal when he heard one, but he had to make sure. 'Promise me I will see him, Bishop.'

'You have my word,' Tomline replied.

It was all John was going to get. This was a battle he could not win, and he had no desire to create a scene, not while William lay ill upstairs. Leaving felt like surrender, but so long as William was alive there was hope, and so long as John had hope, there was time.

****

John passed two carriages going the other direction as he turned down the Portsmouth Road, and recognised their livery. One was Castlereagh's, another Mulgrave's. He did not feel better knowing they would also be turned away when they arrived at Putney.

He stared out of his carriage window at the moving landscape and tried to think calmly. It was difficult. He had been on the outside of his brother's life for so long, looking in with the eyes of a stranger. It had not always been so, and perhaps that was the only shred of comfort he had: even 12 years ago the story would have ended very differently. John had never forgotten his brother's words when William had offered him the Admiralty. *You are my brother, you are my friend, and I trust you with my life.* What had gone wrong?

He and William had spent so much time looking backwards, they had never devoted any thought to what was to come. There had always been tomorrow to make amends, but now there would be no more tomorrows, only yesterdays, and the bitter memories that came with them.

It was the Duke of Rutland all over again. Instead of waiting for William to ask for the help he was too proud to request, John might have given it freely. He might have stopped William destroying himself with drink. He might have saved a life. For the first time the reality of his brother's situation, and his own, hit him with its full force. Pain surged through him and he inhaled so sharply the breath stuck in his throat.

The journey took a couple of hours on the frosty roads, but the carriage still entered St James's Square far too soon for John's liking. His house rose out of the mist, tall, white and austere, just one classical exterior out of many along the pavement. He stumbled up the front steps to his house, feeling sick and wanting nothing more than to be alone, but he had reckoned without Mary, who met him on the threshold of the library.

'John.'

She wore a plain linen day-gown, her hair beneath its lace cap brushed free of powder. She looked just as ill as she had done at the Queen's birthday drawing room; when she saw her husband's expression her pale face grew paler still. John said, 'You should rest.'

She shook her head and clutched her shawl. 'I must speak with you.'

John had never felt less like talking, but he followed his wife into the library. She pulled a chair closer to the fireplace and gave the coal in the grate a half-hearted prod with the poker. The fire's orange glow cast long shadows across her face, exaggerating the rings under her eyes and the grooves round her mouth.

'Sit down,' Mary said.

John hesitated, then drew up a chair. Whatever Mary had to say, he supposed they might as well do it quickly. 'I expect you're about to tell me Harriot Hester eloped with her penniless colonel.'

This was not the time for feeble jokes, and John regretted his words the moment they had escaped his mouth. Mary blinked and he saw that she was twisting a worn cambric handkerchief in her hands, her face streaked with tears. A sudden doubt seized him; it was as though lead weights had dropped into his stomach. Fear filled his veins as fast as lightning. Surely it could not be – he had seen no messenger overtaking him on the Putney road. 'Have you heard from Putney? Is he dead?' She shook her head and the fear gave way to such strong relief John felt weakened by it. 'Thank God. Thank God.'

He closed his eyes to stop the world spinning, surprised at the vehemence of his own reaction. The veil had been whipped away from his eyes and he had seen, so clearly, the prospect he knew now to be inevitable. He pressed his hands together to stop them shaking. A moment later Mary put hers around them, as though to protect them.

'So he *is* dying,' she said.

It would have been too easy to give into the lie, to shake his head, to wrap himself in the comforting fiction that William, though ill, was not yet in extremis. But he could not; he owed it to Mary, his brother and himself to face the truth. He said, simply, 'Yes.'

Mary's eyes widened and she gave him a reproachful look, as though he had killed William with his own hands. Then she drew a long, shuddering breath and burst into tears.

Each sob was another knife in John's heart. He knew he was not the only one who had the right to care about William's situation, but he could not bear to see Mary's distress. 'He is not gone yet. There is still time—'

'Time for what?' John did not really know; the words had slipped out meaninglessly. The numbness that had settled on him at Putney was finally giving way to the burning agony of grief. A sweep of sadness settled over him, followed by the anger that had been his mainstay throughout the years of estrangement: directed, this time, not at William, but at himself. 'I suppose you find it strange that I am so disturbed at the prospect of losing him.'

'Not at all.'

'I confess I do. William and I have been estranged so long. I've lost count of the number of times I wished I did not have a brother.' Mary watched him through her tears. She no longer looked reproachful, only sad, but John had no use for her pity. 'It seems my desire is to be granted.'

'It does not matter what you thought then,' Mary said, unsteadily, wiping her eyes with the inside of her wrist. 'What matters is what you want now.'

'No. I have never mattered. As long as I can remember I have been William's brother; I have never really been anything else. Without him I am nothing but the Earl of Chatham, landless and debt-ridden. It diminished my father and God knows what posterity will make of me.'

'You are not merely William's brother,' Mary corrected him, with a glint of emotion. 'You are also my husband.'

Fondness pierced his grief, suddenly, unexpectedly, as warm as though she had wrapped him in her embrace. 'I will always be that, it is true. I will always be that.'

They sat with clasped hands in silence. The feeble glow from the fire played on the lines of Mary's face, touching on the grey at her temples, the half-dried tears in her eyes. They had been married 22 years. The memory of that happy summer ceremony came with difficulty to John on this cold, dark January day, and yet it nudged at his thoughts. It had been the last summer of innocence, the summer before William took the Treasury. William's 24-year-old face swam before his eyes, already wearing the cautious, shaded expression that later became habitual. *I will do my duty, Your Majesty.*

William had more than kept his word to the King. But what of William's duty to John, the head of his family? What of John's duty to William? John's thoughts splintered on the rocks of his guilt, a guilt that transformed his grief and anger into a debilitating exhaustion that seemed likely to drown him.

Mary saw the grey shadows cross his face. She released his hands. 'John. You must return to Putney.'

He had known she would say this; he also knew it was impossible. 'I cannot. They will not let me in.'

'You said there is still time. Are you telling me you want to wait until there is no time left?'

John opened his mouth to explain, but it was too much trouble even to think about his reasons. They existed and that was all he needed to know. He knew he was admitting defeat, and he hated himself for it, but he was not in control of his life; he never had been. 'It is not so simple.'

'No?' Until now there had been nothing in Mary's voice but sadness. Suddenly, there was an edge. 'I think it is perfectly simple. You're more like William than you will ever admit, despite your protestations to the contrary – so stubborn, so proud! You are afraid to go to him because you think he might forgive you.'

'No, Mary,' John murmured. 'It's not like that at all.'

'Is it not? Forgiveness cannot be commanded at will, John. It is one of the scarcest commodities in the world. It is the most difficult of gifts to give – and it is even more difficult to accept.' She stood up, her face full of love and exhaustion, as though her words took the last of her strength. 'I cannot help you any longer, John. It matters little what William did to you, or you to him. No crime is worth the punishment you are meting out to yourself. Go to him, and make amends.'

Edward Eliot's words in the saloon at Burton Pynsent came to John, borne by a sweep of desolation. He said, 'I must forgive myself first.'

He saw his absolution in the emotion reflected in her eyes. She placed her hands round his and looked at him as though it were the most obvious thing in the world. 'It is the same thing.'

****

After John left Mary remained standing in the middle of the library. She heard horses' hooves, and the carriage-wheels grinding over the cobbles as it carried John back to Putney once more. She had achieved her purpose, but she felt worse than if she had failed. Her head flamed and she could barely breathe.

'Mary?' The door opened to admit Georgiana, untying the ribbon of her hat and pulling off her gloves. 'Did I just see Lord Chatham's carriage? Is he going to Putney? Is Mr Pitt worse?'

'I—' Mary began, but choked off. Emotion coalesced into a hard, painful mass in her throat. She started to tremble. Even though there was no chair behind her she sat down, heavily, on the floor, in a pool of linen skirts.

Georgiana ran to her side. The minute her sister pressed a hand to her head Mary felt the tears come, silently, effortlessly, without a sound. Through them Mary saw Georgiana bite her lip. 'Oh, Mary … Mary, don't. Please don't cry.'

'I'm going to lose him.'

'Who? Mr Pitt?'

'John,' Mary whispered.

Georgiana frowned, and Mary lowered her head onto her sister's shoulder. She did not want to think of what would happen if John did not reach Putney in time.

****

For the second time that day John's carriage turned down the lane leading to the lamp-lit windows of Bowling Green House. He still had no idea how to persuade Lincoln and Farquhar to let him in, nor did he know what he would find when – if – they did so.

Then he caught sight of Charles Stanhope, Lady Hester's second brother, pacing up and down at the gate, apparently unaware of either the cold or the falling darkness. When Stanhope saw John's carriage he rushed towards it and halted the horses.

For a moment John thought Charles was trying to keep him away, and frustrated anger rose unevenly within him. One look at Charles's tear-streaked face turned the fury instantly to ice.

Chapter Thirty

January 1806

'I must see him, Bishop.'

'I do not think it will do any good, my lord.'

'I only want a moment,' John said. He felt hoarse from repeating the same words all evening. At least he could see the Bishop's refusals were devoid of conviction: he was going through the motions and that was all. 'You promised.'

'I did promise,' Tomline agreed heavily, 'that is true.'

He ran his hands through his close-cropped grey hair. He was only six years older than John, but looked like he had aged 20 in the space of only a few hours. John could see Tomline was not entirely with him and it frightened him. Since Charles Stanhope had stopped the carriage in tears John had, at least, discovered that William was still alive, but that his illness had progressed more swiftly than anticipated. More than that he could not establish.

The door opened to admit Sir Walter Farquhar. Tomline rose, but John was too quick for him. His only chance of gaining admittance to William was to secure permission from one or the other of these men. Tomline had proven unwilling, so John would have to work on the doctor. 'Sir Walter, I beg of you.'

Farquhar looked even worse than the Bishop. Despite the cold weather he was not wearing a coat, and his waistcoat was unbuttoned. 'Back already?'

'I told him it was not wise,' the Bishop said. Farquhar focused his unfriendly eyes on John for a moment, and John braced himself for another rejection, another brick wall erected in his path. To his surprise, it did not come. The doctor said, 'Why not? It can't do him any harm now.'

They had moved William into a much larger chamber, with windows on three sides looking onto the garden and heath. Big as it was, the room was warmed to an oppressive degree and reeked of sickness. John did not care. He did not see the table by the fireplace covered with cups, lances and hot irons. He saw nothing but William, lying on the bed with his head thrown back against the bolster, so thin he hardly made an impression on the blankets covering him.

John quickly discovered what Farquhar had meant. Perhaps six hours ago he might have been lucid, but now William was only barely conscious. For ten agonising minutes John held his brother's fever-hot hand, watched the rapid pulse at his throat, and waited for a sign that William had re-entered the room. He waited in vain. Occasionally William shifted and moaned, but his words were always nonsense; his eyes, when they opened, remained unfocused and empty of recognition. All John could do was watch helplessly, waiting for a reaction he knew would never come, yet as long as he was here he would not give up hope. Only when he felt his grip gently prised away from William's loose fingers did John stop staring at his brother's face and look up, blearily, into Tomline's.

He followed the Bishop downstairs in a dream. Tomline pressed a glass into his hand; John drank mechanically, without tasting. His numbness had returned. He knew it would not last, and that he would long for it long after it had worn out, but right now he wished he could feel something, anything, to make the situation seem real. Even now, after everything he had said and seen, it did not seem possible that it could be over. But it was, or at least it would be soon.

Tomline's lined face was full of sadness, but also a surprised benevolence John had not seen there before. Had the Bishop truly believed John did not care about William's fate? The brief pulse of anger, however, sputtered and died. Tomline had every right to think John did not care. Until only a few hours ago, John had believed it himself.

'I am truly sorry, my lord,' Tomline said. 'Had I realised how quickly your brother's illness would progress I would not have turned you away this morning.'

John could easily believe the Bishop was sincere. In any case he had had enough of blaming others for his own predicament. 'I know.'

'I should make sure Lady Hester is supporting herself well enough. Shall I call your carriage?'

John knew he had no further place here, not now William was given over. He was in the way; and yet leaving seemed entirely the wrong course of action. He gazed down at his linked fingers and, beyond them, the buckles on his shoes. 'I would prefer to remain, in case my brother regains consciousness.'

He did not believe for a moment that his brother would come round and he could tell Tomline knew it. This time John did not resent Tomline's palpable astonishment; he was beginning to realise how much like indifference his anger with William must have seemed to those not in the secret.

'Very well,' Tomline said at last. 'I will inform you if there is any change in Mr Pitt's condition.'

Tomline never did return, but John did not mind. In truth, he was hardly aware of what was going on. At certain moments time seemed hardly to pass, while at others it seemed to leap forwards in bounds. He never could recall what he did that night. Perhaps he sat in his brother's striped green easy-chair, watching the fire burn to ashes in the grate and listening for sounds from upstairs. Perhaps he read a book; occasionally he became aware that he had one in his hands, but he never remembered reading a line. Candle after candle burned to a stub in the fixtures. Servants paraded back and forth, going about everyday business as though it were not past midnight. At some point one of them laid out some bread, meat and cheese on a table by the window. John ignored it, even though he had not eaten since breakfast.

The later it got the fewer demarcations there seemed to be in John's mind between reality and unreality. *He's awake, he's asking for you.* He could hear movements on the landing: people tiptoeing as though afraid to be heard, Farquhar's low voice, hoarse with fatigue. *I'm sorry. Forgive me.* But no-one ever did come to fetch John.

Even so, he did not completely give up hope until after four o'clock when a dishevelled and unshaven Farquhar threw open the door. The doctor's face was grey with fatigue. He stared at John without really seeing him, then walked away in silence.

John rose. There were new sounds coming from upstairs, more steps, more whispered conversations, the distant tinkle of bells, and the responding hammer of feet. John climbed the stairs slowly, as though in a trance. He could hear someone calling out for Lady Hester Stanhope's brothers, Charles and James. Lady Hester's door was closed, but John's dispassionate gaze caught the Bishop of Lincoln collapsed in a chair, staring blankly at the candle flame.

A manservant stood outside William's room. He raised a stunned face to John but made no move to stop him. John hardly paid him any attention; he pushed the door open and walked in, his heart hammering in his chest.

It was not yet dawn. The wind had died down; the leaves were no longer beating against the windowpane. The fire in the grate had burned down almost to the end; a few embers smoked gently on the plate. Someone had left a branch of candles on the table. John picked it up and held it over the bed. William's eyes were closed, his chapped lips parted, his brow furrowed as though he were having an unpleasant dream. His hands had knotted themselves around the counterpane, and he lay twisted as though to escape the pain. For all that, he looked like a child who had just dropped into an exhausted sleep.

John put the branch of candles back on the table and wiped his sweaty palms against his coat. As he did so he heard a muffled sob from the recesses of the room. 'Who is there?'

He grabbed the candelabrum and brandished it at the shadows. Curled up on a chair with his knees drawn up under his chin was the 17-year-old James Stanhope.

John had so completely expected to be alone that the sight of the boy startled him. His first instinct was to be angry, but then he saw how upset James was and the emotion evaporated. John put a hand on his shoulder and felt James start at his touch. 'Come away, James. You should not be here.'

James's light hair was plastered to his forehead with tears. He did not look at John, but nor did he look at the form on the bed. 'I've been here all night, watching. I … he …'

The boy's eyes strayed too close to the bed. He trailed to a halt. John squeezed his shoulder. 'They are looking for you downstairs. You should go to them.'

Another tear coursed down James's cheek and he cuffed it away. 'I can't. I don't want to leave him.'

You left me at my most vulnerable moment, without a thought for anyone but yourself. The memory of the words sliced through John's mind, as sharp as a sword-thrust – the echo of that day nearly 30 years ago, when he had made his choice and run away from his responsibilities and from William, who had needed him more than John had ever wanted to admit. He had spent the rest of his life trying to make amends for his error, all while fearing the release forgiveness might bring, for he had spent so long holding onto his pain it had almost become part of himself. Now it was too late.

The realisation tore through John's numb shield so violently he gasped for breath. He looked at the bed and felt something in his heart give way, as though everything he had possessed, and lost, had been brought home to him with the force of a hammer-blow.

But there was one last service he could perform for his brother, even if William would never know of it. He fought down his emotion and turned to James. 'You go. Do not worry. I will sit with him.'

At that moment, they both heard James's name being called again from downstairs. The boy looked questioningly at John, then unfolded his legs and slipped out of the room. He paused at the door, but then he was gone, and John was alone.

He went to one of the windows and opened it. The breeze that struck his face was cold, but not freezing. John turned back to the bed. His brother's gaunt profile lay silhouetted against the candlelight. The flickering of the flame made it look like he was breathing.

'I won't leave you again, Will,' John whispered. 'I give you my word.'

He drew up a chair by the window. He remained there, arms folded on the windowsill, until the shadows started to recede and the servants came in to lay out William's body.

Chapter Thirty-one

February 1806

'One of my prebendaries at St Paul's has found 47 poor men, one for each year of Mr Pitt's life, who have agreed to take part in the procession. They will need serge cloaks, and black staffs.' The Bishop of Lincoln's voice sharpened. 'They will also need, eventually, to be paid.'

John looked down at his clasped hands. Lost in his own internal world, he broke into Tomline's monologue only to nod or grunt to suggest agreement to arrangements he was incapable of grasping fully. 'Of course.'

The Bishop had clearly expected more, but went on. 'As it is to be a public funeral, at public expense, we may be able to source their payment from the parliamentary grant voted to pay off Mr Pitt's debts. If not, we may have to pay them from our own funds.'

'Naturally.' John was heavily in debt himself, but it was too much effort to argue.

'As for the order of service, I will be taking part in the procession, so I have asked the Bishop of London to deliver the sermon. Have you any preferences as to texts? I thought the anthems sung for the late Lord Nelson might be appropriate.'

That got a reaction. John looked up, startled. 'The same service? Will that not seem odd?'

'I rather think it apposite,' Lincoln replied, primly. 'Particularly the closing text: "His body is buried in peace; but his name liveth evermore".'

John returned the Bishop's challenging stare for a moment, then looked away. He knew what Tomline was doing. It was as though the real William had been replaced by a fictional one, the gallant knight who had saved his country and died at his post. John knew he ought to stop this nonsense; a public funeral would rob him of his right to grieve, as though he were expected to mourn the loss of the public man more than the loss of a brother. And yet he did not feel he had the strength, nor, perhaps, the right, to protest.

His only defence was to close his mind to the grief, and the guilt. He spoke at last, his voice bland with tiredness. 'If you consider it good, I have no objection.'

'Would you like to make any alterations to the procession? I sent it to you yesterday.'

John had not even opened the letter. 'It will do.'

'It would help me greatly if you would give me some comments,' the Bishop said, pointedly, but John waved a hand.

'I have faith in your judgment.'

For a moment he thought the Bishop would argue with him. John knew Tomline thought his reluctance to help with the funeral was little more than indifference, and that the Bishop considered him lazy and selfish. John did not care; it could not make him feel worse than he already did. Tomline tightened his lips and bowed. 'I have an appointment with Garter King of Arms this afternoon. I shall inform you of any decisions.'

'My thanks.'

The Bishop paused. 'Farquhar tells me Lady Chatham continues ill?'

'She is rather better today,' John said, woodenly.

'Good. Please pass on my good wishes.'

John remained at his desk for a long space after Tomline left, hands clasped, staring at nothing. There was a difficult decision to be made, and he did not want to face it until he had to. The sound of the Bishop's carriage rolling away revived him. He rose and tugged the bell-pull.

The servant who appeared was in deep mourning, as were all the members of John's household. The usual livery had been replaced with black woollen clothes, black stockings and black shoe-buckles. John looked dispassionately at him. 'Has Lady Chatham asked for me?'

'No, my lord. Miss Townshend is with her.'

'Thank you. Tell Miss Townshend I will come by shortly.'

John spent a few moments putting papers into piles on his desk, flicking dust off the folios. He no longer had official duties to distract him. William's Cabinet had met only once after his death to agree they could not continue without him. On the 1st of February, Lord Grenville had kissed hands as First Lord of the Treasury, with Fox as his Foreign Secretary. John had lost his office and the handsome salary that went with it. He and Mary had been forced to move, quickly, into a much smaller house on Dover Street, for he could no longer afford St James's Square.

At least it would be some time before the duns worked up the courage to knock on the door of a house in deep mourning. The period for the loss of a brother was six weeks; three had already elapsed. Whether he would have cause to extend that period of mourning further John did not know.

****

Mary lay in blackness. The windows, hung with mourning crape, were shuttered completely. A few candles burned in the fixtures, but otherwise all was gloom. It suited her. Somewhere beyond the boundary of her blackened room she was vaguely aware of the world continuing to turn, but nothing could affect her here, shut up safe in her bedchamber. Cutting herself off was the only way to keep her heart and mind from bursting with pain.

Georgiana and Harriot Hester took turns to hold her hand, trying to persuade her to talk, but she did not rise to the temptation to reply. If she remained silent, perhaps they would leave her alone. If she remained silent, perhaps they would not notice if she slipped away and never returned.

She heard a knock at the door, and a voice. 'How is she?'

'Awake,' Georgiana said. 'Sir Walter's laudanum draught worked. The fever has not returned, and she passed a good night.'

'Will she see me?'

The curtains round the bed parted. *John*. Black made him look sallow; he had always looked most handsome in bright, elegant colours. Mary raised her head briefly and he smiled, but she did not have the strength to meet his eyes. She dropped her gaze again to the back of her hands. Her dry knuckles and bitten nails seemed unconnected to her, as though they belonged to someone else.

He leaned over and kissed her cheek, and she flinched. *Go away*. He seemed inexplicably unable to read her thoughts. Instead he sat beside her and took her hand. She hated being touched, but there was no point fighting him, so she let him hold it, hoping he would understand from her stillness how much she wanted to be left alone. *Go away. Go away. Go away*. He stayed.

'Georgiana tells me you passed a good night,' he said. 'I am glad of it. All I want is for you to recover.'

Every day he followed the same pattern, sitting by her side, holding her hand, and telling her everything that had happened. He told her he loved her, and that he missed her. She supposed he hoped that, one day, she might give him a reaction. She tried to close her ears. *Just go away, John.* If she listened, she might give in to the despair, and she dreaded what would happen if she did.

'The Bishop of Lincoln came this morning,' he said. 'Some difficult decisions have to be made about the funeral. I do not know where to put Lord Grenville in the procession. He ought to be with the family, yet I think William would have preferred him to have a greater role. But Grenville disagrees. I think he feels he does not deserve it.'

Mary's fingers lay unclenched in John's hand. *Go away. Stop talking.* But as always, he continued to talk, to fill the silence that was her buffer, her security.

'I have not heard from Lady Hester Stanhope. I think she is still upset we did not offer her a home with us. Perhaps I ought to have done, but I did not think it appropriate when you were so ill. We might ask her when you are better, but I doubt she will accept.'

Mary turned her head further away on the pillow. John said nothing for a space and she thought he had finished. She was wrong. He stroked her hand for a moment, then continued.

'I confess I find it hard to pay attention to the funeral arrangements. Three weeks have passed and I still do not know for certain he is gone.' He paused to steady his voice. 'The Bishop of Lincoln feels I am taking it too easily, and suspect I do not care; but I hope you know otherwise.' He hesitated, his forefinger describing a light circle on the back of Mary's hand. 'I hope, too, you will understand my decision not to attend the funeral.'

Mary's eyes snapped open. She remembered, from a time before the black fog descended over her mind, John telling her how much his failure to attend his father's funeral had cursed his life. His decision to go to Gibraltar instead, he said, had been the origin of all his troubles with William. Now he was going to shirk his responsibilities a second time. Even in death he could not stop himself failing his brother.

How could he do it? Had he merely said it to elicit a reaction? But no, his tone had been perfectly sincere. *Dear God, he means it.* Why was he so determined to punish himself? Did he not see how he had already destroyed himself – how much he had destroyed her, his own wife?

Her voice was cracked and hoarse from lack of use. 'Who, then, will be Chief Mourner?'

It was the first thing she had said to him in days. John raised his hand and stroked her cheek. She flinched and he pulled away, as though afraid she might retreat into herself again if he persisted. 'I do not know. All I know is I cannot go.'

'Why not?'

'There is so much to do. William's debts, for example. Parliament has voted £45,000 towards them, but it isn't enough, and he wanted his servants paid double wages. I don't have time to go. Perhaps it is best if I don't.'

Even in her distracted state she knew he was not telling her the truth. She pushed herself up against the pillow. Unlike the rest of the world she knew how much of a sacrifice he would be making by missing the funeral. Everyone else would assume he was too lazy to attend, and cared too little. It could not be true. There had to be a reason. 'Why, John?'

For a moment he did not reply. Then he said, 'Do you remember our wedding night?'

It was so shocking a non-sequitur that Mary could say nothing but, 'Yes?'

'I gave you my word I would never place my happiness before your own.' His voice grew muffled. 'I broke it. You have stood by me through everything. You told me what I needed to do to make things right with William, but I was so wrapped up in my troubles I listened to nothing but my own anger. I put too much upon your shoulders, Mary. I am sorry.'

The pain in his voice chipped away at her defences a little more. She murmured, 'Why are you telling me this now?'

'Because I now understand what is important.'

'I thought William's funeral *was* important.'

'It is,' he admitted. 'But you are more so.' He finished with a gasp, 'I love you, Mary. I cannot leave you. What will I do if you are gone when I return?'

She tilted her head against the pillow, and as she fastened her gaze on his for the first time since William's death the tears formed in his eyes. He made no attempt to restrain them and they fell, unevenly, on the counterpane, tiny dark discs soaking into the fabric. He truly would do it for her. William was gone, but John was determined to give Mary a reason to remain. This time he was determined to act before it was too late.

He still gripped her hand in his, as though to let it go would be to release her for good; but Mary knew, now, she did not want to be released. He still needed her, and she him, for he alone had the power to close the void inside her, if she let him.

But neither of them could heal their wounds unless John laid his ghosts to rest. She could see he knew it as well as she did; all he waited for was her permission, and her forgiveness.

'I will still be here,' she said. 'I promise.'

He kissed her forehead and gathered her into a firm embrace. It had been so long since she had let anything but misery touch her that Mary was almost surprised to feel the beating of his heart through his black woollen coat.

Chapter Thirty-two

February 1806

The drums began beating at half past 12. Their muffled sound, and the shrill, mournful music of fifes and trumpets, echoed around the barrelled roof of the old House of Lords as Lord Camden draped the folds of the heavy mourning cloak over John's shoulders. It seemed incongruous that the unwarlike, peace-loving William should be laid to rest to the sound of a military band, but there was a very unreal feel to the procession slowly building up. The ceremony had been designed for the burial of a medieval war-baron.

Camden finished draping John's velvet robes and stood back to admire the effect. 'There, I think we are ready.'

'I imagine it will be a good few minutes before we are called up,' Lord Westmorland said. Camden shrugged.

'It is as well to be ready. Is everyone in place?'

Camden moved down the procession, making sure nobody had moved out of the order prescribed by the heralds. Several hundred people were taking part in the ceremony, so many people, in fact, that the participants had been divided between ten different rooms scattered across the Palace of Westminster. Here in the old House of Lords, in addition to John, Camden and Westmorland, there were six Assistant Mourners, twenty-five close friends and family, and a half-dozen members of William's last administration.

A loud sob came from the other side of the chamber. Lord Mulgrave, William's last Foreign Secretary, had been weeping on and off all morning and now reached for his handkerchief again. John wished Mulgrave would pull himself together. Not only were his tears making John feel wretched, but he had overheard several whispers comparing Mulgrave's emotion to his own lack of sentiment.

Nothing could be further from the truth. John had never felt worse. Every detail of the funeral seemed to have been calculated to make him feel ten times as much pain. Arranging to gather here, in the old House of Lords, made sense, for from here he and his companions could move most easily into their place in the cortege, but he could not forget that he and William had watched their father struck down by a fit in this very room.

William's coffin, like their father's, had lain in state in the Painted Chamber for two days, beneath a canopy decorated with the family crest and surrounded by 200 wax candles. John had stood before the ebony casket and brushed his hands over its polished surface times without number. He could not convince himself his brother lay under that glossy lid, could not believe he would never see him or hear his voice again. It was impossible to make anything of it. This was the funeral of a statesman; it was not a funeral for a brother, and John did not feel he had been given a proper chance to say farewell.

John longed for William to be here, to make a flippant comment and break the atmosphere even by a degree, but it was impossible. He had to bear the pain, as he would have to live the rest of his life: alone – or nearly alone, for the thought of Mary, recovering slowly on her sofa in Dover Street, kept him going when he thought his heart might well break.

Outside the drums grew fainter as the procession advanced, slowly, towards the Abbey. The door to the chamber opened and Somerset Herald appeared, his tabard on top of his robes. 'The coffin is ready. Are you prepared?' The silence that followed was broken only by the whine of trumpets and a suppressed sob from Mulgrave. 'In that case, follow me.'

The coffin awaited them in Westminster Hall, carried by a detachment of Foot Guards and covered with a black velvet pall. Four members of the highest ranks of nobility stood at each corner, including the Duke of Rutland, son of John's long-dead friend. John himself took up position behind the banner showing the family crest.

At a signal from Somerset Herald the procession began to move. John's military training came back to him and he fell effortlessly into step. It was almost ridiculously easy to detach himself from the process. All these people surrounding him looked like play-actors in their close mourning, their black velvet cloaks sweeping the ground as they walked.

They descended the steps of Westminster Hall and crossed New Palace Yard. The path had been gravelled and cordoned off with railings, watched over by detachments of the 3rd Regiment of Foot Guards.

Temporary seating had been erected, and, as the procession came out onto Parliament Street, the crowds began to make themselves seen. Despite the cold rain, they lined the whole route, down Union Street, across the Broad Sanctuary, right up to the West Door of Westminster Abbey, which was surrounded on both sides by the 47 poor men with their hats and crested gowns. Here the procession was met by the Dean of Westminster, his prebendaries, and the choirs of the Abbey, St Paul's Cathedral and the Chapel Royal, who fell into step behind the great banner. As soon as the coffin entered the church the choir began to sing, and John had to blink back the tears that rose to his eyes.

How he got through the short burial service he did not know. He sat at the head of the coffin, in front of a table bearing the heraldic trophies, directly under the outstretched hand of his father's statue. Beside him the flags covering his family crypt had been removed and John could see the shadowy oblong forms of other coffins down below. He tried not to look at them, or at the new coffin being winched down to join them.

At last the choir stopped singing. Garter King of Arms stepped out, each slow step echoing from the high vaulting in the breathless silence. His voice rang out solemnly: 'Thus it hath pleased Almighty God to take out of this transitory life unto his Divine Mercy, the late Right Honourable William Pitt, one of His Majesty's most honourable Privy Council, First Lord Commissioner of the Treasury, Chancellor of the Exchequer, Lord Warden of the Cinque Ports, one of the Representatives in parliament for the University of Cambridge, the character to whose memory is inscribed, *Non sibi sed patriae vixit*: "He lived not for himself, but for his country".'

William's secretaries, Joseph Smith, John Carthew and William Dacre Adams, each representing the ancient medieval offices of Comptroller, Steward and Treasurer in William's household, stepped to the edge of the grave. They snapped the short white staves they carried and handed them to the herald, who threw them into the crypt. The pieces bounced off the coffin lid with a hollow thud.

It was over; the funeral service was finished. The heralds collected the trophies. The banners that had been laid on either side of the coffin were taken up again, and the choir began to sing its final anthem. John rose from his chair. Immediately he saw Camden approaching to offer assistance, but John waved him away. He had one last duty to perform.

He moved to the side of the grave. There was William's coffin, and Papa's and Mama's, and Harriot's a little further away. Hetty was buried at Chevening; James Charles lay on the island of Antigua. Only John now remained above ground, the last of the Pitts.

Past and present merged in his mind. He saw, as vividly as though he had been there, young William shrouded in black velvet, white-faced and choking back tears as another coffin was lowered into the depths of this grave. William had spoken of his feelings on that occasion only once, and in anger, but John could still hear his words, as though they had been spoken only moments ago. *I could never rely on you when it truly mattered. Never.*

John had allowed those words to shatter their brotherly bond, yet he knew, now, how easy it was to wound, how hard to make amends. Mary had been right. Forgiving oneself was the hardest thing of all, and now he would never get the chance to tell William how sorry he was. He could only let the grief surge through him, each throb more painful than the last, and wait for it to be over. He did not know if it ever would be.

Outside the rain still fell. Hardly any light filtered through the tiny rose window above the North Transept's enormous wooden doors. A cold draft rippled the folds of John's cloak around his feet. Someone was calling for him; it was time to say goodbye. He shivered against the chill and looked down, one last time, into his family's grave.

'I did not leave you at the very end,' he said, whispering into the depths of the gloom. 'I hope you know it.'

He waited a few moments longer, although he could not have said precisely for what; then he raised his head. Drawing his mourning cloak more closely about him he turned, straight-backed and dry-eyed, to take his place in William's funeral cortege.

Author's Note

After his brother's death, the Earl of Chatham continued for a while in public political life. He served as Master General of the Ordnance under the Duke of Portland and Spencer Perceval, and in July 1809 was appointed to command an amphibious expedition to capture the French fleet, reduce the island of Walcheren, and destroy the defences of Antwerp.

The expedition ended in complete failure, and Chatham disappeared almost completely from domestic politics. He remained in the army, however, and was appointed Governor of Gibraltar in 1820. He died in 1835, 29 years after his brother, and 14 years after his wife Mary. Upon his death, the Earldom of Chatham became extinct.

****

My book *The Late Lord: the life of John Pitt, 2nd Earl of Chatham* (Pen and Sword Books, 2017) is likely to remain the only biography of Chatham for a long while. Chatham's brother and father are much better served in the literature, and I drew most of my initial research leads from biographies of them. The best are:

John Ehrman, *The Younger Pitt* (3 vols.)

Michael Duffy, *The Younger Pitt*

Robin Reilly, *Pitt the Younger*

Marie Peters, *Pitt the Elder*

Brian Tunstall, *William Pitt, Lord Chatham*

Stanley Ayling, *Pitt the Elder*

William Hague's 2004 biography of Pitt the Younger is an excellent and highly readable introduction to the politics of the era.

All characters and events described in the novel are historical; I confess I elevated Mary's father to the peerage a couple of years early for simplicity's sake. All letters quoted are from originals (but I have occasionally condensed them for the sake of readability).

Acknowledgments

I have accumulated many debts in writing this novel. The internet has connected me with more like-minded individuals than I ever dreamed existed. Many friends have read and commented on the work in progress: Maggie Scott; Stephen Bishop; Catherine Curzon; Geraldine Porter; Lillah Irwin; Lynn Robb; Angela Filewood; Helen Pinches; Ashley Wilde; Chris Sorensen; Malcolm Mendey; Lindsay Ryan; Mary Tickel; Piers Bearne; and Cherry Bowen. Huge thanks to Philip Ball, the only person who has managed to work out what John was doing during the Battle of Castricum. Alice Grice and Helen Pinches have been hugely helpful in putting several sources my way. I would also like to thank my Yummy Mummies, who have followed this project for years and kept me (sort of) sane. Thank you, ladies, each and every one.

Finally, there are not enough words to express my gratitude to Stephenie Sverna and Therese Holmes, my spiritual sisters-in-research. Both have read this book from its earliest drafts, and this would be a much poorer novel without Therese's input in particular. I owe them more than I can ever repay. This book belongs properly to them.

About the author

Jacqueline has a PhD in late 18th century British history from Cambridge University. She has been researching the Pitt family for many years, focusing particularly on the life of the 2nd Earl of Chatham, whose nonfiction biography she has also written. She lives in Cambridge with her husband and their two young children, both of whom probably believe Lord Chatham lives in their house.

If you enjoyed *Earl of Shadows*, please share your thoughts on Amazon by leaving a review.

For more free and discounted eBooks every week, sign up to the *Endeavour Press* newsletter.

Follow us on Twitter and Instagram.

15084792R00182

Printed in Great Britain
by Amazon